Praise for *Fi*

"In Maren Cooper's character-driven novel *Finding Grace*, a family secret leads to ruptures and reconciliations."
—*Foreword* **Clarion Reviews**

"*Finding Grace* will ring true for any parent who has shepherded a child through the perils of mental illness. Filled with flawed but genuine characters, Cooper's tale delves into the complex mix of devotion, despair, fear, and hope inherent in unconditional love."
—**Susan Ritz**, author of *A Dream to Die For*

"Cold mothers and troubled children. A father's desperate wish for vital and lasting connections. The peculiar, senseless decision-making of teens who are hurting. Second chances at love. The essence of community. Set on the shores of Minnesota's Lake Superior, *Finding Grace*'s beautiful descriptions of the harsh beauty in the outside world perfectly frame the complex inner worlds of the central characters."
—**Barbara Stark-Nemon**, author of *Even in Darkness* and *Hard Cider*

"*Finding Grace* is a riveting dive into the heartache and terror that parents experience dealing with a child who lapses into mental illness during adolescence. It's a keen portrayal of the ways in which childhood trauma shapes lives. An added attraction is Maren Cooper's wonderfully evocative descriptions of Lake Superior in all its moods and seasons."
—**Ames Sheldon**, author of *Eleanor's Wars, Don't Put the Boats Away*, and *Lemons in the Garden of Love*

Finding Grace

Finding Grace

A Novel

Maren Cooper

swp

SHE WRITES PRESS

Copyright © 2022, Maren Cooper

All rights reserved. No part of this publication may be reproduced, distributed, or transmitted in any form or by any means, including photocopying, recording, digital scanning, or other electronic or mechanical methods, without the prior written permission of the publisher, except in the case of brief quotations embodied in critical reviews and certain other noncommercial uses permitted by copyright law. For permission requests, please address She Writes Press.

Published 2022
Printed in the United States of America
Print ISBN: 978-1-64742-385-8
E-ISBN: 978-1-64742-386-5
Library of Congress Control Number: 2022900129

For information, address:
She Writes Press
1569 Solano Ave #546
Berkeley, CA 94707

She Writes Press is a division of SparkPoint Studio, LLC.

Interior design by Tabitha Lahr

All company and/or product names may be trade names, logos, trademarks, and/or registered trademarks and are the property of their respective owners.

This is a work of fiction. Names, characters, places, and incidents either are the product of the author's imagination or are used fictitiously. Any resemblance to actual persons, living or dead, is entirely coincidental.

When our hope is linked to the hope of others, we become even stronger. Hope builds on itself. It grows. The more we share in hope, the more we see the light, even in the darkness of the midnight hour.

—STEVEN CHARLESTON, *Ladder to the Light: An Indigenous Elder's Meditations on Hope and Courage*, 2021

Prologue

Two Harbors, Minnesota
January 15, 2017

Charlie brushed his thick, sandy hair back as his bleary eyes squinted to study the letter for the tenth time. The gooseneck lamp shone brightly on the stack of carefully ordered letters and printed emails on his desk, framed by a border of biology textbooks covering all other available surfaces. He wasn't exactly sure why these letters, evidence of nothing but wasted time, beckoned him to stay up late into the night—maybe because he needed a distraction from his internal turmoil to wind down at the end of the day. Alone.

Nobody had been around for over a year now.

He flinched out of his reverie with the ringing of the landline. As he rose and his feet found the floor, he registered his truth—nothing good comes from a call in the middle of the night. He didn't dare let his mind lock in on his constant dread—the police had found a body and thought it might be his long-missing daughter, Grace. Instead, he forced himself in a different direction.

Was it Caroline? Never one to live within convention, she'd call in the middle of the night, merely for lack of checking the world clock. Perhaps she was on one of her crazy trips to search for some elusive bird to check off her "world bird list." But she never called anymore.

His nervous black lab sidled up to him, slowing his movement through the dark house to the kitchen and the phone. "Bailey, get out of the way, girl." He attempted to give the dog a reassuring pat and swallowed the hope that it could be his vagabond wife. He grabbed the receiver.

"Hullo."

"Is this Charles Booker?" asked a women's voice, youngish and tentative.

"Yes."

"I have some news, urgent news, about your daughter, Grace."

"Gracie?" He hadn't heard from his troubled daughter in over a year. Their last months together had created an estrangement not yet bridged, etched in his aching heart.

"Yes, Grace is in the hospital and wants you here. She needs you now."

"What, where?" His voice was still froggy. He looked at the clock, which read 3:00 a.m.

"Memorial Hospital, Chicago, south side."

"Who are you?" His mind now on task, he needed information.

"A friend. Get a pencil and I'll give you the address. You need to hurry."

With the order, he scrambled for a light switch and pen, scribbled down the address, and then she was gone. Shocked by the sudden adrenaline rush, he found his hands shaking as he hung up. Then, his knees gave way, and he crumpled to the floor. Bailey was all over him with her warm muzzle and licks, finally giving him the strength to move. He stumbled to Grace's bedroom and took a moment to breathe in her essence, still strong after her flight from him.

He was dressed, packed, and ready to lock up when he registered Bailey. Too early to wake his neighbor. *Damn.* With only one person he could turn to, he gathered some dog food and packed it and Bailey in the car. Lori was always there for him. How much more could he put her through?

At the last minute, he returned to Grace's room. He stopped when he locked eyes on her last school picture, her junior year in high school. Beautiful and fragile. His fault.

He pulled a soft wool blanket for Bailey from her closet. His own blanket of guilt would itch at him for the ten-hour drive to Chicago.

Chapter 1

➤

Kearney, Nebraska
Spring 1996

Not the most romantic place to propose, but Charles Booker knew it fit Caroline perfectly—a rugged bird blind in Nebraska, just before dusk. It was an amazing sight. The sandhill cranes swooped in with their long necks cutting through the sky. Their bodies aligned, following as sharp as knives against the backdrop of the twilight sky.

"Shhh . . . I need to block everything out for this moment." Caroline shushed him as he crouched down beside her, his feet scattering the gathered leaves on the concrete floor of the blind.

He thought, not for the first time, how most men would feel diminished if the woman in their life had a passion so obviously beyond them, but Charlie was awed by Caroline and her brilliant mind. He was just grateful to be in her galaxy and let the energy around her envelop him.

They had waited for hours, and this moment wouldn't last long. At twilight, the noisy, raucous sandhill cranes landed by the hundreds, squeezing in without disturbing their colleagues who had already landed. As the night turned completely dark, the birds' loud cries continued unabated while the final stragglers found their night's home.

Charlie hoped the afterglow of this wonder would serve to keep Caroline in a state of euphoria long enough for him to get the words out before she reverted to the scientist focused on her next challenge. And who knew if that would include him?

Caroline finally put the binoculars down and lowered her body onto the bench. With her raven-black curls tightly pulled back into her hat, she looked like a high school kid even at twenty-five.

After a long, delighted exhale, she jumped up, pulled him to her by his jacket, and gave him a deep kiss. "We did it! Charlie, did you love it? Can you believe it? Is there anything as beautiful as the in migration of the sandhill cranes?"

"It was incredible, just as you said!" He wrapped his arms around her in a bear hug and felt her warmth before plunging ahead, before he lost his nerve. "But, to me, beauty is you, now, in your element. And love is what we have together. And will have, forever." As he spoke, he lowered her to a seated position on the bench and went down on one knee.

"Caroline Lee Tate, would you share your life with me and be my wife?" His words tapered to a whisper as Caroline started to laugh.

"Charlie, you silly man, what are you doing?" She took his face in her hands and gave him a quick kiss.

He knew Caroline well enough not to expect a conventional response to a proposal of marriage, so he held his position on one knee and deftly pulled a little box from his jacket pocket, trying to hide his terror that she would persist in thinking this a joke.

Caroline eyed the box. "Oh, Charlie, you know marriage isn't my thing. I don't think you'd be happy with me. I'm made for the life of a mad scientist, a nomad, wandering the world and discovering its secrets, not playing housewife."

"Caroline, Caroline—I don't want a housewife. I want you! I want you as you are, wanderer, inquisitive explorer. We were meant to be together, don't you feel that?"

Caroline bounced up and walked around the blind, pausing to pick up her binoculars and check out a few straggling cranes. Charlie gave her a few minutes; then he approached her body from behind and put his chin on her shoulder, waiting for her body to relax as he put his arms around her and rocked her from side to side. "Caroline?"

"Charlie, you know feelings are hard for me. But I do feel good when you're around." She lowered the binoculars and turned to him. "You're serious?"

"I am serious. I want you, as you are, I promise. I love you." He took both of her hands and met her gaze. His heart raced.

Finally, Caroline whispered, "Then, yes, Charlie, as long as you promise. I will marry you."

Charlie sealed the deal with a passionate kiss, hoping he left her wanting more, and ushered Caroline into their jeep rental. The celebratory dinner and night of lovemaking boosted his confidence that he could successfully compete for her attentions.

Chapter 2

➤

Kearney, Nebraska
Spring 1996

Soft light framed the window where the cheap drapes gapped in the nondescript highway motel and shone on the ring box on the bedside table. Morning. Caroline reached over to pick it up and peeked at the engagement ring. Ambivalent about the proposal, she had no reservations about the ring. How was it that he knew her so well?

She was not a girly girl, but he got this right—a sturdy but slim gold band with two gemstones side by side in a simple setting, their birthstones. No protrusions to get in her way—this was an everyday ring that could be worn with gloves, on a hand that would be hardworking in the field, and not call attention to itself. She loved it. And, she finally admitted it to herself, she loved that he loved her. And how he loved her. She thought back to her adventurous years with too many boys, then men, to count—always looking for someone who was able to please her.

Then, Charlie's demeanor of a reformed bad boy, with a facial scar to add mystery, and his muscular, compact body and adventurous moves that never failed to please her.

So, why not say yes and make him a happy man? Her brow furrowed as she puzzled this out. Would making him a happy man make her a happy woman? Being tied down was not what she wanted. She needed to be free to go where she wanted and make her way on her own. She thought back to the eighteen months they had been together. He had followed her to her graduate program and stayed by her side even as she barely had time for him. Would that change if they married? What kind of demands would marriage put on her? She needed to be free— free as the birds she studied, to be able to fly away on a whim.

She felt his breath on her neck as he turned to spoon her. "You're awake." He kissed her shoulder and looked over her and saw the ring on her finger. "Oh good, it fits." He pulled her to him and, with one thing on his mind, added, "Just like us."

"Oh, what a terrible line." Caroline laughed at him until she laughed with him as they playfully rolled around the bed entwined in the sheets.

Caroline was coy over the next few months, testing Charlie's promise. First, they agreed not to tell anyone they were engaged. Caroline didn't want to deal with any of the silliness accompanying news of an engagement. She just wore the ring and moved on with her life. As a couple, they were in their own world. They didn't need anyone else. So, that was easy.

Close wasn't her style. She had been orphaned early and raised by an uncle, a priest. Uncle Fritz had been caught unaware by the untimely responsibility and didn't give up on his mission to Natal, Brazil, but carted her along and foisted her on the nuns running the mission school, where she became fluent in Portuguese and Spanish over the next five years. Back in New England, she flourished in high school, but only academically. Socially, she was awkward and isolated. Having come from the mission school, she was a curiosity to her classmates. Making friends wasn't something she knew how to do, and she had nobody to encourage her to do so.

She was cared for by a parade of parsonage housekeepers, supervised loosely by the uncle who died as she left for college. With that inheritance and some of her parents' trust available to her at age twenty, she was able to follow her own path for college choice—Radcliffe—and to take the full-ride biology–ornithology scholarship. She barely touched her inheritance and knew there would be more to come later from the insurance settlement paid out after her parents had died in a small plane crash.

Charlie was also a solo act. A real orphan. He had been abandoned at a fire station when he was born and in foster care until a family with a restaurant kept him long-term. He quickly became valuable to them. It was not a loving environment, but they were nice enough. Scrappy and street-smart, he played the long game. They put him to work, and he developed a social aptitude for customer service that helped them grow into a successful business. Years of having to watch his back made him the perfect workaholic. He knew how to protect himself by becoming indispensable.

When he graduated from high school, they offered to let him work for a franchise of his own, but he didn't want it. Instead, they mocked him as he sought out the school counselor for help with the paperwork and applications for a full ride to Harvard and set out on a scientific course, majoring in biology. When he left, he didn't look back.

Caroline remembered how they met and considered it to be a sign that things could work for her in this marriage. He had come in late to their biology lab.

"Hi, I'm Charlie Booker. Looks like we're going to be lab partners."

Caroline didn't look up from the microscope, so couldn't see she had blocked his passage to the open stool on her left side. She was totally absorbed in her sight lines. "Oh, this is way cool." She moaned with pleasure.

She vaguely registered the professor starting to read the names off of the roster. "Julian Abanto, Tamara Axelrod, Ahmed Aziz—"

Caroline felt a light touch on her shoulder and a gentle whisper. "Excuse me, but I need to move around you to take my seat."

"Virginia Baxter, Daeun Bok." The professor's voice now got her attention.

"Charles Booker."

"Here, sir." Charlie raised his hand.

"And will you be standing for this class, Charles Booker?"

"No sir, sorry to be late, sir." He answered smoothly and with an energetic push to Caroline's chair, he slid into his own seat.

Caroline's face flushed crimson. She couldn't look his way.

Fifteen minutes into the class, the professor directed the lab partners to assemble their workstation. "I see you've already put the specimen on the slide. Must have been something to take all of your attention."

Caroline looked at him sharply, expecting the telltale signs of sarcasm, but Charlie grinned at her with genuine pleasure.

"What is it, exactly? Can I take a look?"

As he studied the specimen, Caroline studied him. A strong jaw, tousled, sandy-brown hair, tall but compact build. His arms were freckled and his hands artistic. Was he like all the others? Arrogant in their good looks and narrow-minded in their views of women? She was happy to have sex with those guys, but that was it.

"This is way cool, but I still don't know what I'm looking at." He turned to her with a lopsided grin and said, "Hello, Caroline Tate. I'm happy to be your lab partner. And I won't be late again." He chuckled.

She finally smiled. "I'm sorry, Charles. I sometimes get lost in things. I apologize for being distracted and getting you in trouble." She registered his double take. No doubt he was checking her out, but she saw a twinkle in his eye.

"Not necessary to apologize. No big deal. I get into trouble all the time. But, it's Charlie to you." He stretched out his hand to shake hers. "I have a feeling we're going to do great things together."

And they did. Lab partners, study buddies, friends, and then more than friends. Such a natural progression that Caroline didn't think twice about it. Until now. She chided herself for being surprised by the proposal. When he picked up and followed her to her graduate fellowship in Iowa, it was a commitment most would have seen as the next step toward a life together.

But Caroline didn't track the way most people did. She remembered the time the high school counselor had sent a note home to Uncle Fritz suggesting that he consider a psychological assessment for her. He didn't know she had steamed the envelope open and read its contents before handing it to him. When she found it crumpled in the trash by his desk in the study, she chose to interpret the action as disagreement with the school counselor rather than indifference. From that day on, she ignored any other opinions about how she should behave and embraced her unique view of the world. *On her own.*

However, Charlie was someone she let in a bit. She was surprised but happy he followed her to Iowa. That must mean something. She didn't like the idea of being without him.

Then two weeks later, fate intervened.

"Ahhh. It arrived. Aren't you going to open it?" Charlie teased as he spied the official university letter on the kitchen table as he came in from his run. He grabbed a towel to mop his brow, his T-shirt glued to his enviable chest. "You've only been waiting for it for three weeks."

"I'm scared to open it. What if it—?"

"Caroline Tate. Review the historic data. You've never been turned down from an opportunity you sought. Not ever. You won't be this time, either. Your references are impeccable. Your preparation complete. You are ready for this, and they want you. I'm sure of it. In fact, so sure, I'm going to open it myself." Charlie grabbed the letter and ran into the bedroom.

She chased him and got there just before he closed the door. He grabbed her and pulled her to the bed with him. "Let's do this thing."

She grabbed it from him and gently opened the flap. She made a show of unfolding the letter but shared it to read together.

Miss Caroline Tate,
We are happy to inform you that the faculty of the University of Minnesota Duluth has endorsed your appointment as a tenure track professor of biology with a special emphasis in ornithology.

If you accept this offer, we would like you to be in Duluth to start September 1. We will pay for your moving expenses—

"Hallelujah! I made it! I was so worried. I can hardly believe it came through." She drew a long breath, hugged him, and gave him a big kiss. "Charlie, have you ever wanted something so much that you couldn't imagine life without it?"

"Yes, Caroline, I have indeed." He sidled off the bed to open a dresser drawer and pulled out a letter of his own. "I can't imagine life without you, married to you. It's time."

He opened the letter dated one week ago and showed it to her.

Mr. Charles Booker,
We are happy to inform you that you have been accepted as the high school biology teacher for the

academic year starting in September. We recommend that you take time to relocate to Two Harbors this summer, as classes start immediately after Labor Day, and teacher preparation begins ten days before that.

"Two Harbors is twenty miles north of Duluth; it was the only opening I could find in the area. We can live in Duluth or Two Harbors. But, Caroline, I think we should arrive as a married couple."

"You did all of that, sure that I would get this job?"

"Yep, I did."

Caroline smiled so big she thought she would swoon, and then teared up. She swallowed hard, put her hand up his dank T-shirt to pull it away from his chest to take in his musky smell. She said in a husky voice, "Charlie, you stink. Let's go take a shower, and then let's go get married."

Chapter 3

Two Harbors, Minnesota
Fall 1996

"Is this Mrs. Booker?" Charlie called her excitedly with the news.

"This is Caroline Tate Booker. Who's calling, please?" She laughed with him as they both loved to hear the sound of their married names. "I miss you! How's it going?"

"It's done. They accepted our offer on the house."

She screamed in delight.

"And they brought the price down based on our agreement to replace the windows and furnace. So, I figure we can swing the financing with our new salaries and replace the furnace right away, and then wait a year or so on the windows."

Charlie had found the perfect lakefront house for them on the North Shore Scenic Drive between Duluth and Two Harbors. The previous owners, an older couple, had built it themselves forty years before, and it was in need of some upgrades. However, the location was all they had dreamed of since they had accepted positions in the northland.

Caroline had said, "As long as we're near one of the Great Lakes, let's get as close as we can get."

Charles complied. He had traveled out twice to get the job done.

"Fifteen minutes max travel time for each of us, and a double garage."

"That's perfect, Charlie. I gotta go to this meeting. I'm so proud of you. Thank you, darling. I'll see you in two weeks."

A week later, the furnace was installed, and he was on hand to accept their meager belongings from Iowa. When she arrived, he had flowers on the kitchen table and a big red bow on the tree outside the house. It was the lakeshore that drew her.

"I can't believe you got us such a great spot!" Caroline ran the length of the shoreline and scanned the lake, her hair whipping in the wind. "It's beautiful!"

He joined her at the edge of the yard where the high weeds bordered the rocks leading to the lake. "Yes, it is. The lake changes constantly. I've yet to see two days in a row where it appears to be the same color." He pointed south. "There's Duluth. Most nights you can see the lights from the city. On the horizon straight across from us is Wisconsin." He pointed again. "Sunrise direction."

"I love it. We need to get some of those classic Adirondack chairs so we can sit out here and watch the water every day! Maybe right here?" She gestured to a spot that provided a perfect view and was somewhat protected from the wind by a stand of fir trees at the northern border of the property.

Charlie grinned. He had hoped for this response and was delighted with her enthusiasm. "Yes, of course we will. Now, let's go show you the house."

He gave a short, guided tour that quickly ended in the bedroom, and they spent their first afternoon as homeowners making it their own.

The next day, Charlie gave Caroline a tour of the town. Two Harbors had a small-town feel, with the area near the ore docks lively with tourists. Locals, who frequented the hiking trail nearby, could catch a view of the big boats navigating in by the lighthouse. The tugboat, the *Edna G*, was on permanent display in the harbor. It didn't take long to show her downtown, consisting of a street or two of businesses, a hardware store at the heart of the activity, a few gas stations, one supermarket, and a few restaurants on Highway 61, the highway that bisected the town. It was not a big city but had everything they needed.

Caroline was keen on visiting Hawk Ridge in Duluth the first week they were there. When her face lit up, he knew it would be one of their haunts. She had a fondness for raptors, especially peregrine falcons. She was entranced with their resurgence from near extinction, their speed and adaptability to new environments, which kept her interested in searching for them wherever they might be found, as they were known as wanderers.

Charlie had been to his school a couple of times to meet with the principal, Patricia Benson, and to have a look around his classroom. After they toured his big, boxy room with rows of lab tables and cupboards labeled with sharpie ink, he realized how much he had to do to get it set up in the next ten days.

Patricia said, "Make sure you bring your wife to the annual teacher back-to-school potluck dinner. What's her name again?"

He wondered how inviting Caroline would go. He wasn't in the habit of requiring things from Caroline.

Patricia seemed to sense his hesitation. "Well, it's important that you introduce her to the other teachers and their spouses. This is a small town, and it's good to know one another. We've been teaching the children of this town for eons and know all of the families here. You'd be surprised how helpful it is to be able to call on a colleague, especially during your first teaching year." She peered at him from the clear glass above her bifocal lens, sizing him up.

Charlie could almost read her unspoken thoughts.

This guy barely finished his classroom practicum.

True.

He had supported them in Iowa with a restaurant manager job and managed to add enough to their savings to secure a down payment for the house. He had barely finished the required teaching credentials before applying for this job.

"Support from your wife in this first year will be very important." She smiled then, a halfhearted attempt, and added, "By the way, there's another new teacher starting this year, the physical education teacher and basketball coach. This isn't his first teaching job, but he and his wife are new to town as well. You may want to get to know them. He and his wife are expecting a baby, too, sometime this school year. Name is Craig Barnes."

Charlie raised an eyebrow.

Patricia added, "Breaking into a small town can be a little rough. It would be good to have company on that road."

They arrived late. Caroline, her unruly hair held back in a headband, quickly disappeared to check out his classroom, and Patricia took him around to make introductions as people mingled.

"This is Caroline?" Patricia extended her hand as Caroline returned and approached the small circle around Charlie. "Welcome to Two Harbors."

"Thank you. I know we'll be happy here," Caroline said, as she shook Patricia's hand and beamed up at her husband.

An involuntary giggle from Jesse North as she studied Caroline had them all turn toward her. She quickly recovered as her husband, the math teacher, helped her out. "Oh, my god, you two are so young. And we are so . . . not! It's so exciting to have such a nice young couple reinvigorate our little town."

"Young but accomplished," Patricia inserted.

Jesse recovered and added, "Caroline, what do you do?"

"I'm on the faculty at UMD in biology. Ornithology is my specialty. I'm super excited to be living here with all of the natural wildlife and ecological diversity."

Just then, Patricia pulled over another couple to make introductions. "This is Craig Barnes, our new basketball coach, and his wife . . ." Patricia gestured to her as she turned into the group beside her husband.

"I'm Lori Barnes. Nice to meet you all."

Charlie did his best to take a look at this flaxen-haired, willowy young woman without focusing on her baby bump. He shook Craig's hand. "Sounds like you and I are the newbies this year. Glad I'm not the only one."

Craig asked. "I understand from Patricia that you're from New England."

"Yes, we both grew up in the East but spent some time in Iowa for Caroline's PhD program. We like the Midwest, and after Iowa, we're excited to be near so much water. How about you two?"

"We're both Midwesterners. Met at Mankato State. Lori is in early childhood development, and this is my third year coaching."

Jesse giggled again. "Looks like you two have been doing a bit of child development. When is the baby due?"

Craig took his wife's hand and smiled. "Ah, that would be soon, just another few months to go."

Light laughter followed, and the grouping scattered. Craig pulled Charlie aside, "You play sports in school?" Craig put his finger to his eyebrow and pointed to the same spot on Charlie's face.

"Oh, this?" Charlie stroked the one-inch-long scar cutting through his sandy-brown eyebrow, along the orbit of the eye. "Nah, schoolyard fight. I was a badass in my day." He made light of it, hoping Craig wouldn't probe. He was not going to tell this guy the story of how street fighting was a survival skill.

None of his foster placements could support a way of life for him to go out for sports in school.

His mind quickly found the image in his memory. It had been a schoolyard fight he would never regret. He had been fourteen years old and lived with a foster family that had two other foster kids. Joseph, a small kid at ten, was being bullied in an isolated corner of the playground of his school when Charlie had arrived to walk him home. The taunts and laughter still echoed.

"Joey. C'mon, you can do better than that!" Two larger boys held his arms back while a third, older than him, was pulling his pants down. Joseph was trying to wrestle himself free. "Where's your mommy or daddy to save you? You don't have real parents, do you, bastard?"

Without hesitation, Charlie threw himself at the bully, taking him down to the hardpacked ground. Charlie got a first punch in, shouting, "Pick on someone your own size" before the bully grabbed a rock and smashed its jagged edge at Charlie's face, carving an inch-long slice through his eyebrow. The immediate bloom of blood sobered the trio, who ran away before Charlie could get to his feet.

When he did, he saw a crying Joseph cowering in the dirt, his pants down to his ankles. Rather than following an instinct to chase the boys down and take his revenge, he focused on Joseph. He comforted him by talking to him gently, cleaning him up, trying to make him feel cared for and protected, which he did that day and for as long as he was in the same home with Joseph.

Bravado didn't come naturally to Charlie, but he defended himself and others as needed. He never sought out a fight, but sometimes it was the price to pay for being an orphan in a cruel world. He vowed to leave that world behind and have his own family to love and protect someday.

Fortunately, his last foster placement had put him in a safer environment. Working with college kids in their restaurant, he learned to model his behavior and manners by watching them until he was often thought to be one of them.

"Well," Craig smiled. "Maybe you'd like to come out and help me sometime on the court."

Charlie thought he would like these people. He couldn't get a read on Caroline, but she seemed to say all the right things.

When they were on their way home, he asked, "What did you think of the party?"

"I assume we only need to do that once a year, right?" Caroline scanned the sky through her window, already searching for something new on the horizon.

Charlie had always been the more social of the two, so he was delighted when Caroline announced she had invited a faculty associate to come to see their house over drinks.

Charlie made sure they had wine, beer, and snacks on hand.

Geri and her husband, Frank, were East Coast people, and while they swapped tidbits of experience to find a match, they finally hit upon the common bond of baseball at Fenway Park. "My cousin was a ball boy at Fenway, and every summer my parents let me take a trip to Boston for a game. Got to sit in the dugout once!" Frank gushed.

"That's special! I didn't get that close up. I did get to a game or two during my college years. Charlie, remember that game when you tried to catch the foul ball and almost fell from the balcony?" Caroline laughed and put her arm around him. "Must have been sometime after we became inseparable, right?"

Charlie marveled at how this woman was increasingly coming into her own. He hadn't witnessed this side of Caroline and realized each of them was still evolving. When he remembered how much trouble he had gotten into to make himself noticed, he winced; all due to the deficit he felt with no family ties—or at least no family that wanted to be tied to him. Once he met Caroline, he knew she would make him whole. Now they were forging a new life together. Who knew what would come next?

As they toured the house, Geri remarked, "Nice family house. Three bedrooms so you shouldn't need to move once you have a baby or two."

Caroline laughed heartily at that. "Oh no, not me. I'm amazed I'm married. Babies are not in my future."

It was an offhand remark, and the party went on. But Charlie wasn't there anymore.

Later, after Geri and Frank had gone, Charlie left the house alone for a walk to get his emotions under control. When he returned, he found Caroline in the office, working.

"Nice people, aren't they?" she asked without looking up. "Geri is my guide to the politics of the department, so I want to make sure I stay close to her."

"Caroline." Charlie stood in the doorway.

"She's been there for years and knows her way around, that's for sure."

"Caroline. Do you really not want to have a baby, ever?"

She finally looked up. "What?"

"A baby. I thought we would have a family. Pretty soon, actually. Isn't that what you want?"

"Oh, Charlie, no. I don't want a baby. I've never wanted a baby. I thought—"

"How would I know that? We both grew up so alone. I assumed you would want a family. Don't you want to make a family with me?"

She crossed over to him and attempted to bury her head in his chest. "Charlie, you are my family. You are more than enough for me."

Charlie's body was unbending. For the first time in memory,

he was not willing to comfort her. "What if I want a baby Caroline? What about me?"

He felt her body recoil from him, and she sobbed as she backed away from him. "Charlie, are you saying that I'm not enough for you?"

As her tears started, Charlie's resolve melted, and he gathered her in his arms. "No, darling, of course not. You know you are everything I've ever dreamed of. I love you more than you could ever imagine. It's just that I also dreamed of having a mini-Caroline around as well."

"I'm sorry to disappoint you. Maybe you shouldn't have married me." Caroline was in full hysteria now, and he guided her to the sofa to sit beside her until he could calm her down, reassuring her that she was more than enough for him.

After she fell asleep on the couch, Charlie picked up the snack dishes from the living room and cleaned up while he thought about his miscalculation. How did he get this so wrong? He assumed she wanted a family like he did because she, like him, had none. He remembered the long road he traveled before he dared to propose and wasn't ready to surrender on the baby question quite yet.

He brightened. This was just the next challenge to overcome.

The lake was beginning to earn its reputation for extremes. One day, the wind would hit the lake where churning waves threatened the shoreline. The next day, the sun and bright-blue sky would change the color of the still lake from blue-gray to turquoise. They loved it when the wind whipped the waves and howled around their house so that it felt like they were alone, surrounded by the elements. Their days became routine. Charlie left for school just after seven in the morning. Caroline could go to work later but stayed later, too, not arriving home until close to seven at night.

"What time will you be home tonight?" Caroline was up and drinking coffee with him one fall morning, as usual, but this curiosity about his day was out of character.

He was suspicious. "About the usual time."

"When would that be?" Caroline busied herself buttering her toast and avoiding his eyes.

"Are you saying you don't know when your husband usually arrives home, Mrs. Booker?"

"Just answer the question, will you?" False bluster was also out of character for her.

"Well, today is a normal day, so I would guess, but I can't be sure of the exact time. Do you need an exact time?" He folded his paper noisily. "If you told me why this is important, I could be of more help to you."

"Not exact. Approximate would work." She finally gave in to the joke and laughed at herself.

"Well then, around four. Does that work for you?" He got up and kissed her solidly on the mouth, grabbed his jacket, and left the house.

Charlie pulled into the driveway at 4:09 p.m. and was surprised to see Caroline's car already there. Then he remembered her strange behavior at breakfast. He couldn't remember Caroline ever pulling off a surprise and wondered if everything was all right. He hustled into the house.

"Caroline? Are you here? Is everything OK?" The kitchen was empty, but he could hear shushing in the living room. He followed the sound.

A blur of black fur and skidding puppy paws came toward him on the wooden floor. He crouched to meet this fur ball and accept kisses and loving noises from a beautiful black Labrador pup with white markings on her muzzle. "Well, hello there, how are you?" He looked up to see a fidgeting Caroline taking in this introduction.

"What do you think? Do you like her?" Caroline's words tumbled out as she quickly put her hands in her pockets.

"Wow, what's not to like? What's the story, Mrs. Booker?" Charlie couldn't remember Caroline ever giving him a surprise gift before. He smiled broadly.

"Well, meet Abigail. I brought her home to be part of our family, silly." Caroline's attempt at nonchalance was foiled by the tight line of her mouth until she joined the puppy on the floor and grinned.

Our family doesn't sound silly at all. Charlie eased down to the floor, and the puppy climbed all over him. "What a fine idea. Abigail is a great name. Couldn't have named her better myself. Does this new family member have any supplies?"

"Ahh, yes, the breeder sent me home with a bag of puppy food, and I have this leash, too." Caroline proudly pointed to the leash on the piano bench.

"Good job." He put the puppy down and pulled his wife in for a hug and whispered, "Thanks, Caroline."

Chapter 4

Two Harbors, Minnesota
January 1997

Charlie knew that January on the north shore of Lake Superior would be cold. He didn't know that such glacial chill could penetrate the marrow of your bones and freeze the lake out fifty feet or more most years. The whipping wind on his face reminded him that his windows needed to be replaced.

One night, Charlie came in from a frigid walk with Abigail and pulled off his boots. When Caroline called to him, he walked into the bedroom and found his bride in fingerless gloves reading a book with the pillows bolstering her up and only her head peeking out of the piles of blankets atop the bed.

"I'm cold. Please come to bed and keep me warm."

"Well, that's not an invitation I can refuse." He was quickly in his boxers ready to head her way.

She closed her book and turned out the light. "I forgot to take my pill. Would you bring it to me? It took me ten minutes to get my feet to thaw in here."

"OK, so where am I looking? In the medicine chest—the little wheel, right?"

"Yes, it's the next number in order. Thanks."

Charlie found the birth control pills easily. He gazed at the wheel.

"Do you think we made the wrong decision to replace the furnace before the windows? Would that have made a more comfortable January for us, do you think?" Caroline asked.

It took him a minute to see they were similar in size to the low-dose aspirin.

"Sorry, what did you ask?"

It took him another minute to check his conscience. He badly wanted a family. He knew Caroline needed one, too, she just didn't know it yet. Both of them had an emptiness to fill. Wouldn't this one act be viewed as worthy to get them there? He quickly dispelled an unformed worry that he could be caught in this betrayal.

She repeated her question, and he grabbed a Dixie cup from the holder, filled it with water, turned off the bathroom light, and carefully navigated across the dark bedroom to Caroline's side of the bed. As he gently proffered the pill and water he reassured her, "Well, my dear, I think we'd be frozen if we had no furnace, and with just these rattly windows, we have a chance of making it to spring."

And he made sweet love to her, which warmed her down to the bottom of her toes.

Charlie liked this little trick so much, and Caroline was so eager to be waited on, it became a routine. As the weeks sped by, he almost succeeded in ignoring the little voice in his head saying, *This is not your choice alone.*

Finally, the lake froze over, and the big ore boat traffic stopped. Their habit of watching the boats progress across the lake out their windows was interrupted, but they still delighted in watching the landscape change into a virtual ice land. They could make out the city lights from Duluth and loved watching the mist hover over the lake where there was still open water. Ice shards picked up the sunlight in incredible patterns.

The days started to get noticeably longer again in February, but it was still so chilly in their house with the windows seeping air in that their nighttime ritual of cuddling in bed to keep warm became a necessary delight for both of them. Charlie continued to wait on his wife, bringing her pill to her every night.

"I'll really miss you when you go to Brazil. How will I keep warm?" Charlie asked, as he awakened and whispered to Caroline after one such night of lovemaking. The air temperature in the bedroom was still forbidding.

"I'll probably be overheated by the temps there in March. Hope my system can handle the contrast." She dipped a toe onto the fuzzy rug on the floor, then stood to find her slippers. "You could come with, you know. We could take a side trip to Natal. I could show you where I lived with Uncle Fritz."

Charlie muttered, "Yeah, sure." He knew that was an empty invitation. First, she was an add-on to a National Geographic birding tour, solicited by a former professor colleague who wanted to initiate her into the life of sharing her passion for birds. Cushy trip to guide well-heeled birdwatchers. Second, he couldn't get away. His break didn't coincide with hers, and he needed to use the time to stay ahead of his class during his first teaching year. Developing lesson plans took an incredible amount of time and more of his energy than he had expected. Plus, her way was paid, and they could not afford paying for him, not with the mortgage and windows to buy.

"Charlie." She turned to him and threw her pillow at him. "Hey, you knew who I was when you married me. I'm a nomad and an adventurer. You promised, bud."

He grabbed her at the waist when she leaned in and pulled her back into the bed. "I love you just the way you are, Mrs. Booker." He took her hand and stroked her wedding band. "But I'll miss you." *Will she always be so eager to leave me?*

While she was gone, he did miss her. He had window companies prepare bids for replacement. Abigail was company, and he did get ahead on his lesson plans. He recognized how empty he was without Caroline to fill him up, her neediness a balm to his deep need to care for her.

Chapter 5

Two Harbors, Minnesota
Spring 1997

She needed him to care for her when she returned from Brazil, exhausted and possibly ill with a virus.

"It's so good to see you." She gave him a weak smile as they waited for her luggage. "I missed having you with me."

He gave her a long look and gently touched her flushed face. "I think we should go right to a doctor. You don't look like yourself. How long have you been sick? Do you think you picked something up over there, or could it be a reaction to those shots you took before you left?"

She tucked into his arms and smiled. "I missed having you worry over me. I just want to go right home to bed. I'm really tired."

"OK, but if you are not feeling better in a day or two, promise me you'll let me take you to a doctor?"

"Yes, of course." She took his arm, and he handled the luggage as they made their way to the car. She used her last reserve of energy to tell him how much she'd enjoyed the rain forest and traipsing around searching for birds. "They've asked me to come on their next trip. I'm so excited."

Charlie frowned and turned to look at her. He was about to tell her she couldn't agree to that without talking to him, but she looked so ragged that he was worried about her and didn't say anything.

After sleeping through the next day, Caroline felt marginally better in time to start the next semester the following Monday. She was still tired and nauseous on occasion. When she didn't bounce back after a week, she agreed to go to the doctor. They were new to the area so Charlie did the research on their insurance and chose a family physician in Two Harbors. She agreed to meet him there after work for her appointment.

She looked drained as they did the preliminary check-in. Her hair had lost a bit of its shine, and she had become thin.

"Wow, I can't believe I lost that much weight in Brazil. I'm down eight pounds."

Dr. Riley, in his mid-forties with graying hair and deep-set eyes almost hidden by wild, bushy eyebrows, waltzed in with his crisp white coat and immediately put the patient chart down to chat with them. They spent the first few minutes discussing how the Bookers were getting along in their new home.

"Two Harbors is a nice little town, sometimes too little, but you'll sort that out as you live here." He chuckled. "So, what brings you in here, Mrs. Booker?"

"I'm not sure. I'm really tired all of the time since I got back from a birding trip to Brazil, and I've been feeling nauseous sometimes. Looks like I've lost some weight." Caroline's voice was softer than usual.

"Here are her most current medical records, Dr. Riley. She also had to take some pretty heavy-duty drugs to go to Brazil, and that information is here, also."

"OK, well, let's take some blood and a urine sample and see what may be going on with you. I see your temperature is normal." He looked through the papers that Charlie had given him. "No children?"

"No."

"Birth control?"

"Yes, pills."

"Before we look too hard at Brazilian viruses, we'll look closer to home. The nurse will come in to take blood and instruct you on the urine specimen. I'll let you know in a day or two what we come up with, and what that means, all right?"

Two days later, the doctor's office called and asked them to come in to go over the results.

What results couldn't be left on a phone message? Charlie tried to distract himself by grading papers late into the night, but the words became jumbled on the page. He sat up until the early hours gazing at the lake, then fell asleep on the couch. By the time they went into the doctor's office that Saturday morning, he held Caroline's hand to steady himself as they waited for Dr. Riley.

"Well, the blood work came back clear from any viral or bacterial infections, foreign or domestic, so you're all right on that score." He looked at them, and then smiled. "I've got good news for you. Mrs. Booker, you're pregnant."

Caroline dropped Charlie's hand and stood up so quickly she got light-headed and fell back down in her chair. "What? That's impossible. I can't be pregnant. I'm on the pill."

Charlie could feel his heart beat wildly as he alone celebrated the news. *I did it!*

"So you said. But even oral contraceptives are not fail-safe. You are eight weeks into your pregnancy. Congratulations."

Caroline put her head between her knees, her curls hiding her face. "No, I can't be pregnant. I can't be."

Charlie stared at the doctor and stroked his wife's back. "Unbelievable," he whispered.

Caroline swiveled up out of Charlie's reach and said sharply, "It certainly is!"

"Well, believe it. I've experienced this occurrence a few times during my career. It's always a surprise, but, of course, I'm hoping it's a happy one for the two of you." He looked from Charlie to Caroline, who was again head down. Charlie avoided his eyes.

"So, no issues with any of the strong meds or inoculations she had before she left to go to Brazil?" Charlie couldn't help thinking, *Is there any risk to my baby?*

"Are you asking if there is any potential ill effect to the fetus due to the vaccines and meds she needed before and during the trip?"

Charlie looked down at his wife and continued to stroke her back. "I guess I am, yes." Then quickly added "But, my primary concern is for Caroline."

"I believe Caroline is fine on that score, but I'll be watching her for any ill effects. As for the fetus, I did check all of the contraindications on the meds that were listed in the file you brought in, and pregnancy was not mentioned. That should mean we are safe on that score."

"Should mean?" Charlie's heart went to his throat as he struggled to get the words out.

"Well, early fetal development is always a vulnerable time. But there's nothing known that we should worry about."

"Mrs. Booker, Caroline, I'll need to get you in for a physical exam, and then we can establish a schedule of appointments for you and get you on prenatal vitamins. Do you have any questions for me right now?"

Charlie couldn't breathe. *What have I done? How could I ever have thought she would be happy with this?*

She lifted her head up to a forty-five-degree angle to look straight at him. "How could this happen?"

Charlie forced the image of a Dixie cup and pill from his mind.

"I know it's a big surprise, and that you will need to do some thinking and planning about what this means to you both. Oral contraceptives are about ninety-nine percent effective. That leaves the magic one percent. This appears to be what has happened here, dear."

Dr. Riley rose to leave and said, "Congratulations to you both." He left them in the room alone.

Caroline rose slowly and whispered. "Get me out of here."

Chapter 6

Two Harbors, Minnesota
Spring 1997

Caroline felt herself being helped into her coat and ushered out of the office. Charlie hesitated by the reception desk, but she shut down any idea he had to make another appointment by the withering look she cast his way. "I need to leave now." Her steely voice dropped an octave lower.

"I know this is a shock to you, to us, Caroline." Charlie was eager to talk as he pulled out of the parking lot.

"Don't even start." Caroline hissed. *I hate him, and Dr. Riley, too.*

Charlie kept his eyes on the road as he drove home in silence, scarcely glancing her way. Finally, he tried to take her hand as he walked beside her toward the house. "Caroline, are you OK?"

"No, I'm clearly not OK, and I don't want to talk about it." She brushed his hand away and firmly said, "Go," her voice a low growl.

She walked into their shared study and closed the door. Her body robotic, she opened up her computer to bury herself in research. Gathering information was her default whenever she felt challenged. This time, she wasn't sure what would help her.

First, she researched pregnancy and the pill, only to find that Dr. Riley had been correct. It wasn't 100 percent effective. She admitted to herself she must have known that when she first chose a method of birth control, but that was a long time ago. *Damn him for being right!*

Then she searched on miscarriage. She was heartened to find the incidence of miscarriage high but as she reviewed the common causes, knew it would be pure luck if she couldn't carry this baby to term.

If she didn't want to leave it to chance, there was another option. *My research must be thorough.* Her fingers stopped midair and she looked around the room as she considered typing abortion into the search engine. She hated the fact of her inner conflict. But there it was, all those years growing up in the church at war with her mantra of being her own woman.

On the cusp of breaking down into sobs, she caught her breath and self-soothed like she had so many times before, this time promising herself, *Motherhood will not be my future.*

Not sure how she would avoid it, she put it off to another day. Her heart rate normalized as she regulated her breathing. She calmly closed the search down and moved to her observation notes from the Brazilian rain forest to lose herself in her passion.

An hour later, she felt Charlie's presence in the house before she heard him rattling pots and pans, then putting groceries away. *He must have gone out to the store.* She heard him talking to Abigail in the kitchen as he fed her and then heard his footfalls on his way to her.

She was ready.

"I suppose you feel victorious that your macho sperm vanquished my chemical line of defense when you knocked me up." She greeted him with a cold stone voice and watched him enter the room and move toward her.

"Caroline, it will be OK. I know it wasn't your dream, but we'll sort it out. Maybe you'll be happy about it soon."

"That's one thing I won't be, Charlie, happy about it. Ever. I can't have a baby."

"Caroline." He was close and getting closer.

"I'm not supposed to be a mother. It's not right for me." Whispering now, she felt his heat as he closed in on her, pulling her to him and out of the chair.

He stroked her hair and held her tight as the tears of confusion came. "Hey, baby, it'll be OK. We'll sort it out." After a few moments, her tears subsided, and he tenderly moved her aside. "I have some chocolate chip cookies in the oven. Can you smell them?" He led her by the hand to the kitchen table.

How can I stay angry with him? It would be like kicking a kitten.

As she sat at the table eating cookies, she was reminded of Mrs. Mason, the only one of the series of her Uncle Felix's housekeepers Caroline remembered fondly. Trudy Mason had been lovely. A grandmother herself, she had raised four of her own and knew how to connect with a child. From age nine to eleven, Caroline felt almost loved. Mrs. Mason got her up and off to school with a smile and a lunch worth trading at school, greeted her with cookies and milk after school, got her through her homework, and tucked her into bed with a story or a laugh.

Cheered by the comfort of that image, she smiled at Charlie, then suddenly, her mind clicked on a memory that fed her fear. Mrs. Mason convinced her uncle to take in a parishioner's daughter for a few days when she had been thrown out of her own home once she was discovered to be pregnant. *Being pregnant means being vulnerable. Losing control!*

She shivered at the thought. "I'm scared."

"I know. We both are. It's new to us. But we'll be fine. Right now, you need some rest, right? I'm thinking a nap." He led her into the bedroom and settled her into bed. "You know I'll take care of you."

"Thanks Charlie." Caroline settled in.

Chapter 7

Two Harbors, Minnesota
Spring 1997

Charlie lay beside his wife and pulled a coverlet over the both of them. He was exhausted from lack of sleep the night before, but he couldn't relax until he put his mind right about what was happening.

It was the unknown that bothered him. While Dr. Riley was sure Caroline was OK, he hadn't been quite as convincing about the fetus. *What if there's a problem with the baby?*

He knew he had to tread carefully with Caroline about the baby and focus on her given her state of mind. She pulled the coverlet tighter around them, and he succumbed to the warmth of his bed and his wife. *One thing at a time.*

Charlie was undecided about what to do, so by default, he waited Caroline out. He didn't initiate another conversation about the pregnancy. They spent a quiet Sunday with *The New York Times*, and some classroom prep for their upcoming weeks. Charlie served Caroline breakfast in bed, and they went on a short walk with Abigail. A full weekend without nausea, and Caroline looked less drained.

"Remember, I have Journal Club so won't be home until around nine tonight," Caroline said as she headed out the door with her briefcase the following Monday morning.

"Are you sure you feel up to it?"

"Yes, of course. Why wouldn't I?" Caroline's defiant glance dared him to specify any reason she would be changing her routine.

"No reason. Just . . ." He kissed her on the lips. "Just glad you're feeling better."

That evening Charlie stopped at the hardware store in Two Harbors to pick up some rock salt for their driveway. He bumped into Dr. Riley, debating paint color with a young girl.

"Gwen, you really think you want your room to be this dark purple color?" Dr. Riley was showing her the color wheel. "Maybe this lighter shade would be better?" He did a double take when he saw Charlie and said, "Hey, nice to see you. Do you have a minute?" Then he directed Gwen to look at more colors and took Charlie by the arm around the corner.

"My daughter, Gwendolyn. Wants a purple room, tweens." He laughed. "I'm glad I ran into you. I haven't heard from your wife yet. We should get her in for an appointment." He lowered his voice. "I know the news was a shock."

Charlie clearly interpreted this as an opening for a longer discussion, but he wasn't prepared to take it. "So, your daughter Gwen will be in my classroom in a few years. What is she, twelve?"

"Eleven going on eighteen, I think." Dr. Riley laughed. "Children are a trip, that's for sure.

But you know that well, as a teacher, I suppose."

"I enjoy teaching. I learn a lot from them and love what I do." Charlie preferred talking about school rather than his wife's mood. He smiled at Dr. Riley and recalled the teacher he had in middle school who had looked beyond his status as a foster kid and encouraged his interest in science. He shifted his bag of rock salt to his other hand. "Well, I should get going. Nice to see you."

Dr. Riley reached out and touched Charlie's jacket at the shoulder. "Mr. Booker, please know that I can help in any way that you and Mrs. Booker would like me to help." He let go of the jacket and met Charlie's eyes. "Is she feeling all right?"

"Yes, yes, she's feeling much better. Had a restful weekend. Thanks." Charlie's smile faded as he made his escape. *Yes, Two Harbors is a small town.*

He drove to the harbor and watched the lighthouse beam streams of white light on the dark water. On the horizon, he saw the lights of Duluth to the south. He needed to be invisible for a moment. He turned off the car engine and let the stillness envelop him as he gathered his thoughts. He allowed himself a moment to indulge in his impending fatherhood, a miracle under the circumstances. But it was clear to him he would have to focus on Caroline and to welcome the baby so that she would learn to share his dream. *Can I do this? Hell, yes, I can!*

He had gotten this far. He relaxed into a "won the jackpot" smile. He couldn't remember ever being this happy. Maybe when Caroline agreed to marry him, but this was even better. His smile faded as he realized the pregnancy would always be clouded in his mind with his trick to make it happen. He felt his body grow rigid as he turned his torso to look to his right and to his left, peering out his window, on guard for anyone able to see the guilt he knew must be apparent on his face.

Instead, he saw a young family about to cross in front of his truck. Dad and Mom each held a little one's hand tightly on their way from the breakwater toward the lighthouse. His heartbeat slowed, and his body relaxed as he accepted this as a signal. A child, a family the redeeming outcome of his action. Now, he had to let go of his guilt and get Caroline on board with building their family.

Resolved, he started up the car and drove home, put rock salt on the worst of the driveway, and made himself a dinner of ham and eggs. He had just enough time to prepare for Caroline before she arrived home at nine thirty.

Charlie made paper-bag luminaries from his store of lunch bags and lined the walkway from the garage to the house. The night was brilliant with starlight reflected on the open water of the lake. Flickering light from the candles appeared magical against the black of the landscape toward the shore. He watched for her to drive up and met her at her car.

"Welcome home, my love."

"What have you done?" Caroline's face was screwed up tight, until he gently helped her out of her car and gave her a warm hug.

"I'm merely celebrating the greatest surprise of my life. The woman that I love more than life itself is carrying our child. It's a miracle."

"I'm so confused." She tilted her face toward him, and he kissed her full on the lips.

"Let's get you into the house." He took her hand and strolled with her carefully between the luminaries and opened the door to the inviting aroma of warm chocolate.

"And feed you a brownie. A celebratory food that you love. You are still down some weight, so you can enjoy with ice cream, if you'd like."

She laughed. "So, you're trying to fatten me up?"

"No, I'm celebrating with the woman I love and treating her with the joy that I feel about our new situation."

With candlelight and the good china gleaming, they shared warm homemade brownies à la mode and had their first real talk about the baby.

"I still don't know how to feel about this. It was never something I wanted." Caroline lifted a forkful of brownie.

"I know."

"I doubt if I'll be any good at it."

"I know you doubt yourself, but I don't."

"I won't give up my career."

"I don't expect you to."

"I want to be the nomad adventurer of my own dreams."

"I know and will support you." Charlie reached over to take her hand.

"I'll be miserable as a pregnant woman."

"Not if I can help it."

"I'm not good at housekeeping or taking care of you, so how can I take care of a baby?"

"I'll take care of it."

"There is another option." Caroline pulled her hand back from his.

"That would be?" Charlie was afraid of her answer.

"You know—"

"Please don't say adoption." Charlie's words jumped out in a rush. He knew she couldn't defy the early grounding of the church and mention abortion. "That's the one thing I couldn't manage. Adoption is for people who don't want their children or can't raise their children. That would be a lie. Because I want this child, and I can raise this child. I know deep down that you do, too. Caroline, I'm willing to make it work on my own, until you realize it, too."

"Do you mean that? You'll raise this child, and I'm free to be me?" Caroline stopped picking at the brownie crumbs on her plate, her eyes fixed on him.

"Yes, I promise." The words came fast; he didn't pause to consider their full meaning. Right then, it was just another pledge he made to his wife. "Would you like more ice cream?"

"No, I'm good." She pushed her dishes forward and leaned back in her chair, a smile brightening her weary face. "Thank you for all of this."

"And now that it's past ten, let's get you to bed. By the way, I ran into Dr. Riley at the hardware store in town. He asked about you. I'll call tomorrow and make an appointment for you. I love you, darling. I'll take care of you."

As he cleaned up the kitchen and collected the luminaries, he congratulated himself. *I can do this. I know I can.*

Chapter 8

Two Harbors, Minnesota
Spring 1997

Caroline awoke to Charlie's voice on the telephone confirming the doctor's appointment for later that day. Now that he had promised she could offload baby duties onto him, she was going to test him.

"I'd like a brownie for breakfast please, warmed up, and I suppose I should have some dairy, so how about some ice cream with that, again this morning."

"Do you think that will agree with you? How are you feeling?" He came to the bedroom doorway and peered in at her.

"I'm fine. And until the doctor's appointment, let me have my way with my diet, please." She blew him a kiss as she rose and disappeared into the bathroom. She stretched wide and hugged herself, relaxing in the knowledge they had reached an understanding that met her needs. She had a life to live, and Charlie had promised her she could still have that life.

"You are a very healthy woman. You are ten weeks along in your pregnancy. You may find that the nausea comes to an end within the next few weeks. I also would like to see you start putting on weight. Have you ever had any issues with appetite or eating disorders?"

"No. Charlie feeds me very well. I just don't eat when I'm not hungry." Her eyes strayed to Dr. Riley's paunch, straining his white coat buttons.

"So, the due date is when?" Charlie asked.

"Mid-September."

Caroline exhaled loudly. "Oh, good. Then I can still meet my commitments of birding trips midsummer and late October."

"If you remain healthy and have the energy, I see no reason why you can't." Dr. Riley faced her after entering information in her chart. "Unless the trips are in locations—"

"No, they are both stateside. Fortunately." She smiled at Charlie, whom she had surprised with this news.

"Dr. Riley, are you sure the exertion of travel and the long days that go with guiding a group of birders is really a good idea late in the pregnancy?" Charlie asked.

"Well, putting aside the October trip, which may be complicated for a nursing mother, and possibly interfere with the bonding process . . ." Dr. Riley stood and handed her the prescription for prenatal vitamins, "the midsummer trip is really only a problem if Caroline isn't feeling energetic enough to make the trip. Pregnant women do amazing things."

"Oh, I'll be up for it. You can count on that." She beamed at them both. "I don't plan to be a nursing mother, so you needn't worry about the October trip." She took Charlie's hand and smiled at him. "Charlie will handle the bonding."

Charlie looked away and mumbled, "Yes, whatever that means, I'll do it."

Dr. Riley scanned their faces. "This is a journey that is just starting for you two. There will be lots of decisions to make along the way. My advice at this point is to take it one step at a time." He smiled at them and added, his body angled toward the door. "Do either of you have any other questions at this point?"

"Just one, Dr. Riley." Caroline gathered the fabric of her patient gown to her and folded her arms in front of her. "I understand I can get my tubes tied immediately after the birth, is that correct?"

Dr. Riley did a turnabout. "While that is possible clinically, it is unusual, especially with a first pregnancy. Many couples wish to keep their options open pending the unknown health of their baby, in those first days. Even if you think you only want one child, tube reversals are difficult and a sometimes unsuccessful solution should you change your mind later. Why don't you think about this? There's no hurry."

"I won't change my mind." Caroline's voice was firm as she looked directly at Dr. Riley.

Charlie was stunned but so close to his goal he didn't say a word as Dr. Riley left the room.

On the drive home, he asked Caroline, "You committed to these bird trips without telling me?"

"I thought I had told you. Glenn was surprised and impressed with my performance as a guide and wants me to take on any trip I can. So, these are the first two that we agreed on, but I have an open invitation for more. I'm thrilled."

"When did you commit to these trips."

"When I was with Glenn on the last one. I didn't think you'd mind." She reached over and kneaded his shoulder, her voice a caress. "You are always encouraging me to do what I want to do. Aren't you?"

"You committed before we knew you were pregnant."

"Oh, my god, yes. I still can't believe I'm pregnant!" She laughed. "As you said, quite the miracle." She continued to knead his shoulder. "I can use the trips to further my research—maybe get another journal article or two."

She noticed Charlie's hands tightening on the steering wheel and his shoulders tensing up.

"I chose the midsummer one so that you could come with me. Glenn says there's a chance to get a discounted price on the trip for you." She leaned over to kiss his ear. "I was hoping you'd come with me. You won't be in school then."

"And October? How will that work?"

"I really don't know, haven't thought about it. I do have professional leave for both trips, but that's all I've done." She dropped her hand from his shoulder and checked her watch. "It's nearing dusk. Can we drive to Split Rock and check to see if the peregrine falcons are around? Thinking about my trips makes me want to bond with my favorite wandering birds."

Knowing he wouldn't refuse her, she dug out her binoculars and directed him to the spot.

Chapter 9

Tucson, Arizona
Summer 1997

Mud season on the North Shore gave way to a late spring. Finally, there were a string of days warm enough for the new windows to be installed, and it clearly made the house cozier. The locals had warned Charlie heating season ran through June, and they were right. He was on a mission.

He needed the house to be warm and snug for his baby's first winter. This, he could do. It was just a matter of money and effort. Keeping Caroline happy and getting her on board with welcoming a new baby in a way in which she would learn to share his dream was more elusive.

She was healthy, he knew that. Once they finally agreed on a nutritious diet that gave her enough calories and made sure she took her prenatal vitamins, her energy level stabilized. While she complied with the schedule for doctor visits, she was dispassionate about the data collected or tracking progress, uncharacteristic of Caroline the scientist. Dr. Riley never missed a chance to praise his patient and explain fetal development along the way. "Congratulations, you're doing beautifully. Your weight is on target, and fetal growth is good."

But Caroline never missed a chance to share her distance from the entire situation. "Charlie's doing, not mine."

He juggled the housework and cooking with a full teaching schedule. Caroline rested a lot and became irritated by the attention she received from fellow faculty.

"They accept me now that I'm big with child, as if I've succumbed to the natural order of things and am no longer a threat to their kingdom. Even Geri is giving me advice about things that I don't care about, like it's a female rite of passage. I hate it. What do I care about diaper brands?"

"I think they're just showing interest. Most people think having a baby is a big deal. You should enjoy it."

She didn't resist him, but she didn't make any effort to get ready for this baby. He still had to line up day care for late September, as he assumed Caroline would stay home for a few weeks with their new baby.

She refused. "I'll be physically ready to go back to work in a week and will go crazy if I have to stay home for more than two weeks." She looked at him with panic in her eyes, as if he had asked her to give up her career.

"Caroline." He drew close and massaged her shoulders until he felt them loosen up a bit, then kissed her neck. "A few weeks will be good for you, the baby, our family. How about you try it? You may even like it."

"Two weeks. That's all I can do." She pulled away, standing as tall as she could but listing a bit with the midbody weight. "You are the baby parent in this family, I'm just the vehicle. You promised."

He planned to go on the birding trip in mid-July, not because he wanted to experience the birding wonders but because he wanted to take care of his wife, by then close to eight months pregnant.

"You'll love it! I can't wait to go and find the sparrows," Caroline said, as they arrived in Tucson and met the shuttle to take them to the ranch, which was home base for this particular birding trip. The timing was designed around the black-throated sparrow, a smartly patterned bird that thrived year-round in the Sonoran Desert and also in the much sparser plant growth of the Chihuahuan Desert farther east.

Upon arrival at the ranch, Caroline had Charlie check them in while she went off and rounded up a few birdwatchers who were reviewing the schedule board. As he approached, there she was, a slight woman in khaki and hiking boots with an oversized shirt open over her T-shirt-covered swollen abdomen, more animated than he had seen her in months. She was holding court with her fellow bird-watchers, who listened with interest. Charlie felt slighted at her exuberance about this trip and the chance to catch a glance of some rare sparrow rather than the impending birth of their own child. However, her enthusiasm was catchy, and the group was in her grasp by the time Glenn Lightner, the tour organizer and chief ornithologist, came over.

"I see Caroline is taking care of all of you, as she tends to do."

Caroline faced him after he had already swooped in for a hug without seeing her body in profile. Glenn gave her a very close hug. "Wow, this is different." He pulled away, but not before everyone saw his expression of surprise as he panned her full body and took in her physique. "My, my . . . How far along are you, Caroline?"

Caroline hesitated while everyone watched her.

Charlie entered the circle and stretched out his hand to Glenn. "Glenn, I'm Charlie Booker, Caroline's husband, and the father of our child," he gestured toward Caroline and grinned, "expected in a couple months."

With that, the birdwatchers chuckled and scattered after Glenn reminded them they would have their first lecture just before the social hour at five o'clock. A few lingered to chat with Caroline.

Glenn asked Charlie, "You're a schoolteacher, right?"

"Yes, just finished my first year of teaching high school biology. I'm on summer break. Decided to accompany Caroline and try to catch sight of some five-striped sparrows."

"Uh-huh." Glenn stretched to his full height of six feet five inches, towering over Charlie. He took off his sunglasses and leaned in, whispering, "Glad you're here. I didn't know she was pregnant. All she ever talks about is birds—never seen such passion." Glenn hesitated and Charlie sensed that he was trying to reconcile his personal knowledge of Caroline and how she would take to motherhood. "Son, I've been married for twenty years and have raised a couple of very independent daughters. I'm aware of how women can 'do it all.' Just didn't anticipate this particular track with Caroline. More power to her."

Charlie nodded. "She is an amazing woman."

Glenn rubbed his chin. "I assume this means she will cancel out on the October trip?"

"Well, actually, she's still planning on it. Maybe you could suggest to her—"

Glenn shifted his weight. "Well, that's not my business. She'll realize soon enough whether it will work for her. But for now, I can count on you to watch over her, right?"

Charlie was speechless for a moment, and then they both started to laugh. "Yeah, right," Charlie said. "As if Caroline listens to anyone."

After witnessing the constant activity and work involved, Charlie continued to worry about Caroline's insistence on her bird tour so soon following the birth of their baby. He finally admitted to himself he was a bit unsure about handling an infant on his own in that first stretch. Even though he had promised her he would be the main parent, what would that mean in the early weeks? He hoped to engage Dr. Riley in helping to persuade Caroline to change her plans.

When Caroline and Charlie returned home from Tucson, he had a message that distracted him from his own worries. They were unpacking as they listened to the voicemail.

"Charlie, this is Patricia. I'm calling with very sad news. Craig Barnes has died after a head-on collision with a deer on the highway. It was instant, and he was alone in the car. Call me when you return, and I should know about funeral arrangements."

"Oh no!" Charlie sat down on the bed with a plop. "I can't believe it. He's our age, Caroline."

"Who is he? Did I ever meet him?" Caroline was throwing dirty clothes from her travel bag into the laundry basket.

"Yes, you met him at the teacher get-together last fall. He and his wife were expecting their first child. Do you remember?"

"Not really, but that's too bad. I'm sorry." Finished with her unpacking, she stowed her bag in the closet. "Don't plan on me attending the funeral—didn't know the guy, and funerals aren't my thing."

Charlie barely registered her as his mind shifted to another child growing up without a father.

Charlie attended the funeral alone, as planned, and took in the image of Lori Barnes holding her six-month-old daughter. Red-eyed but poised, she was almost regal in bearing as she calmly responded to those paying their respects after the service.

At the lunch in the church following the service, he chatted with his fellow teachers. Patricia, the principal, said, "Lori evidently wants to stay in Two Harbors. They had just bought a house, and she's not sure how she can swing it. She may decide to leave town."

Someone else asked, "Does she work?"

"She was taking time off to be with the baby. She's certified in early childhood ed, so she's clearly employable. Wow, what a bad break," Patricia said. Then she took Charlie aside and added, "By the way, Mack is taking this particularly hard. I know you two may not know each other well, but you're colleagues, and he could use as many friends as he can get right now. Can I count on you to reach out to him? I'd appreciate it."

"Sure, Patricia. I will." Charlie glanced over to focus on Mack, the math teacher, and his wife, huddled with Lori. Mack and Craig had been inseparable this school year, and Charlie had envied their tight friendship as he watched from his solo perch. Besides, if the principal had asked him for a favor, he couldn't say no. He made a mental note to approach Mack at school.

Chapter 10

Two Harbors, Minnesota
August 1997

Patricia had connected Charlie with Lori, knowing he needed help with day care, and she needed an income. He hoped the flowers he offered as she opened the door signaled kindness rather than desperation. She gestured for him to come in while she finished a somewhat heated telephone conversation.

Finally, she put the phone down and walked to him, physically shaking off the tension of the call. "Charlie," she said, extending her hand in greeting, "those are beautiful. Thank you."

"I was at the funeral but couldn't get over to the house after. I hope you like these. They're supposed to last awhile in a vase."

She took the flowers, smiling. "Thank you. C'mon in, Ashley's sleeping. Let's go into the kitchen. I've got some iced tea if you'd like some."

"Thanks for agreeing to hear me out. Patricia was careful to manage my expectations." He smiled back, suddenly feeling shy, as if it were a first date and he needed to make a positive impression.

"Well, I'm not sure of anything right now." It would have been impossible for Charlie not to have heard the phone conversation Lori had just finished with her father, so he didn't need any more explanation. Her father was clearly after her to move back to Iowa with the baby, rushing her to make a decision.

"Fair enough. I'll just tell you what my situation is, and you can decide if it's something you can help me with. If not, no problem." His gaze wandered beyond her to the sheetrock stacked on the studs between the kitchen and the back entry. "Looks like Craig had a project going when. . . ." His voice trailed off.

Lori busied herself finding a vase, not meeting his eyes. "He and Mack were just starting the addition." She pointed to the expanse. "We wanted it to open into one big great room with a screened porch for the back end of the house."

He sank onto one of the kitchen stools, leaning his elbows on the counter. "Give you lots more family space, if you did that."

"Well, not sure I'll need 'family space' and not sure how it'll get finished now." She set the flowers on the kitchen island between them. "You have a baby coming soon, I understand?"

"Yes, any time now. I haven't got childcare sorted out. My wife will be traveling within three weeks of the birth, and she won't be taking any time off, so I need care around my schedule, as I'm the major parent."

Lori's eyes widened. "Really, how does that work?"

"Not sure. Figure I'll learn fast." Charlie shrugged and took a sip of iced tea. She was certainly straightforward. He liked that. But he wasn't sure about what to share about Caroline, so he didn't.

"Um," he cleared his throat, "I was thinking that since you have your baby, maybe you could take mine in and have two to care for? I'd pay you well. We can keep it short-term if that's what you want."

Their eyes met, and Charlie saw some of the lost soul in her that he felt in himself. She squeezed the lemon into her tea. "Do you have a backup plan if I say no?"

"Nope, can't say that I do. But, like I said, I'll figure something out." He smiled shyly again. Charlie read her delayed response and scrunched brow as puzzlement. Perhaps she was wondering how he would figure something out if she said no. He waited her out, hoping she was tempted. After hearing how she reacted to the pressure her father was exerting, he wanted to offer an alternative.

Finally, she asked questions about hours, expectations, and whether he really meant it when he said that it could be a temporary arrangement while she sorted out her future. They discussed each item.

She surprised him by saying yes. After he left, he wondered if it was because it allowed her to extend the lifestyle she would have had if Craig had not died. A school schedule, babies, one more than she would have herself. Or was it because she felt a kinship with him, so vulnerable himself.

As he drove home, he pondered the irony of recent life events. In a moment of opportunity, he grasped the chance to become a father and hoped for the best. *How can I feel relieved that Craig's death turned out to be a lucky break for me?*

The next day was a teacher planning day. Charlie searched for Mack and found him in the teacher's lounge.

"Mack, I understand you and Craig Barnes were friends at college." Once Mack met his eyes, he added, "Sorry for your loss." Charlie positioned his body to shelter Mack from the group of teachers a few feet away who huddled at the coffee pot.

"Thanks. Totally tragic. Still can't believe it happened." Mack's canned words were a contrast to the emotion on his face, as he turned away quickly.

"So, then if you were friends in college, you know Lori pretty well, right?"

A quick nod from Mack. "Lori's great. And now Ashley to raise alone on no income. She seems to be feeling a little lost right now."

"Not sure if you know this, but Lori is going to be taking care of my new baby, who should arrive any day now. Just made the agreement with her yesterday."

Mack's face immediately brightened as he stretched to his full six feet two inches and grabbed Charlie's shoulder. "Really? Man, that's great. I didn't even know you and your wife were expecting. Congratulations." He reached out his hand to shake Charlie's. "You know she's an early ed teacher, right?"

"Yes, I do. So, I'm very happy that she's available." Charlie could almost see the wheels turning in Mack's head as he processed the positive synergy of this new arrangement. An income for Lori, at least for the short term, while she sorted out her future without Craig.

Just like that, Charlie had made a school friend.

Chapter 11

"Charleeeee." Caroline screeched again, with everything her swollen body could muster, and finally he came to her.

"Caroline, darling. What is it? I'm here." He opened the shower door ready to rescue her from whatever peril she was in now.

"Where were you? I needed you." Caroline stood in the steady stream of warm water, hair plastered to her head, stark naked with her belly stretched around the beach ball soon to be their child.

Charlie placed his hand on her shoulder and softly said, "I'm here now, Caroline. I took Abigail out for a quick walk. What do you need?"

"I dropped the shampoo and can't pick it up. And it's all your fault." Caroline spit out the words.

"OK, I see that's a problem." He kicked off his shoes, grabbed the shampoo and leaned into the shower. "Let's get this done before we run out of hot water. So sorry, babe." He gently worked shampoo into her hair, caressing her scalp and whispering in her ear, "I'm here now."

Caroline soaked up his tenderness as her due, disregarding that he was now totally drenched. "I'm carrying your child. Abigail is a dog. I'm your wife."

"I'm taking care of both you, and Abigail and will take care of the baby, too. I only have two hands and twenty-four hours a day!" Charlie controlled his sharp voice through gritted teeth. "Give me a break, Caroline!"

She glared at him and scrambled out of the shower, clumsily reaching for a towel while water dripped from the dramatic contours of her body, leaving a pool of water on the floor. As Charlie stripped off his clothes and cleaned up the bathroom, she climbed into bed and reflected on her situation.

How did this happen? She hated being pregnant—celebrated not for her intellectual contributions but because she was a female captive to her biology. She hated it. Her natural tendency to fight back and show them all, to win regardless the odds, was shaken by her own self-doubt. She had been mortified when her colleagues started a baby pool and collected money in a piggy bank for a bet on the birth date, giving each a reason to size her up every day for whether she would go their distance. But the worst was when a disgusting junior faculty member patted her stomach, as if her baby bump were community property.

She couldn't count on her body now—cumbersome in these last days of pregnancy and a little muddled. Her energy was sapped by taking a shower and she was humiliated by not being able to bend down to pick up a dropped bottle.

Would she get through the birth with its blood and gore? The rituals that came with it were bad enough to endure. She had turned down Geri's offer of a baby shower, but still people persisted in dropping off gifts to her at the office, now sitting in a pile on top of the piano in their living room.

She felt the warmth of Charlie's body as he joined her in the bed and spooned her from behind, evidently sorry for his show of anger.

"You're cold. Get away," Caroline said, still annoyed by his outburst.

"I'm cold and need to warm up by my red-hot wife."

Caroline halfheartedly back-kicked him. "Get away from me until you can tell me you're able to have this baby yourself."

He cuddled her and nibbled her ear. "Wouldn't that be something? Man bears child after wife pregnant for nine months." His chuckle started as a low rumble as he patted her stomach and kissed her shoulders and neck.

Her body was always the key to changing her mood. She finally giggled as she allowed herself to be comforted by the only man she had ever conquered. "You would if you could, I know."

"Damn straight, woman." He molded his body to hers and her breathing slowed.

"Caroline. Your due date is only a week away."

Caroline felt her body tighten. "Don't remind me."

"Are you scared?"

"No, I know you'll be there with me." She hesitated slightly. "Four weeks after that is my next birding trip. That's what keeps me going."

She felt his body shift slightly away from her. "Let's just keep that as a hope and not a certainty. You may not—"

"You promised, and I'm holding you to it." She wasn't sure what he would have to do and didn't want to know. It was his problem.

Chapter 12

Y

Two Harbors, Minnesota
September 1997

Charlie was finally able to get his sullen and bulky wife to leave the house for a drive. He helped her down the recently reinforced porch steps. A moist lake breeze carried the last of the light scent of daylilies from the garden border. The singsong of finches provided a muted backdrop to the gentle grind of a rotary mower kicking out the fallen blades in the yard across the road.

As he helped her into the car, he tenderly pulled an errant cottonwood wisp from the barrette that kept her black curls from her eyes. He slowly breathed in the familiar scent of her rosewater shampoo, mixed with freshly cut grass. He drove slowly to town passing by the neighboring mom-and-pop resort noisily having their busiest week leading up to Labor Day. A family gathered near one of the housekeeping cabins, some playing cards at the picnic table, two young women playing with their babies on a blanket nearby. He slowed to watch the beginning of either a pickup baseball game in the park or a batting practice. He heard the unmistakable whack of a solid long ball with no soft thud of a glove following.

"Someday our kid may play baseball in this park." He put his hand on her knee and smiled hopefully.

"Maybe with you," she said gruffly.

"Caroline, I'm not going to let you bait me into an argument. I know you're uncomfortable, but we're close now." His voice was a sweet caress to her stony facade. *What's behind this? If it's insecurity, hey, I feel it, too.*

She removed his hand from her knee.

He swallowed hard. *Pact be damned. How far can she take this?* He took a deep breath and exhaled slowly. *Waiting her out is always the way to go.*

On their way to the harbor, Charlie pointed out the cars unloading colorful kayaks at the cove for the annual Kayak Festival. "Calm water won't last long today. There's a change in the weather coming. I can feel it."

Wildflowers, daisies, and yellow tansies danced over the meadow, but her eyes were skyward, as usual. He saw her give up quickly with no bird sighting but show some interest in a monarch butterfly bobbing up and down on a search for nectar.

At the approach to the wooded area closer to the harbor, birch and aspen trees were beginning to show the first signs of red and yellow and seemed to stretch to meet the sun while it was still warm. Their evergreen cousins threw cones to the ground to secure their future. He saw her scan the branches looking for birds, but there were only gulls heading toward the water.

Charlie pulled the car over to a slow stop and pointed excitedly to alert her to twin fawns with their mother peeking out from their forest home. The rich loamy smell of dirt and weeds invaded the car as he opened the window.

They parked at the harbor of mighty Lake Superior, suspiciously calm close to shore with dark clouds moving in. They watched a hulking ore ship languidly make its way into port. They listened to the chug and hum of motors starting as a few hopeful fishermen left the marina. A few more watched the sky as they made their way in. The wind picked up, bringing the stench of gasoline their way.

"I feel like a DQ." Caroline surprised him with her first smile in a week. "I have a craving for the crunchy sweetness of a chocolate dip cone."

He happily drove the mile to the Dairy Queen and tucked Caroline under an umbrella to duck the plop of first raindrops. She headed to the restroom, and he ordered.

In the next five minutes, the granite sky unleashed a torrent. He had finished his cone by the time she came back. Her eyes were as wild as the storm, and her wet skirt clung to her inner thighs.

"We need to get to the hospital." She took her dripping cone from his hand and made a hook shot into the garbage. "Now."

Charlie ushered Caroline into the emergency entrance. As the maternity nurse, Melissa, offered her a wheelchair and started to wheel her away, she bolted upright searching for Charlie, who was just about out the door. "Charlie, where are you going? Stay with me."

He sprinted to her and leaned down to give her a hug. "I'm going to move the car into the parking lot, and I'll be right up. I promise."

Charlie pulled himself away and left a voice message for Dr. Riley as he headed out to move the car. Alone, he allowed himself a moment to breathe deeply and assess. He would grade his plan to keep Caroline happy until she could share his dream of welcoming their baby only a C so far. Her demands on him were more than he expected. She was still not showing any interest in the baby to come. When she saw their baby, all would be well. He knew it!

Adrenaline rushed through his body as he finally let his mind take him to the goal and accept the message that it was game on. Every muscle in his body felt alive. He would have kicked his heels in the air if there hadn't been other people in the parking lot. Finally! A child of my own! A real family!

He found Caroline in a heated exchange with the nurse trying to get her into bed. "I can do it myself." Half in the wheelchair, she kneeled over in pain. Fortunately, the nurse was still holding onto her side when Charlie closed in. "Charlie, I need you."

"I'm here now. Let's get you into the bed. Melissa is just trying to make you comfortable."

"Not likely to happen! Where is Dr. Riley? Let's get this done."

"Mrs. Booker, this is your first baby, and the contractions are still five minutes apart. It will be a while before Dr. Riley comes. Let's get you into a gown. We'll take good care of you."

Hours later, Melissa was abused as expected by a recalcitrant Caroline who repeated loudly and often, "Make sure Riley ties my tubes. I'm never doing this again." She added to no one in particular and anyone within earshot, "I'm not nursing this baby, so don't try to make me."

Hours after that, Caroline demanded whatever drugs could kill the relentless pain, and by turns, yelled at Charlie for his role in her predicament and beseeched him to comfort her. She remained adamant about having her tubes tied, and in her pain and panic, wouldn't agree to push until Dr. Riley, now summoned, promised that he would oblige.

"Mr. Booker, is that what you want, as well?"

Charlie looked at his wife, who was laser focused on his every move and word, even as her pain tore her apart. He locked eyes with her and relented.

"Yes. Whatever Caroline wants."

Once Caroline heard those words, she unleashed her body's reflex to push and gave it her all. Three pushes and there she came.

Grace Tate Booker. Perfect in every way.

Caroline finally agreed to hold the baby the next day after she had eaten breakfast and taken a morning nap. "Looks like my uncle Fritz—no hair and a frown." As the baby searched around for a breast, Caroline thrust the baby out to hand her off to Charlie. "Your department, Daddy."

Charlie locked eyes with his newborn baby girl and felt a surge of pure love. He knew then that it had all been worth it. He would be hers for life.

Charlie slept on a cot and stayed at the hospital all three days to soak up whatever he could about caring for a newborn. He learned how to bathe her, swaddle her, feed her, and the first steps to get her on a schedule. He had read a mountain of books, but watching the nurses was helpful.

On the third day, while Dr. Riley was preparing to discharge Caroline, the doctor took Charlie aside for a private conversation. "How are you feeling about going home with your baby, Mr. Booker?"

"I think I'm ready." He smiled, with a touch of pride. "I've got the swaddle down, and they're sending me home with plenty of formula."

"Son, I notice you are saying 'I' not 'we.'" Dr. Riley put his hands in the pockets of his white coat. "I'm not sure whether your wife has started to bond with the baby yet, and frankly, I'm not sure what to make of her resistance to motherhood. Is her attitude about this consistent with her personality generally, or have you seen any other signs of . . ." Dr. Riley moved closer and added, ". . . a mood disorder?"

Charlie felt his face contort slightly. "Caroline is perfect, Dr. Riley. A bit unconventional but brilliant. She'll be fine as soon as I get them both home. I'll be taking care of the baby. That's our agreement."

"Do you have any support from family or friends?"

"We're going to be fine. Thank you." Charlie was not likely to share his orphan story with Dr. Riley, who seemed to consider the entire community his family. He turned away then, and Dr. Riley touched his shoulder to add one last comment.

"Let me know if you need help. Postpartum depression can hit hard, and I want you to know you can always call on me."

Charlie's bravado didn't last long. The first night home was a long one.

After the ten and one in the morning baby calls, it took a minute or two for Charlie to register Grace crying for her feeding at four fifteen.

Caroline said, "Charlie, the baby's hungry or something." She rolled over on her side away from him. "Could you just sleep in the other room or on the couch so I can get some uninterrupted sleep?"

He pulled his weary body out of bed, noting Caroline had issued an order, not a request. The next day he called on Lori Barnes for help getting the baby nursery set up and supplied. He needed to sort out the layout and knew who would be there for him.

Chapter 13

Two Harbors, Minnesota
Autumn 1997

Caroline heard the knock on the door when she was toweling off after her shower. She could hear Charlie's happy voice greet Geri, and her delighted response at meeting the baby. She combed her wet hair, struggled into her pre-pregnancy jeans, and studied her body in the mirror. Ten days out from delivery; tubes tied and lactation avoided. Her boobs looked great while still temporarily engorged. Belly was starting to shape up, but slower than she liked. She still couldn't button the jeans. *Amazing what a baby could do to a body, like a barnacle hanging on and leaving you with less muscle mass. I hate it. I need to get back to me, but maybe keep the boobs?* She smiled at herself in the mirror. Time for her to make an entrance.

"Hi Geri." She interrupted the gibberish language going on between her husband and her guest, gushing over a seven-pound baby.

"Caroline. Hello." Geri pulled away from Charlie and Grace to greet her. "She's beautiful! Congratulations!"

"Thank you." Caroline shrugged. *She should congratulate the sperm for the win against the pill, not me.*

"You look great! How are you feeling?" Geri asked.

"Pretty good. I'm really ready to go back to work. Getting a little stir-crazy here." Caroline gazed at the baby, and then cast a questioning look toward her husband.

"Caroline has been a star. Tough labor, but she managed it beautifully. Look at her, radiant and already slim again. She's amazing." Charlie managed to shift his full attention to adoring his wife while continuing to hold the baby in his arms, rocking her slightly.

Despite her attempt to detach from all the fuss, Caroline felt herself perk up at the praise. "Geri, come in and sit with me. Tell me what's been going on at the department. What should I know before coming back on Monday?"

"Oh, wow, I didn't know you were coming back so soon. How will you manage that?" Geri asked. "I took a full three months off after my babies were born."

"Well, Charlie has it sorted out. He'll be home for another two weeks, and then he has a sitter close to his school all lined up." Caroline led Geri past the windows along the living room as she talked and saw a car turn into the driveway. "Charlie, did you expect Lori Barnes to come out now?"

What is she doing here? Her eyes recorded Lori's every movement out of her car—the bounce of her blond hair as her willowy frame moved gracefully to unbuckle her baby from the child seat in the back. *Why does she have to be so gorgeous? Why not a grandma-type rather than this young widow to care for Grace?* She took a cleansing breath to shake the image of Lori. One thing she had learned in the last week: babies took a lot of work, and Charlie would need help with that. *Still, better her than me.*

"Oh, yes, she's bringing me a few supplies. Sorry, forgot to mention it." Charlie's voice waned as he headed into the baby's room to put her into her crib, then went out to help Lori.

Caroline watched as he and Lori shared a laugh while he approached her car. She remained standing a beat too long as she registered a warning that she would have to be watchful. Turning quickly, she gestured for Geri to sit to discuss more important matters. "I need to make an appearance at the office before I leave for my birding trip the following week. Have to keep Phil Peterson happy with me." Caroline grimaced, thinking of her department head.

"Oh, he's supportive of mothers. He'd give you all the time you need," Geri said.

"For a baby, yes. But my passion is birds, and I intend to follow that wherever it leads me. I don't want trouble from the likes of Phil." She noted Geri's quizzical expression and added in a calmer tone, "What?"

"Caroline, I know you are not asking for advice here, but—"

"No, I'm not, but go ahead." Caroline was bemused and curious.

"I'm not telling you to be conventional. I don't think that would work for you, anyway." Geri smiled. "But you may want to play up your maternal side a bit with Phil. You want him to support you, so play into his stereotypes. I think it will pay off and get you more leverage to do what you want to do career-wise."

Caroline heard her voice rising. "That's ridiculous. I am who I am, and I'm not about to change for Phil Peterson." As she registered the sound of the back door opening, a strategy came to her, and she felt her heart rate stabilize. *I'm not about to change, but I can certainly manipulate him.*

Charlie approached Caroline and gently placed his hand on her shoulder as he and Lori came in. "Geri, this is Lori Barnes, and her daughter, Ashley. Lori will be taking care of Grace for us while I'm teaching."

"Nice to meet you, Lori." Geri stood and extended a hand in greeting to Lori, who shook it and then lifted a fold on her chest-mounted baby pack to share a peek at Ashley. Her big brown eyes surveyed the scene from her perch. "How lovely that Grace will have a companion to watch and play with every day. What is she, about six months old?"

"Close. She's seven months now," Lori said.

"We're very lucky," Charlie said. "Lori has a degree in early childhood education. It's incredible that she's available to care for Grace. I'm not sure what we would've done without her." He smiled at Lori, and then added, "So, let's survey the nursery, and you can show me where the baby swing should go."

Geri whispered to Caroline. "Is that the widow of the Two Harbors schoolteacher that got killed?"

"Yes, head-on collision with a deer. Died instantly," Caroline said. "She needed the income after he died. They had just moved here and bought a house."

Geri took it all in and then said, "Such a tragedy. You should make sure Phil knows about how you are helping her out. He'll remember the story of the accident."

Caroline smiled and decided against adding a comment. She needed Geri to help her navigate the office, and even though she wanted to disregard this pedestrian thinking, Phil Peterson could be a roadblock if she wasn't careful.

I can play this game, for now, anyway.

Chapter 14

Two Harbors, Minnesota
Autumn 1997

Caroline's first trip away was just three weeks after Grace's birth. Upon reflection, Charlie thought it was the happiest week of his life. Although there was a crazy schedule of feedings and weird learnings about the basics of human biology, he was immersed in a bubble of love. Caroline was off on her bird trip. She couldn't hide her enthusiasm in leaving the new bundle of baby, and Charlie thought she might even have been eager to leave him for a week. That left him free to adore his daughter fully without measuring equal amounts of attention on his wife, who never failed to need him while he was tending to Grace. Free of that tension, he celebrated his fatherhood, now certain he was born for the role.

He was unsure whether motherhood just didn't come naturally to Caroline or whether her mind was so averse to it that any possibility of her warming to the role was closed off. She ignored her daughter's cries, took no interest in the subtle changes Charlie pointed out each day—a longer morning nap, a more focused gaze, a tighter grasp of his finger, and how much more quickly he could comfort her in the middle of the night.

He tried not to worry over Caroline's obvious detachment and realized it was likely to continue beyond any distraction from her coming bird trip. Fortunately, his love for his daughter allowed him to take the easy path by blocking out thoughts of a future marred by this selfless servitude to his wife. *Almost.*

One more week of parental leave to soak up this newborn experience. By day four, he had figured out the best way to make time for a shower, and he had read enough to know he should sleep when Grace slept. He wasn't sure, though, how that would work when he went back to work in a week. Thank God Lori would be there to help him then. He thought again how fate was so fickle. He was benefiting from her misfortune.

He knew he had tempted fate himself to become a father. Every morning that he woke up to his beautiful daughter, he was grateful he had risked it.

He was sitting in the nursery rocker feeding Grace when he heard a car driving in. "Well, Gracie, are you expecting anyone? I'm not." He rose and carried his daughter to the door and was surprised to see Dr. Riley.

"My, my. A doctor who makes house calls." Charlie's quick smile suddenly faded. *Am I being monitored?*

"Mr. Booker. And Grace. May I come in?" Dr. Riley was holding the screen door open while Charlie stayed inside, cradling Grace.

"Of course. Come on in, and call me Charlie."

"I hope you don't mind my surprising you this way. I just wanted to see how you two were getting on. Lori Barnes mentioned to me at church that you were on your own with the baby for a week, and I thought you might appreciate a quick look-in."

"Ahh, so you and Lori go to the same church?" Charlie inquired with narrowed eyes. *Why are they talking about me?*

"Well, you know small towns. There's a church on every block, but yes, Lori and Ashley were welcomed into our Lutheran congregation and now are solidly a part of our church family. She thinks you're doing beautifully, by the way, and is excited about caring for Grace." He stared directly at Charlie, "She didn't send me to snoop, but when she mentioned you were on your own, I thought it would give me an opportunity to talk to you alone."

Charlie led Dr. Riley into the living room and hoisted Grace over his shoulder, positioning her on the burp pad and patting her back before finishing her bottle.

"Well, we're doing fine. Absolutely fine. I'm soaking up, literally and figuratively, this newborn experience!" Charlie laughed as he pointed to the burp pad, which had not quite caught the earlier spit-up.

"I know you'll do fine, Charlie. I can tell you want this baby and will do whatever it takes to raise her well." Dr. Riley paused. "I'm more concerned about your wife. She didn't come in to talk to me before she left on her trip. I wanted to assess whether she had any postpartum depression, which would explain her lack of interest in caring for the baby."

Charlie had forgotten Caroline was supposed to see Dr. Riley before she left. "Well, I know she was very enthusiastic about her trip. Birding is her thing, and I support her interests. Simple as that."

"How is she with the baby?"

"Fine. She's happy that the baby is healthy." Charlie chose his words; his intuition warned him not to be defensive. "I know it's not something that you are used to, Dr. Riley. But Caroline and I agreed that I would be the main parent. I wanted this. I feel fine about it. I'm actually in baby bliss right now."

"I see." Dr. Riley smiled. "You do seem to be very happy, Charlie. Are you getting enough sleep?"

"Of course not." They both laughed at his response. "I know that's normal. I spend all of my waking hours just watching the miracle of this baby. I don't need a clock. She owns me. That must mean something, right, Doc?"

"It does." Dr. Riley checked his watch. "I'm so happy for you. I know you'll make a great father." He rose and walked around Charlie to take a quick look at Grace, who had fallen asleep on her father's shoulder.

They walked toward the door together, and Dr. Riley added, "By now you know this is a close community. We try to look out for one another. Lori will be a great help to you. But please remember you can reach out to me as a friend, anytime. Good luck." Dr. Riley opened the door and turned. "And Charlie, do have Caroline come by to see me, will you?"

"Yes, I will. Thanks for the visit, Dr. Riley." Charlie patted Grace and smiled.

"Goodbye, and call me Walt."

Charlie walked Gracie across the living room a couple of times and watched Dr. Riley's car pull out onto the highway back toward Two Harbors. He took a deep breath and eased himself down into the rocker without disturbing Grace. In a fifteen-minute visit, his emotions had evolved from suspicion at being monitored to almost feeling cared for by the family doctor. Trust didn't come easily to Charlie, but he felt like Walt Riley was someone whom he might trust, someday.

Then he remembered Riley had made him promise to send Caroline in for a visit, and his grasp on Grace tightened. *How in the world will I do that?*

Another week, this chore may have been hard to consider, but this being the happiest yet in his life, he decided to accept Walt's visit at face value and think about how to deal with Caroline tomorrow. He slowed his breathing to match his daughter's. *Today is for Grace.*

Chapter 15

Duluth, Minnesota
Spring 2000

Bird trips away became a regular occurrence. Reluctantly, he admitted to himself life was easier when Caroline was out of town. Then, he could express his joy with his daughter wholeheartedly.

"So, don't worry about me if you don't hear from me on this trip. I'll not be in a zone for easy communication and want to be single-minded about birds, OK?" Caroline was gathering her gear from the car as Charlie pulled her close for one last embrace before she left on a three-week tour of the Amazon with Glenn and the latest bird tour.

He watched her stretch to her full five-feet-two height and pull her backpack on. Amazing how light she could pack for three weeks in the jungle. "So, Glenn's office is the hub if I should need to reach you in an emergency, right?"

She nodded, then pushed him against the car, her hand stroking his groin, gave him a deep kiss, and in her sexy low growl whispered. "I'll miss you."

Then she was gone. No hugs or blown kisses for Grace who sat patiently in the car seat next to Abigail, who had been licking the car window trying to get someone's attention during the clutch engagement at the rear of the car.

Charlie caught his breath and returned to the car. He leaned back to give Grace a kiss and hug, patted Abigail's head, and began to sing a nonsense song, making up lyrics as he drove. He could feel the tension in his shoulders relax, as it always did when Caroline flew off on one of her bird adventures. Three whole weeks of being able to put Grace at the center of his universe without worrying about Caroline's reaction. Plus free time to spend with Mack and Lori and their kids doing family stuff. Or whatever else he could dream up.

Off-key and this time rhyming to "Baa Baa Black Sheep," he used it to engage Grace in looking out the window and recognizing things as they drove. Now three years old, she had an expanding vocabulary and loved to repeat things that Daddy sang to her.

"Where's Mommy going now?"

"To the Amazon." He sang to her. "To the rain forest, where the trees grow big, and the frogs are red, and the fish can eat pigs." He looked back at her as she started to giggle, and Abigail howled.

"Daddy, fish can't eat pigs!"

Charlie's laugh trailed off as he registered his daughter also found tension release with his wife now gone. His pact with Caroline tested him in ways he had never imagined. He marveled at her ability to ignore the school calendar and what that might mean for their family schedule. She never volunteered to start dinner or go grocery shopping when he was running late. Only once, when he had the flu, did she make sure that Grace was fed and taken to Lori's until he was able to resume his duties. Then she gave him a kiss on the forehead and said, "Back at it, Daddy. Glad you're all right."

But he had committed himself to this life and pushed aside fleeting thoughts of resentment or worry of how this dynamic might affect his daughter.

Chapter 16

Duluth, Minnesota
Spring 2000

As she reached the gate, Caroline put her passport with her other papers and reorganized her backpack. It would be a long plane ride, but at least no change in time zones. Thank God for these trips. She wasn't sure how she could cope without them. The novelty of Duluth had worn off; she yearned for the adrenaline rush of these adventures that took her to new landscapes and threw her in with people who didn't reek of small college academia. She wasn't sure how many more stuffy faculty meetings she could handle. She recalled last week's meeting, which had crawled along on the titillating topic of whether office hours should be extended another fifteen minutes each week. She was doodling in her notebook and a million miles away when Phil Peterson called for her opinion. *What a control freak!*

At least she knew how to manage him. As her reputation grew, she was careful to share credit with her department chair, which he seemed to enjoy enough to allow her to take these frequent trips. Geri watched her back while she was away from campus, which helped.

If she were free, she'd be traveling the world now, writing books and picking up teaching gigs to finance her lifestyle. Now with blogs and internet online teaching, she could be anywhere. But she wasn't free. She was married. To Charlie. She loved Charlie as much as she loved anybody. And she wanted him to travel the world with her.

The gate seating was filling up. A young couple eyed the last seats available, and Caroline moved her backpack to allow them to sit.

"Thanks," the twenty-something said and turned to his partner. A nose ring suited the confident young woman dressed in a flowing skirt and hiking boots, who had the guy's undivided attention until his phone rang.

He held it so both of them could hear. "Yes, we're at the gate. Meant to be!" He laughed, his available arm around her.

She joined in and put her hand on his thigh. "Thanks so much for taking Cleo. We owe you! We'll go retro and send you a postcard from Rio, but watch for our email updates."

The guy added, "Who would have believed I could get this assignment? And with enough in the expense budget to take Hallie with me?" Another lighthearted laugh.

The steward announced priority seating to prepare to board. Hallie poked him in the arm.

"Oh yeah, Hallie just reminded me, there's more cat food in the broom closet right by the basement door. Thanks, man, we'll see you in ten days!"

Caroline stared after them as they stood to board. *I want that life.* Footloose, adoring husband. Free to travel. But Charlie would never leave his students or Grace, even for a short trip.

An image popped into her head from last week. Caroline had to be in the office early and was running late.

"Charlie, I need you to move your car. You're blocking me in the driveway." She blustered into the house and shouted "Charlie!" She shouted loudly a second time, and when he still didn't answer, she pulled off her boots and trudged through the house to find him. "Where are you? You need to move your car!"

She found him sitting on the bathroom floor, with his index finger pressed to his lips "Shhh . . . we're having some success here. But need to give her a little more—"

Caroline looked over at a naked Grace, sitting on the potty chair, taking her sweet time. Through clenched teeth she spouted, "Charlie, if you won't move your car, then get me the keys . . . now!"

Grace's face crumpled and tears started to flow. Charlie spoke slowly and softly, first to his daughter, "Gracie, it's OK, sweetheart," and then to Caroline, "My keys are on the kitchen counter. Sorry about the car, but I've gotta stay the course here."

The memory jogged her back to her new reality. *How many concessions do I need to make for my daughter, a child I never wanted?*

For now, she had her trips and, with any luck, she would find a male conquest on the bird tour that would hold her carnal interest for the duration of the trip.

She finally had an offer to guest lecture at Florida State University for a full semester with time to research spoonbills and their habitat. The gig came with the loan of a faculty house vacant due to a sabbatical leave for the professor courting her down to Florida. After reading the email offer, she slipped out of her office and ran out to the quad to hug herself and laugh out loud. She wouldn't show such emotion to her colleagues.

She accepted before talking to Phil Peterson or her husband. It wasn't a choice she would allow anybody else to weigh in on. She would do it. If Charlie would agree to come and bring Grace, fine. If not, she'd survive.

If this went well, if they liked her enough, there was a strong possibility she would be recruited to fill a position there and be able to leave this small town and godforsaken climate. She would miss the lake, but she would have the ocean in Florida.

She drove home early to surprise Charlie, then remembered he wouldn't be home yet. She drove into Two Harbors to meet him at school. It was early spring and a beautiful drive. The trees were just starting to show new buds, and the wind had tamed down a bit.

In her enthusiasm, she waltzed into the school and to Charlie's classroom without checking in. She looked through the glass of his classroom door and located her handsome husband helping a student at his lab station, both in safety glasses, heads bent over a specimen on the table. An ache in her lower torso hit her suddenly; her body tingled with desire. *Must be the setting*, she thought. He wasn't in the kitchen or taking care of Grace. He was doing something apart from that domestic life she now so often equated with him.

Caroline knew her libido was one of her unique features because she had been told by more than one conquest over the years that her eagerness was a turn-on that brought out the best sexual performance of her lovers. She preferred one-night stands or brief flings and didn't like clingy men. But, once Charlie came along, he provided the right combination of sex and adoration, both of which she needed as a steady diet. What Charlie was too blind to suspect, Caroline didn't divulge. Somehow, Charlie had parlayed his unconditional love for her into marriage. Even with Grace in their lives, Caroline still usually managed to get what she needed from her willing, if now often exhausted, husband.

If he weren't around, she would get it where she needed to get it. She had enjoyed a torrid affair with a married man in Iowa after Charlie left for Minnesota. Brief but memorable, just the way she liked it. Variety thrilled her, and the idea of a new partner was addictive. Pursuit wasn't necessary, especially on the birding trips. There was always a solo male looking for it. She gave out the signs, never trying to disguise them.

If it weren't for the adolescent eyes looking over at her as she gently knocked on the glass, she would have swooped in and taken him in the storage closet beyond his desk. She took a deep breath and strolled in slowly, quietly stalking her target. Charlie ushered her in and introduced her to his class.

"Hello, Mrs. Booker. Nice to meet you." The student closest to her came up for air, then turned his eyes, veiled in safety glasses, back to his work.

Charlie had the class continue and led Caroline over to the corner by his desk. "Caroline, is everything all right?"

"Marvelous, actually." She cupped his behind with her arm facing the wall. "Just came to pick up my man. When can you leave? I have designs on you. Let's duck out and find a private spot for a special date."

Charlie stepped back quickly. "Caroline." He looked over his shoulder to see if any students were watching, then turned to her. "That sounds lovely." He reached over and touched her arm gently. "But school is out in ten minutes, and I promised Lori I would pick Grace up right after so she could get to her quilting class."

Caroline felt her body go rigid and tears of rejection welled in her eyes. "Of course." She hissed at him. "Of course Grace is more important than your wife. Nothing new today."

She stomped out, slamming the door behind her so loudly that she missed the aftermath of fifteen adolescent heads that popped up from their specimens and watched the door rattle on its hinges.

Chapter 17

Two Harbors, Minnesota
Winter 2004

The best part of Charlie's day was when he went to Lori's to pick up Grace. It was a routine the girls seemed to highlight as well. He always made a lot of noise out on the front step, stomping his feet and whistling or singing a tune to let them know he was coming in. Then, he would ring the doorbell, and the squeals would start.

"Daddy's here!" Grace would come running into his arms, followed by Ashley. "Charlie's here!" Then the girls would each take a hand and escort him into the playroom or wherever they had something to show him. Today, it was fresh bread from the oven, last week, snickerdoodles, one of their favorites.

He rounded the corner with the two seven-year-olds, and Lori beamed, putting an egg wash on two steaming hot loaves of bread just out of the oven. "Hi, Charlie. Look what the girls did today."

"Daddy, I learned how to knead a loaf of bread. And Ashley got to put flour on the countertop so we could keep it from sticking."

"Gracie helped me measure the ingredients." Ashley brushed her hands together to remove some flour residue.

"Girls, this is amazing. I can hardly believe you made this. It's beautiful." He hugged each of them. "Just like you two!"

More squeals. "Daddy, Lori said we could take one home."

"Whoa, really? That is so kind! Thank you."

"How was your day?" Lori asked.

"Not bad, how about yours. Girls well-behaved today?"

"Yes, actually, we had fun. We mixed up this bread dough before school, and it was ready to bake later on. They did a good job." Lori put the egg wash remnants in the sink.

"Great. Now it's time to go home, Gracie. Let's get your jacket and backpack." He ushered her to the hall closet to get her things, but Ashley had other ideas.

"Mommy, can't Charlie and Gracie stay here and have dinner with us, just like a regular family?" Ashley took Charlie's hand and peered up at her mom. "I wish Charlie was my daddy."

The moment was long enough for Charlie and Lori to look anywhere but at one another but not long enough to get their answers synchronized. They both spoke at once.

"Honey, Charlie and Grace have a mommy waiting at their house for them." Lori went down on one knee to put an arm around her daughter.

Charlie leaned down and softly cupped the back of her head. "We're kind of a family, right? I see you every day. You and Gracie are best friends, and I love you, just like a daughter."

Grace came up from behind them with her coat and backpack on. "You'll always be my sister, Ashley."

The moment passed when Ashley broke away. "Gracie, don't forget your bread!" She raced to the kitchen, Lori trailing them, leaving Charlie in the wake of emotions he struggled to control. He wondered again whether Lori had tried to meet anyone. *Best if I don't know.*

Lori met him at the door to say goodbye, holding a freshly

baked loaf of bread in a brown paper bag. "Here you go! Enjoy." And after a slight pause. "Will Caroline like the bread?"

"Nah, she doesn't eat gluten." He raised his eyebrows, realizing he may just as well have said, "She doesn't do family." He took his daughter's hand as they headed out the door. "Hey, that just means there's more for us, right, Grace?"

"Right, Daddy."

By now, it was routine. Charlie and Grace would pick Lori and Ashley up on Sunday mornings, and they would all go to church. It started when Gracie thought she was missing out on something fun that Ashley got to do—Sunday school.

"Maybe we should try it, Caroline." Charlie tempted his wife to attend the Sunday service at the Lutheran Church, so Grace could go to Sunday school with Ashley at the same time. "It would be a good way for us to participate in the community, and it's not the Catholic Church. I wouldn't ask you to do that." He knew his wife would never go in another Catholic Church. After her lonely childhood going to Catholic schools and living in a parsonage with her uncle Fritz, she would never return to that cold and rigid life.

"Not interested." Her head was deep in a bird journal.

"Dr. Riley and his family are members. They have a youth group, a youth choir, a lot of my students go to that church—"

"Don't care. Not going. Knock yourself out."

He wanted his daughter to have some understanding of religion, and Lutherans were plentiful in Two Harbors. His orphan upbringing didn't involve much churchgoing, and yet he liked sitting together in community with a hodgepodge of people all in one place. He grew to appreciate the rituals of the service, the glimmer of the offering plates, the way the light played through the stained glass windows, and mostly, the quiet fellowship.

He found it ironic that Caroline's wanderlust might be a rejection of her upbringing in a ritual-bound environment, but that he found comfort in the routine traditions of a church community.

Caroline came to church twice a year. Once for the Christmas pageant at the urging of her daughter, proud of her various roles and costumes, and to Easter Sunrise service to watch her daughter hunt for eggs.

One year, Lori made elaborate angel costumes for the girls, who were eight at the time. The girls couldn't sit still and pranced around one another watching the delicate wings move in tandem with their steps.

"Daddy, are you sure Mommy will be here on time?" Grace asked.

"Yes, Gracie. Mommy said she would get here. She had to teach a late class, but she knows how beautiful you will be and will surely be here to see you." Caroline had promised to make it to the evening performance, but it was snowing, and she had a long drive. Still, Charlie hoped, for Gracie's sake, that she would keep her word.

Aside from a minor mishap with Grace stepping on Ashley's angel train, nearly causing them to topple like dominoes, the angels made their entrance on cue, sang the song in tune, and looked angelic, if a little overexcited.

Lori and Charlie sat in their usual pew, proudly watching and sending encouraging smiles to their daughters. Charlie saw Grace look to the door several times, but he didn't want to appear agitated to his daughter. He didn't turn around to check for Caroline during the service.

As they went downstairs to pick up their angels, a newer church member, Alice Johnson, approached them just as they were greeting their girls. "Oh, what a lovely family you make. Your daughters are beautiful angels! Would you like me to take a family picture of the four of you?"

Before Charlie could correct her, Caroline rushed in from nowhere, pulling her husband and daughter close and smiled brightly. "Yes, do take a family picture, but this is the family. This is my husband, Charlie, and my daughter, Grace."

"Oh, I'm so sorry." Alice's face turned red, and she mouthed the word, "Sorry," to Lori, who had moved a few steps away, giving Caroline her place.

"Lori is our childcare provider, and that's her daughter Ashley." Caroline kept hold of her family while she distanced them from Lori, who took Ashley's hand.

Alice's hands were jumpy, and she jostled the camera before she was finally able to take the picture.

Then Charlie said, "Would you mind taking one more picture of all of us?" He took Ashley's hand, which was connected to Lori's and pulled them into the family circle and handed Alice his phone. He tried to signal his support to Lori, but she didn't meet his eyes, just gave Gracie a quick hug and left.

"Mommy, where were you? Did you see me?" Grace's big eyes peered up at Caroline.

"Of course I did. I said I would, and I did."

"I didn't see you come in, and I kept watching for you."

"Well, you missed me, I guess."

"Did you hear the song?"

"Of course I did, Gracie."

"What was the song?"

"Gracie, you were beautiful. Let's go home. It's snowing hard outside, and it's getting late. Come home with me? Or with your dad?" Caroline held out her hand and smiled coolly at their daughter.

"I'll come with you, Mommy. I don't want you to be lonesome." Grace took her mom's hand and gave her dad a small smile.

The drive was slow, and Charlie followed closely behind his wife's car. After taking Abigail out for a quick walk, he ducked in to tuck Grace into bed.

"Daddy, I don't think Mommy saw the pageant."

"What? Why do you say that?"

"Well, I sang the first verse of "Hark! The Herald Angels Sing" to her on the way home and she said that was the song the angels sang in the pageant." Her eyes were downcast.

"Well, she maybe just made a mistake, honey."

"No. She also didn't see that I tripped and almost fell. Mommies see those things." Her voice faltered. "She wasn't there."

"Well, my love, I know she wanted to be. I was so proud of you, my beautiful angel." Charlie kept his voice light and gave her a warm hug.

"Daddy. Thanks for being there." Grace's eyes glistened.

"Wouldn't miss it, sweetheart. Love you. Sleep tight."

But Charlie slept poorly, thinking about Grace's hurt feelings and how slighted Lori must have felt. *How could Caroline be so thoughtless?* His mind flitted around until finally he drifted off after landing on the realization, *How could she be anyone but herself?*

The next morning, Charlie stopped to pick up coffee for himself and Lori before dropping Grace off before school. When they arrived at the house, she raced off to join Ashley and Charlie handed Lori a hazelnut latte. "Could we chat a minute in the kitchen?"

"Thanks for the coffee. How did you know what flavor to get?" Lori asked, playing with the sleeve on her coffee cup.

"I'm observant," Charlie said slowly, waiting for her to look up at him. "I wanted to apologize for what happened at the pageant last night." He waited for her to respond.

"Apologize for what? For the way Caroline marginalized me and my daughter? For the inelegant way she made it perfectly clear we were not family but put me in my place by labeling me the babysitter?" Lori's words came fast and hot. Then stopped. She turned away from him.

He moved toward her and touched her shoulder to turn her back to him. "Yes, Lori, for that. I'm sorry." A tear slid down her lovely face. "You know I think of you as extended family. If it weren't for you, I wouldn't be able to be the parent I am to Gracie. I'd be lost." Charlie spoke softly but with feeling. As he spoke the words, it became clear to him what he had expected of Lori all of these years, and he knew he owed her a debt he could never repay. She had taught him almost all he knew about parenting—swaddling, toilet training, disciplining, and how little girls should be allowed to try all activities and have trucks, not just dolls. She taught by example; he had watched how she cared for Ashley. They were a team, and he hoped he had shown his appreciation over the years, but he was now forced to see the situation from Lori's perspective.

He had been desperate to get Lori's help when she was her most vulnerable after Craig's death. Lori had pulled him and Grace in and taken care of them selflessly for all these years and made a different kind of family for all of them. Now, he realized he had taken advantage of her to respond to his own needs, perhaps even prevented her from moving on. Managing Caroline was his burden, but how could he not see what it had cost Lori?

"I never would have learned about how to avoid peanut allergies or how and when to introduce new foods, how to make a princess crown . . ." He finally saw a grin and heard a chuckle.

"Well, you could still improve your crown making." Lori exhaled and smiled. "Thanks for noticing."

Charlie was relieved, and an idea popped into his head. "Hey, Caroline will be gone all spring semester. Let's take the girls somewhere special for spring break. Waddaya say?"

Lori looked at him with a bewildered gaze. He thought he had hurt her feelings but wasn't sure how. "Lori?"

"Think this through. What would Caroline say? I notice you apologized, but she didn't. How will she handle us taking the girls on what the world would consider to be a family vacation?" She picked up her coffee and walked out of the room.

As he watched her walk away, he suddenly felt his heart skip a beat and then fall heavily, as if down an elevator shaft at full speed. In that moment, he saw himself turning a corner but couldn't see where the road would take him. He wasn't sure if he dared to invite anyone along.

Chapter 18

Two Harbors, Minnesota
Winter 2006

Grace crept down to the floor in her parents' study, sat cross-legged, and carefully placed the sheaf of photos on the Turkish rug just beyond her. Her mother's pictures. From her last birding trip. Prohibited. But so pretty, the colors so vibrant. Grace couldn't help herself. She barely dared to breathe.

It was Abigail who gave her away. The sound of her claws on the wooden floor morphed to a slow dog exhale as she lowered her aging body to the comfort of the carpet beside Grace and put her muzzle in Grace's lap.

"Abigail, shhhhh. Get out of here, girl. You're going to get me in trouble." But Grace was all bark. She leaned down and put her forehead on the dog's head and patted her on her back. "Aren't they pretty?"

"Gracie?" her father's voice called from the hallway. "Grace, where are you?"

She considered a getaway attempt. With Abigail, though, she knew it was impossible. She put the photos under the edge of the rug and gave herself up. "In here, Dad."

"Ahhh . . . there you are. I see you have a friend with you." Her dad bent down to tousle her hair and give Abigail a pat. "So, whatcha doin' in here?"

"Nothin.'" Grace gave him her most angelic smile.

Charlie sat next to them on the rug. "Find any dust bunnies under your mom's desk?"

"Nope." The less she said the better. In her ten years of life, she had learned this truth with anything related to her mother.

"Did you come in here to find a book?" Her father's voice was as soothing as Abigail's fur.

"No."

"Well, as long as you're here already, would you like to sit at my desk and check out my study plans for next semester? Or help me record grades into my record book?"

"Can I help you record grades?" Grace bounced up so fast that Abigail was forced to move quickly away. As she did, the force of her body weight moved the rug and a corner of a photo peeked out from under it.

Grace saw her father look down and didn't dare follow his gaze.

He bent down and lifted the corner of the rug, retrieving the bird photos from beneath it.

"Hmmm . . . What have we here?" He looked at the photos. "Sweetheart, you know your mom doesn't want you messing with her stuff, right?"

Grace looked down at her feet. For a long moment neither of them spoke. Then she mustered the courage to ask, "Dad, *why* doesn't Mom let me look at her stuff? I'm not little anymore. I just wanted to see the bird pictures from her trip. Why can't she share them with me?"

Her dad seemed to choose his words carefully. "Hey, baby. Your mom just wants to make sure the pictures are carefully preserved for her books and lectures, that's all." His voice was warm but not convincing.

"Dad, will Mommy ever love me?"

"Gracie!" Her dad put his hands on her cheeks and bent down to her eye level. "Your mom loves you. Of course she loves you."

"No, Dad. She doesn't. You love me. She barely puts up with me."

"Oh, Gracie." Her dad hugged her tight. "Your mom has a hard time showing her love.

Gracie had seen enough over her years to know her mom loved her dad and showed it all the time with affection. She even patted Abigail once in a while. But she barely touched Grace. Grace wasn't good enough for her mom.

Will I ever be?

Chapter 19

Gooseberry Falls State Park, Minnesota
Winter 2006

"I'll just take Grace with me. No big deal. It's not ideal, but it can work, right Grace?"

Grace's eyes, wide open now, moved from her mother's inscrutable face to her father's worried brow.

They had just learned Ashley Barnes's sore throat had been diagnosed as strep, so the plan to have Grace stay there for the weekend had been abandoned. The Annual Winter Bird Count and Charlie's departure for a scheduled winter overnight with his biology class were happening the same day. Caroline wasn't going to miss her bird count.

"Grace will enjoy it, right Grace?" Caroline pulled on her winter gear from the closet. "Unless you want to take her with you on the winter camping adventure with your class?"

Caroline didn't expect an answer from Charlie who stood by their stunned ten-year-old daughter. "Where do you keep her long underwear and insulated pants? We'll need those for today. It's not going to get above five degrees, and there's a wind."

"Are you sure that's a good idea?" Charlie asked, raising his eyebrows and looking pointedly at Grace.

"We're perfectly capable of having a day on our own, aren't we, Gracie?" Caroline stopped short of adding, "Just because I'm not Lori Barnes, doesn't mean I can't take care of my own daughter," but she sensed Charlie and Grace were both unsure. *How hard could this be?*

Charlie had just enough time to lay out Grace's winter gear before his ride came. He kissed them both goodbye and loaded his own camping gear into his fellow teacher's truck, off on an adventure with sixteen adolescents to Wolf Ridge Wilderness Camp for the weekend.

Caroline drove to Gooseberry State Park to meet up with some local birders so they could divvy up the area to be surveyed. Caroline bounded ahead and stopped to check out a pileated woodpecker hammering a damaged branch near the top of a white pine. The bird spooked as Grace breathlessly tried to close the distance between them. "Mom, wait up."

Caroline's scowl in response kept Grace a few feet behind her. As they approached the bird count circle, one of the men, Ed Gallagher, said, "Wow, it's Caroline and mini-Caroline."

Caroline pulled her daughter forward and put an arm around her "This is Grace. She's joining us today." She took one of Grace's hands in hers and swung them both as her face lit up. Grace's dark curls were barely visible, but her facial bone structure and dimples were clearly a duplicate of Caroline's own.

"I really like your binoculars, Grace," someone said.

Grace proudly lifted them up to show the pink straps. "Dad gave them to me for my birthday."

Caroline dropped Grace's hand and took a step away. *Almost worthless as field glasses, but that's what he wanted to give her because she liked the pink.*

"Well, it's gonna be cold out here today. Let's get down to business," Ed said. They agreed on the assigned areas and a time to meet again and drove off in their vehicles or to walk to the nearby terrain.

Caroline drove to the parking area closest to the lakeside pavilion and parked the car. The air was so cold their breath was visible, and within steps each had ice mustaches around their roll-up chin covers. The lake was still mostly open, with ice crackling near the sides of the Gooseberry River running slow toward Lake Superior.

"OK, Gracie, let's get bundled up and go count some birds. Remember, today is about not looking for any particular type of bird but just to make an accurate count of birds that you see in the sky or in the trees, understand? Then later our results will be added to the Audubon's national headquarters website." Caroline had been participating in this ever since they moved to Minnesota but had never taken Grace with her.

Caroline wound the scarf around her daughter's neck and tied the hood tight around Grace's head, already covered with a woolen hat. "That should do it." She tapped the top of Grace's padded head and beckoned her to follow. *Who knows? Maybe this mothering thing will be better now that Grace is older.* They trudged through deep snow to a spot protected from the wind, and Caroline said, "Now, stay here, and I'll come get you when I'm done. Count what you see, and we can compare numbers later."

"OK, Mom. This'll be fun! See you later." Grace waved and her mom headed away from her.

Caroline took her snowshoes from her pack and stayed on the crusty layer of snow to follow the deer trail closer to the lakeshore, about ten minutes away from her daughter. The wind was quieter here, and she was able to shut out the rest of the world and listen to the swish of the brittle bare branches of aspen trees swaying in the breeze, and finally the telltale screech of a red-tailed hawk crossing above.

Two hours later, the buzz of her phone alarm surprised her. Time had passed so quickly. She quickly packed up her binoculars and headed back the trail to find her daughter, anxious to share notes with Grace.

When Caroline got back to the spot, Grace was not there. *What now? All she had to do was to stay put.* She registered her body temp growing chilly and started looking for tracks in the snow that she could follow. *Damn, Grace, where are you?*

The wind had picked up and peak sun was starting to cloud over—it would be very cold soon. Unable to identify a fresh set of footsteps, Caroline sorted out her options when her phone chirped. A text from Ed Gallagher. "Missing a little girl?"

Caroline's body temperature rose, her face flaming. She quickly replied, "Where is she?"

Ed wrote back, "We're at the meeting spot."

"On my way." Caroline texted quickly, removed her snowshoes, and trotted up the trail to her car.

Caroline scanned the adult faces expecting judgment but was surprised they appeared to be in a jovial mood. Grace was telling them about the birds she had seen and missed her mother's approach.

Ed looked up first and said, "I was driving back from my spot and came upon her on the road. She was cold, so I picked her up. She's a trooper."

"Thanks, Ed." Caroline wanted to grab her daughter and leave, but someone suggested going into the trailhead store for hot chocolate, and Grace got swept into the wave. All Caroline could do was follow.

On the drive home, Caroline was quiet. Grace chatted away until she picked up her mother's mood and quieted herself.

"Don't you ever do that again!" Caroline snapped.

"I'm sorry, Mommy, but I had to pee. I went up to find that outhouse near where we parked. When I couldn't find it,

I just squatted behind the pavilion. I was on my way back to my spot when Mr. Gallagher drove up."

Caroline didn't respond and didn't look at her daughter.

Gracie tried to apologize again, and then again, and then started to cry.

Caroline felt her face flush red hot. She ignored Grace's repeated attempts to apologize and shouted, "I will never take you birding again, ever!"

She shared only silence with her daughter.

Chapter 20

Two Harbors, Minnesota
Spring 2010

Snickerdoodles lined up on the cooling rack in Lori's kitchen island. Ashley, Grace, and Lori were playing a game of hearts and sharing memories of Abigail, who had been put down the previous week.

"I still don't understand how you can put a dog to sleep and not help people go to heaven when they're ready," Grace said, still comforted by the peace she saw in Abigail's eyes when she and her dad had held her as the vet made the lethal injection. By then, unable to walk unassisted and moaning in pain when she did need to move around, it seemed like a blessing to be able to help her out of her misery. When her kidneys started to fail, it was time.

Ashley replied, her brown eyes clouding over a bit, "Yes, Mom, do you remember how hard it was when Grandma was so sick and finally decided not to have any more of those treatments for her cancer?"

"Yes, I certainly do. Such a hard time for all of us and lots of trips to Iowa to visit. It was hard watching, and for Grandpa, it was even worse. When she finally put her foot down and said she chose a life of quality over more time in pain, it was a difficult decision for her to make, and even then, her passing didn't come easy." Lori concentrated on the cards in her hand.

Grace sought to lighten the mood. "Do you remember when Abigail came with us trick or treating and barked when she didn't think we were getting a good treat? She'd stick her muzzle between us on each stoop, checking out the goods before she let us move on."

"Kit Kat bars were her favorite, and she was good with peanut butter anything." Ashley laughed. "We wouldn't let her have chocolate, so, how do you think she knew those were our favorites?"

"C'mon girls, you know Abigail spoke your language. She followed you like a shadow who protected you and loved you both unconditionally," Lori said.

"Just like a mom!" Ashley sneaked the queen of spades into a trick her mom had to take, thereby foiling any attempt she had to win this hand.

As Lori shrieked in surprise, Grace thought again about how this daughter–mother relationship was so different from her own. Caroline had no time for cards or board games and wouldn't let Grace share in her passion of birds—well maybe the occasional trip to Hawk Ridge or hiking, but only with her dad along. The disastrous winter bird count destroyed any possibility of Grace going with her mother on her own.

She remembered when she was eight and Ashley and Lori had given her glittery nail polish and suggested she have a "girl party" with her mom.

"I don't approve of that vanity," Caroline had said when Grace invited her mom to paint their nails together.

Finally, she learned not to expect time or attention from her mom. She couldn't recall the last time she'd cried about it or the last time her dad had comforted her and tried to make up for it. She smiled at the image of her dad's painted finger and toenails, and how they didn't have any nail polish remover at home, so he had to borrow some from Lori one Monday morning before school.

"Gracie, I can't teach my classes with nail polish on!" her dad had giggled with her as they recognized the problem.

Yes, she knew she had the best dad in the world. Ashley didn't have one at all. *I'm lucky.*

"Where is everybody?" she heard her father's voice call from the front of the house.

"We're in here, Dad." Grace walked to greet him, reminded of how much she loved him. "Why didn't you come in the back door?" Ashley and Lori followed.

"'Cause, this big box was on the front doorstep. Mail delivery, do you think?" Grace watched her dad's eyes twinkle as he took in the girls, with a big smile, and then she saw his sly smile only for Lori.

Then they all heard it. The unmistakable whimper of a puppy. All eyes went to the poorly disguised dog crate wrapped in color comics from a Sunday paper and topped with a big red bow positioned to hide the handle.

"Ahhh." Grace and Ashley ripped off the paper to get to the pup, whose response was such exuberant tail wagging that her entire body was in motion.

"Dad, I can't believe it. You said we had to wait." Grace said, but her attention was all over the new puppy.

"Charlie, she's beautiful." Ashley hugged him. "What a great surprise. Where did you find her?"

"Well, Ashley, it was your mom who found her. She knew someone in town who had a cousin." He paused. "Lori, you tell it. I won't get it straight."

"So, you girls know the receptionist at Dr. Riley's office, Charlene? Her cousin lives in Silver Bay, and her dog had a litter of Labrador puppies. The timing was just about perfect." Grace watched as Lori shared a conspiratorial look with her dad. "We needed a canine friend, right?"

The two giggling girls, on the floor playing with the puppy, replied quickly, in unison. "Yes!"

"So, I think we made them happy, Lori," Charlie said. "Don't I deserve a snickerdoodle or two?"

Grace watched the two adults head for the kitchen, like she thought parents would do at a time like this. Her dream of having a mom like Lori was one she had learned to hide over the years.

When she had been around three or four and so proud of a picture she had painted, she'd raced into the house in front of her dad to share it with her mom. "Mommy, look at the picture I painted at Lori's house. I have two mommies in it!"

Caroline took the picture from her, and her face turned white. She dropped it to the table as if it were on fire.

"See, Mommy." Grace pointed at a short stick figure with a glob of black hair and a mouth in a horizontal line, with an arm pointing to a tree with a bird in it. The other figure, taller with long, blond hair, wearing an apron and a smiley face, was holding the hands of two little girls. "This is Ashley, and this is me." Grace pointed everyone out, but her mom had left the room.

The loud slam of the office door startled her. "Daddy, doesn't Mommy like my picture?" Grace's lip trembled as she looked up at her dad.

"It's a great picture, Gracie. Can I take it to my classroom and hang it near my desk there?"

Sometimes, like today, it was hard to keep the mother love she had for Lori to herself. She thought her dad knew because she could see her dad loved Lori, also. They didn't talk about it, though.

She and Ashley made a list of names for the new pup and discussed them until they agreed. They wanted a name that honored Abigail, so they chose the next letter of the alphabet and a name that wasn't very common. Bailey. They tried it out on the pup and their parents, and all agreed it was perfect.

It was only that night, when her mother called from Costa Rica where she was guiding a birding tour that it appeared it wasn't perfect. Grace heard only her dad's side of the conversation, but that was enough.

"Calm down. I know you didn't want another dog. It just seemed like the right thing to do. . . . No, the dog will not keep me from traveling. Lori agreed to help. . . . No, Lori and I don't make all the decisions. . . . I'm sorry I didn't discuss it with you first, but the timing was a factor in getting the puppy. . . . You don't mean that. . . . Caroline . . . Caroline . . . are you there?"

Grace walked quietly into the study to find her dad pacing and running his hand through his hair, shaking his head. "Dad?"

"Oh, hi, princess, I didn't hear you come in."

"Is everything all right?"

"It will be, princess. Not to worry. Mom's just a little surprised. That's all."

Grace knew that was not all. "Dad. Thanks for getting Bailey for me." Her voice came out a squeak of emotion.

Her dad walked the short distance to his daughter and gave her a big hug. "For us, Gracie, for us."

She accepted her dad's affection and tried not to worry about how he would have to make peace with her mother about the puppy. She went to the piano and played the music that soothed her most, starting with scales and working through to the sonata she loved best. Bailey slept beside her on the needle-point-cushioned piano bench.

Chapter 21

Two Harbors, Minnesota
Spring 2013

"Charlie, remember our agreement. You promised I could be a nomad, and you would support my adventures. This is just another one." Caroline's black hair bounced as she moved to the edge of the bed and stood naked, her slight body still taut in all the right places, her breasts standing proud. "You promised."

"We hardly ever see you. Gracie needs you now that she is a teenager. I'd like you to be here more." Charlie raised himself up enough to grab her arm and pull her back to him.

Caroline beamed at him; she could never refuse him sexually. "Hah, that's a joke. That girl has never needed me. You are all she's ever needed or wanted. The parent in you is dominant, but right now, I need a lover." She lowered herself to him and nibbled his ear. "Don't think I'll give in on my next move. You two can come visit me over school break, and I'll still be home for six weeks in the summer. I'll tell Grace in the morning." She headed to shower.

Grace and Charlie were already having breakfast when Caroline, her hair wrapped in a towel, strolled out of the bathroom and filled her coffee cup.

"Well, aren't you two the early birds." Caroline ruffled Charlie's hair and whispered, "Morning, lover."

"It's a school day, Mom. We have to leave in about ten minutes." Grace, now close to Charlie's height, took a bite of toast.

"OK, then." Caroline stood at mock attention saluting her daughter and announced, "So, I've been appointed to a two-semester visiting professorship at the University of Lisbon."

Caroline caught Grace's surreptitious peek at Charlie. *Dad to the rescue, Gracie?* But he picked up his plate and rose from the table.

Finally, Grace spoke. "Congratulations, Mom, if that's what you want. Is it?"

"Yes, of course it is. I only do things I want to do. This is a prestigious opportunity, and I would be foolish to turn it down." Caroline felt her voice rise in defense of her decision. She positioned her body between Charlie and the dishwasher, blocking his path, expectation in her eyes.

"Gracie, this is a great thing for your mom." Charlie reached around her to load his plate in the dishwasher and then put his arm around his wife. "She'd like to know how we—how you—feel about her being gone for that long."

Caroline picked up his cue. "Yes, of course, I'll miss you, Grace. I'd love it if you and your dad would come and stay with me over breaks, and I'll be back next summer for a few weeks. How does that sound?"

"Well, to be honest . . ." Grace walked her dishes to the kitchen sink, dropping them loudly, "it doesn't sound any different than the last year or the year before that, so I'm not sure that it matters what I think. You'll do it anyway."

She's got that right. Caroline watched and waited for her moment.

Grace was on her way out of the kitchen when Charlie grabbed her arm. "Gracie, I just had a crazy idea. What about if you and I joined her? You could take your sophomore year in Lisbon, and I could ask for a sabbatical from the school. How does that sound?"

Caroline waited a beat too long before she said, "What a great idea!"

Grace replied with a sarcastic chuckle. "Yeah, sure, Mom."

In a late attempt to show maternal feeling, Caroline added with scant conviction, "We would have lots of time together."

"Not sure that would be a good thing. But thanks for the invitation." Grace's well-modulated voice contrasted to her mother's in tone and control.

Caroline missed the snark in Grace's comment until she added, "Dad, how about if you go, and I'll stay with Lori and Ashley? They'll take me in, I'm sure. They've always been there for me."

Gracie walked toward the door. "Dad, I'll be in the car. Just have to grab my backpack."

Caroline's breath grew shallow. She resisted the temptation to keep the discussion going for fear Charlie would force the issue, and she would be stuck with her daughter in Lisbon. She liked the option of just Charlie coming, even if it had been Grace's idea. Grace had spoiled it by mentioning her "real family," and Caroline hated the idea of Grace being with Lori and Ashley as Lori's daughter for an entire year.

Lori was always around—for years and years now. Caroline always came in second in a competition she herself had created. *Count to ten.* Images of dress-up parties, baking, and crafting floated to the surface. She registered each of them, took a deep breath, and dismissed them with one thought. *Still, better her than me.*

Charlie took her in his arms and said, "She may come around. Let me talk to her more about it. I think it could be a wonderful year. It would be good for her to have a year abroad before college. Love you. Will you be here when we get home tonight?"

Caroline gave him a deep kiss. "Charlie, forget the year abroad idea. Clearly, she's not interested." She pulled away and made a quick decision. "No, I won't be here tonight until late. I'm going to meet up with Geri for dinner to catch up."

She walked to the door and watched Charlie get into the car beside a sullen teenager who wouldn't be coming to Portugal for her sophomore year of high school. *Too bad.*

Chapter 22

Two Harbors, Minnesota
Autumn 2013

Of course, Caroline went to Lisbon that fall after having been gone much of the summer on a bird tour. He never doubted that she would. While Grace didn't seem to mind, he wasn't sure how she felt about much of anything these days.

"Grace, how about we go hiking this weekend? That stretch of trail near Tettegouche should be beautiful about now." He started the conversation on the drive into school. Life was logistically easier now that she went to the high school where he taught every day, but lately she was hard to reach. She claimed to be too busy with homework to play board games or even watch their favorite TV shows together. He noticed she wasn't spending much time with personal grooming, but lots of time in her room with the door closed, even to Bailey. Car conversations were his best bet.

No answer. He looked over at Grace who was staring out the window. He couldn't even see her blink. "Gracie?"

She turned toward him finally. "Hmmm? What Dad?"

"What's on your mind, princess? You look like you're on a different planet." He leaned toward her and pushed a strand of hair behind her ear.

"Nothing." Grace flinched and turned toward the window again.

Charlie pulled into the Holiday station. "Hey, your choice. Pump gas or go get each of us a donut?"

Grace didn't move. "I don't feel like a donut."

Charlie was tempted to reply, "You don't look like a donut either," but he knew his usual banter with his daughter wasn't the right move. Instead, he filled the tank and skipped the treat.

"Something going on with you that we should talk about?" He sat in the truck before starting it back up, waiting her out.

"No," she answered, her voice monotone as she looked at her side mirror. "Dad, there's a car behind you trying to get to the pump."

"Oops. Thanks." He smiled at her as he started the engine and headed to school. "So, what do you say about that Tettegouche hike this weekend?"

"Ahh . . . maybe, but I have a physics test Monday to study for so maybe not."

Charlie eagerly grabbed onto a topic to pull her out. "How do you like Mrs. Spencer? Is she a good teacher?"

"She's OK. I don't like physics." Grace still looked out the window.

"Well, I can help you with it. Should we plan a study session together this weekend?"

"Maybe."

They drove past Dr. Riley's office and saw him pull the door of his clinic open. Charlie honked and waved. *Walt knows about kids; maybe I should talk to him.*

He upped the stakes. "Since we have a three-day weekend coming up, we could take a trip out of town? Maybe go to the Twin Cities? Or we could go up the shore to Isle Royale—make arrangements to get on the island. Maybe see if Lori and Ashley would join us?"

"Haven't thought about it yet," Grace muttered.

"You know what else happens this fall now that you're sixteen?"

Silence.

"You can take your driver's test!"

Finally, a grin appeared on his daughter's face. "Forgot about that. That's cool."

Later that day, his friend Mack, Grace's math teacher, pulled Charlie aside in the teacher's lounge. "Got a minute?"

"Sure." Charlie led him to a grouping of chairs in the back of the nearly empty lounge.

"It's Grace," Mack said softly.

It took Charlie a moment to get over the surprise. Grace was an excellent student and always well-behaved. Math was one of her strongest subjects. "Really? What's up?"

"Well, I just wonder . . . have you noticed that she's a little down lately?"

"Moody, you mean? Like all teenage girls?" Charlie shrugged his shoulders and felt some relief.

"Not that. I mean, yes, I see the variation in moodiness with students at this age, boys and girls. Lots of hormonal changes. Life starts to get more serious and has them worrying a bit more." Mack rubbed his chin. "But I'm talking more than that with Grace."

"So tell me." Charlie leaned in.

"It's somewhat subtle, I'll admit. She seems disengaged in class. No real interaction with other students and never raises her hand anymore. Just sits there, staring off into space."

"Is she keeping up with the assignments? Have you noticed a drop in her performance?"

"I'd say she's hit and miss. It's too early in the semester to know how much she's missing conceptually, but she has a few assignments that have been turned in late and not done well. Not her usual work." Mack pulled himself up straight and took a minute before he continued. "Charlie, do you remember Peter?"

Charlie's shoulders fell and he and Mack shared a knowing look.

"We all missed the slight changes in his personality. How he kinda closed up on his friends and stopped being social?" Mack continued.

Charlie did remember. Two years back, a student—a senior—had committed suicide. It was a total shock to the school and the entire community. He had been diagnosed bipolar the year before, and his parents had supported his treatment. But nobody had been told at the school, and it wasn't until after his death that Patricia, with the permission of his parents, took the opportunity to hold a series of educational sessions with the faculty and the student body about warning signs for suicide.

Disengagement and lack of interest in previously pursued activities topped the list. Both Charlie and Mack had taught this student for years and hadn't seen it . . . until they looked back.

Charlie turned away first, looked down at his shoes, then grabbed Mack's shoulder. "Thanks, Mack. I appreciate you telling me this." The bell rang, signaling the next class period and the men went their separate ways. Charlie's world shifted as he realized Mack had tied together some of what Charlie had seen in Grace, but not fully registered, until now.

At lunch break, Charlie went to Lori's preschool classroom, where she had been teaching for eight years. He loved that she was still so close, even though he didn't see her every day. He tried to see her as much as he could without causing problems for either of them. He slipped into the class from the back of the room and watched as she magically helped the children put their rugs down on the nursery play area for nap time. When she moved toward him to turn the lights down, she smiled at him and his heart missed a beat, then steadied.

God, I miss her. Does she know that?

"You do such a nice job with these little people." He had learned over the years how she appreciated recognition of her own value, and still a single mother of Ashley, he knew she didn't get it from very many, just like he didn't.

"Thanks." She smiled again. "What brings you to my territory this fine day?"

"As usual, I need some advice." He grinned, then got serious. "Have you noticed anything going on with Gracie lately? Beyond just being fifteen, I mean?"

"Hmmm. I don't see her so much anymore."

She studied his face; she knew him well. Grace and Ashley had been as close as sisters, but he hadn't seen them together for a while, and Ashley hadn't been to a sleepover for months.

"Ashley tells me Grace is busy with other things when I ask about her. Is something going on?"

"Not sure. Mack just told me he's a bit concerned about her. Evidently she seems disengaged in his class." He looked at her and saw encouragement for him to share more. "I'm a little worried. Not sure what that means, or what I should do about it."

"Seems to me you should check it out a bit more." She started slowly. "Maybe observe her closely yourself and ask a couple of other teachers. If you'd like, I could be a resource, too. I'd be happy to help." She leaned in close enough for him to catch her scent as she squeezed his shoulder in encouragement.

"Yeah, that sounds good." He exhaled loudly as he tried to ignore the unexpected tingle radiating from his shoulder. "Just having you say it out loud helps. Thanks. That's what I was thinking, too."

A soft giggle arose in the sea of nappers; it was time to leave her but not without a plan to find this comfort again soon.

"Could you and Ashley come for brunch Sunday after church? That could be a good time. Are you up for that?"

"Of course. I'll bring a pie. Cherry?"

Charlie felt his facial muscles relax. He smiled at her and walked out as she went to check on her nappers.

Chapter 23

Two Harbors, Minnesota
Autumn 2013

Grace couldn't sleep. Too much on her mind. Then, she lost track of what was on her mind or who. She drifted off but woke up with a man's voice yelling at her. Trembling and afraid, she realized it must have been a bad dream. Was it her dad's voice? Seemed like there were two voices. Her dad was never angry with her. Why would he yell at her?

She heard the furnace go on. Bailey's dog tag jangled as he looked up at her from his bed. The swish of a branch brushed against the window. Too loud, too close. How could she ever sleep?

She heard her dad calling to her as he opened her bedroom door. "Good morning, sleepyhead!"

"Dad, not so loud," she snapped at him. "I barely slept. Everything is so noisy."

"Sorry, princess. Just thought I better get Bailey out. You can take your time. We leave for church in an hour."

She groaned. "Do I have to go?"

He approached the bed, then touched her forehead. "Are you feeling OK? Coming down with something?"

Her body flinched. The last thing she wanted was to be touched, even by her dad. His face was so close, she could see where he had missed a spot shaving. *I should tell him. He counts on me.* She couldn't summon the energy.

"No, I'm fine. Just sleepy. I'll be ready."

"Great! Remember Lori and Ashley are coming for brunch. I'm going to work on my kitchen prep. Love you!"

He left her room with Bailey, and she tried to rally. But she was so tired. Finally, she skipped a needed shower and threw on yesterday's clothes to join her dad at the door just in time to leave.

She felt herself drifting off in church, and her father's elbow nudged her awake. She sat with her dad, Lori, and Ashley in their usual pew in front of Dr. Riley and his family. Everything was so familiar and yet muted and loud at the same time. She tuned out the clank of the offering plates as they were placed at the altar and the organ music cueing the choir to start, while keeping her eyes open.

After church, Lori and Ashley followed them back to their house for brunch.

"Girls, would you wash up and then help me finish setting the table?" her dad asked.

Ashley elbowed Grace and giggled. "Some things never change, do they, Grace?"

"No, not really."

Ashley was pretty like her mom, with a slim build and the same incredible yellow-white hair. The only feature from the dad she'd lost was her beautiful brown eyes.

"What have you been up to? I haven't seen you at soccer recently. Did you quit the team?" Ashley asked.

Grace looked behind them and put her finger to her lips. "Shhh. Dad doesn't know. He'll freak out. I just need a break."

"I won't give you up, girlfriend. But are you OK?"

"Yeah, just feel a little strange, not sure why. I'll be fine. I always am." She grabbed a towel.

"Well, you know you won't be able to keep the soccer team secret from your dad. He's at the school every day, and we do have our first real game next week." Ashley waited her turn at the bathroom sink and caught Grace's eye reflected in the mirror.

"I know, I know. I just need a little time. I don't want him to worry."

"Should I be worried?" Ashley turned to look at her. "You know I'm your sister, right?"

"Of course." Grace let herself be hugged, but when Ashley pulled away, she said, "Hey, sister, you could use a shower."

Chapter 24

ㅅ

Two Harbors, Minnesota
Autumn 2013

Over the next few weeks, Charlie watched Grace become more and more detached. Her grades continued to slip, and when not in school, she spent almost all of her time alone. He was still reeling from the surprise he got when he attended the first girls' soccer game of the season. It was a beautiful fall day, one of Minnesota's finest. He had strolled from school out to the soccer field and scanned the girls in play, then the sidelines, looking for Grace.

When he didn't spot her, he approached Ashley. "Hey, where's Gracie? Isn't she playing this game?"

Ashley just shrugged as she was called into play. The parent of one of his students overheard the interaction. "Haven't seen Grace at all. Heard she didn't come out for the team this fall. Too bad. We could use her." She pointed to the field as the opposing team made a goal.

Charlie doubled back into the school and searched for his daughter. No luck. Finally, he found her in his truck, with a math book on her lap. "Why, Gracie?" was all he said when he climbed in beside her. She had mumbled something about prioritizing school over sports while she quickly opened the book.

How did I miss this for three weeks?

And now, she had failed her driver's test.

"Grace, what happened with the test? You studied for it. What was the problem?" Charlie had asked her gently that evening as they ate dinner together. He ate, and she moved food around on her plate.

"I was tired. I got confused. It was so noisy in the test area," Grace replied slowly, in a whisper. He wasn't sure if she was embarrassed, but she wasn't defensive. She was uninterested.

"Well, princess, I know you'd like to be able to drive the car. Do you want to take it again?"

"Sure, I suppose." She pushed her plate away, poised to get up from the dinner table.

"This time I'll prep with you so it's easier when you're in the room with the test. How does that sound?" Charlie moved to her and stroked her dark hair, noting it stuck to her scalp in places. "How about if you go take a nice shower and get into your PJs before tackling your homework?"

She leaned into his chest, her voice muffled when she finally spoke. "I don't want to shower. The water comes out too hard, and I can't keep track of what's going on when it's so loud. I get scared in there."

"Gracie, honey." He held her close and rocked her. "I'll tell you what. I'll draw you a nice warm bath and you can soak in it and shampoo your hair in the tub. OK?"

She didn't respond.

He pushed beyond the fear to ask the question in his head. "Are you worried about the sound of the bathwater?" She relaxed in his arms, and he felt her head nod slightly while he held his breath.

"Then I'll go start the water running and close the door on it. When the tub is filled and warm, I'll have you take your bath. A plan?"

"OK, Dad."

"Good girl." He gently pulled away from her and went to start the water, something he hadn't done since she was six years old, when she insisted she was big enough to take a shower. Too independent at six, but too compliant at sixteen? Something was clearly off. *Thank God I'm taking her to see Dr. Riley tomorrow.*

He joined her in the hallway after starting the bathwater and closed the bathroom door. His phone rang and after a quick look, he let it go to voice mail. *Caroline. Not in front of Grace.*

"Gracie, go ahead and get ready for your bath. I'll keep checking the water."

He considered calling Caroline back. She was probably making her weekly call in at his request. Instead, he stationed himself in the hallway between the bathroom and Grace's bedroom, his eyes rotating between the two doors, his heart, as usual, torn in two.

The calls had become a formality. Caroline mostly talked about herself. "You'll never guess . . ." she touted her travels and new experiences, while he felt it more and more a chore to sound amazed and proud of her. "No, do tell me about it, please!"

His mind flashed back to the angry exchange that had led to the uneasy truce between them—the question of whether Portugal would be a family move for a year's sabbatical for all of them together or whether Caroline would go on her own. Unwilling to leave the decision to Caroline alone, he kept at her until she finally snapped at him. "She doesn't want to go. She's made that clear!"

"You haven't really tried to interest her in going. You need to invite her, make her feel that you want her to come with you to Portugal, paint the picture of a year abroad for her." Charlie risked coaching his wife.

"I'm not going to beg her. She's no longer a baby! Leave it."

After several days of waiting for her to approach Grace, Charlie countered with the plan to take an extended Christmas break so that he and Grace could visit Portugal with a side trip to Spain while they were there. Caroline agreed.

After the tension around Caroline's decision to leave them for a year, it had become more difficult to pretend any normal semblance of family. She never asked specifics about her daughter, so it was easy not to report about what was going on with Grace. After a few attempts to steer the conversation to their daughter, Caroline's disinterest was obvious, and his hesitation much easier. *How can I explain when I don't even understand myself?*

While she still signed off every call with, "Can't wait to see you both at Christmas. Love you!" it rang hollow, even to his loyal heart.

No, I can't deal with her tonight.

He kept the bathroom door opened a crack so he could monitor Grace in the bathtub. Only after hearing the gentle splash of soap and water and a shampoo bottle cap opening, did he allow his body to sink quietly down to the floor, his legs rubbery. *How can I keep her from falling apart? How did we get here? My fault.*

He thought back to the many nights he would try to get her to talk to him, to do a puzzle or watch one of the TV shows they had watched together a million times. She just wasn't there. Several times, he had raced into her room following screams of, "Leave me alone! Go away!" to reach for her flailing arms before they could connect with him as the perceived enemy.

"Gracie, it's me. It's Dad. Everything's OK." He would have to pin her arms to the bed in order to calm her and wait until her eyes lost their vacant stare. Then she could focus enough to realize he was not one of the wicked characters she told him were "arguing over my body." She couldn't explain what the dreams were about, but they scared her to the point of desperation. She slept with Bailey on her bed, a light on, and her door open.

She still played the piano every day, mostly scales and soft music. When she played, she seemed to go off somewhere, not like her usual playing that could get raucous and loud.

Once in a while, she would agree to do something with him, and then he saw she was just going through the motions, for him, no doubt, smiling a faint echo of her smile to please him.

It was Lori who moved him to action. She had been aware of the change in Grace's behavior since the brunch several weeks before and had advised him to get her into Dr. Riley for a checkup. He had put it off, hoping it was just a phase and would be over soon. He couldn't face the possibility that he had somehow broken the baby he had brought into this world.

Finally, an emphatic Lori appeared at his homeroom after school and insisted he make an appointment, or she would call Dr. Riley herself.

"I keep thinking she'll snap out of it." He didn't meet her eyes.

She persisted. "If one of our girls had broken an ankle in soccer or had a cough that wasn't going away, we would get it looked at. Just because you can't see what's hurting doesn't mean there isn't something to be done about what's going on with her."

"I failed her, Lori."

"This isn't about you and whatever you feel guilty about. It's about Grace. You need to get her to Dr. Riley, now." Her voice was sharper than usual.

"I shouldn't be a father." He cast his eyes down to his feet.

"Oh, for God's sake, Charlie. Snap out of it. All parents feel like failures from time to time. We all just do the best we can. Now, will you make the call, or will I?" She stood with her hands on her hips, unrelenting.

They were interrupted by a student reentering Charlie's homeroom for a forgotten backpack, and the moment was gone. Lori looked at her watch, and he remembered this was her quilting night. "OK, I'll do it. Thanks for helping me see straight." She hurried off, and he made the call, while her strength was still lingering in the air he breathed.

After he made the appointment with Walt Riley, Charlie wondered if Lori had said something to the doctor already. The Rileys sat behind them at church every Sunday, and he recalled the conversation he'd had with Walt last Sunday after church while they chatted during coffee hour.

"How does it feel to have a sixteen-year-old daughter? Can't believe Grace is that old. Means I'm really getting old." Charlie knew Walt had a way of sneaking up on you with his conversation starters.

"It's great. Soon she'll be able to drive." *If she ever passes the test, that is.*

"Yes, parenting teens is a challenge." Walt took a sip of his coffee and looked over at Grace standing apart from Ashley, whose youthful laugh punctuated her animated conversation with the Swanson twins. "It's when individual identities come forward in a variety of ways."

"How would you describe Grace's personality right now, Charlie?" Walt turned back to him.

"Well, I think she's finding her way, as all young girls do, eventually." Charlie's hopeful response bought him enough time to deflect Walt for the moment, and then, Walt's wife, Claire, came by to join them.

"What are you hearing from Caroline? I understand you and Grace are joining her for the Christmas holiday in Lisbon?"

"Yes, that's the plan. Caroline is doing beautifully. Loves it there." Charlie shifted his weight, frowned, and looked over at his daughter. "We miss her, of course, but we'll see her soon."

How on earth will I handle that trip?

As Charlie and Grace headed into Dr. Riley's exam room, he looked over at his daughter. At least her hair was shiny, and her clothes were clean. He had grown used to the dullness of her eyes, and the flat affect of her conversation, but Dr. Riley noticed right away.

"Gracie! Gracie! Do you know that it was sixteen years ago that I delivered you as a healthy baby girl? What a happy day it was." He did a quick and dorky version of his happy dance to show his exuberance and laughed heartily—an inviting laugh.

Charlie couldn't help but laugh, but Gracie merely smiled and turned away.

"So, Grace. Are you happy?" Dr. Riley boldly asked.

Grace looked from her dad to Dr. Riley, but she didn't respond.

Dr. Riley turned to Charlie. "Now that Grace is sixteen, I'm going to ask that you wait in the reception area. Grace and I will have a chat, and I'll call you in later. OK?"

Charlie left them and waited thirty minutes in the reception area. In the interim, his mind felt like a ping-pong ball batted around by champion players.

When he was called back in, he immediately noticed his daughter's body was more relaxed with her legs crossed at the ankles. She welcomed him with a small smile.

"Grace and I had a good talk. She shared a lot about how she's feeling right now. I asked her permission to share this with you." Dr. Riley looked at Grace.

She nodded.

"This information about Grace is to be treated confidentially among us. Grace wants you to know how she feels and asked me to tell you for her."

Charlie swallowed hard. *Why can't my daughter tell me herself?*

"Gracie has been feeling sad for several months. She's not sure why. She feels like she's living in a muffled world where nothing really matters, and she's not sure why she is here."

Charlie gasped at that, then clenched his jaw as his eyes teared up.

Grace looked to Dr. Riley to continue and not at her dad.

"She worried that if she told you, that you would feel responsible for her sadness, and she didn't want you to. She knows you love her and do everything for her that a good dad should do, and she loves you very much. She didn't want you to feel bad about her feeling bad."

Charlie felt a tear start to fall, helpless to stop it. "Oh, Gracie. Oh, baby, I'm so sorry."

"Charlie, Gracie wants you to help her get better. She needs you to be strong for this next part. Are you willing to help her?"

"Of course!" He practically leapt out of his chair, but one glance at his daughter and he could see from the way she looked at Dr. Riley that she wanted him to continue to be the expert in the room, so he stayed put.

"Gracie and I have come up with a plan that we'd like you to support." Dr. Riley looked at Charlie and then continued after he nodded his agreement. "I'd like to refer Grace to Dr. Lloyd Chester, a psychiatrist in Minneapolis. He specializes in adolescent mental health issues and is the best there is. I've been sending patients to him for years and recommend him highly. The problem is that he's very busy. Even if I persuade him to take Grace on ASAP, there will still be a wait. That's just how it is for these services."

Charlie stopped breathing at the word "psychiatrist" and didn't inhale until he heard the words "the best there is." *My baby needs a psychiatrist?* He felt his leg jumping and pressed both feet down hard against the floor.

"Charlie?" Walt finally spoke.

Charlie felt Grace's eyes on him. *I can't fail her now.* He sat up straight. "Whatever it takes, Walt. Let's do it."

"OK, I'll get that ball rolling tomorrow," Dr. Riley said. "Now, since that will take a while, my practice is typically to prescribe an antidepressant medication in cases like these. I believe it will help Grace through her sadness earlier than waiting for her first appointment with Dr. Chester. Are you with me here?"

He tried to remember the last time Grace had been on medication and came up blank. She was up-to-date on immunizations, but they had steered clear of much of anything else if it could be avoided. He knew little about antidepressants beyond that they came with side effects. *Is it safe?* Charlie drew a deep breath. "What do I need to know about the meds? I know there are lots of them out there." He raised an eyebrow.

"Yes, there are. I'll follow up with you later on the options and dosages and so on."

"I'd also like to know how Grace feels about this. Gracie?" Charlie asked.

"I'd like to try the medicine, Dad." She spoke clearly.

"Then yes, Walt. Let's have you prescribe something." Charlie said.

"I will," Walt replied to Charlie, then turned to Grace. She nodded at him, some unspoken agreement between them.

"Just one more thing, Charlie." Dr. Riley cleared his throat and started strong. "Gracie doesn't want to go to Portugal for the holiday break. She feels she would be better off here."

As hard as it was to hear, Charlie knew he should have anticipated this. *Of course she wouldn't want to go. Why would she want to spend time with a mother who cares so little about her that she ignores her even when she lives in the same house? We'll just stay home.*

Dr. Riley continued. "She wants you to go. She wants you to go visit Caroline and have a great time. She thinks going would hurt her now. She will feel terrible if you don't go. She wants to stay with Lori and Ashley."

Charlie sought his daughter's eyes, and she whispered, "Please, Dad."

Chapter 25

Two Harbors, Minnesota
Autumn 2013

Grace started to take an antidepressant. Before the medication could have any possible effect, Charlie noticed a difference. She seemed lighter somehow, even in the way she walked, something as subtle as lifting her feet higher. She seemed to glide while before it appeared as if she had to carry her slumped body around like she had weights on her ankles. He attributed it to the visit with Dr. Riley. He hoped it was relief that she could get help but knew it might be because she didn't have to go see her mother.

He searched his brain for a way to stay home over the Christmas holidays—he couldn't see himself leaving her, even if that's what she wanted.

Walt reached out to have coffee the next Saturday afternoon, "as a friend," he had said on his voice message. They met at the Rustic Inn in Castle Danger, and Walt ordered two pieces of pie with their coffee. "Save me from eating both, Charlie. My waistline doesn't need two pieces of apple pie, even as good as this is." He pointed to his belt buckle and chuckled. "So, how's it going?"

"Not well. My daughter is in terrible pain, and I can't fix it."

Walt smiled and leaned back. "I'd be surprised if you were doing cartwheels about now. Any parent wants to protect a child from the dangers of living, including an illness, even a mental illness." He took a bite of pie. "How is Grace doing?"

"Better. She seems to be relieved. I can't believe I held off so long before I brought her in. What was I thinking?" He fumbled with his car keys, then put them in his pocket.

"It's hard to recognize behavior change in an adolescent. Variation in mood is totally normal in that age group. Don't beat yourself up about that."

"I beat myself up about not providing a healthy family environment." Charlie took a long swallow of coffee before adding, "Caroline is complicated and never wanted to be a mother." *And I forced it on her.*

Walt chewed slowly. Charlie felt his scrutiny and waited for him to respond.

"Do you think Caroline's frequent absences are the issue, or is it Caroline's lack of motherly attention wherever she is?"

"That's a terrible thing to say." Charlie tossed his napkin onto the table. "How could you possibly think that?"

"Hey, slow down. I'm not trying to rile you. I'm trying to open your mind to a different way of seeing things for your daughter's sake." Walt put his fork down on his pie plate.

Charlie felt his shoulders release as he took a deep breath. "What do you mean?"

"I mean that, from the beginning, starting with the pregnancy, Caroline took little interest in anything about the baby. It was all about her. When she delivered the baby, she didn't focus on bonding. Instead she made herself scarce during the immediate weeks following the birth."

Charlie said nothing but shifted in his chair.

Walt continued. "It's no secret in this town that you took on the role as parent while Caroline concentrated on her career, birds, whatever, and didn't spend much time with Grace, avoided her, even. Just because you didn't mind taking the responsibility of parenting full on doesn't mean that your wife's emotional neglect of her child didn't go unnoticed in the community or by her daughter."

Walt stopped talking while the server poured them fresh coffee. "The community has your back, Charlie. They see things, and they want you to succeed with Grace. We all do."

"It's not Caroline's fault." Charlie picked up his cup and held it in front of his face like a shield, defending Caroline . . . a default position that came naturally.

"There's no judgment in my comments. It's your marriage and your life. My interest here is in making sure that you recognize that in your daughter's eyes, in Grace's eyes, she feels diminished with Caroline around. She idolizes you and has tried her best to minimize what she needs so that she doesn't upset the balance between her parents. She's a very smart kid, but it's taking a toll."

Charlie rubbed his forehead and checked to make sure there wasn't anyone within earshot before he asked Walt a question he had not dared ask himself. "Do you think Caroline is making Gracie sick?"

Walt smiled kindly. "No, no, not at all. Grace has an as yet undiagnosed mental illness. I hope to God it's something that Dr. Chester can help with soon. But, I'm saying that, in the interim, don't underestimate Grace's plea for help. She couldn't face you directly with it and needed me as an intermediary."

Walt reached over to touch Charlie's arm. "I strongly advise you to agree to her wishes not to visit her mother at Christmas and that you should go, as she requested. It will help her feel empowered to make a change for her own benefit. We need her to feel like she has value, her opinion counts, and she has some power in her life." Walt held his gaze, his hand still on Charlie's arm.

It took him a few minutes to respond. With a silent shiver, he felt any remaining pretense drain out of him. "I don't know what to say."

"Well, then how about eating your piece of pie, before I do?" Walt inched the pie plate over toward him with a light chuckle.

Charlie didn't make a move toward the pie. He felt queasy but curious. "Did you know that I was thinking of not going to Lisbon?"

"I figured as much. I understand a father's instinct to stay home and take care of his kid. But, in this case, I know it's the wrong thing to do." Walt motioned to the waitperson and asked her to put the piece of pie in a take-away carton and the moment instantly changed. "I want you to take this pie home for Gracie."

Charlie grinned his relief. "Thank you. I'm grateful for your care of us, as a friend and as a doctor." Charlie felt like a student who had just failed an exam but was being given time to prepare for the retake.

"I know it wasn't easy to hear, but you're welcome. Now, I want you to do me a favor. I want you to make arrangements with Lori and Ashley for the holiday break in the next couple of days. I want Gracie to hear from you that it is arranged for her to stay here and for you to go to Lisbon, as she asked. Can you do that?"

"Will she be OK while I'm gone?" Charlie's raspy voice was a clear plea for reassurance.

"Yes, she will. We'll see to that. Come January, you'll be able to take her to see Dr. Chester and start to sort out what's what with Grace. I've pulled the strings that I can pull, and that's as early as I can get her in for an appointment."

They walked out together, and Walt handed him the pie. "Now, make sure Grace gets that. I'll be asking her at church in the morning." He chuckled and waved goodbye.

Charlie watched Walt drive away, shaking his head. *How does Walt always manage to do this to me? Make me think 'til it hurts and try to pull the best out of me.* He knew that making arrangements with Lori was the easier of the two tasks before him. Lori would happily take Grace for the holiday break. It was explaining the change of plans to Caroline that he dreaded.

But, there was nothing he wouldn't do for his daughter. Wasn't that the point of being a father?

Chapter 26

Canary Islands
December 2013

"What do you mean she's too ill to travel? What's going on?" Caroline sat at her office desk scanning a document on her computer while talking to Charlie on the phone. Her usual check-in call was not going as usual; normally, she could review a paper or two while she was on the line with her husband. She got up from her desk and stomped around her office.

"I didn't want to worry you, but she's not been herself for these past few months, and I thought it was just teenager stuff. I took her in to see Dr. Riley—"

"What did he say?"

"He said that she's sad, unusually sad, and needs help. He prescribed an antidepressant and we're waiting for an appointment with a psychiatrist in January. Somebody Walt refers patients to, somebody he trusts."

Caroline's mind cast about for proof that this could not be true. She grasped images of a triumphant Grace happily beating her father at chess, totally absorbed in learning a new piano piece, and as an angelic toddler singing gaily while playing with her toys in the bath. *Riley's an idiot.*

"What does he know about depression? He's not trained to identify depression. He's a family doc, for god's sake. Why do you think he knows what he's doing?" Caroline had never thought much of Walt Riley. Way too nosy and bossy for her taste. She remembered how he hinted that she had postpartum depression after Grace was born. *Must get kickbacks from the pharmaceutical companies for prescribing antidepressants.* "I don't like it. I don't like it one little bit."

"Walt thinks it's a good idea for me to come to visit for the holiday break on my own. Leave Grace here and make the trip myself."

Caroline stopped breathing. *Could Walt Riley really be giving me this gift? I might not respect him, but this is a brilliant idea.*

"Caroline?" Charlie waited.

She considered what a mother's reaction to this should be, and said it, lightly, before she lost her conviction. "Maybe I should come home for the holidays?"

"No—that's not a good idea. It's fine that I come there. Grace understands." Charlie blurted with unusual finality.

"What does that mean, Grace understands?" *What's really going on here?*

Charlie slowed his delivery, as if trying hard to convince her. "She knows I've been looking forward to the trip and seeing you. She wants me to do it and would feel worse if I don't go."

Caroline processed that for a moment, almost ready to celebrate that she wouldn't have to deal with her daughter. "Where will she be when you're with me?"

"Lori will take her. She and Ashley are pleased to have her join them for their holidays. And Grace is happy to be there with them."

"Of course Lori will take her." Caroline felt her face break into a gleeful smile thinking about two blissful weeks alone with her husband, sparing her the mind-numbing church pageant, trips to light displays, cookie baking—all to be enjoyed by her daughter along with Lori and Ashley. "She'll be happier with them." She didn't realize she had spoken out loud until Charlie continued.

"Walt assured me he'll be available if there's an issue while I'm gone, but I'm still concerned." Caroline heard a break in Charlie's voice. "Caroline, we'll have to talk about this in more depth when I see you. I'm really worried."

"Of course we will." Caroline assured him, while her mind raced to new possibilities for two weeks with Charlie alone. "We'll have plenty of time to do that while you're here."

"Good, thanks." Charlie sounded distracted. "Sorry, I've gotta go. I need to check on Grace."

Before signing off, Caroline added, "I think I'll look into flights to the Canary Islands. If it's just the two of us, we could take a little sun break and do some birding. How about that?"

"Whatever." Charlie dismissed her and hung up.

It took Caroline a lot of effort and money to get the Canary Island tickets at this late date, but she needed a break from her research, and her body trembled at the mere thought of a rendezvous with her favorite lover. With the extra travel time, they would have only ten days together, but it would be like a second honeymoon. She couldn't remember the last time they had been off alone and together.

Caroline made arrangements for Charlie to join her at an exclusive resort near a nature preserve on the Island of La Palma. She expected him to be waiting for her in their bungalow when she got there. She thought ahead to the hot tub in their suite and a romantic night to renew their relationship.

But Charlie was late. His connection from Madrid had been canceled, and he wouldn't arrive until early the next afternoon. By the time he did, she was tired of waiting and annoyed.

She heard the taxi approach the bungalow and stepped out to the beautifully landscaped and fragrant walkway expecting an enthusiastic greeting from her husband to change her mood. Instead, Charlie nodded her way and then took forever to sort out the correct payment with the driver and attend to his luggage.

She waited for the passionate embrace she expected as he approached, but he skirted her, held his bags tight, and walked by her toward the door. She swiveled to face him, her hands on her hips. "Finally. I can't believe you couldn't get an earlier flight out. Did you even try?"

"Caroline. I'm here now." His voice was flat and just above a whisper.

As he carried his bag toward the door, she could see he looked tired and unkempt. She attempted an inviting smile, but Charlie didn't react and just followed her into the bungalow. "Wow, this is fancy, Caroline. You went all out. What's the occasion?"

Caroline snapped at him. "Well, I haven't seen my husband for five months, and I thought he might be happy to see me."

He shrugged and took a deep breath before he replied, "I did try to get an earlier flight. Tried hard. But, right now, I'm exhausted. Let me take a shower and a little nap, and we'll start fresh."

The "little nap" became seven hours of hard sleep. Caroline left to go to the clubhouse to swim in the pool, then returned to the suite and spent a couple of hours reviewing a paper she was preparing for submission. He finally awoke when she was noisily booking a local bird guide to take them around the island the next day. She wasn't about to waste her vacation.

"Finally!" She rumpled his hair as she sat on the bed near him. "I was wondering if you were ever going to wake up."

"What time is it?" Charlie asked.

"Eight o'clock. Time for dinner. I'm starving." Caroline was anxious to salvage their evening.

Charlie didn't move.

"Hey, let's go get some food." Caroline bit her tongue and tried to stay calm.

"Ahh, I'm not feeling great, Caroline. I have a headache. You go get some dinner. I'm so lagged. I'm just not up for it."

Caroline took her hand back as if scalded and popped up like a petulant child. "Charlie—c'mon. I waited all afternoon for you to wake up."

"Sorry, Caroline. I can't." He finally opened his eyes to look for his phone, scrambling to find it on the bedside table. "I've gotta call home and check on Grace. You should talk to her, too."

"No way. I'm going to get some dinner. It's my vacation!" She turned in a huff and left him alone. By the time she got to the clubhouse, she had cooled down enough to ask for a table for two, confident he would follow her shortly. He didn't.

The bird guide knocked on their door at six in the morning. Charlie had been up for hours. Caroline's only greeting to him, following a full body assessment of his gear, was, "Those hiking boots should work. Better bring a hat for the sun. You brought one, I hope?" She headed out to the jeep, following the guide, already shouting orders.

She intended to make her husband suffer by ignoring him, but he didn't seem to mind. He appeared to be in a daze, and after a while, she lost herself in the fabulous fauna of the island and the spectacular birds to be found. She liked the guide and, without consulting her detached husband, hired him for several more days.

Still complaining of a headache, Charlie took another nap when they returned, which further complicated his jet lag. Caroline sulked, ordered room service, and finally went to bed herself, leaving him a room service sandwich.

By the third day, Charlie and Caroline were finally on the same time clock but not in sync. *Where has my adoring Charlie gone? And how do I get him back? What's wrong with him?*

Her mind spun with questions she couldn't answer. When he arranged a romantic dinner on the patio of a restaurant near their hotel on the beach, she finally exhaled. *That's more like it!*

By the time their entrées arrived, Charlie was nursing his third gin and tonic.

"I've never seen you drink this much. What's up with that?" Caroline didn't drink at all and noticed that the more he drank the quieter he had become. She took a bite of her locally harvested fish and was ready to swoon. "This is incredible. You'll have to have a taste."

Charlie didn't lift his fork. "Caroline, you haven't asked me once about Grace. We were supposed to talk about the situation while I'm here. Aren't you concerned about her? About how she is?"

Caroline noticed then that her husband was tightly wound, probably from the alcohol. "You shouldn't be drinking this much." She took another bite. "I can see it's affecting you. Of course, I'm concerned about our daughter. What mother wouldn't be?"

"Well then?"

"Well then, what?"

"Well then, ask me how she is. You haven't even tried to talk to her."

"Don't be silly. You've talked to her practically every day we've been here. If something were wrong, you would clearly tell me. I trust you, silly man." She chuckled.

"Aren't you worried about her?"

"Of course I am. But you said that she will be seeing a psychiatrist in January, so we'll see what needs to be done then." She took a third bite and added, "Your dinner is going to get cold. Eat it while it's hot."

"I'm not hungry." He looked off the patio toward the ocean, his dark mood a foil to the beauty of the sunset over the water.

"Leave Grace out of it. We're here alone. Let's enjoy it. We'll find out soon enough what's wrong, if anything. It's probably something from your unknown ancestors—a mental weakness of some kind. We can't know until we know." She took another bite. "It can't be from my side of the family. My parents and Uncle Felix were totally solid and healthy, as am I. You, on the other hand, have no idea."

"Is that what you think? That I may have defective genes? Really?" He spoke quietly but with an edge.

"That's not at all what I said. I merely said we won't know anything for several weeks. Remember Grace wanted us to enjoy our holiday?" But as Caroline finished her sentence, Charlie had already left her alone at the table in the moonlight shining over the bay.

The next morning, Caroline decided to change things up. Charlie was sleeping in the second bed in their room, having come in much later than she had. She threw off her nightie, slipped into bed beside him, and tried to wake him by nibbling his ear. He turned his head the other way.

She persisted and began to stroke his shoulder, then kiss his neck, working her way down his flank. Finally, he responded but not the way she expected him to. "Caroline, not now."

He turned his back to her. Not to be spurned, she started slowly stroking his body gently until she reached his crotch, and then, interpreting his passive acceptance as encouragement, she urged him on. "I've needed you, Charlie, and you need me!"

Her eager insistence finally aroused him. She bit his ear, sharply, and he yelped. He turned her around and pinned her, thrusting hard and fast into her arched body until she screamed in relief.

He got up and pulled a sheet around his torso, leaving the room. "Is that what you wanted, Caroline?" His voice was rough, untamed, the question rhetorical.

Yes, she did want it.

The last few days of their Canary Islands vacation was about sex and very little else. No more talk of Grace. Caroline hired her bird guide during the day, while Charlie walked the beaches alone. They didn't fuss much with dinner, but Charlie always celebrated sunset with a few cocktails.

The sex, new every night, had the same theme—hesitation and capture. Release elusive. Satisfaction for one.

Chapter 27

Two Harbors, Minnesota
January 2014

Even though Charlie had been in almost daily contact with Grace or Lori, he was desperate to see his daughter. The moment his flight left Spain, he felt like a fly released from a spiderweb. Now that the mathematics of his marriage to Caroline had been exposed, he refused to participate in her rigged equation any longer. *But what damage have I done to my daughter?*

Grace was his priority, and he would do what needed to be done to take care of her.

It was his ambivalence about Caroline that had overwhelmed him. He had loved her since the day he'd spotted her in the biology lab. She was an original, living in her own world, oblivious to others, always totally focused on something new and different. Her total disregard for day-to-day pursuits that had other college students all twisted up was enough to keep him in thrall. Now, he saw how she had barely taken notice of him, no matter how hard he had worked to become indispensable to her.

However, she had always been honest with him. "I'm a nomad. I want to travel the world and follow my path wherever it takes me." She was doing that now. He couldn't be surprised by her lack of attention to a domestic life that he had forced on her, a child that he'd wanted, a family life that he'd craved and she detested.

But now that Grace was a victim of this situation, he knew how messed up it was and more dangerous than he could have imagined. He knew it was going to blow up, and he wasn't sure where the pieces would land. He did know that he would catch his daughter first.

Upon arrival, Charlie searched for Lori. She stood with their two girls waiting for him at the arrivals section of Duluth International Airport. Her bright smile was the beacon he homed in on as he then found the strength to search his daughter's face for the trusting love he needed. He reached to her for an embrace.

"Gracie, I missed you so much." She felt a little stiff in his arms, and he released her after a quick squeeze. "Let me look at you. He tweaked her nose. How are you, princess?"

Grace responded with the slightest of smiles, but Ashley shoved her way beyond Grace to give Charlie a heartfelt welcome hug. "Welcome home, Charlie! You look sun-kissed next to us pasty Minnesota girls!"

"Speak for yourself! I'm not pasty! My complexion has a rosy glow from the snowshoeing we enjoyed this morning. So does Gracie's!" Lori put her arm around Grace as she talked and winked at Charlie. "So, how jet-lagged are you? We thought maybe you'd want a home-cooked meal before you tuck in for a long sleep?"

"You have no idea how good that sounds. I've been on four flights in the past twenty-four hours and can barely think straight."

"School starts again day after tomorrow," Ashley said.

"Lori put a pot roast in our Crock-Pot this morning, Dad, so we can go straight home and eat." Grace's voice sounded stronger than it had when he left home, and her shiny hair was up in a ponytail.

"You're incredible, Lori. That sounds perfect after all of the foreign food I've tried, and no real food for the last day of traveling—exactly what I need." He caught her eye then, trusting that years of nuanced communication between them would convey his gratitude.

Lori dropped them off at their door. She was about to leave when she rolled down her window. "Almost forgot to ask. Caroline is well?"

"Yes, she's well. In her element," he replied wearily. *Clearly where she should be.*

Sensory overload hit Charlie as he opened the door. The aroma of roasting meat and vegetables mixed with the high-pitched excited yips of Bailey, who climbed over the luggage to get to him. His eyes teared up as he sat on the bench and let Bailey slobber all over him as Gracie watched.

"It's good to have you home, Dad."

"I'm so happy to be home." He switched gears from worrying about the mess of his marital situation to pure relief that his daughter was speaking in sentences and looked better than when he'd left her.

Over dinner, Grace told him that she was able to play the piano the way she wanted to again. "It's not too loud now."

"Hmmm. What do you think that means, princess?"

"Don't know, but Lori thinks I'm better."

"Well, that's good. How are you feeling about school on Monday? Ready?"

She tensed up but finally replied with her eyes cast down to the floor, "I'm pretty far behind."

"You're a smart kid. You'll catch up when you can catch up. The important thing is that you are improving, and that's cause for a celebration." He pulled a wrapped present from his bag and presented it to her. "This is from your mom and me."

He saw a slight flinch of his daughter's body when "Mom" was mentioned, but she opened the gift. He wasn't sure he could maintain the charade that Caroline had a role in the gift choice for their daughter. Fortunately, Grace didn't ask for details.

Grace opened the packing to uncover a beautiful scarf woven from the alpaca found in Spain. Beautiful magenta, pink, and purple hues, with a lovely border of deep royal blue. She looked up to him with a big smile. "Wow, Dad, it's beautiful. I love it."

They called it an early night since Charlie was exhausted. He took a moment to call Lori before he went to bed. He couldn't tell her the real reason for his call, but he was close to admitting it to himself. The contrast between her and Caroline in this stressful time made it clear to him that his heart was transmitting a message. "Just wanted to say thanks again, Lori. I couldn't get through this without you."

"Of course. You'd do the same for me if I were in a pinch," Lori replied.

"Yes, I would." Charlie couldn't imagine that, as it had always been him needing her, but he liked the idea that she depended on him, as well. "Good night, Lori. I'll call you tomorrow to get an update on how things went. I'm dragging now."

They skipped church the next day so he could catch up on time zones and housekeeping, and get ready to return to school. Grace came with him on errands. Charlie watched her carefully and reserved time to call Lori later in the day to get a full report.

"I do think she's a little better. She showed renewed interest in playing her usual music on the piano and seemed to enjoy the regular Christmas festivities. But I'm glad you've got the appointment soon. Something is still not right."

"Such as?"

"Well, she didn't want to go out with Ashley and their friends to a movie in Duluth. Wanted to hang with me, which was fine, but not her usual behavior. I think she sorta forced herself to look happy for me on occasion. Felt watched, I think, or monitored."

"Thank God for that! I don't know how I can ever thank you for watching over my daughter while I was on a vacation." Charlie flinched at hearing that word. "If Walt hadn't advised me to go, you know I wouldn't have."

"Yes, I know. By the way, Walt and Claire invited us over for dinner once and we, of course, saw him at church activities. Each time, I could see that Grace was pleased to have him around, and each time, he made it a point to check in with her. I think that helped. He is such a friend to you, and so caring for Grace."

"I know. He's been amazing."

"One more thing you should know." She hesitated a few seconds. "How did she sleep last night?"

"Well, I was dead to the world. So, I honestly don't know. I went to bed before she did and woke up once she was already up. Didn't mean to, but it just happened."

"I'm sure you were exhausted."

Lori always seemed to assume his best intentions. "I was, but so relieved to find Grace intact and so grateful to you and Ashley for keeping this as normal as possible. I didn't sleep well while I was gone." He left the question in the air. He had never confided in Lori about Caroline and wouldn't start now. If Lori was curious about why he hadn't slept well, she would remain curious.

"Well, she had a hard time at night. Bad dreams or worries kept her awake, then she'd fall asleep and wake up wild. When we comforted her, she retreated into her shell. It didn't happen every night but enough for me to do something about it."

"Yes. She has suffered from nightmares for a while. What did you try?"

"I bought one of those background sound machines that you plug in to block out other noise—it's like white noise. You know the type?"

"Yes, I do. You can choose waterfall, birds chirping, that type of thing?"

"Yes. Exactly. It seemed to help. I sent it home with her. You may want to ask her if she's remembering to use it. She commented that it helped her block the bad voices." Lori paused.

Charlie's heart stopped beating. He sensed Lori right there with him. "Oh, my god. I'm so scared. My daughter is hearing voices." He heard his own voice as a controlled scream.

Lori soothed with a soft whisper. "Charlie, I'm with you. Walt is with you. We need to take this one day at a time."

He was able to mumble, "I know. Thank you."

"When is the appointment again?" Lori's voice sounded anguished, as if she had barely battled the desperation out of it.

"Two weeks."

Could they make it that long? And if so, then what?

Chapter 28

Two Harbors, Minnesota
January 2014

Charlie welcomed the routine of the winter semester. Everything from the discipline it took to create review exercises to getting each class ready for new learning to the horseplay he witnessed in the hallways as kids greeted their classmates after a break of two weeks kept him focused on current issues.

Still, Grace never left his mind.

The first day back, she had been very distant in the car and wouldn't eat any breakfast before they left. He was unsure how to handle the situation, but she had functioned this way for the last few months. He now counted the days until the doctor's appointment. He tried to coddle her into eating that night, and she did finally eat a bit. It was only when she played the piano two evenings later that he saw any animation from her. And then, it was frenzy or a solo note played over and over.

"Grace, do you want me to help you with any of your homework?"

"No."

"Do you have any?" he pressed, after reminding himself, *She's not like glass; I won't break her by asking.*

"I'm tired." She went into her room. That night was bad.

Charlie woke to Bailey's bark and ran into Grace's room to find her cowering in the corner of her closet, her hands over her ears. "Gracie, Gracie, I'm here. What is it, baby?"

He reached out to comfort her, and she screamed, "Get them away from me. Get them away from me!"

Bailey barked loudly and then lay down and crept into the closet near Grace. Charlie also lay down near Bailey and started to whisper gently to Grace. "Gracie, baby, it's OK. I'm here. Daddy's here. You had a bad dream, but I'm here. Bailey's here. You're OK."

Grace rocked her body back and forth and mumbled, "What do they want? Make them go away."

"Who, sweetheart? It's just me and Bailey here with you. And we love you and will protect you. There's nobody else here."

After fifteen minutes of trying to comfort a hysterical Grace, she finally pointed at her bedside table. Moonlight through her curtain shone enough so that Charlie could see the table and lamp. He could also see the sound maker that Lori had given Grace to help her go to sleep. "Them," she croaked. "They're in there."

"The sound maker? That's just a machine that puts out white noise to help people sleep. There's nobody in there."

She became more agitated with his explanation, and so he tried a new tactic. "Would you like me to get rid of it?"

"Get rid of them." Her voice was now a hoarse whisper.

Charlie jumped up, ran to the bedside table, and unplugged the noise machine. He showed her the disconnected plug and said, "See, the noise is gone. There's nobody there."

Grace reacted by slumping into a ball and starting to sob silently. Charlie stood still as his senses recalibrated to the sudden change from background noise and screaming to the only sound in the room being Bailey licking his daughter as he cuddled close.

Only after he could hear his own breathing did he think he could move and act. His fear was acute, his heart beating wildly. He moved to his daughter and dog and huddled with them until his exhaustion caused him to move her to her bed, where all three of them lay together through the remaining hours of the night.

When morning light replaced the moonlight, Charlie woke abruptly, disoriented. A quick look brought it all back. His fear instantly palpable, he pulled Bailey out of the room with him and made two calls. First, to school, and then to Walt Riley.

As he finished his calls, he gazed out at the lake, today's robin's egg-blue shade a soothing backdrop to the bare branches of the stoic paper birch trees standing guard by the house.

Lori called during her lunch break. "How's Grace?"

"Honestly, I'm worried sick. She had a very bad night."

"I'm so sorry. Mack told me you weren't here at school today, and I just had to call. Is there anything I can do?"

"Thank you, but no."

"I'm so sorry. I thought she was stable. Do you know if something triggered the nightmare?"

He hesitated to tell Lori about the sound maker. "She was convinced that there were men arguing, fighting about something to do with her, and she thought they would attack her."

"Oh, how frightening for her. That sounds something like what happened here, but not quite as bad, I guess. Was she using the sound maker?"

"Yes, actually she was. After you told me it had worked well when she was with you, I had high hopes, but she told me the voices were coming from the device. She didn't calm down until I unplugged it. Then she just broke down. It was horrible to see."

She gasped. "Oh, my god, I'm so sorry." Her voice broke. "I didn't think . . . I should have known—"

"It's not your fault. You couldn't have known. You never

need to explain your motives with Grace. I know you love her and would do whatever you could do to keep her safe."

They shared a painful silence, then Charlie said, "So, I'm not leaving her side until we have a plan to get her help. I hope we can hang on until then."

"I understand. Did Walt give you any idea about how this will go?"

"Not really. His priority was to shake Dr. Chester into action. He knows she's in bad shape. Without saying it aloud, I believe he's trying to push for a hospital admission where Chester is. He doesn't think it would be a good idea to hospitalize her in Duluth, as he wants her with him. He thinks highly of the guy. And I trust Walt, so I'm in his hands."

"Will you please call me when you know, and if there is anything I can do?"

"Of course. I've got plenty of groceries, so we'll be fine. I'm going to stay very close to Grace and wait on Walt's call."

Charlie quietly opened Grace's bedroom door to take a peek. Her dark curls swirled over her face. He stepped close enough to hear her softly breathing. Such a contrast to her agitation last night leading them to huddle together in a closet. He thought back to his earlier conversation with Walt Riley, whose rapid-fire grilling had stayed with him: "Any reason to think she's not been taking her antidepressants? Any worry that she may be taking more than the prescribed dosage? Have you been watching her take the meds?"

He finally relented when Charlie retrieved the bottle and counted the pills. "I've been doling them out and watching her take them, Walt, and you know Lori did that while I was gone."

"Yes. I checked on that with Lori myself," Walt replied softly, thinking aloud. "We could try a different med, but I don't like what's happening. She's devolving quickly. She should be in a controlled environment for treatment."

"What does a 'controlled environment' mean?" Charlie asked.

Walt ignored the question and asked his own. "What role will Caroline play in Grace's care going forward? Were you able to discuss her situation?"

"You'll be dealing with me; Caroline will not be involved." He chose not to tell Walt that Caroline had called twice since he returned from Portugal. *And I'm not calling her back.*

"Please do everything you can to get Grace the help she needs." Charlie signed off.

Grace napped much of the day and didn't want to talk about the events of the previous night. By the time she headed to bed, Charlie was exhausted by the day's worry and his own lack of rest. He kept both bedroom doors wide open and finally fell into a deep sleep.

It was so deep that it took him a minute to register Bailey's barking. Then he raced out of bed. Disoriented in the dark house lit only by moonlight streaking through the windows lakeside, he moved toward the barking and noticed Grace's empty bed on his way. He ran for the back door and could see Bailey near the water. He turned on the spotlight, pulled on his boots, and ran into the night.

As he neared his dog, he saw his daughter, in the water, wading out from the shore.

"Grace! Gracie! Stop!" He yelled but with no response, quickly focused his energy on the uneven descent and clumsy sidestepping he needed to move across and beyond the ice-covered rocks and shards to get to open water. By the time he got to her, she was up to her neck. Thirty seconds later and he wouldn't have been able to reach her.

"Gracie, it's Dad. Come with me." He pulled her back, her body willing but her eyes vacant. He moved as fast as possible, knowing she had been in the bone-chilling water for several minutes. Once they reached the shore, they fell twice on the icy rocks. Bailey's pleading bark kept them moving forward.

The distance to the house was almost too much. Grace was now a dead weight for him and too heavy to carry fast enough to prevent hypothermia. He left her momentarily to get blankets. One to place around her, and one to slide her on the slippery snow and ice toward the house.

Once inside, he stripped her of her pajamas, noting her feet were bloody and raw. Hard to believe she could walk barefoot across the jagged rocks and sharp ice shards without registering the pain. Then he recalled the zombie-like state she was in when he reached her and started shivering uncontrollably. He led her to the couch and tucked her in with blankets, started a fire, got the teapot going, and pulled his own wet clothes off to change into sweats.

He looked at the clock. 3:30 a.m. But he already knew it was time. *What were the words Walt finally used when I pressed him about what precipitates a hospitalization for someone in mental distress?*

"When someone is a danger to themselves or others, it's time for the hospital."

Chapter 29

Lisbon, Portugal
January 2014

Caroline sensed a monumental shift in her relationship with her husband during their time together in the Canary Islands but decided to dismiss it as a sign that Charlie had finally realized what he was missing by not joining her in her new life and was too proud to admit it. He was unhappy about that and not her. *He'll come to his senses and be with me someday soon.* Once she was finally able to get what she needed from him, she didn't obsess about the details.

Until she couldn't get him on the phone. At first, she guessed he was playing a game with her, and she was confident she would win it, as usual. But when the date for Grace's psychiatric appointment came and went without word from him, and the next of her countless phone calls went to voice mail, she threw her phone across the room and broke a vase. *Enough!*

Her pride precluded her from calling Lori. She called Walt Riley. Relentlessly. Every hour on the hour, his office, then his home. Finally at four o'clock in the afternoon, he called her back.

"Caroline, this is Walt Riley. I understand you called."

She instantly railed at him with all of her pent-up complaints. "You have no business treating my daughter for anything beyond a nosebleed. Who do you think you are, diagnosing depression? Do you think everybody is depressed? Just because they are not as clueless-happy as you are?" Finally coming up for air, she paused briefly, then asked, "And why is Charlie not taking my calls? What's going on?"

Walt calmly stated, "Grace is in the hospital. She was admitted a little over a week ago. She is very ill. Charlie has been with her."

She finally listened and calmed enough to ask, "Well, what's wrong with her?"

"They are observing her and sorting that out." He hesitated slightly. "Right now they are trying to rule out psychosis."

Caroline gasped.

"She has exhibited almost all of the classic symptoms—difficulty concentrating, depressed mood, suspiciousness, withdrawal, sleeping too much, delusions."

His voice dropped and Caroline concluded she would only get his version of the story.

"They're ruling out any other organic causes for her symptoms. It'll likely take a bit more time."

"Where are they?" she yelled, though she added silently to herself, *I should have asked more questions when Charlie was with me. Walt is useless.*

"They are at University Hospital. Dr. Lawrence Chester is her psychiatrist." He cleared his throat. "You are best off talking to Charlie directly. It would be hard to get information otherwise."

Caroline's venom returned. "Don't you think I've tried that? You fool!" She hung up.

She was on a flight to Minneapolis–St. Paul International Airport that night. Within twenty-four hours, she demanded to see her daughter at University of Minnesota Hospital.

"May I see an ID, please?"

Caroline's ire was hot, and the jet lag hangover wasn't helping. "I'm her mother, and I demand to see her," she snapped.

"I'm sorry, ma'am. We don't have your name as the responsible parent. I have no authority to release any information to you."

Caroline's withering look was meant to intimidate this functionary into gaining access. The receptionist remained unfazed. "Let me have someone from customer support help you out." The receptionist picked up the telephone and simultaneously pushed a panic button under her countertop, while glancing over at the security guard stationed by the door.

"You have no right to keep me from my daughter. I demand to see Grace Booker. I am Caroline Booker. I just traveled across the Atlantic Ocean to be here," she screamed.

The burly security guard approached her and cut her off from the receptionist with his body. "Ma'am, I need to ask you to calm down. Let's go over here and we'll wait for customer service to help you out."

Upon this attempt to physically bar her from the reception desk in the middle of her tirade, Caroline planted her solid but small frame and wouldn't budge. "This man is preventing me from seeing my daughter. I demand to see my daughter."

The busy lobby was now part of the performance in a one-act play. All heads had turned to watch the possible altercation between the small woman with the loud voice and a burly security guard. In the next thirty seconds, a matronly woman with a calm demeanor and careworn expression sidled up to Caroline and whispered, "Come with me, or we will throw you out of here."

Caroline lifted her chin up, swung her bag in an exaggerated arc, and followed the woman to a small room off of the lobby. She sat down and eyed the coffeepot on the table before helping herself noisily.

"Now, what can I help you with?"

Caroline repeated her entreaty. Pulling her ID from her pocket, she handed it to the woman when asked. After a few minutes, the woman calmly said, "Yes, I see that your daughter is a patient here. Is your husband, Charles Booker, her father?"

"Yes."

"You haven't been in touch with him?"

"No, he won't return my calls."

"Are you two separated?"

"No, of course not. I just work in Europe at the moment. My expertise as a bird specialist is in demand in many parts of the world." Caroline huffed. "Women can be mothers *and* experts, you know."

"I see." The woman frowned openly and peered at Caroline from behind her glasses.

"Well, your husband is the responsible parent and therefore the parent on record as our contact. I'm afraid he will be the authority for us regarding your access."

Caroline sputtered. "Then get him the hell in here."

"Mrs. Booker. You need to understand that in situations of parental estrangement we need to keep the best interest of the child as our ultimate goal. Surely, you want what is best for your daughter, right?"

"Well, produce him, then. I'm not leaving." Caroline took off her coat, sat back in her chair, and sipped her coffee. She was good at war. *Bring it on.*

"I'll see what I can do." The woman, Ms. Childress according to her name badge, exhaled wearily, as if she had seen this situation play out before. "It is likely he is not in the hospital, and visiting hours are restricted on that ward." She stepped out to make a few phone calls, leaving Caroline stewing in her office.

Twenty minutes later, a stern Ms. Childress returned with the security guard looming behind her by the door. "I've reached your husband, and he's on his way to the hospital. When he arrives, I will allow you two to use this office to talk. I warn you now. This is a hospital. Your daughter and many others are patients here. We will not allow any disruptions and are absolutely willing to enforce our ability to remove you from the premises. Do you understand me?"

"Well, who made you queen?" Caroline laughed and spread out in her chair. "I need more coffee. Send your bodyguard to replenish the supply, won't you?" She raised the thermal pot.

Chapter 30

Minneapolis, Minnesota
January 2014

Charlie tried to make sense of the timeline while he drove slowly from his temporary quarters in Minneapolis to the hospital, thankful Mack's friend had put him up without questioning for how long. *Caroline will want to know. I've been here a week, a little more?* He visited Grace every day and would continue until he felt she was turning a corner.

Right now, he had to consider how to deal with Caroline. He didn't want to waste time second-guessing his decisions to date, but it was difficult not to. *Would any of this have been easier if I had called her immediately? Who would that have helped?*

Instead of calling Caroline after he fished their daughter out of Lake Superior, he had called Walt. He thought back to Grace's explanation for fleeing the house in the middle of an early January night.

"They were after me. They were going to get me." The defeat in her voice had caused his body to break out in a cold sweat.

The call to Walt was followed by the swift arrival of both Lori and Claire Riley to take shifts in supporting his care for Grace until she could be hospitalized at University Hospital in Minneapolis, two days later.

When he received the call from a Ms. Childress about Caroline, he put in a panicky call to Walt. Walt had called him yesterday to warn him after talking to Caroline, but Charlie hadn't expected her to fly in. *Why didn't I call her then?* He wasn't sure what she was capable of now.

Walt was quick to react. "Charlie, I'm not sure it will be good for Grace to see her mother. Let me put in a quick call to Dr. Chester and call you right back." He had called back within twenty minutes with Chester's concurrence. "Do not upset Grace with a visit right now. She is too vulnerable."

Walt added, "I pressed him a bit, knowing Caroline may not give up so easily. He said that it's up to you, Charlie, but you could choose to raise the question to Grace. Does she want to see her mother? If Grace gets agitated or is able to articulate that she doesn't want to see Caroline, then it's clear. If Caroline isn't satisfied with that, then Chester reluctantly agreed that Caroline could see Grace if they can arrange a setup for one-way viewing."

"My God, that makes it sound like Grace is a zoo animal." Charlie's voice was as rough as his nerves. "What do you think?"

"Well, I don't think the middle of a psychotic break is the best time to arrange a reconciliation between mother and daughter, so if Grace isn't up for a visit, I guess I'd allow the 'viewing' if it meant that Caroline would be satisfied enough to leave the situation alone for a few months while we try to get Grace through this challenge."

Ms. Childress arranged for someone to meet Charlie at another entrance and escort him up to Grace's ward. The place was just changing over to the evening shift, so staff was going into report. Grace's nurse saw him arrive, and they huddled in a room off of the nurse's station so he could explain the situation. She had more empathy in her eyes than yesterday.

"Yes, Mr. Booker. Dr. Chester alerted me. He told me about the plan. Are you here to talk to Grace about the possibility of seeing her mother?"

"I am. How is she today?"

"About the same. No interaction to speak of. But she's willing to take the meds. Sleeping a bit too much, but that's to be expected right now. This is a good time for you to be here. We're going to try to get her out of her room for dinner tonight. So, we have some time for your visit. Let me go and see her, and I'll bring you to her in a minute."

Charlie nodded and thought about how to introduce this idea to his daughter. Grace hadn't seen her mother since the summer before and had avoided seeing her over Christmas break. How would she react to the unexpected request now? Any mother would be worried about her child. But Caroline wasn't just *any* mother. *This is my fault. I should have kept her in the loop. Surely I could have managed her, but how could I know what was coming? I was trying to protect Grace from her unpredictable mother, and now that is more important than ever.*

Grace's nurse came to get him and ushered him to her room. "She's not very alert, but she knows it's you coming to visit."

He hadn't seen Grace yet today and was happy to find her out of a hospital gown and in sweats, her hair clean, her injured feet still bandaged but in soft slippers. He hoped for at least a facial expression of recognition as he approached her, but she didn't look up when he entered the room.

"Hi, princess, I'm here to see you," he whispered to her and she turned toward him slightly. "Can I give you a hug?" He knew to ask permission. He was advised that her sensory overload was acute and speaking softly and respecting her personal space were important right now to give her a sense of control over a world she believed had turned on her.

Grace crossed her arms in front of herself but nodded her head. It made for an awkward show of affection, but Charlie would do whatever he could to keep his daughter in his world.

He pulled back and sat next to her on her bed. Just breathing the same air was a comfort. He tried a little small talk but got no response. Finally, he decided it was time to broach the topic.

"Grace, I have some news for you. It will be a surprise. Your mom flew home to see you." He stopped briefly when his daughter moved away from him on the cot and stared at the wall. "And is here at the hospital now."

Grace began to shake and rock from side to side.

"Would you like to see her?" He knew the answer before she spoke, but he willed himself to finish his task.

The rocking speeded up and the shaking was horrible to watch. "No," she mouthed, voiceless.

"OK, OK Grace. I won't make you see her. I'll send her away." Charlie didn't hesitate to assure his daughter that the one thing his wife had asked for, he would prevent. His shoulders slumped, and he quietly slipped out, aware that she wouldn't relax until he was gone and that he may have forfeited his goodwill with her carrying the message for his wife.

He trembled as he left Grace and needed to compose himself before he approached her nurse. "I'm afraid she's agitated. This may not be the night for her to join the others for dinner."

"So, do you want to go to Plan B?" she asked.

"I hope not." The idea of Caroline viewing Grace without her consent chafed. He steeled himself to convince Caroline that she should return to Europe and leave the care of his daughter to him, as she always had.

Caroline was set up in her own little anteroom near Ms. Childress's office, working on her laptop when Charlie arrived.

"Caroline," he began.

"Well, could it be? Mr. Charles Booker. My husband. My daughter's father. Evidently her keeper." She closed her laptop and stood up. "How dare you keep me away from her?" she shouted at him. "How dare you not return my calls?"

Charlie let her tire herself out before responding. He was experienced in dealing with her tirades, but this time he wouldn't take her onto his lap and stroke her hair while she vented. He simply couldn't reconcile that behavior with his need to defend his daughter. He stood and took the verbal abuse.

At one point, the security guard knocked on the door to check on them as even the soundproof walls weren't enough to contain Caroline's outburst.

"Get the hell outta here!" she shouted at the guard, but once Charlie told him things were under control and closed the door himself, she started to calm down.

"Caroline, Grace is very sick. They are almost certain that she is suffering a psychotic break. She is very vulnerable right now." His voice was flat but solid, so he continued, "She doesn't want to see you. The doctors advise that we don't push that point."

"Who do these doctors think they are, God? What do they know? I'm her mother. I gave her life. I have a right to see her." She pushed her chair back, poised to get up to fight.

Charlie didn't trust himself to respond. He pulled his sweater sleeves farther down his arms to cover his shakiness. "We don't want to push her over the edge."

"What is that supposed to mean?"

"It means that she is suicidal."

"What?" Caroline sat up in her chair.

"She's on suicide watch right now."

"Why?"

"Because she already tried once."

Charlie took a deep breath and tried to keep his voice steady while he looked her in the eye. "In the days before her scheduled appointment she had what they now call a psychotic episode, and while I was with her all of the time, one night she walked out of the house and down to the lake and into the water before I realized she wasn't in bed."

Caroline sat completely still. "I don't believe this. It can't be true," she whispered, looking past Charlie.

Charlie gave her some time. He hoped she was having a flashback to the morning thirteen years earlier when their daughter, left in the care of her mother while he went back into the house to make their picnic lunch, had toddled down to the only access point to the lake. It was summertime and a warm day. Day lilies bordered the lawn closest to the lake, very inviting to a toddler. By the time Charlie returned to the yard, Grace was already in the water and all he could see was her little head bobbing up and down with the waves. Caroline had moved to the side yard with her binoculars, lost in her own world. He let her stay in the memory for a few minutes before he continued.

"Bailey's barking woke me. If there hadn't been a full moon, I wouldn't have been able to save her." He looked away, his voice wobbly. "She thought monsters were after her."

Caroline listened to his every word. After a moment she said, "My God. She's crazy."

Charlie flinched at the expression but didn't miss a beat. "There are a range of possible diagnoses, some for diseases without a cure, but clearly there are effective treatments."

"Such as?"

"Medication, of course. She's been on one type of antidepressant, but it can take a long time to get the right combination of drugs. Cognitive therapy is another treatment to address everyday challenges of living with a mental illness." He didn't want to overstate it, but he knew he was close to the desired outcome with his wife. *Butt out. It's best for Grace if you do.* "But first we have to get her through this acute phase. Keep her alive basically, until treatment can help her live her life."

"The life of a crazy person," Caroline said, as if reciting the phone book.

"That's a terrible thing to say. This is Grace you're talking about. Our daughter's life!" Charlie shouted.

Caroline leaned in close. "As if she's ever really been *our* daughter."

Charlie watched the transformation of his wife as a calm set over her. He could see her switch gears, as if she had pulled a lever to reverse course.

"You look like hell." Caroline threw one more taunt.

"Thanks. I feel worse than that."

When Caroline looked at him, and then at her laptop and small overnight bag, he added, "I'm bunking at one of Mack's friend's house in the basement. I could get you a hotel room for tonight if you'd like."

"Well, that's welcoming." She rose but kept her distance and put her laptop in its case. "Don't bother. I'm going back to the airport for the first flight back. You can take care of your daughter."

Chapter 31

Minneapolis, Minnesota
January 2014

Caroline carefully attached her laptop to her overnight bag and turned toward the door without a backward glance at her husband of over sixteen years.

When she left the building, the brisk air hit her as a reprieve from the overheated lobby. She took a cleansing breath and gave herself a good shake. She saw a taxi lineup and headed over, her mind racing.

The air was gloomy with dusk and the swirl of snowflakes that could snarl traffic over the next several hours. It was late in the day, and she hadn't made flight arrangements. She considered her options.

Before she left, was there anyone she wanted to see? Anything she wanted to do? Any shopping she wanted to do for US goods before she flew back to Portugal? There was one interesting possibility. She picked up her phone and punched in a number.

"Glenn, it's Caroline Booker."

His voice was deep, husky, pleased. "Caroline, what a surprise. How are you?"

"Good, all good. Listen, you know I'm working in Europe now, right?" Caroline's voice was flirty, sensing the interest she was hoping to find.

He chuckled. "I've been following your globe-trotting academic career. Where are you calling from?"

"Minneapolis. I've got a few days before I need to be back, and I wondered if you would be interested in meeting up somewhere?" Caroline had sensed Glenn's romantic interest in her since their early birding days when he was mentor to her protégé. It had never been the right time.

But it was now.

Chapter 32

Two Harbors, Minnesota
June 2014

Grace felt sunlight on her face, the first indication that she was no longer in rehab. She had dreamed of this moment—waking up in her own bedroom, sun streaming in from her window, the smell of her dad's morning coffee. She pulled her covers up and snuggled in the familiarity. As she moved, Bailey's soft muzzle and then wet tongue on her wayward arm completed her image of homecoming. "Come on up, girl. Nice of you to let me sleep in." Grace lifted her head up to invite Bailey who eagerly leapt from the floor onto the bed and slobbered all over her.

She inhaled the smell of coffee. Grace wasn't sure about all that had happened in the last five months of hospital and residential treatment. But she knew that mornings didn't start this way. When her dad had picked her up yesterday, she felt like she was walking out of a cloud or out on a performance stage with all the manmade fog they put around actors or singers to make it look dramatic. Home now, she was worried about a case of serious stage fright.

Lori and Ashley had been great. To celebrate her homecoming, they had arrived at her house with pizza. Lori's hug was as warm as ever, her telltale glossy eyes told Grace all she needed about her constant love. Ashley held back a little at first, but then when Grace asked, "Ash, what have you done to your hair? I love it! Especially the orange stripe," both girls turned to Lori. "I can't believe your mom let you do it!" Grace said. They giggled together at the feigned look of outrage as Lori played along.

Why did I risk this life?

She remembered the look on her dad's face when he told her he was admitting her to the hospital for her own good. They would help her, and he couldn't help her anymore. He was crying, and she was numb.

She also remembered her dad telling her that her mother had flown in from wherever she was. *I'm so glad nobody forced me to see her.*

Then her memory went blank. She remembered kindness. The doctor was kind and gentle. She remembered endless days of sleep and no energy. She remembered group therapy. Going home wasn't so scary once her dad told her that her mom was staying in Portugal and wouldn't be coming home in the near future.

Until she had met Abby, her roommate at rehab, she wasn't sure she would make it through. A couple of weeks in, Grace returned to her room after a particularly rough counseling session. Abby had been waiting for her, holding an envelope in her hands. "Hey, Grace, I want to show you these old pictures my grandpa sent me."

But Grace climbed into her bed and turned to the wall. "Not now."

Instead of a nasty response, Abby gently put a blanket over her and let her be.

Later, when Grace did take a look, her interest perked up. "These are old pics of my grandma and grandpa and me as a baby." Abby pointed to each.

"Where's your mom?" Grace asked.

"My mom wasn't around. Ever," Abby said. "That's a good thing for me."

Grace's mouth dropped open. "Because?"

"She was a drug addict and using through her pregnancy. I nearly didn't make it...a preemie in the hospital for like months. She's dead," Abby stated. "What about you? I've heard you talk about your dad. What about your mom? Do you have one?"

Grace wasn't sure how to respond. *Do I have one? Do I wish I didn't have one?* "I do, technically, but she's really never around, which is fine with me." Grace felt her body relax. "She hates me."

Rather than responding with shock, Abby said, "Well then, wanna join me as a 'motherless child'?" She put her arm around Grace, and the club of motherless girls was formed.

From that day forward, they watched out for each other, helped each other with their schoolwork, shared their secrets—a bipolar diagnosis for Abby, a suicide attempt for Grace. They guarded each other against self-shame, a constant battle.

She waited to get up from bed until she heard her dad's movements in the kitchen. She put on a sweatshirt and padded to the kitchen, Bailey trailing. "Morning, Dad."

He was reading the paper and drinking coffee. He turned to greet her. "Morning, Gracie. How'd you sleep?"

"Good. Nice to wake up with sun on my face from my own window again."

"I bet it is." Her dad reached out for a hug and patted her back. "I can't tell you how happy I am to have you home."

"That makes two of us." Then she saw Bailey sitting patiently by the door. "Well, that makes three of us. I'll let him out."

"Usual eggs, princess?"

"Yes, please." Her dad had been making special eggs for her forever. It's one of the things she really missed over her last months' odyssey. Scrambled with a splash of salsa and rye toast.

While they were eating, she tested her idea. "Dad, I know

this is a catch-up summer and I'll be doing lots of schoolwork. Can we also try to fit in having me take my driver's test again?"

He didn't choke on his eggs but took a long time to chew before responding. "Well, I guess we can look into it."

"Dad, if you're worried about the meds I'm on, I already checked that part out with Dr. Chester. I'm safe to drive." She looked at him eagerly. *How can I get him to trust me again, when he's just months out from saving my life?*

Charlie smiled. "It's nice to see you interested in driving. Yes, let's add that to the summer's plans."

"That way I can drive myself to therapy in Duluth, so you don't have to do that."

He immediately replied, "I don't mind doing that. I'm just happy to have you home and be able to continue your therapy close by."

Grace wasn't sure her dad would realize that her driving to therapy meant she'd have the opportunity to see Abby there. He had expressed little enthusiasm about her continuing her friendship with someone she had met in residential treatment. She wasn't even sure he knew that Abby lived in Duluth.

The following Sunday, she returned to church after many months away. The stage fright was back, but she expected it. *Best get it over with!* She had gained weight from the meds and inactivity, and while she now attended to her personal grooming, she was sure her appearance would be a shock to people.

Her dad and Lori must have planned how this would go. Lori and Ashley met them at their car, a united front entering the church.

As they approached their pew, Dr. Riley and his wife, Claire, stood up to greet her. "Grace! We missed you!" Grace was happy the welcome was over by the time the service started, and she was able to get back into church mode, with the comfort of the ritual and being surrounded by people she loved and who loved her back. She had missed it.

At coffee afterward, Grace asked Ashley if she would be willing to go hiking with her. "I feel like I need to get back to the Superior Hiking Trail for some proper exercise. Been cooped up too long."

She saw Ashley flinch at the expression "cooped up" and realized it may have scared her friend to think about her hospitalized for so long. Ashley surprised her by looking into her eyes. "I'd love to hike with you. What's your schedule like this summer?"

"Well, Dad's helping me get back on track with schoolwork. All of the teachers have given him lesson plans and assignments for me. The plan is for me to be caught up with my class by fall. So, I'll be busy with that, and I have therapy once a week in Duluth. How about you?"

"Working at the Rustic Inn this summer. Early shift. We could hike in the later afternoon sometimes?"

"That could work." Grace smiled at her friend and pictured her with a bow in her hair as a toddler, hiking with her at Hawk Ridge, and playing soccer on the school team. *I'm trying to come back, Ash.*

As they were leaving, Dr. Riley took her aside. "Gracie, Dr. Chester has provided me with your after-care plan and I'm aware of the Duluth therapy setup. Know that I'm here should you need me. OK, kiddo?"

"Thanks, Dr. Riley, I will." Grace smiled at the doctor who had delivered her into the world and saved her when he delivered her to a physician who could help her. She loved that he called her "kiddo."

By midsummer, Grace had her license to drive and access to her mother's car. She was making such progress on her schoolwork that her dad trusted her with some freedom. She and Ashley were doing things together, and the hiking with her and regular exercise with her dad helped her get back into shape. She made a weekly trip to Duluth for therapy and was finally able to see Abby.

Abby understood her. They were both afraid. Afraid that they would slip back into the surreal state where their minds betrayed their will. Therapy helped, but the fear was always there. Abby's grandparents worked, so there was never anybody home when Grace went to visit her. They just hung out and smoked.

Everybody in treatment smoked. Before Grace got sick, she thought it was a habit that only losers had. The reality was that, deep down, Abby and Grace shared that, too. They knew they were both losers, abandoned by their mothers. At least Grace had her dad. Abby didn't even have that.

When school started in the fall, Grace didn't see Abby so much, but they talked on the phone a lot. Grace's dad allowed her to invite Abby to stay the night once, although she knew he didn't approve of the friendship. Abby declined the invitation. Once, back when she was in rehab, she had a day pass and she asked him if she could bring a friend with on their planned outing to the Arboretum. He had whisked her away, saying, "Nah, let's just get away from here, just the two of us." She had read his anxious body language as fear of contagion from her fellow residents.

She kept quiet about Abby and figured out how to see her on the sly. Grace used her mom's car to get away from her dad's watchful eye. She didn't like lying to her dad; she knew it was wrong. But she also didn't want him interfering. Her social life was her own business. He would never understand why she needed Abby. Every now and then, she needed relief from his constant watchfulness—it was like he thought she would break. She could barely take a shower without him hovering near the door, and he required her to keep her bedroom door open at night, with a night-light on in the hallway between them.

They were still trying out various medications for her, and she didn't like how she felt all of the time. Drugged. Tired. She had a hard time staying with any workout because her body would fatigue easily, and she gained and lost weight depending on what she was on.

Her dad kept asking her if she was OK, and her therapist wanted her to talk about her mother all the time. *Enough already. She's a bad mother. End of story.*

"You're late, Gracie B!" Abby tweaked her friend as she jumped into the front seat of Caroline's car. "Such a sweet ride. Your mom may be a monster, but at least you get to use her car!"

Grace smiled, understanding Abby's void without her own mom. *But at least she doesn't have a mom who hates her. I'd never get to use her car if she were here.*

"I only have an hour or so; I'm supposed to be shopping for jeans." Grace raised her eyebrows in a sideways glance at her friend.

"I have a joint to share. Wanna go down to the lake—that spot by the flats? Wind's right for it today. Should be good cover."

Grace nodded and took the next left toward Superior Street and the lake, switched on the radio, and they were on their way, singing with the music and assured that, in their own company, they could count on no judgment for the hour ahead.

Chapter 33

Two Harbors, Minnesota
Autumn 2014

The lingering smell of cigarettes was hard to miss when Charlie put a load of dark clothes into the washing machine. Just in time, he pulled out a pack with one remaining cigarette from Gracie's favorite worn jeans. He swallowed hard and tried not to breathe in until he left the laundry room. He knew he should forbid her to smoke, but he didn't have the heart. He was so grateful she was alive, and she had so many challenges as it was, he couldn't make a stink about the lousy cigarette smoking. He heard her put her dishes in the sink and went to deliver a drive-by kiss to the top of her head. "I love Saturday mornings, don't you, princess?"

"I do. Ummm, I'm thinking I'd like to go into Duluth to do some clothes shopping for school. Is that all right? You're going to breakfast with Walt, right?"

"I am." He turned to look at her. "Would you like to see if Ashley wants to go with you?"

"Nah, she's probably working today. It's not a big trip." She looked at him as if she suspected he didn't trust her. "How about if I stop to get some of that caramel popcorn at the candy store on Superior Street on my way back?"

"Oooh, would you? That would be great!" He opted for the happy daughter rather than raise her defenses. He knew he had to build her up to keep her strong.

"So, how's Grace?" Walt asked, as he took a quick look at the menu at the Vanilla Bean, their favorite breakfast place. "She keeping up with the meds and therapy?"

Charlie chuckled. "Why do you even bother looking at the menu when you know you're going to order the Swedish pancakes and sausage?" He put his own menu down. "And, yes sir, Gracie's doing pretty well." He smiled at the doctor. *How would I have made it through the winter without him?*

Charlie's ability to dip into his parental leave on occasion was a godsend as he had traveled back and forth to the Twin Cities for the last five months. Mack, Lori, and Walt kept the community informed with the least damaging information and had helped prepare everyone for Grace's welcome upon her return.

"Any worries?" Open-ended questions were Walt's specialty.

"Nothing new. I've told you about the smoking, which I hate."

"Right now, it may be a comfort to her. Is she complaining about any side effects from the medication she's on right now?"

"Off and on. She doesn't like the weight fluctuation. I get that. I know that she's tired a lot, and that gets in the way of her exercise, which then doesn't help her with the weight."

"So, they're still sorting out the best combination for her?"

Charlie nodded, then frowned. "I don't know what to expect. I know her adolescence has been interrupted big time, but beyond supporting her through all of this, the other big worry I have is that she still doesn't seem as comfortable with kids at school as I'd like to see. Whenever I see her at school, she's alone. Other kids are huddled up together all the time. Her social life isn't very lively for a seventeen-year-old girl. Should I be able to expect it to be?"

Walt took his time answering, attending to spreading butter and syrup on his pancakes. "Well, it's not been a year yet since her break, and remember she was away from school for several months. Probably vital months for adolescent social connections. Now, at seventeen, many of the kids are more independent, with jobs, their own cars, all of the digital gadgets they get into. She missed out on the sports connections. I'd give it some time."

"Thank God she's still tight with Ashley." Charlie put his fork on his plate. "But I worry about Grace's friendship with this Abby from residential treatment. It sounds bad, but I don't want her to isolate herself from the kids she grew up with and take up with a troubled kid instead. Doesn't it almost compound her own issues?"

"Something to watch, of course, but they could be a good support for one another. Think of what they've been through."

Charlie nodded. "I guess. Just makes me nervous. I should probably make it my business to get to know her grandparents."

"That's a good idea. Might be good for you to see how they are coping. Then you wouldn't feel isolated yourself, and your connection with them may provide some peace of mind if the friendship continues."

Over a second cup of coffee, Walt asked, "So, what are you hearing from Caroline?"

"Absolutely nothing. Haven't heard from her since she was here last January."

"And?"

"That makes me happy. I don't have room in my head to deal with her right now." Charlie looked down into his coffee mug.

"Has Grace asked?"

"No. Before her discharge, I did tell her I didn't expect her mom to be home this summer, which seemed to relax her. Otherwise, I haven't talked about Caroline since I told Grace she made a surprise trip in January and she had declined the opportunity to see her mother." Charlie spoke quickly and immediately noticed

Walt raise his eyebrow. "And, yes, I imagine it is a topic that she discusses with her therapist."

"But not with you?"

Charlie shook his head and slid the bill to his side of the table.

Grace wasn't enthusiastic about his suggestion to have Abby and her grandparents come to dinner. "It's nice of you to think of that, Dad, but they are very busy people and not very social, I don't think it's a good idea."

"Well, if Abby is a friend of yours, I'd be happy to get to know her family." He tried again but was relieved that he might not have to meet them. "Is she still a friend of yours?" He hoped he didn't sound too curious.

"Oh, sure, a little bit. I don't see her very often anymore."

"We'll let it go then. What do you think about inviting Lori and Ashley over for a special dinner soon, sound good?"

"Of course. They're family." Charlie could almost see her unspoken words in a cartoon bubble over her head.

I wish.

Chapter 34

Two Harbors, Minnesota
December 2014

It was still there. On top of the piano, in the midst of the rest of the junk mail. Why didn't he open it? Gracie had even attempted to pound the keys so hard that it would fall to the floor, and he would have to pick it up and touch it again. He must have known it was there. She certainly hadn't picked it up with the rest of the mail and left it to linger there.

For days she could feel herself grow more agitated. Her concentration was off, or, rather, all she could focus on was the letter from her mother, and what it said. Finally, after three long days, she was at a breaking point.

As they drove home from school on a Wednesday night a few months after her seventeenth birthday, she remained quiet.

"Hey, princess. You're awfully quiet. What's going on?" her father asked as they left town and turned onto the highway toward home.

She looked out the window and didn't speak to him during the drive, even though he attempted to coax her into conversation several times. As he stopped at the end of the driveway to pick up the day's post from the mailbox, she said, "You can't open that mail until you open the letter that's on the piano and has been for the past three days."

"What?" Charlie looked perplexed.

"The letter from your wife, my mother." She opened the car door and ran into the house while the car was still hovering by the mailbox.

She watched him keep to his steady pace, park the car in the garage, and bring his briefcase and her backpack in to set them on the dining room table.

She felt her breathing quicken and her heartbeat accelerate as she saw how calm he was. She stood with her arms crossed until he approached her, and then she pointed to the piano. "Open it."

"Gracie, I will. But I don't like to see you this upset. Please, let's just relax." He tried to take her into his arms, but as he got closer, she dodged him and stumbled toward the piano.

"Open it." She caught herself and waited to see whether her father could be trusted.

"Baby, I'm so sorry this has loomed so large in your imagination. I clearly didn't intend to have you be upset by it. I forgot it was there, actually. I know what's in the letter, so I didn't worry about opening it." He approached her again and had almost cleared the distance between them.

"What are you saying?"

"Your mom sent a letter from Portugal, but she grew impatient and couldn't wait for it to get here, so she called me at school last week." His voice was gentle, and he reached for her hand.

"What does she want?" Her voice caught, but she let him take her hand.

"She wondered about holiday plans," he whispered and held her hand.

"What about holiday plans?" Her voice was barely audible, her body rigid.

"She had this idea about going to Majorca." She noticed that he did not say who was included in this idea.

She kept her eyes on her father's to gauge his commitment to his words. "And?"

"I told her we weren't interested in traveling over the holidays." He kept his eyes on her and took her other hand.

She almost collapsed as her body went limp. He guided her to the couch, where they sat. Her breathing slowed as she tried to process what he said. But her mind zeroed in on what he didn't say. *She wants him, not me.*

"She asked about you, princess." He took that moment to smooth her hair and stroke her arm. She couldn't risk turning to look into his eyes, fearing the duplicity she might find there.

She heard voices that night and disrupted the household with her nightmares. In the morning, she learned two things. The letter was no longer on the piano, and her father had made an emergency appointment with her therapist.

Her father drove her to Duluth to see Mrs. Schiff. She could see curious eyes on her from the office staff as she arrived with her father. She had relapsed, and they knew it. Her father had to come with her this time; she couldn't drive herself. She was so tired she could barely walk. They sat in the waiting room, and she pulled her hoodie over her face and slumped down in her chair.

Mrs. Schiff was a gentle woman, and Grace liked her. But Grace didn't want to see her today. She knew that today, Mrs. Schiff wouldn't allow her to hide from a conversation about her mother. Her father would have seen to that.

"Hello, Grace." She came to the waiting room to greet them and escorted Grace into her office after a smile and a nod to her father.

"How are you?"

"Tired."

"Can you tell me what happened last night?"

"You already know. I had nightmares, was being taken away, and terrible people argued over who owned my body."

"Similar to past nightmares?"

"Yes."

"Do you have any idea why this happened last night?"

"I won't talk about her, so don't ask me." Grace stayed on her standard script. It had worked for almost a year.

"Grace, I understand you were upset about a letter that your father received from your mother."

"I won't talk about her, so don't ask me." Grace pulled herself up into a ball on the chair as best she could, given that it was a hard wooden chair. She sometimes wondered why there wasn't a couch in a therapist's office. She could use one to take a nap. She pulled her hoodie over her face and repeated her stock phrase. "I won't talk about her, so don't ask me."

They picked up a new prescription for her before driving home. She stayed home from school for three days with her father constantly watching her. She was compliant and took the meds, but she wasn't too fuzzy to hatch a plan. Her father could leave her and join her mother at any time. *I know he loves me, but she's working on him to leave, and she'll win. She'll do whatever it takes. She doesn't want me; she has only ever wanted him. I'm spoiling his chance for happiness with her. I can't stand between them any longer.*

She needed to get out of here. Abby was right.

Chapter 35

Two Harbors, Minnesota
Winter 2015

After the relapse and resulting increased dosage of her meds, Grace slept all the time, and even when she was awake, she walked around the house in a trance—no playing with Bailey, no banter or games. She and Charlie were more like roommates—roommates who had not signed up to live together. It was such a contrast to the obvious pleasure she'd felt when she'd finally come home months earlier, after her hospitalization and stay in rehab. Then, it had been only a matter of reintroducing her to things she loved and watching her regain her footing. Charlie had been fooled into thinking things could get back to normal. Now he realized he was wrong.

Lori tried her best to help by hosting a slumber party. When Grace declined to help make cookies and curled herself into a ball before their movie marathon was to start, she decided against suggesting ideas for other outings for Grace and Ashley with lots of girl stuff.

Ashley finally said, "Mom, let's not push it. I think she just needs some space right now." Ashley also needed her own junior-year experience, taking college entry tests and sorting through the myriad assortment of college applications. Charlie was flattered when she asked him to help her put together her application package.

Charlie, Ashley, and Lori had been sensitive about Grace's feelings and tried to keep this activity secret until Grace finally said to them, "It's OK, Ashley. I know you'll be going off to college, and I'm happy for you. It's not my path. Don't worry about it."

As to what Grace's own path would be, nobody talked about that much. It was the absence of a path that tore Charlie apart. As usual, he consulted Walt about how he should handle it.

"Has she expressed interest in going on to school?"

"No, she doesn't express interest in anything, really." Charlie knew he looked like hell; the constant stress was causing him to lose sleep and weight. "She still plays the piano, sometimes like a fiend and sometimes like an angel."

"I wish I could give you a straight, logical direction here, but unfortunately, I can't. I can tell you that she may not be ready for the rigors of higher education at this point. Has her interest in schoolwork picked up at all?"

"No, and frankly I've stopped pestering her about it. It's like the teachers have all given up on her, and they're all just going through the motions." Charlie hesitated, to gather his courage. "Is it possible that things will click in for her again, and she will get back to being my Gracie?"

Walt's voice softened. "Hard to say. It's a long and twisting road. Unfortunately, you two have just started the journey. What I do know is that Grace is very lucky to have you in her corner. Having said that, let me give you some advice. You look terrible. If you don't take care of yourself, you aren't much good to her. I want you to make an appointment with me. We need to make sure there's nothing going on to cause you to be losing weight."

"My worry is causing my physical issues, nothing more." He knew he was depressed but didn't want any meds—he wanted to feel this situational pain. He was to blame for it.

"Dad, I'll be fine. I have a movie I want to watch. Bailey and I will just hang out." Grace encouraged him with more positive emotion than he had seen lately. "Prom is not my thing, and you promised Ashley you would be there."

Charlie hated to leave her alone on prom night but had lost the battle to have her go. No date, and the one friend she could count on, Ashley, was going with a date and other couples. She would feel out of place, even more than usual, and he didn't feel he could force it. It was his year to chaperone. It was not always a choice assignment and he had eagerly signed up for this rotation year to coincide with his daughter's first prom. Plus, Ashley had asked him to come over to the house for pictures before the dance. He couldn't let her down, couldn't let Lori down.

"Mr. Booker, could you help me with this boutonniere?" Alison, one of Charlie's students, caught him in the front yard of Lori's house.

"Sure, Alison." Charlie eagerly joined Alison and her date, pleased that his role as teacher would carry him through this pre-party, eclipsing the fact of Grace's absence. Years ago, he had been excited about the prospect of his daughter's prom, having not experienced one himself. *Shake it off, Charlie. It's Ashley's night!* He walked onto the porch, lit with twinkling lights for the festivities, and found her.

"Ashley, you look beautiful." Charlie took her hands and pulled her in for a careful hug and whispered, "I know your dad would be so proud of you." When he let her go, Lori and Ashley's eyes glistened, as did his own. Ashley's date took a picture of the three of them. The lump in Charlie's throat finally disappeared when Lori mouthed, "Thank you," to him as he helped her as cohost in serving sparkling juice in champagne flutes for the guests. Charlie owed them so much; the least he could do was savor this moment of celebration with them.

He knew all of the kids in attendance and their parents, who *oohed* and *ahhed* as they walked around the room complimenting all of the kids. In their fancy heels, three of the four girls were taller than the boys, all of whom could maybe pass for thirteen. The girls dressed for glamour, with slits up their thigh and hair and makeup for magazine photography. "Mr. Booker, will you take a picture of us?" was a common refrain as he made the rounds as an extra hand alone.

Later, in the decorated school gym, Lori had chaperone duty along with Charlie. With the youthful vitality all around him, he was able to relax and enjoy the evening. Mack approached him and captured his personal conflict by saying, "This has gotta be hard for you, man. Thanks for being here for all of us."

Ashley asked Charlie to dance a slow dance, and then brought him over to her mother. "You two dance. I bet mom hasn't danced for centuries." Ashley flitted away, and Charlie felt like a shy boy at his first dance with a chance to make time with his dream girl.

Without saying a word, Lori backed up a step and shook her head slightly to let him know that he need not dance with her, but in that same moment, Charlie relished the chance to put his arms around her. "Care to dance?" he asked, and held out his hand, just as the music started playing "At Last."

Her touch sent an immediate signal to his body that enveloped him in warmth and comfort, like coming home, if he had ever really had one that nurtured his soul. He couldn't stop staring into her eyes, and while he did manage to lead, he was like Jell-O by the end of the dance. *If only . . .*

He wasn't sure he could let go of her.

"Wow," was all he could say.

"I knew you would be a good dancer," Lori whispered in his ear and slowly pivoted away from his embrace.

"Care for another?" Her hand was still in his.

Lori walked them off the dance floor and made her excuses about going to check on the refreshments. Charlie was still somewhat stunned by the end of the prom and drove home wondering how he could ever erase that dance from his sensory system, knowing he had to do so.

His dream state lasted until he got home and found only Bailey there. The DVD movie was on the dining room table, with no note or sign of his daughter anywhere. Only one lamp in the living room was lit.

He quickly turned the outdoor lights on and let Bailey out. "Where is she, girl?" He ran down to the shore looking for a sign. She was not in the water. It had rained the day before and there was still moist sand between the rocks by the access point. No prints. And no barking.

He took a minute to think, then ran back up to the garage. Caroline's car was gone. He cursed at himself for not noticing. He had parked his car outside and not in the garage. How much time had he wasted? It was now one thirty. Where could she be?

It was a moonlit night. The stars glowed, and the waves gently lapped on the lake. He tried to calm himself. She wasn't with Ashley. *Who could she be with*? He couldn't bring himself to consider the alternative—that she was with nobody and had already—

Abby. He needed to contact Abby. He pulled out his phone, grateful that he had pushed for contact information for Abby and her grandparents.

The call went to voicemail. "Abby, this is Charlie Booker, Grace's dad. I'm worried about her. Is she with you?"

His second call was to Abby's grandparents. After seven rings with no answer, he was ready to give up. He tried again. This time, someone answered after five rings.

"Hullo. Who's this?" an older man's voice asked.

"Hello." Charlie realized he didn't know Abby's last name. "I'm so sorry about calling this late, but my daughter Grace is a friend of your granddaughter's, a friend of Abby's."

"Abby?" the voice now was a bit more audible.

"Yes, your granddaughter Abby. I'm worried about Grace. She's not at home, and it's close to two in the morning now. I'm wondering if she could be with Abby?" Charlie heard the sound of footsteps on the line.

"I don't know. I'm not sure if Abby is here or not. What time did you say it was again?"

"Ten to two in the morning."

"Sunday morning, then?" The voice was gaining strength. "I'm checking to see if Abby's here."

Charlie heard a door opening. His heart was in his throat. "Sir, is she there?"

"Yes, yes, she's here and sound asleep. Do I need to wake her?"

Charlie was frantic but not heartless as he heard the man explain, "She's been good lately. Not sneaking out as much. As far as I know, she's been here tonight. I just got home from work after my shift at eleven. Didn't check on her then but looks like she's pretty peaceful right now. And that's worth a lot."

"Then don't wake her. I'm sorry to bother you."

"No bother, I know what it's like. Good luck to you."

"Sir, can you tell me where Abby goes when she sneaks out? If you know?"

"Well, could be a variety of places, but usually wherever someone's selling some marijuana."

With the mention of marijuana, Charlie's breath stopped. "Marijuana?"

"Oh, yeah, Abby's a user. Says it helps her cope." He hesitated. "That doesn't mean your daughter is. I don't think I've met her. What did you say her name was again?"

"Grace. Grace Booker. They met in aftercare." Charlie's panic grew more acute when he realized this man had never met Grace, and Grace had described Abby's grandparents as if she knew them.

"Nope. Never met her. Sorry."

"Thank you. I'm so sorry to wake you."

"You may want to call the Duluth police. They have brought Abby home a time or five. They are pretty good with these vulnerable kids. Give it a try if she doesn't show up."

Charlie heard the pounding of his heart but couldn't bring himself to call the police. *How could I have been so careless as to leave Grace home alone tonight?* He raced to his car and drove toward Duluth. He scanned the road and the pullouts carefully. When he got to the Scenic Café, he let out a whoop when he saw Caroline's car parked in the parking lot of the restaurant. No other vehicles were around, however, and he didn't immediately see anyone inside.

He turned his car around and parked lakeside. He grabbed his flashlight from the glove box and jumped out to scan the lake under the look-out. There wasn't a body on the rocks or in the choppy lake. *Where would a body be?*

He was about to give up and call the police but decided to check the car more closely. He had Caroline's keys on his ring. He approached the car, which had been parked sloppily on the far side of the parking lot, away from any restaurant light.

He opened the driver's side door and as the interior light came on, he gasped as he saw his daughter sprawled on the front seat. "Ahhh. Grace." Her head tilted away from the steering wheel. He quickly touched her, and his knees gave way in relief when he felt her warm breath as he rolled her head toward him. "Gracie!" he shouted, his voice a yelp. "Gracie!"

He ran around to the passenger side to get better access to her and climbed in the car. His feet kicked something on the floor that rolled, a nearly empty vodka bottle. He pulled her body to a seated position close to him and started to gently nudge her awake. "Gracie, Gracie wake up." He held her tight, too tight.

Her first words were, "I can't breathe."

His first thought as he heard her was, *I'll never breathe easily again.*

Chapter 36

Two Harbors, Minnesota
Summer 2015

The next morning came the reckoning. Charlie, bleary-eyed from lack of sleep, sat across the table from Grace, unkempt and dragging, and demanded an explanation for her outing.

Grace was not talking. She wouldn't meet her father's eyes but asked for and received two aspirin to address her hangover. The harangue continued for another fifteen minutes.

Charlie again repeated himself. "I need to know why you refused to go to the prom and then went off on your own."

"I don't know, Dad. I just felt like going out."

"After you told me you would stay home and watch a movie? You lied to me. Where did you get the booze?"

Up until now, Grace seemed not to track his interrogation, but he noticed that her eyes darted quickly to the cupboard above the good dishes, the ones they never used. He walked over to open the cupboard, which was where he kept his meager supply of liquor. Her eyes followed him. In that moment, he wished he had kept a better inventory in his head because he truly did not know if anything was missing. He recognized the fancy brand of bourbon he'd gotten for his last birthday, but that was it. "Did you take a bottle from here?"

"Dad, I'm sorry. Can we just forget it? I made a mistake. Last night was a mistake."

"We learn from our mistakes, and I'm not convinced you've learned from this one. I still don't know why you did it. If you can't explain why you did it, then how on earth can you learn and move on?" His fist hit the table hard, shaking it.

Grace started to cry, loud sloppy sobs. She pushed her chair away from the table and screamed at him. "Because I'm a loser, Dad, that's why!" Gracie blurted out in full sobs. "I just needed to get out of the house. I'm not a prom kind of girl! I don't know what kind of girl I am."

She ran into her room and slammed the door.

That summer was hell. Charlie sought advice from Walt, Dr. Chester, and Mrs. Schiff. Nobody had anything very helpful, just cautious comments about hanging in there. He had expected her to be happy that she had survived her breakdown and rehab had her moving in the right direction. Caroline was nowhere in the picture. Now, he wasn't sure if she was moving at all. *Is this just typical adolescent behavior made more complicated by her anxiety and depression?*

He didn't dare let Grace out of his sight. He couldn't renege on teaching summer school, but he forced Gracie to go with him each day. He signed her up with a tutor to try to get her caught up for her senior year, but she wasn't interested. The tutor quit when Gracie barely opened a book in the first four sessions. They were housebound except for school and therapy appointments. No hikes, kayaking, or social connections. He had reduced her phone privileges and allowed her only an hour a day, which he knew she spent talking to Abby. He insisted on an open-door policy so he could keep tabs on her and wasn't above listening in on occasion. He didn't like what his fear had done to him but wasn't willing to take any more risks.

This fear made him harsh and unreasonable. He installed new locks on the doors that only he could open. He became her keeper, and she resented it.

Finally, in August, Lori and Walt conspired to get them out of their self-imposed isolation.

Walt called. "Charlie, you need to come to the fiftieth anniversary party for the church. It'll be good for both of you to get out and be around people. No pressure, just casual mingling."

Lori dropped by with a homemade blueberry pie. "We miss you two. Please come to the party." She spoke to both of them. No mention was made of the two months they had been missing Sunday services.

Charlie watched his daughter carefully. Grace searched Lori's face hungrily for a human connection that she missed. He immediately felt chastened.

"Grace, would you like to go?"

"I'll go if you want to go." She kept her eyes on Lori.

"OK then," Lori quickly said. "We'll see you Sunday afternoon at two o'clock."

Charlie walked Lori out to her car; he felt as if he had just caught a life preserver. He smiled shyly and leaned on her car door.

"Yes," she said. "I miss you, too." She touched his arm before he moved in slow motion to open it for her.

After Lori left, Charlie felt a change begin. "Grace, would you like to go hiking at Split Rock today?"

She thought before responding. "Can I hike without a leash?"

"Can I trust you without a leash?" He gave her a shy smile, and as it was returned, a reprieve was born.

Three days later, they went to the church anniversary picnic and were welcomed warmly.

"Missed you, Gracie." Ashley hugged her friend and led her away to catch up.

Charlie noticed the group of other young people watching Grace. She had made some effort with her personal appearance, and while not blooming with health and vitality, she appeared at least on the outside to be a normal seventeen-year-old eager to catch up with her friend.

It had been a long summer by North Shore standards, so the church grounds remained resplendent with lush grass and vibrant trees and no visible fall color yet. Croquet and volley-ball games had been set up beyond the church toward the south side of the property, and a round of picnic tables with colorful tablecloths clustered around a rustic table covered with trays of food. Two grills stood off to the side, and Walt and a few of the men were turning brats and burgers. Claire and Lori were among the women arranging the food on the buffet table.

With his friends close and his daughter within his range of vision, Charlie breathed deeply and felt his rigid body relax. Later, Walt recruited him to help with clean-up duty. "Good that you came out today. I see a change in you in just these few hours."

As they were loading up the leftovers Lori insisted they take, Grace said, "Dad, Ashley told me about a new hair salon in Canal Park, and I was hoping I could try it out."

"Are you talking about that new place, Stylin'? I've heard good things about it. Are you thinking of a totally new style?" Lori asked.

"Yes, I think I need a new look for a new year," Grace said. Charlie had watched Grace's attempts over the years to change her hair to avoid the obvious similarity to her mother's black curly locks. No doubt she wanted it overhauled again.

When he heard the old Gracie respond, he didn't hesitate. "Sure, go ahead and book an appointment. Let's try to piggy-back on a trip to the clinic."

Chapter 37

Two Harbors, Minnesota
August 2015

Charlie accompanied Grace into the salon, a girly place with no waiting area. He asked how long it would be, and they agreed he would stroll on the Lake Walk and return in an hour.

The lake was rough, the air chilly. He put up the collar of his jacket to ward off the wind as he started back. His daughter seemed almost intact. Her interest in a new hairstyle seemed indicative that she was eager for a fresh start.

Fifty-five minutes later, he returned to the salon. No Grace. "Where's my daughter?" he asked gruffly. The stylist jumped.

"Umm, she declined to have her hair blown out and left."

"When? When did she leave?" Charlie tried to control his panic.

"Probably fifteen minutes ago, maybe twenty?"

"Did she go out the front door?"

"No, she went to the restroom back there, and out the back, I think."

Charlie ran out the back door. A small parking lot led to a road leading to Lake Avenue. He looked around for her, at first thinking she may have gone to the ice cream place next door or taken her own walk on the boardwalk. Then why would she have gone out the back door?

He tried to think calmly for the first twenty minutes. Then, he realized that twenty minutes added to the previous twenty was close to an hour; she could be anywhere. He thought of her phone—at home as she was still only allowed an hour a day, so she hadn't brought it with her. If she had planned to leave, someone could have picked her up easily and be forty-five minutes away by car.

Where is she? Who's she with?

He called Abby and got voice mail. Then he called Abby's grandfather, Lucas. Charlie had been in contact with Lucas after Grace's prom night misadventure in May. They had commiserated on the challenges of keeping their girls safe. Charlie had needed to vent, and Lucas was a willing teacher, especially about Abby's access to marijuana. He knew there was some talk of Two Harbors kids getting it fairly easily, but he had never been curious enough to ask much about it.

"Almost anywhere, really. The Lake Walk leading to Canal Park. Superior Street near the convenience store. Another likely place is the skyway—kids can score easily there. There's an escalator from the main floor to the second-floor atrium that can be lively. The cops tell me there's really no way to know who will be showing up, but the kids seem to know. How? No idea."

He told Charlie how Abby had been picked up twice for possession of marijuana, and both times he had convinced them that she could be monitored at home with intense supervision, like closely watched probation. But with her bipolar diagnosis, they told him that the next time, she would likely be detained at the Arrowhead Juvenile Center and her mental health status reevaluated.

"Frankly, I'm at the point that I'm not going to fight it if they lock her up. I'm not sure I'm up to what it takes to stay on this situation. Not sure if I'm helping her at all." He had leaned in and whispered this to Charlie, defeat showing in his eyes.

Charlie called Lucas at work, a number he had been given for just such an emergency. "Lucas, my daughter has given me the slip. Not sure where she is. I just tried Abby's line, and she's not answering."

"Tell me where you are right now."

"Canal Park. At the Lake Walk across from the lighthouse. Do you know where Abby is?"

"No, I'm at work. Let me call my wife and see what's what. I'll call you back in five."

He did. "Karin hasn't seen Abby since this morning. She has Karin's car. Said she was gonna go up to Miller Hill Mall to pick up some job applications."

"Did Abby say anything about Grace?"

"Not a word. Listen, I'm going to leave work and help you look. I'll be there in fifteen minutes."

Lucas picked Charlie up. They drove around, searching for Karin's car. They checked downtown, Miller Hill Mall, and any other place either could think of, but didn't see it.

At dusk, Lucas said, "There's one other place. I don't want to think it, but I'm going to check out the bars over by the docks in Superior."

Charlie knew what that meant, and neither man wanted to say it out loud. The dive bars near the docks on the Superior side were a haven for criminal behavior—illegal entry, prostitution, drug sales, and easy alcohol access to minors. If Grace and Abby had picked up a tip about a bar in Superior serving underage kids, they could be in way over their heads.

He called Lori in an effort to calm himself down and with the slim hope that there had been some plan he was unaware of that could explain where Grace might be.

"Oh, Charlie. No, I don't have a clue where she is. What can I do?"

"You're doing it now. Just hearing your voice helps. Thanks. I'll let you know." He needed the courage as they drove around checking cars in front of the bars, and then walked into a few to check faces. Still nothing.

Finally, Lucas said what Charlie knew he didn't want to say. "I'm not happy to do it, but I think we'll have to call the authorities. They know Abby well, and they'll find her. If she's drunk and in trouble, I guess it's time for her to go to lockup."

"We don't even know if Grace and Abby are together. Are you sure you want to do this?"

"It's not something I want to do, but it's something I have to do."

The police found the car at three in the morning parked under a railroad trestle near Two Harbors. Charlie got the call while sitting with Lucas on his porch. The girls were found fifteen minutes later near a smoldering bonfire. The configuration of stump seating and empty bottles of beer and liquor around the fire indicated there may have been a couple of others at the gathering, but they had left by the time the police arrived or were alert enough to run off before getting caught. Grace was belligerent and tried to run, and an officer had to chase her down. Abby had passed out on the ground.

Lucas drove them to the station where they could see their girls brought in and booked. Grace didn't look up when her father tried to talk to her. Her new cut was a shock to him; angular and shaved on one side of her head. They would be held for a night or two and then brought before a judge to determine the next steps.

The senior of the cops said to Lucas," Sorry, man, but at least she's safe." And to Charlie, "Your daughter tried to run. Not sure what that'll mean to the judge. But, again, she's safe for now."

Safe for now, but for how long?

Chapter 38

Two Harbors, Minnesota
Autumn 2015

Charlie had never been in the Lake County Courthouse in Two Harbors. As he walked up the stairway to the stone building with a rotunda, his jaw clenched. *Can I do this?* He found Lucas and the attorney waiting for him outside the assigned courtroom. Lucas looked smaller, as if he had lost some physical stature over the past two days. They entered the courtroom.

At the sight of his daughter walking in wearing an orange jumpsuit, he gasped. The attorney had prepared him, but it was still shocking to hear the charges: underage drinking and suspicion of marijuana possession for Abby, underage drinking for Grace.

The judge addressed Abby's charges first, and Charlie watched as the attorney had to guide an ashen Lucas to a standing position as the expected sentence in Juvenile Detention was announced. His turn came, and as he approached the bench, he saw Walt and Lori sitting near the back of the courtroom. He felt his back straighten as he neared the judge.

"Mr. Booker. This is your daughter Grace's first offense. I'd like to order intensive probationary supervision. In order for that to work, you, as her parent, need to cooperate fully with the probation officer and assure compliance with the rules he sets forth. Not every parent can do this successfully. Are you willing and able to take on this responsibility?"

Charlie nodded and said, "Yes, sir. I am willing."

"And able?" the judge prompted.

Charlie thought back to the past weeks and months of the virtual lockdown he had put Grace in already. If he answered honestly, he would say, "To the best of my ability, which is evidently lacking." However, he replied, "Yes, sir, and able."

Arrangements were made to release Grace, and Charlie paid her fine. While he was given a packet of paperwork and the attorney told him where to sign, he looked up to catch the door closing behind Grace as she was led from the courtroom to change her clothes and retrieve her belongings.

Shaky on his feet, he was sure of only one thing. He couldn't give up.

A sullen Grace sat next to him in the truck as he pulled away from the courthouse parking lot. Thick fog got worse as he drove toward home on the highway that followed the lake. He hadn't felt this alone since before Caroline. Then, his sole motivation had been survival, to create a life of his own, be his own person. When he had met Caroline, his motivation was to be her person so she would need him and give him value. When Grace was born, he found the true purpose in his life. *Now I've failed her.*

His thoughts darkened as he wondered if he would have folded in the courtroom had Lori and Walt not been there.

Suddenly, his headlights caught the second of two deer crossing the road. He braked hard and flung his arm over to cushion his daughter from any impact, the protective-move instinctive. He avoided hitting the doe, but it stalled his truck. "Are you OK?"

She nodded, still holding onto his arm. He calmed himself and his breathing finally and restarted his car quickly when he saw lights coming up behind him. *Get her out of harm's way.* It was still and always would be his job as a father.

With Grace tucked safely in bed that night, reality crowded in again. His wandering mind caught a fragment from over a year ago, something he had pushed aside while busy with his daughter's illness and treatment. Now, it came back. Caroline's throw-away sarcastic comment about Grace's still undiagnosed illness.

"Probably something from your unknown ancestors—a mental weakness of some sort."

He remembered being helpless to fire anything back at her in his defense. He didn't know. He didn't know anything about his birth mother or father or any other family member. He had nothing.

Caroline had rubbed it in. "My parents and Uncle Felix— totally solid and healthy, as am I. You on the other hand, have no idea."

She was right. His shame about his "foundling birth" was never very far from the surface. He thought back to the many times over the years he had ducked any social conversation that veered too close to his family origins. Even now, the warmth of Lori and his friends, the support of the community, Walt—all of it felt like more than he deserved. He had a better understanding of how families should operate and how friends should support one another. He grieved for his own childhood. It was like an open wound that kept festering. He needed to clean it out. Maybe then he could find the strength to face the challenge of his daughter's future. Maybe he could discover something from his medical history that would help them navigate her future.

A mix of curiosity and hope burst through his body as an adrenaline rush, and he decided to celebrate the feeling. He unearthed the fancy bottle he got as a birthday gift and poured himself a bourbon, switched on his computer, and turned on the gooseneck lamp in the study. With Bailey settled at his feet, he tried several search engines to determine the best way to find meaningful answers.

Three hours later, he had information but no answers. Lots of helpful advice for adoptees, but he had never been that lucky. He started a new document, "What I know," and wrote down the names of all the foster families he could remember.

1. Aronson (age 14–18)
2. Merkle (age 13–14)
3. Schmidt (age 12–13)
4. Hansen (age 10–12
5. St. Joseph's Home for Boys (age 5–10)
6. Unsure, at least several placements

He stared at the list, his lips quivering as a single tear fell onto his shirt. *How did I survive that much upheaval?* He got up and walked around the house, stopping to look out at the unusually placid lake; more tears fell as he allowed himself to release his pain.

When he went to bed, for the first time in months, he slept soundly with no interruptions, real or imaginary.

The next day he started fresh with a pot of coffee and a sense of purpose. He thought about his birth certificate. Perhaps it held a clue. He dug it out of his home safe. He felt a sharp pain in his chest seeing the words "foundling child" where his parents' names should be. That was expected, but he was hoping for a trace of something that would point him to the fire station where he had been found.

His mind clicked onto a new possibility. He could search for the men who found him. One of those stations filled with firemen had the experience of finding him, a foundling, on their step one day. They had even given him his name. Charles Booker. No middle name. Maybe one of them knew about his birth parents and could help him. He slowed down his thinking to consider if it was possible. Before he started searching fire stations, he thought it best to contact the St. Joseph's Home for Boys. Who knew if the fire station was even in Boston?

Somewhere in his consciousness, he knew this effort was merely a distraction. But he knew he needed one badly.

Chapter 39

❯

Two Harbors, Minnesota
Autumn 2015

A night in holding sobered Grace up fast. First buoyed by relief that Bobby had fled the scene before the police had arrived, her own failed attempt at escape had led to a humiliating ride in the back of a police car with Abby, jolted awake and crying loudly. By the time they arrived at lockup, Grace had vomited all over her clothes and was still woozy when led into the building.

"This one needs a jumpsuit." The officer had kept his distance from Grace as he signed her in before leaving her with the next keeper. The raw facts of her arrest now swirling in her head, Grace couldn't sleep beyond a few naps, interrupted by strange noises and muffled sobs, sometimes her own. If she felt jailed living under her father's watch, she hadn't known what jailed really meant.

The next day, she had appeared before the judge. She didn't dare look at her dad directly, but each time she peeked, he turned his head away from her.

When the judge asked her, "Will you cooperate with the supervised probation and plan that your father will have in place at the request of the court?"

She took a beat too long to respond, and her father elbowed her.

"Yes, sir," she mumbled and looked down at her feet, her mind stuck on the inevitable prison her father would build around her.

Abby wasn't so lucky. She was placed in Arrowhead Juvenile Center for four months. But maybe that was lucky—she was so close to turning eighteen, they could have sent her to an adult facility. Only her grandfather's pleas to the judge had avoided that.

Grace got through the moment thinking about how this could work for their plan—to meet up after Grace turned eighteen, very soon. She would have time to get to Chicago and set them up before Abby was released. Now she just had to make sure Bobby got her there to be the link with Abby.

What was truly lucky was the timing. She thought back to the night before. The plan had been finalized just before they were picked up. It was crazy easy how it came together once they were all together. Abby and Grace had been playing with the notion of running away for months. Abby wanted to start a new life somewhere fresh and was excited that she had, in Grace, someone who also wanted to leave town and her current life behind.

My mother won't wait that much longer to lure my father to join her. I need to leave first!

Once Abby's friend Bobby came into the picture, Abby presented him as the solution to put the pieces together.

"Bobby's a sure bet to help us get out of here," Abby assured Grace. Abby knew Bobby from school. Older and running with a party crowd, he had been her source of marijuana for years and could get alcohol, too. At first, Grace was cool to the idea of sharing their plans with anyone, and she knew Abby had a crush on Bobby, which may have clouded her judgment. But Grace was getting desperate with her father's shackles, and as he was more and more disappointed in her, she knew it wouldn't be long before he left her to be with her mother.

It turned out that Grace liked Bobby, which surprised her. After a couple of beers, Grace started asking him how a plan might work. He had an easy, confident way about him and talked about how he could help them get to Chicago, where anyone could get lost. "You'll need some money to get you started."

The girls looked at each other. Grace had money in the bank, not a lot, but a few hundred dollars. *How will I ever get at it?* She knew Abby spent every penny of her allowance as soon as she got it.

"Anybody got something to sell, to get you a stake for your fresh start?"

Grace pulled Abby away from the bonfire for a summit before Abby drank too much. "We could take my mom's car and sell it." Abby hugged Grace and proceeded to get drunk while Grace and Bobby exchanged phone numbers and put the finishing touches on a plan.

That plan kept her motivated. By early October, her weeks had become routine. School and home, school and home. A visit by her probation officer, Mr. Rogers—his real name. Sessions with Mrs. Schiff were now weekly with the addition of alcohol counseling by another therapist in the office.

Her father was distant with her, which made life easier. Constantly holed up in his study, with the door closed into the late hours, he had her locked down, evidently confident she wouldn't run. *Shortsighted.*

School was a waste. She didn't even bother pretending interest. Everyone avoided her; even Ashley had given up on her. Her dad's efforts to have the teachers give her a break were now haphazard. She wasn't making any effort, and they all knew it. She was like a walking ghost.

Her phone privileges were down to once a week, and she always called Bobby on the sly, easy now that her dad no longer listened in.

Any pretense of companionship was gone now. Her father barely spoke to her, and if he did, she saw the pain in his eyes. Beyond the day-to-day conversation about routine, neither was willing to engage in any talk about the future.

Finally, her birthday came and nobody recognized it as a celebration. They went out for pizza with Lori. Ashley had plans with her boyfriend and didn't break them to spend a dreadful day of obligation with her delinquent friend Grace.

A week later, as planned, Gracie took her chance when it came. Weeks earlier, she had finally discovered her mother's car keys and hidden them in her escape kit, along with money, her meds, a change of clothes, and the letter that kept her motivated. She needed to keep the weight down to travel light.

She had heard her father go to bed after one o'clock. It was Sunday, so he would sleep in. Bailey was with him. The wind was howling—sounded like a nor'easter coming, a precursor to the November gales ahead. She carefully opened the window in her room and jumped out, ran quickly to the garage, and quietly drove out of the driveway, the wind drowning out any sound from the car.

Just as planned, she drove to Superior and met Bobby at the prearranged spot. They drove to Eau Claire and sold the car to a guy at a ramshackle garage for half its value, no questions asked. Grace cut up the car registration card and her ID and threw them both in the trash at a rest stop.

They hitchhiked to Milwaukee and crashed with a friend of Bobby's. Party time. Grace was so relieved she celebrated, and after a few beers, she gave Bobby an exuberant kiss on the mouth. "I can't believe we did it! Abby will be so excited, Bobby!" After all, he wasn't Abby's boyfriend, and she would be back in their circle soon. A little kiss couldn't hurt.

After a few more beers, Grace was flying high, any inhibitions abandoned. *I deserve this!* That little kiss led to more and turned into a full make-out session. By the time Bobby led her to the bedroom, she was tracking with how good she felt and eager to follow him wherever he took her next.

When she woke up, she didn't know where she was, but she hurt. When the previous day's events came back to her, she realized her escape from home had come at the cost of her virginity. *Not exactly the way I pictured my first time.* Before her mind could hold too tight to the rush of regret, she heard shuffling in the next room and knew she needed to wake up fast. *Time to toughen up, Gracie, you're on your own now. You did it!*. No longer the spoiler between her parents, her dad could finally be with her mom. They could be happy, and she would no longer have to live with the guilt of keeping them apart.

"You're hungover, Grace," Bobby entered the room and counted the money in her backpack.

"Not Grace. I'm now Janie. Grace is gone." She tried to stand up but wobbled and vomited on the floor.

"Jesus—you're a mess. That your first time?"

Gracie laughed bitterly. "Don't flatter yourself."

Bobby took a tissue and dabbed at the vomit that had dribbled on her chin. "Listen, kid, you can stay here until you sleep it off. Then, we gotta get you outta here. These guys will take advantage of you." His voice had a hint of tenderness with an edge to it.

"What? Where are you going?"

"I'm heading to Kansas City. Can't get you to Chicago. But I'll help you get to the bus station. And give you half of the car money. That should get you started."

He handed her some bills, and she nodded slowly, looking around the room. Now that she was awake, she saw what a dump it was. She made a face, and Bobby must have noticed because he said, "Hey, are you sure you want to go through with this? I can put you on a bus back to Minnesota, just as easily as to Chicago. It's a big city."

"No!" She grabbed his arm. "You need to stick with the plan. Get me on a bus to Chicago, and I'll be there waiting for Abby. That's the deal. You need to connect with her to let her know."

Her alarm must have set him off, and there was no more caring in his voice. "Then let's go. Get up and move your ass."

Chapter 40

Two Harbors, Minnesota
October 2015

Charlie woke up shivering. Bailey's body encircled his feet at the end of his bed, and they were warm. He hadn't put his pajamas on before falling into bed. In his underwear, his mouth dry from drinking at his computer, he pulled the covers up over his body, like a cocoon or a casket. *Why is it so cold?*

Bailey jumped down and headed for the door. Charlie grabbed his flannel robe from the closet hook and opened the door to the hallway. He stubbed his toe on the threshold while trying to tie his robe. "Damn!" He held his toe and felt how cold the wood floor was on his bare feet. Had the heat gone out? He remembered howling wind last night. A blast of cold air hit him from Gracie's open door.

"Grace, why is this window open?" He closed the window, noting that her bed was slept in but empty. He shouted out for her again as he went through the house looking for her. He checked the doors, still locked from inside with his key. She couldn't get out. Then it finally hit him. The window. He retraced his steps to her bedroom and opened the window again. Looking down, he saw it was a bit of a jump but not a hard fall if she was determined to leave. Aspen leaves swirled in the yard under the window, so there was no way to see any sign if she had.

He unlocked the back door and ran to the churning lake, Bailey with him and barking each step of the way. Had she done it this time? Succeeded in taking her own life? He could see nothing to indicate she had been down there. What could he see if she had been? The rocks were not icy this time, and when she'd attempted suicide last time, that hadn't stopped her. He continued to shout her name until he started to hyperventilate. *How did I let this happen again?*

He ran to the house to get to a phone, but in a moment of clarity, he opened the side door into the garage. He stopped, panting again. Caroline's car was gone, but he had Caroline's keys. His mind raced as he ran into the house and opened the cough-drop tin he had hidden under some papers in his bottom desk drawer. Empty. The keys to Caroline's car were not there.

He fell back in his desk chair and let out a muffled sob. "This can't be happening!" He looked at his desk clock, which read 11:00 a.m. He had slept in, and his daughter was missing. He had slept in because he'd drunk too much bourbon and spent too much time going down yet one more rabbit hole trying to find the fire station where he had been abandoned.

The first thing he did was call Lori. "She's gone. Gracie is gone." The knife-edged sound of his own voice surprised him.

"What do you mean, she's gone?" Lori was near hysteria. "Charlie! What do you mean?"

"She snuck out her bedroom window. She took Caroline's car. She found my hidden keys." He kept to the facts now knowing that time was not on his side. "I need help, Lori."

"Yes, yes, you do." Lori's words were slower now, as he knew she was already problem-solving. "Here's what we'll do. I'll be out very soon, and I'll bring Mack with me. We'll sort this out." Her voice was soothing. "Stay there."

Charlie called Lucas next. By the time he got dressed, Lori, Mack, and Walt were driving up in one car. She had probably corralled them at church after the service. Just as he finished telling them what had happened, Lucas drove up, and he repeated his story.

Lori made coffee as they discussed what to do.

"Have you called the police?" Walt asked. "Shouldn't we do that ASAP?"

"You can do that, and I'm sure they will take the report, but Grace is now eighteen. That means she's no longer an adolescent runaway. She's just a girl who left home without telling anyone," Lucas said, the only one in the crowd to know how juvenile court worked.

"She's also a vulnerable kid," Walt countered.

"Yes, she is. But the vast majority of runaway kids have reasons for running that include abuse, addiction, and mental illness. Unfortunately, Grace is not unique in this situation," Lucas said.

"There's got to be something that we can do," Mack said.

"Yes, of course. Charlie, you should call the police and have them come out to take the report. The highway patrol can pick her up if we give them the license plate number since in their eyes she's driving a stolen car," Lucas said.

Lori gasped. "What? She'd be arrested for stealing the car?"

Mack asked, "You mean, it may get them to act fast if they are looking for a stolen car and not a missing kid?"

"Essentially, yes." Lucas said. "It's your call to make. If you want to get your daughter back, the car is the best bet. Whether they think you will or won't press charges depends on what you say."

Charlie felt like a sleepwalker. He was in the room with these people, these friends, who were talking to him about something he didn't understand and didn't know how to navigate. He walked out of the house and down to the shore. Lori followed him and stood by his side, putting her arm around his shoulder. The wind had died down, but it was chilly. Lori leaned into his body heat. "It's not your fault. You know you did everything you could think of to keep her safe. If she was intent on leaving, you couldn't stop her."

Charlie wanted to believe her. But he knew the truth. He knew what he had done. "It's my fault."

"Why do you think that? Nobody else does. Tell me." Lori kept her hand on his back rubbing it gently.

He stepped away from Lori and started a soliloquy. Whispering as he started, he was near shouting by the end. "It's obvious. I stayed up late drinking and focusing on a pipe dream that kept me dazed and not concentrating on her safety. I slept late, and she slipped away through a window. I can't even tell you, within several hours' time, when I last saw my daughter. I am a terrible father." His energy sapped, his head fell as did his tears. "I never should have been a father. I cheated fate to become one, and this is what I get."

Lori went to him and hugged him tight. Once he was composed, she walked him back into the house. "So, gentlemen, what's the plan?"

Walt took Charlie's car and drove into Duluth to the known haunts that Lucas directed him to check. Mack took Lori's car and drove back up the shore toward Gooseberry and Split Rock.

Lori stayed with Charlie to wait for the policeman to come take the report. Lucas had called the station and asked for the officer who had been on duty when they'd found Abby and Grace the previous spring.

Lucas was Charlie's hope. He was on his way to see Abby in juvie. Maybe she had some idea about what might be going on with Grace, and where she might be heading. He figured he should get a call back from Lucas in a little over an hour. He hoped they had been in touch. Grace hadn't taken her phone; in fact, hadn't been using it much. She hadn't been asking to use it now that he thought about it. *Because she didn't need a phone where she was headed?*

Patrolman Slater arrived, and Lori offered him coffee. They sat at the kitchen table, and Charlie watched him take notes as he relayed the facts of his daughter's departure.

"So, what time did you notice Grace was missing, Mr. Booker?"

Lori answered too quickly. "This morning, right Charlie?" She looked at him for validation.

"Ma'am, I need to have Mr. Booker respond directly. Protocol. I hope you understand." He smiled sweetly at Lori and then asked, "And how are you related to Grace again?"

"Of course, I understand. I . . ." She hesitated, then spoke more slowly. "I've been close to Gracie since her birth. Her childcare provider all through her youth and a close family friend." Her eyes welled up. "She's like a daughter to me."

"And Mrs. Booker?" The officer now looked at Charlie directly. "Where is she?"

"My wife is in Portugal. She's a professor of ornithology at the University in Lisbon."

"Is there reason to think Grace would try to go to her? Or that Grace and her mother had planned for a trip that you weren't aware of?"

Charlie found a spot out the window to focus on when he replied, "No, that's not a possibility."

"Why is that?"

"My daughter and my wife are . . ." he searched for words, "are not close. Grace would not try to go to her mother, and her mother would never reach out to Grace." It was ludicrous to consider a scenario where Caroline would reach out to Grace without him.

"Boyfriend?" Officer Slater looked at Charlie first, and then at Lori.

"No." They both replied in unison.

He read from his notes and repeated what they had told him. "Correct?"

Charlie nodded.

"I think I've got what I need. Anything else you want me to know?"

"You know the rest. Grace was on a supervised probation after the incident this spring, and she also suffers from depression. She's on medication right now but could be at risk if she stops taking it or if her depression spirals out of control. Her condition is changeable." Charlie sounded like a zombie, even to himself.

Officer Slater stood and thanked them for the coffee. Lori asked what would happen next.

"Well, most runaways turn up within forty-eight hours. Technically, Grace is not a runaway as she is eighteen. However, the juvenile record from the spring incident and the fact that she took a car without permission makes it possible that she could be arrested."

"I won't press charges against my daughter." Charlie came alive. "Never."

"I understand, Mr. Booker. I'll do what I can. Given the length of time she's been gone and the means at her disposal, the car . . . she could be quite far away by now. If she had a good plan, that is."

Officer Slater shook Charlie's hand as he left. "I'm sorry, sir."

Chapter 41

After Slater left, Charlie felt like a caged animal waiting for a door to open. He wore a path through the house scanning out to the road, and then to the back to focus on the lake, not as choppy now, but there was nothing to see. He wasn't sure Grace hadn't ditched the car somewhere and then doubled back to take her life here, where he wouldn't expect it.

"Charlie, I'm making you something to eat. You've got to get something nutritious in you." Lori opened the refrigerator. "Wow, there's not much here." She wasn't sure she had said that out loud until he walked over to her and softly said, "I can't eat anything. Sunday is usually shopping day so—"

Lori ignored him and took out some eggs, butter, cheese, and milk. "An omelet and toast—and you *will* eat." She looked up at him. "What did you mean when you said something about spending time on a 'pipe dream.' What are you working on?"

Charlie turned away to check his phone yet again. Still no call from Lucas. Standing at his stove, making him a meal, Lori was the closest friend he had, a support to him through all of his life as a father. But she didn't know the real truth about his birth. Nobody did. He didn't know himself. He was afraid to talk about it. Caroline knew, and she had used it against him in the most painful way.

Lucas saved him by calling. "No Lucas, I haven't heard from anyone. Did you talk to Abby?"

"Yes, I just left her. She's upset. Tells me she doesn't know anything," Lucas replied.

Charlie waited for more, but finally had to ask, "Lucas, do you believe that?"

"I do. She looks to be feeling a bit put out that she doesn't know anything. Feels trapped in juvie and would like to help find Grace. Thought they were friends."

"I thought so, too." Charlie tried to keep his voice even. "Abby was my best bet at helping to find her."

"I know. I'm gonna check a couple of other places, and then I'll come out to your place."

Lori ushered him to the table where a steaming plate of food waited for him. "I heard. I'm sorry. But Grace wasn't communicating much now with Abby in detention, that much I know. Let's not lose hope. Eat."

Charlie ate a few bites, and then, with Lori sitting and waiting, he finally spoke to her about his history. The abandonment, the children's group home, the never-ending foster families. He spoke for forty minutes until he was empty. He was surprised at her equanimity when he had finished.

"So the pipe dream is to find someone from the fire station? Or is it to find your birth parents?"

He met her eyes and then searched her beautiful face, this solid, accepting woman who cared about him, and felt his burden lighten. *She knows me better than Caroline ever did—I don't hide anything from her.*

"I don't really know. It's a long shot either way. I wouldn't even be thinking about it if Caroline hadn't said—" He stopped mid-sentence. He had never knowingly complained about Caroline to Lori, never spoken ill of her peculiar mothering style, her odd behavior. He hadn't ever spoken to her about the fact that Caroline had now been absent for close to two years.

"What did Caroline say?" Lori's voice was gentle, her eyes kind as she asked.

"Well, she said perhaps my genetic pool wasn't great, and that Grace's issues were a result of that." Charlie looked sheepish. He felt he was in dangerous territory.

Lori gasped. "Oh, my God, that's a terrible thing to say. For anyone to say."

"Well, she was worried about Grace." Defending his wife was a hard habit to break.

"Let's examine this for a moment. First, just because you don't know who your birth parents are doesn't mean that you have a faulty genetic pool. It's unknowable, right? Isn't it?" Lori's anger was building.

"Yes, I guess so."

"Second. I did a lot of reading about mental illness when Grace was so sick. The causes of these diseases are still not known. The research suggests that a very small percentage of children born of parents with mental illness go on to develop it. While there may be a familial relationship, it is not causative." Lori articulated her points firmly as if to a classroom of students. She stood up and walked around the kitchen.

Charlie sucked in his breath at her expression of clear support for his daughter; the stark reality of how it must have been for Lori to watch the dynamics of his family play out with no ability to protect his daughter, whom he knew she loved. *Lori and Caroline. Such different women, such polar opposites as mothers.*

Lori wasn't done. "Nobody can say if there is a familial strain here on either side. For somebody to accuse you of something that is totally out of your control . . . well, it's despicable.

I'm so sorry she did that." She gathered his dishes and busily filled the dishwasher and scoured the omelet pan.

Charlie sat with his confusion. He knew he should dismiss Caroline's comment as a throwaway dart she'd aimed at him in the place she knew would hurt the most. He wasn't sure whether the objective of his pipe dream was to determine who his parents were, get information about his own genes, or just thank those who found him.

However, he was more sure than ever that Lori was in his corner.

It was after eight o'clock when Walt, Lucas, and Mack shuffled in with nothing promising to report. Dark came early in October, and they weren't sure what more they could do that day.

Charlie told the group about his interview with Officer Slater. "They'll look for the car, but I've told them I won't press charges. He says runaways are usually found within forty-eight hours, but he did warn me that the car gives Grace the means to get far away quickly. I can't accurately state how long she's been gone . . ." His voice caught, and he whispered, "It's my fault."

One by one, his friends responded with their own version of assurance that he shouldn't blame himself. After a moment, he rallied. "I thank you all so much for helping me today. It's time to call it. Slater said he would phone if they got anything, anything at all, and he seems to be a man of his word. That's about all we can do right now."

As they filed out, Mack said he would call Patricia and alert her that Charlie wouldn't be at work tomorrow, but Charlie surprised them all by saying, "Yes, please do, but tell her I'll be in mid-week. We should know something by then. If not, this could be a long haul, and I'll go bonkers sitting around here waiting."

After his friends left, Charlie reviewed a list of actions taken today, sure that he would be lacking in some obvious way.

Call friends—check. Police report—check. Car info reported to highway patrol—check. Likely haunts visited—check. Runaway's friends interviewed—check. Information disseminated to interested parties and school friends—check.

He had already let his daughter down by failing to protect her; he couldn't let her down again by failing the action plan to find her or making it difficult for her to come home safely. *If she's still alive.*

He walked through the house turning every light on, then went to the garage and put on the outdoor lights that lit the driveway and the path to the lake. Standing near the lake and watching the waves, his mind flitted to the possibility of her body washing ashore at some point in the future. He pushed the thought away and returned to the house. He had one more call to make. It would be near dawn in Lisbon. Better to get this over with.

"*Olá,*" a man's sleepy voice said. "*Olá? Quem é?*"

Charlie hung up the phone. Must have misdialed. He checked his phone's history. No, he hadn't mis-dialed. It was Caroline's number.

His body started to shake; he barely made it to a chair before he collapsed. He thought back to the last time he saw her—at the hospital—when she left in a huff. *Was that scene our last one?* At the time, he had been relieved. He put his head in his hands, trying to close out the world.

My family.

Chapter 42

Lisbon, Portugal
Autumn 2015

Caroline, still in a sex-induced sleepy haze, was slow to rouse at the ringing of her cell phone but rolled over on her side to take it just as she heard Mateo, her grad student, click it off after his brief pick-up greeting. "*Quem é?*" she whispered, her voice husky with the night's activity.

Mateo stroked her undraped breasts, taking advantage of their reawakening to continue the night of lovemaking. She couldn't resist, as all of her senses were overpowered by the pleasure of sex with an eager young man whose sole objective was to satisfy her every need and get a letter of recommendation to his PhD program.

She remembered the call after Mateo had left her the next morning. She always had her lovers leave early. She didn't want anybody to get too clingy. She checked her phone history for recent calls. The Two Harbors house phone. She shuddered and sat down quickly on her bed. She hadn't thought about Charlie in months. She didn't know what to think about him, didn't want to think about him, so she didn't.

She opened the curtains to view the avenue outside her window. *I can be wherever I want to be. I have nobody tying me down, and no ties to anybody. That's what I want. What I've always wanted.* She tossed the sheers back, held her head up, dropped her robe, and headed to the shower. As the water caressed her body and she washed its crevices, she smiled, pleased with herself. *I love that he was thinking about me. Let him. We'll see how long it takes before he calls again.*

It took him another week. This time, he called while she was just preparing to leave for campus. "Charlie, it's been a long time. I haven't seen you since the hospital. Are you calling with a belated apology for how you treated me?" she teased him.

"No, I'm calling to tell you our daughter is missing." Charlie sounded odd, his voice raspy.

"What do you mean, missing?"

"Exactly that. She ran away a week ago and hasn't returned. We haven't found her and don't know where she went."

"So, you haven't found her body?" Caroline jumped to another suicide attempt first.

"We haven't found her, no. She used your car to run away and sold it. There's no trace of it or her. We have no reason to think she committed suicide, but the police haven't found her."

Caroline let him talk about the night Grace left, the hunt for her, and what Charlie was considering for further efforts, while she thought about what this meant. *If Grace is no longer in the picture, will he want to come to me in Portugal and revive our marriage?* "It sounds as if she decided to live her own life and doesn't want to be found."

"I'll never stop looking." Charlie sounded defiant.

There was her answer. Caroline's anger peaked and then burned out when she decided this was the last time she would allow him to declare his ultimate loyalty to his daughter over her. Her self-control was not perfect. "You're a fool. Give her up. She doesn't want you and your life, your idea of the perfect little family. Even sick she doesn't want you! You're too blind to realize that you could have been with me. Now, I no longer want you, either. Goodbye, Charlie!"

Chapter 43

Duluth, Minnesota
Winter 2016

Three months after Grace disappeared, Charlie attended Abby's funeral. She had overdosed with pills, a presumed suicide, although there had been no note. Lori insisted on going with him. The church, built on the hill near Hawk Ridge, was too big for the attendees. Just as the world had been too big for Abby.

In his own muddle of grief, Charlie pulled himself together to reach out to Lucas immediately after hearing the news, and the two men cried like babies over a few beers in Lucas's garage shop.

Lucas had helped Charlie search for Grace for weeks after she went missing. Putting posters up, going door-to-door in neighborhoods near where known "parties" were held. After a quiet conversation with him, Lucas had made drop-in visits to the Superior bars where runaways sometimes found a way out of town. Charlie needed to be there for him, now.

Surrounded by tools that looked to be frequently used and lovingly hung by hooks above the table with a saw positioned at one end, they sat across from a sawhorse that held their beer and an ashtray for Lucas's pipe. Charlie realized he had rarely seen Lucas at rest and never knew he smoked a pipe. The image of Lucas, silver-haired and bleary-eyed, hollowed out in front of him, made him wince. What if he was seeing a future version of himself?

Over the next several hours, the story came out. "She was doing OK in juvie. On her meds, doing her schoolwork—not doing it well, mind you, but she wasn't getting into trouble with the truly bad kids in there."

Charlie listened as Lucas continued. "Karin and I took turns visiting, so one of us was there almost every day. We brought her the food she liked. Picked up McDonald's or pizza for her. Her grandma brought her home-baked cookies. Food in the place was awful, I guess. She was grateful."

"One of life's simple pleasures. I'm sure it felt good that you could see her smile when you brought her something she liked."

"Yes, it did." Lucas stopped and smiled. "She didn't have a happy life. Her mother, my daughter, left her with us and went off with a no-good guy, not the father. He was a different no-good guy." His face clouded over. "Her health issues didn't show up until later, but you know that story."

"I wouldn't let them do an autopsy and cut my girl open." His face fell, then he straightened, his eyes defiant. "Didn't even want them to do the drug tests, but they insisted—said they needed to for the cause of death."

Charlie's intuition told him Lucas needed a witness for this story, so he waited for the older man to find his words.

"It didn't matter to me what she took. She was gone." Lucas stopped to dry his eyes with his handkerchief. "I know she did it on purpose—she had all of her meds available to her; she could take her own life anytime she wanted. What I don't know is why she wanted to take her own life now. That's what hurts so bad.

"I had some hope in me this time. Hope that when she finished her stint in juvie that her plan of getting a job and finishing up her GED would do it. She sounded excited when we talked about a course at the vocational tech school in welding—always respected my job." He moved forward and cast his eyes to the floor, his voice ragged. "I thought it might work."

Charlie hated himself for what he had to do next but forced the words out. "Lucas, did Abby ever say anything more, once she got out, about Grace?" Abby had been home from juvie for only five days when she died. He knew she had taken the news of Gracie's leaving home hard. According to Lucas, at the time Abby found out about Gracie disappearing months ago, she wasn't even able to respond. "She was speechless and started to cry. When I pressed her about if she knew anything that might help us find her, she clammed up completely."

Lucas took a long pull from his pipe. "I didn't ask her anything else about Grace. Couldn't. I'm sorry. It was so hard when she found out Gracie went missing that I couldn't risk it. Needed to keep things positive. If I'd known what would happen, I would have—"

"Of course, Lucas. I know. Forgive me for asking at a time like this, but I needed to know."

Charlie reached out to put a hand on the older man's shoulder, now shaking with his sobs.

Finally, Lucas found his voice and sat straighter in his chair. "I can't believe we've lost them both. I have to believe that Gracie will come home at some point. We can't lose them both. Life isn't fair, but it can't be that unjust."

Karin knocked on the half-open door before entering, giving the men a needed break in their wake. She escorted Officer Slater in, the policeman who had found the girls the night of their campfire party months ago.

"Gentlemen, I'm sorry to intrude. I know this is a tough time. I needed to come and talk to you and Karin, Lucas, and when I saw Mr. Booker was here, I decided to take a chance and ask if we could all talk together. It concerns both girls."

Charlie bolted out of his chair at hearing reference to his daughter. "Have you found her? Is there news about Grace?"

"No. No. I'm sorry to get your hopes up, Mr. Booker. It's about a cell phone number that was on Abby's phone when we found her body. There was one number on it that she repeatedly called, and it's disconnected. Just wondered if you knew anything about the number." He showed both Karin and Lucas the number written on a piece of paper.

They looked at each other, then back at the cop. "No, doesn't look familiar."

"I thought it was worth a shot. Thanks. I'm sorry to interrupt at such a bad time."

Charlie walked the officer out to his car. "Can I ask why it's so important?"

"Well, you remember the night we found your girls out by the railroad trestle?"

"Yes, of course.

"You may remember that we saw signs that there may have been a couple of others at that party. I was just checking to see if there was any possible link back to your daughter or a third party, that could tell us more. Maybe even about where Grace may be."

"Show me the number." Any hope for Charlie was like salve for his open wounds.

"Sure." The officer showed him the number.

"No. It doesn't look familiar." Disappointed, but not surprised, he looked up at the officer, his eyes beseeching.

The officer mumbled, "Sorry," and walked to his car. Then turned and said, "Doesn't mean that Grace's story will end up this way. Remember that."

As Charlie walked back toward the garage, he saw Karin and Lucas clinging to each other, rocking side by side, crying together. He couldn't bear to interrupt their intimacy, so he slunk away.

Chapter 44

Navy Pier, Lake Michigan
Spring 2016

Grace found herself sitting on a bench facing Lake Michigan. She pinched herself to make sure she was actually alive and not in a dream state heading to heaven. Or hell. She didn't know how she had gotten there.

She was still groggy from the partying last night, and her mind drifted. Where was Abby? She should have been released from juvie a couple of months ago unless she had done something bad to extend her sentence. She worried Abby had been released and had changed her mind about joining Grace. The possibility made her sad, and since she no longer had her meds to keep her on an even keel, she tried not to think about it.

Grace had been a good friend to Abby. She had stuck to the plan. With the car money in her pocket, Janie Blank, no longer Grace, had found a cheap room to rent and a job washing dishes for cash, no questions asked. She had quickly bought a cheap phone and called Bobby to give him her number so he could connect Abby to her, as agreed. But that had been months ago, and Bobby's phone was now disconnected.

When she ran out of meds, she ran out of routine and couldn't keep her job or her cheap room. She found her way to a homeless shelter and spent her days trying to determine whom she could trust. Sometimes she made bad choices for immediate needs like curbing her anxiety, causing her to party or have sex with someone for the promise of a joint or alcohol or even a cigarette.

It was midmorning by the sun. She looked around. Fortunately, no people. She grabbed the dirty blanket she had used to sleep on and wrapped it around herself.

The lake was gray today, thick with waves. The sky above filled with fluffy clouds that seemed to be reaching upward. Gulls swung across the sky and over the shore—sandy by this stretch near Navy Pier. Then she remembered. Navy Pier was where a few of them had ended up panhandling yesterday. She thought back to the trip she and her dad took to Navy Pier on their vacation to Chicago when she was ten, so long ago now.

Her own lake was prettier. Wilder, Lake Superior was not as citified as this one. She missed it. The rocky shore, jagged edges, trees growing right out of the rock wherever there was a bit of soil. Hawk Ridge—you could see for miles from that vantage point. If you were lucky, you saw raptors crossing over, their majesty a testament to the power of the natural order.

She couldn't think of Hawk Ridge without thinking of home. She pushed down the sob that rose in her throat. She could never go home again because she was too messed up. Her father was the only reason to go home, but he was probably with her mother now. Their crazy daughter was no longer keeping them apart.

Where was Abby? Why wasn't Abby here with her? She should be out of detention and here with her now. Bobby had promised.

Grace kept her eyes on the lake even after she heard a swarm of tourists coming her way.

She rose, walking backward as far as she could, so she could keep the lake in her sight for as long as possible. Maybe today she'd try to find that walk-in clinic she had heard about, see if she could get some meds. She dismissed the thought again. *I can't chance being found. I'll give Abby another day.*

Chapter 45

Boston, Massachusetts
Spring 2016

May. Eight months since his daughter had run away from home. Barely functional, he made it through school and back home, not much more. Today, he left as early as he could, but Mack, limping from his old football injury, still caught up with Charlie in the parking lot.

"Hey, buddy!" He hopped up to him and paused, out of breath. "The smelt are running this weekend. How about if we go and get our share? I could pick you up." The run-on sentences slowed to a stop, and the enthusiasm drained from Mack's voice as he saw Charlie's face, now unguarded without any kids around.

"Thanks, but no. I've got some things to do." He had an upcoming trip to Boston planned.

Mack put one hand on Charlie's arm. "It'd do you good."

"Nah, it probably wouldn't." Charlie gave him a half-smile. Mack was a good guy, a good friend. "But you go, have fun."

"Anything I can—?" Mack stopped mid-sentence, as Charlie bent to unlock his car door. "OK, take care."

When he got home, Charlie took his Adirondack chair down by the lake. He felt closer to her there than anywhere else. Looking out at the waves, sometimes lucky enough to watch an ore boat glide across the water, he could revisit their father–daughter adventures together. He sat for a long time while Bailey chased the gulls or a squirrel and day turned into night. When he couldn't take the chill anymore, he headed in, to consider his chances for sleep. His commitment to stay away from alcohol was tested on nights like this.

It had been months since he had fought the battle and won. His drinking had been bad by the time Grace had run away. He'd been hiding from her and the pain in his life by using liquor to get away from it. He had promised himself he would give it up then, blaming himself for shutting Grace out so she felt she had no recourse but to run away. He hadn't touched the bottle since the night before she left. *I need to stay sharp, just in case she calls*, he reminded himself.

When Charlie stepped off the bus, he nearly got clipped by a teen-age kid going fast on a bicycle. The kid was carrying a box that was twice as wide as the bike, his vision impaired by the parcel.

"Watch it!" Charlie yelled, planting his feet firmly to catch his balance, while behind him, the bus moved out fast, leaving him in a wave of exhaust. The kid didn't even look back, outracing the accelerating bus, and Charlie had just enough time to jump up on the curb before another bus pulled in to disgorge passengers.

To his right was a small grocery store with carts lined up outside and a bench where an old man in a Red Sox ball cap sat smoking a pipe and reading the newspaper. The gentle breeze of the spring day brought a whiff of the tobacco toward him.

"Excuse me," Charlie said, stepping up to the old man. "Do you know where Fire Station Seven is?"

"Over one street and down two more to the left." The man pointed and eyed Charlie, "You got a fire to report?"

"Just doing a little research."

"Well, you won't find anybody there for your research project." The man coughed once, hacking out a glob of spit. "That station isn't active anymore. Consolidated with the one over on Delisle Avenue."

Charlie felt the news like the sideswipe he'd just survived from the kid and the bus. He stared at the old man, trying to formulate a question.

"I know a bit about that fire station," the man said. "I worked there for forty years. Want to ask me your questions?"

Charlie nodded and approached the bench, sitting on the far edge. "What did you do there?" After the roller-coaster ride he had been on with the St. Joseph's Home, he was leery of bait-and-switch tactics—nothing but a cycle of angst for his effort.

"I was a fireman. Finest work a human can have." The old man coughed again and nodded.

Charlie let the silence sit between them for a full minute before speaking again. "Well," he began, "I have a crazy mystery to solve involving that station."

"You gonna ask me?" The man folded his newspaper and put it on the bench between them. "I'm waiting."

"Forty-three years ago in 1973," Charlie said slowly, "a baby was left on the stoop of that station. Do you know anything about that?"

The old man looked across the street, then straightened the newspaper. "Was it a boy?"

"Yes."

"A healthy boy?"

"Yes."

He nodded. "I heard about it. Caused quite a stir in the station. Chaz, the guy who stumbled upon him in the cardboard box he was left in, almost threw that box in the garbage. When the baby started to cry, it spooked him like crazy. The guy went to Mass every day for an entire month begging forgiveness for what he might have done." The old man gave a raspy laugh. "After that everybody called Chaz "Baby Man." The old man continued to laugh, barely getting the words out, even as he missed the body language of distress by his bench mate.

"Pretty funny story, huh?" Charlie was stony, his words flat.

The old man stopped laughing, pulled a pipe from his jacket pocket, and began to stoke it. "When you work in a life-and-death situation, sometimes you look for humor wherever you can find it."

Charlie waited.

"The baby ended up fine. Chaz, the fellow who found him, ended up drinking too much and leaving the work. Last I heard he left the country—went to Australia to look up an uncle."

"And the mother?" Charlie got the words out, barely above a whisper.

"Social services tried for a long time to find a relative. Went after it for over a year. Not sure if they ever found out anything."

Charlie nodded. It was what he'd expected. Not hoped for but expected. His body sagged along with his spirits.

"Son," the old man said gently, "I'm not sure about the reason for your research, but I can tell you that sometimes mysteries are not meant to be solved."

Charlie locked eyes with the old man.

Chapter 46

Lisbon, Portugal
Spring 2016

" This is Louis Keith calling for Caroline Tate Booker. Please call me back at your earliest convenience." Caroline pressed off, silencing the phone message, and pulled another dress from its hanger. She folded it, placing it carefully in the suitcase she was packing for her trip to the Maldives to search for crab-plovers.

Louis Keith, her attorney, would have information for her when she called him back, and a smile of satisfaction curled her lips at the thought. He hadn't wanted to do it her way at first, but he hadn't wanted to be fired, either.

So what if she was toying with her husband's emotions? So what if he got angry with her? She was ignoring their daughter's existence in her settlement of their divorce, her last vindication. Grace was no longer a minor. She would not give Charlie the satisfaction of making the divorce anything other than a dissolution of their marriage. It had nothing to do with Grace.

Choosing her favorite merino sweater from the drawer, she pressed its softness to her face for a moment before it followed the dress into the suitcase. The settlement would prevent her having anything to do with Grace's problems in the future. Charlie had made plenty of promises to her that he had broken.

I'm well rid of both of them.

Chapter 47

Two Harbors, Minnesota
Summer 2016

Bailey bounded ahead of Charlie when he opened the back door after coming home from summer school. "Here you go, girl." He watched the dog weave and wag through the trees bordering the property nearing the lake, the sun sparkling in reflection on this stunning day. Ever hopeful, he headed to the mailbox. *Maybe I'll get a letter from Gracie.* He took a first sweep through the stack and didn't find what he longed for, but instead found a business envelope from a law firm.

> *Dear Mr. Booker,*
> *We have been retained to represent your wife Caroline Tate Booker in her divorce suit. As she wishes to terminate the marriage and resides outside of the United States, she has asked us to act on her behalf in this matter. Please call our office at your earliest convenience or should you wish to retain counsel, please have your counsel call us as soon as possible.*
> *Sincerely,*
> *Louis Keith, Attorney at Law*

He paged through the document attached. Legalese aside, it appeared to list the assets that had been acquired during their marriage and the liabilities as of the date of the intended divorce filing. Nothing surprised him, not the act of it or the contents of it, until he came to the heading "Dependents" and noted the blank lines for names under the heading. On the top line was written the word "Zero."

He calmly tucked the divorce papers back in their envelope and walked away, as if in a fugue state. Opening the bottom drawer of his desk, he pulled out the half empty bottle of bourbon, set it atop his desk blotter and stared at it. *She knows exactly where to stick the knife.*

Caroline had just negated their daughter's very existence. He had spent the better part of twenty years raising their child, now expressed as a zero on legal paperwork. A laughable move, really—not only illegal, but something Caroline knew he would not stand for—clearly designed to taunt him.

He tightened his fists as he fought to calm himself. He went out to the deck to watch Bailey until his emotions wound down. And as he did, only the guilt remained. He had tipped the balance in nature's favor, not allowing Caroline the right to determine her own fate as a woman on whether she wished to be a mother or not. He always came to the same conclusion. It was unforgivable. Still and always.

He was going to the kitchen to get a glass when Lori called.

"I have to run home to Iowa and see to my dad. Evidently he had a bad fall and my brother and I need to see what needs to be done to care for him."

"I'm sorry to hear that," Charlie said, grateful for her voice. "Would you like me to drive you down?" With the words barely out of his mouth he realized two things—he couldn't do this because he was teaching summer school, yet he really wanted to meet her father and brother and to help her.

"Oh, that's a sweet offer." Lori paused. "I appreciate the thought, but it's likely not the right time for you to meet them. I'll probably need to be playing the bad cop on this visit."

"Well, I'd be happy to support you in whatever you need, you know that, right?" he said softly.

"I do know that, yes," she whispered.

Charlie kept her on the line for as long as he could. After assurances that she would call him as the trip progressed, he finally let her go.

The conversation ended any further thoughts of bourbon. The natural high he was on just by talking with her reminded him what life could be—he would not do anything to risk any potential relationship with her. She asked so little of him.

While Caroline asked everything. Charlie pulled on a reserve of strength to diminish the hurt of Caroline's action to just another of her selfish acts and decided to act quickly on the divorce.

The next afternoon, he dropped off the divorce papers with Mitch Crowley, the only lawyer in Two Harbors, who agreed to represent him and get the matter finished quickly.

The following Saturday, the Vanilla Bean was bustling when Charlie walked in and found Walt holding court with a table full of retirees, chatting him up about joint pain and exercise. "Can't hardly walk this time of year, Doc. You want me to fall and break a hip?" one white-haired guy with a bit of extra weight teased him.

"No, but there's exercise equipment at the Senior Center, and you know it, Bud." Walt pointed in the direction of the center, then greeted his friend. "Save me from these freeloaders, Charlie, they keep asking me for medical advice. Can't a small-town doc just go out for breakfast without being hounded?"

The table erupted with laughter, and kept their own conversation going long after Walt and Charlie had ordered their food.

Walt looked at him and smiled. "You seem in a better place. Do I have that right?"

Charlie took his time to think before he answered. "Yes, I think I'm getting there. Sorting out a few things will help."

"Things such as?" Walt queried.

Charlie couldn't dodge his friend. "Caroline has asked for a divorce."

"Thank God almighty!" Walt proclaimed, more loudly than he should have, then added softly, slapping Charlie on the back, "It's about time!"

Charlie squirmed away from Walt's hand and surveyed the restaurant for onlookers. "It was a complicated relationship."

"No kidding!" Again Walt was enthusiastic. Then, as if noting Charlie's reaction, he said, "It's just that it seemed so obvious that the marriage was over. How are you feeling about it?"

"Resigned to it. Relieved, I guess. I'm glad it's coming to an end, actually," he heard himself ramble.

"You're my friend, and I'd like for you to have some happy years going forward. This seems like a natural time to make the break, right?"

"Yes, it does." He paused. "I always felt like I was letting her down."

"You got the woman pregnant, but that's nothing more than biology. She seemed to never get over that. You'll be so much better off with closure." Walt searched Charlie's face. "For what you've been through, you deserve to move on."

Charlie flinched. If ever there was a time to admit his despicable action it was now. *Nothing more than biology . . .*

Walt was on a roll. "You and Lori can get together now. You have a second chance. I hope you take it."

Charlie was stunned with Walt's comment about Lori. "What was that you said about getting together with Lori?"

"Oh, well, I shouldn't be meddling." Walt fiddled with his silverware. "It's just that you two . . . well it just seems like . . . everybody thinks you should . . ."

Charlie felt like a high school kid whose crush was out in the open. Were his feelings for Lori so obvious? "What? Who's everybody?"

The moment was lost when a young mother brought her coughing baby over to grab Walt for a quick look.

By the time Walt had finished his table-side consultation, Charlie had made a decision.

"Walt, you always see through me. And you're right. I do have feelings for Lori." He smiled shyly. "But the timing isn't right yet. Gracie still takes up so much of my emotional bandwidth, it just hasn't seemed fair to Lori. And now Caroline . . ."

Walt comforted his friend. "Let it play out. You two will find a way at the right time."

When Charlie left the restaurant, he finally felt ready to stop drifting and move with purpose. *We will find a way*, he told himself, *no matter how long it takes.*

Charlie met with Mitch Crowley a few weeks later. They had been discussing the paperwork for thirty minutes when Charlie said, "I'm ready to give her the divorce. Let's just cut through all of this and get it done."

"Mr. Booker, I know that's your desire, and I will do that for you, but there are a few things that I found out that I want you to be aware of before I start negotiating on your behalf." He read from his notepad. "First, there's the fact of her abandonment of you and your child, Grace. Second, I have discovered that she has not disclosed the receipt of a sizable trust fund in the assets listed here, which you would have claim over as they were received during the course of your marriage."

Charlie's surprise must have shown.

"Were you aware of the trust fund that Caroline's parents had set up for her?"

"No, I know nothing of a trust fund." He wondered how many other secrets Caroline had kept from him over the years.

"It could have been an oversight, but it's also possible, given that she has also not acknowledged your daughter, that she is using the divorce as a vehicle to avoid any financial responsibility to you or her."

"I won't argue that. I have enough resources with my house, my job, and my own savings, modest as they are. I don't need nor do I wish to haggle over Caroline's trust fund money." Charlie had already concluded that while some might think he should fight for more on behalf of his daughter, he knew Grace wouldn't want any part of it.

Mitch sucked in air and seemed to count to ten silently, before he continued, "Mr. Booker, let me tell you about the size of the trust fund."

"Not interested. By the way, Caroline's car that was listed as an asset is gone. It was stolen and never recovered." Charlie was taking a final look at the list of assets, ready to pack up and be off.

"Two million dollars."

Charlie looked up.

"The trust fund. Two million dollars. I could get you at least half of that."

Charlie cast his eyes up and landed on a painting, a family portrait, on the wall. He thought of the term abandonment. Was that the correct word for what Caroline had done? Her self-styled removal from him and their daughter, the scene at the hospital when she tried to see Grace, her repeated appeals to him to leave Two Harbors and their child to join him in her adventures. She wouldn't see it as abandonment. She would see it as him making a choice of their daughter over her. *Odd,* he thought, *how she didn't value family, even though she was now a wealthy woman as a result of parents she didn't remember, taking care of her from the grave. How could I have been so blind to our clashing values for so long?*

Charlie couldn't turn away from the painting, his mind reeling at the contrast between it and his own fractured life.

"Mr. Booker?"

Charlie said to Mitch, "You look like these guys."

"That's my grandfather and my father when he was a kid. My grandfather started this law firm."

"Nice." Charlie smiled politely as he always did when acknowledging someone's roots. "No, I don't want to go after the trust fund."

Chapter 48

Chicago, Illinois
Summer 2016

Grace was in trouble, and she knew it. She put her hands over her ears and sat with her head between her knees trying to block the blaring, screeching noise of the early evening traffic. The loud voices in her head had forced her out of the homeless shelter a block away to hunker down on a street corner nearby; she couldn't seem to drown them out.

This is a panic attack. Just breathe and it will subside. She thought back to the panic attacks she had before she got help from Dr. Chester and how scary they were. She tried to wait it out.

Someone grabbed her arm, pulling on her. "Hey girl, what's up?" A guy she recognized from the street slurred his words. "How 'bout we see if we can score a little coke?"

She hid her head and tried to make like a snail, so that he couldn't keep touching her, but as he continued, the voices got louder, and his eagerness forced her agitation to get the best of her. In one lightning move, she bolted up and away, without looking at traffic, into the street. Alert drivers diverted their path, and she darted and dodged, until she fell, and passed out.

She awoke in a small room with frilly curtains. She had a bad headache but was relieved she was no longer in the grip of a panic attack. Her months on the street precluded any immediate level of trust; she was on alert. She heard someone in the hallway, and then saw a tall woman with wild, red hair peek in on her.

"Ahh, you're awake."

"Yes, and, where am I exactly? Who are you?" She sat up too quickly and shored up her aching head with her hands, then noticed her forearm had been bandaged.

"You are a guest at Angie's Refuge. I'm Daisy Morse, the director. Our program, Angels for Angie, helps young women off the street when they are ready to be helped. I believe you are ready to be helped. Are you, Janie?"

"What does that mean?" Grace asked, curious about this upbeat woman in charge.

"I find help means different things for every girl. There's no one path." Daisy corrected herself. "Well, the one path for everyone is to get you off the street and help you find a safer, healthier path to follow. Does that make sense?"

"Who's here?" Grace saw her backpack hanging on a hook along with a white fluffy robe one hook over.

"Other young women like yourself."

Grace didn't dare ask if that included runaways, so she changed direction. "What happened? How did you find me?"

"Well, we have a relationship with Sandy, who manages the homeless shelter you were staying at. She told us about you a few days ago and said you may need some help sorting things out." Daisy took her time, assessing Grace's comprehension as she spoke. "We were about to seek you out when Sandy called us this evening after pulling you from the street. I understand you were running into traffic, perhaps feeling unwell?"

Grace tried to remember what was happening before the panic attack. She had recently moved to a different shelter and spent most of her time with a mixed-age group who sometimes panhandled together and shared food and drugs when they could get them. With her meds gone, she tried to keep her twin demons of anxiety and depression at bay with whatever she could find on the street. She remembered taking something that afternoon, but couldn't remember what it was. She looked at Daisy and took a deep breath. It was getting too hard.

Finally, Grace spoke. "What does helping me mean?"

"That's for you and me to determine." Daisy smiled. "I suggest you take a shower and get a good night's sleep, and then in the morning we take you to the community clinic we use to get you checked out. Sandy thought maybe you have some anxiety issues?"

Grace felt her body go rigid at the mention of the clinic. Surely they would do a drug screen. She stood up to go for her backpack, poised to flee. Daisy calmly added, "Whatever we find out at the clinic will not rule out giving you help. I promise."

The standoff lasted for a full minute. Daisy spoke first. "The bathroom is two doors down, and you'll find a fresh set of PJs and some extra clothes in the chest, here by the door. Breakfast is at eight o'clock." She turned to leave, then added, "The robe is for you, too."

Do I trust her? I'll decide later. For tonight, she decided to enjoy the privacy of a bathroom door she could lock, a fluffy white robe that smelled of lilacs, and the relief that she was still alive. She knew her body was in bad shape. In the shower, she saw how skinny she was. Her hip bones jutted out, and her wrists were bonier than she ever remembered. Her skin was pasty and covered with acne, which she had never had before.

Her last thought before falling asleep was about breakfast and not whether she was safe for the night.

"Did you know you are eight weeks pregnant, Janie?" the youngish doctor in a white coat and Harry Potter glasses asked.

That question, delivered after he had reported out many other results on her overall condition, caused Grace to let out an involuntary, "Whaaaa—!" She had been worried about the drug screen and not this scenario.

"I guess this is a surprise to you." He gave her a minute to nod, then looked at his watch. "I'll tell you what. I'm going to have the nurse come in and get you set up for prenatal care, or if you'd like to digest this news and consider options, we can set you up with a counselor for that conversation. I'll be back in five." He left her in the room, alone.

How could I be pregnant? I suppose I could be pregnant. Her mind seized up at the thought of a baby, so she tried to focus her mind on sex. She hadn't had much of it. Her face flushed remembering her rude introduction with the unreliable Bobby who stole her virginity without knowing it. She didn't like to think about it but as she did, she realized that she had given her virginity away and cheapened herself in the process. She had been too naive to think about protection and both of them too drunk. She counted the months on her fingers. *Too long ago to be considered for a pregnancy risk.*

Since then, maybe two or three guys, equally forgettable. She remembered one guy, Jude or Jay, just after she moved into the first shelter. She was really anxious about the unfamiliar surroundings, and he took care of her. He had moved on soon after they met, but not before she'd allowed him to comfort her through a particularly rough night of bad dreams. It had seemed a natural flow to move from hugging to naked exploration to sex. But he had left the city a couple of days later. He might have been a friend, even a lover, had he stayed.

A few days after that, there was a night she wished she could forget. She was so down that she needed something, anything to get her through. She wasn't sure what the local dealer gave her, but he wouldn't give it to her without sex. She had gone back for more another time. Unprotected sex was the least of her worries; she was living an unprotected life. *I hope he isn't the father of my baby.*

"My baby" she whispered to herself, then repeated, loudly, "My baby." She wrapped her arms around herself in a hug. Tears streamed down her face until a strong sense of resolve strengthened her spine and she dried her tears. If she had been unmoored these past few months, she now saw an internal compass appear and knew she would do whatever it took to create a new life for herself and her child. *I'll take care of you, baby!*

Grace sat still when Daisy popped her head in. "May I join you?" She quietly took the chair next to Grace. "Remember when I told you that nothing we found out in the checkup would count against you for our program?"

Grace shifted in her chair and waited. She knew they had found a mix of coke and something else in her system but not much. She was malnourished and had a skin rash that needed to be treated. Being pregnant was beyond anything she had considered.

"Janie, thank you for being forthcoming with the doctor about your past mental health stresses. He's referred you to the psychiatrist they work with here, and we've made that appointment for you. It helped that you told him about your meds, so we should be able to get you back on track with that tomorrow. We'll get you eating better and ointment for your rash. Your health comes first, and we'll help you with all of that."

"So, he told you I'm pregnant?" Grace held her breath expecting the worst. *No way this will work now.*

"Yes. He did, and that's not a deal-breaker for the program." Daisy crossed her legs and leaned back in her chair. "Do you have questions about what to do?"

Grace exhaled, and the words tumbled out fast. "Of course, I have loads of questions. But the most important is to make sure that my meds don't harm my baby."

With no immediate response, Grace watched for Daisy's reaction, which started slow, as if she needed a moment to realize Grace meant to keep the baby. Daisy's mouth curled into a lovely smile.

"OK, then, the questions can be handled along the way, right?" Daisy asked, still smiling.

"Yes." Grace dared smile back, relief flooding her body. She hadn't made a pact with someone since Abby, but she had just reached a common understanding with Daisy. It felt good.

Four weeks into her stay at Angie's Refuge, Grace was expected to follow the routine of the house. Keep her room clean and tidy, take kitchen duty as assigned, show up to her counseling sessions, and comply with the no drugs policy, except to stay on the meds she'd been re-prescribed. She had worried about how she would be accepted by the other girls but shouldn't have been. Once the meds smoothed her out, she took a chance, baked brownies, and put them near the piano while she played some free-form music, and it brought a few of them together. She started making some friends among them.

Her invitation, "Should we make this a weekly thing?" was welcomed, and Tuesday evenings became music night. News of her pregnancy also spread fast, and it seemed to prove a tonic for all of them and resulted in lots of advice on how to eat and take care of herself. Best of all, she started building trust with Daisy and their plan to help her: counseling, getting her GED, and being a good citizen in the community of Angie's Refuge.

Daisy continued to probe for more personal information. "Is there anyone we should communicate with on your behalf?" or "Anyone you would like me to contact?" Even as Grace grew more grateful to Daisy every day, she couldn't share the truth of her family or where she was from. She had given up on Abby and didn't keep her alias for her friend. She kept it so her dad couldn't find her, or worse, discover he wasn't even looking.

Four months in, Grace felt better than she had for years.

"Look at you, Janie!" Hannah, one of the girls in residence, fawned at her reflection in the full-length mirror in the hallway. "You are truly preggers, momma-to-be!"

Grace blushed at the compliment. Amazing what her body could accomplish when she treated it well. She was gaining back the weight she had lost living on the street, and her skin was improving with the balanced diet. She found joy in playing the piano and was pleased the girls liked listening to her.

She had confided to her counselor about her family issues and found relief when she took a risk and talked about her mother. Once she started, she couldn't stop. She described her mother's detachment, her emotional neglect, and her lack of physical intimacy with her daughter as a contrast to her attachment to her father.

The counselor described how not all mothers were good at it. The counselor gave her some books about toxic mothers, and Grace consumed them.

"Have you thought much about what kind of mother you want to be?"

Grace didn't have to work very hard at this one. "Yes, I have," she said and went on to describe Lori.

Six months in, Grace was about to get her GED. The GED test had been tough, but she felt pretty good about it. It was interesting to her that so much of what she had learned from Mack and the other teachers at Two Harbors High School had stayed with her. She hoped to thank them someday.

Today, she had promised the girls that she would bake snickerdoodle cookies for them. She was pulling out ingredients when Daisy joined her in the kitchen.

"How do you feel about the test today? Glad it's over, I bet?"

"So glad it's over. I think it went pretty well. I guess I'll find out tomorrow."

Daisy pulled up a chair. "Do you have a minute to chat?"

"Sure." Grace owed Daisy so much, she was feeling increasingly bad about not sharing her true identity and family story with her.

"Just wanted you to know how proud I am of you. I'm feeling confident you will have passed that test—you're a smart girl. I'm so glad you finished it."

"Yes, me too." Her hand went to rest on her stomach.

"Won't be long now." Daisy chuckled. "Have you given any thought to what happens after that?"

Grace hid her eyes in a cupboard searching for a bowl. "Not much." She was nervous about where this was going.

"Well, you've had a lot going on. Getting off the street, learning how to live in community with other girls, completing your GED." Daisy counted on her fingers, wanting more of a response from Grace. "I want you to know that you are free to stay here as long as you'd like. When you have some thoughts that you'd like to bounce around with me, about going forward, I'm here."

Daisy rose and patted Grace on the back. "Snickerdoodles! Excellent!"

That night, Grace took out the badly worn letter she'd stolen from home—one in a series of letters from her mother pressuring her dad to leave Minnesota to join her. Rereading it, she thought of the counselor's words.

"Your anxiety and depression may have exaggerated your worries here, Janie. Perhaps you should keep that in mind."

She couldn't continue to miscalculate. She thought back to her badly formulated runaway plan. How could she really expect to have Abby join her in Chicago? Counting on Bobby had been ridiculous. It was time for her to grow up. *I want to do things right from here on out—and that starts with being a good mother.*

To accomplish that goal, she knew she needed her father. Would he help her? When she had come to Angie's Refuge, it was as Janie Blank, still not ready to be found as the screwed-up daughter she was, or to learn that he had given up on her and was out of the country with her mother. Now, months later, could she really expect him to welcome her with open arms, with a baby of unknown paternity?

She badly wanted her father to see her as a daughter who, though she had failed him, recognized it and had accomplished what seemed impossible a year ago: GED in hand, stable and no longer a suicide risk but eager to build a new life for herself and the baby she carried. She swallowed hard when she thought about all she had put him through. Every time she thought about it, she started to shake. Still, memories of his unconditional love for her fed hope that he would be there for her and accept the news of the baby. *Please, Dad.*

At the right time, she would reach out to him.

Grace stepped lively on the way home from the bus stop the next day. In addition to officially receiving her GED, she would be spending the following week at a series of vocational sessions to jump-start her future. Right now, she needed ideas about something she could do without spending years in school. She wasn't sure how much money she would need to make a life for herself and her baby. So much depended on whether her dad would be willing to take her in. Just a couple of years ago, he would have been helping her consider college choices.

The prenatal child-rearing class she was taking awakened her to what it would mean to have a baby to care for and how much she would be asking of her father to welcome her back with a child. Being a grown-up was hard and scary.

As she rounded the corner to the house, she saw balloons tied on the stoop lining the steps up to the front porch. A large sign decorated the front door.

"Congrats Janie! Happy Graduation!"

Gracie hadn't felt such warmth since she was part of the church community in Two Harbors, surrounded by an intimacy of shared values. She pictured Sunday services with Dr. Riley's family pew behind theirs. She and Ashley, Dad and Lori a family unit within the congregation. Her confirmation celebration, along with Ashley and the Swanson twins, a rite of passage that seemed more important now.

It's time, she thought. *I need to go home.*

Chapter 49

Dauphin Island, Alabama
Summer 2016

Caroline's fancy new title, International Ornithology Director for the National Audubon Society, suited her as did the respect it demanded. Telling people the truth and hectoring if it came to it—often her Achilles heel in her past relationships—worked for her here, and she loved the nonstop travel. Home, still Lisbon right now, could be anywhere or nowhere special.

The job also motivated her in ways she hadn't envisioned, primarily to address the effect of civilization's encroachment on bird habitat. Right now, she was en route to Dauphin Island, Alabama's only barrier island and a vital stopover for migratory birds, to assess recent storm damage to the Audubon Bird Sanctuary there.

She arrived in Mobile after midnight and didn't get on the ferry to the island until late the next morning. Debris, flotsam, driftwood, garbage, and small beached boats still lined the shore as they approached the dock. As she waited at the meeting spot for her Audubon driver, she noted how the island bustled with clean-up activity, even though the storm surge had hit just thirty-six hours earlier.

"Dr. Booker?" A tall, balding man in an Audubon cap approached her while she watched the activity on the landing. "Happy you made it, ma'am. My name is Roy. My jeep is right over here." He hoisted her bag over his shoulder and led the way.

The air was clear, as the humidity was spent. The sun smiling above them gave the hope of a new day, renewal against the odds.

Twenty minutes into their drive, they were stopped by a line of cars waiting ahead of them; they left the jeep to investigate. They both stopped as the cacophony of bird noise, hanging in the air ahead of them, jammed their consciousness. Now walking abreast of one another, they quickened their pace, ending at a run when they saw what was ahead of them.

An Audubon jeep, exactly like Roy's, was tipped on its side, blocking the road ahead. The driver of the jeep, surrounded by people out of their own cars, was on his phone while gesturing wildly to the people attending him. Following his finger pointing to the over wash by the side of the road, Caroline saw approximately ten bird cages with live birds in various levels of water, unable to fly or swim, and in danger of floating away or drowning. Back in the jeep, she saw another half-dozen bird cages full of agitated birds banging into each other in the crowded spaces. One pathetic mother cormorant trying to shelter her chicks with her wing caught Caroline's attention as she considered the selfless instinct.

Roy took off running, and Caroline kept stride. The driver saw Roy coming toward him and yelled, "Get the birds, Roy, gotta get the birds." He dropped his phone and attempted to rise but quickly sat back down, putting his head between his knees.

Caroline's body revved up with a wild dose of adrenaline. She didn't waste any time. "Roy, you get in the water, I'll get a line going to get the birds as you hand them up out of the water."

Roy jumped to it and headed into the water, wading to the deepest part and the farthest bird cage.

Caroline shouted to the people in the cars. "Get out of your cars. We need to make a human chain to get these birds to safety. Use gloves if you have them or a jacket or shirt to protect your hands as you approach the cages." Several people stood waiting for some instruction so the line was ordered fairly quickly.

"You, sir, please make sure they line up the cages here on the side of the road." Satisfied that the birds in the water were to be rescued soon, hopefully soon enough, she approached the tipped jeep to see what needed to be done. Other than a jumble, the bird cages were still intact, their occupants agitated and scared.

From one of the cars, a teenage girl approached her. "Let me help. What can I do?"

Caroline quickly put her to work. "I'm going to hand you each of these cages, and I want you to move them to the side of the road over there." Caroline pointed. "Wait." She approached the driver, who looked shaken but not badly injured. "Give me your handling gloves."

The driver complied. Caroline walked away and asked, "Did any of you call an ambulance for this driver?"

She heard, "Yes, I did" behind her as she approached the girl. "Here, put these on. You can't be sure you won't be injured by a frightened bird."

The girl put the gloves on and Caroline pulled both her canvas hat and her own handling gloves from her pockets. "Now watch how I handle each cage and follow my example. Can you do that?"

"Yes!" the girl replied, beaming.

Caroline approached the jeep slowly and started making clucking sounds in a medium register, lowering her voice. The cages were leaning helter-skelter, and she needed to take care with the order of movement lest she wobble a cage unnecessarily. She worked slowly and steadily until the most precarious of the cages were moved. She had watched her young apprentice handle the first one, gave her a couple of instructions, and then they worked together seamlessly until the jeep's back end was emptied, and the girl rejoined the group of helpers.

While they were busy with that job, an ambulance came to pick up the driver, a police car and tow truck came to clear the road, and Roy had finished rescuing the bird cages from the water.

Meanwhile, Roy had requested police support to allow the large Audubon truck stuck back behind the line of cars to snake its way up to load the birds. He approached Caroline and said, "Dr. Booker, the vets are waiting for our arrival. The truck is making its way to us. We'll be able to load soon."

As Caroline wrapped up her work, she remembered her helper. The girl's gloves were on the ground by the jeep; she could see her walking back to a pick-up truck, her mother's arms around her. For a moment, Caroline thought she looked like Grace, something about the way she walked. With a start, she realized the obvious. She was nothing like Grace, as she had her mother's arms around her.

Chapter 50

Two Harbors, Minnesota
Autumn 2016

Grace's birthday came. Nineteen years old. Then the first anniversary of her disappearance. His search for his daughter was going nowhere. Charlie was getting through his days, but barely.

When Lucas reached out to him, he couldn't turn him down. They met at the Castle Danger Brewery for a beer. The mix of people, young and old, seemed to lift him from his lethargy and remind him that people were living their lives around him. Some were playing checkers or board games while others just sipped their beer, gazing out at the lake. Today, whitecaps caused a frosty mist in the gray of November. It was hard to decipher which way the weather would go—stormy or calm. The sky played coy.

"Any news from Officer Slater?" Lucas asked.

"Nothing worth noting," Charlie replied. "The guy continues to keep an active search going. That's something."

"Yes," Lucas said. "No news at least keeps hope alive."

"I somehow thought there might be contact around her birthday, but nothing."

The older man scrunched his eyes tightly. "I think you need to prepare for the fact that you may have lost her. You're still a young guy with a lot of life left. If Grace is found or comes back, she'll have wanted you to be living it. You need to consider moving on."

Charlie didn't respond.

"You know, Karin and I went to a grief counselor after Abby's suicide. She dragged me to it, never thought much of that stuff. I have to say, it helped. Made me think of things beyond my own grief. Reminded me that life is for the living. Helped me through my guilt."

"She's not dead. I can't go there." Charlie's voice was shaky, and he wasn't sure he could continue the conversation.

"No, of course not." Lucas reached out and tapped Charlie's hand, which was squeezing his beer glass. "Not saying you need to. Just saying a counselor may be helpful—not a grief counselor—sorry I worded it that way. I wouldn't suggest in any way that you give up hope—just that you find some help coping with the uncertainty. That's all."

At those words, Charlie breathed easier, and after a moment or two of silence, he was grateful when Lucas changed the subject.

As he drove home in the rain, he considered Lucas's message. Coming from a man who had lost a daughter and granddaughter, Lucas was the voice of experience. Was he right?

Maybe it was time. Time to sort things out. Who could help? *Walt, of course. He'll know the right counselor for me.*

"Smart move. A counselor would be helpful for you right now. I know just the guy." Charlie heard Walt shuffle papers as he waited on the telephone line for a name and number. "Ah, here it is. Dr. Jerome Gilleck. Good guy. He's located in Duluth, trained in St. Louis. Moved here to practice after he fell in love with the North Shore on his honeymoon twenty some years ago. I've referred many to him over the years. You'll like him."

Charlie made two quick calls before he lost his nerve. The first, for an appointment with Dr. Gilleck, and the second, to arrange a coffee date with Lori.

He misdialed her number the first time. *What am I doing? Yes, it's a risk, but it's time.*

Oblivious to his fear, Lori rebuffed the coffee date. "I'd rather have a beer if that's OK? Maybe the brewery? Pick me up?"

She hadn't been home from Dad duty for long and welcomed the opportunity to vent about the hard time she was having dealing with the family dynamics around shared decision-making and care of her father with a brother she never felt close to.

She summed up her mood. "I just don't know when life gets easier. I do know you have to grab whatever joy you can when you can." She took a long swallow of her beer, as Charlie barely sipped his.

The boisterous crowd required leaning in for intimate conversations.

Here goes. He started slow and shared his frustration with the search for any of his own family. "I know I need to let that and other things go, and I need help to sort some things out." He took a deep breath and took the first step toward the future. "Lori, I'm going to see a counselor."

Lori's eyebrows shot up. "What was it that pushed you to do that?"

"Caroline." He wanted to get past this, so he opened the door early. "The marriage has been over for a long time, but finally the divorce will happen. I need to get my head straight around that. Not the fact of it, which I welcome, but her divorce suit failed to even mention any children born during our marriage. She didn't even acknowledge Grace as her daughter."

Lori studied him in the dimming light of the room. "It's always been about Caroline. Now that Grace is gone, are you prepared to let go of your wife?"

"The quick answer is yes. I'm just waiting for the final divorce paperwork to sign, but I sense you're asking something more. What do you mean?"

"Caroline always seemed to have extraordinary power over you, way beyond what one would expect. She always treated you badly, terribly, never keeping up her end of family obligations, leaving you to raise Grace on your own. When Grace got sick, she totally vanished." Lori gripped her beer tightly and exhaled loudly. "It was hard to watch."

"You think she's still in my head? Is that it?"

"Yes." Lori got the word out.

"If she's still in my head, you worry that I'm not ready to move on, for someone else to take over my heart?"

Lori could only nod in response, her lips trembling.

"Lori, my heart is already filled with you. Has been for a long time. I couldn't let my head go there," Charlie whispered and watched Lori hide her tears by looking out of the window. He reflected on the many years he tried to make a happy family with Caroline and Grace, the tragic years of trying to get Grace the help she needed, and the final reckoning with Caroline when he wouldn't leave Grace.

"You see, I made a big mistake in my marriage. I made the assumption, since Caroline grew up without parents, and I was an orphan, that we shared a common desire to have a family. I couldn't have been more wrong about that. The worst thing about it was that she told me many times that she was an adventurer, not somebody designed to tend a home and have a family. I pressed it, assuming she would change her mind when a baby arrived."

Lori pulled her jacket tighter against the chill of an open door as a large group entered. He went on. "As you observed, it didn't work out that way. I carry a lot of guilt over that and will no doubt carry it always. It's why I'm going to counseling." He looked away to gather his thoughts. "I'm ready to move on. I feel that I am. I hope you can believe me."

A server jostled the table near them, picking up glasses to make room for the group, and Charlie glanced at Lori, who met his gaze. "I hate to admit it, but I don't have any idea about your romantic life after you lost your husband. Tell me?"

"That would be a very short conversation." She laughed. "You should ask Ashley sometime about the men in my life. Nobody memorable, that's for sure."

"Really? No interest or no prospects nearby?"

"Probably both. Internet dating is not much fun, and Two Harbors isn't exactly full of eligible men." She chuckled.

"Yet you stayed here." He searched her face.

"Yes. I thought of leaving a few times." She looked away. "You get used to a place, you like the people. Hard to leave the life you've built after a while."

He caught her eyes and held them. He hoped it wasn't too late to make this right. "Lori, I feel like I have been given the gift of a second chapter. I hope you find it in your heart to give me a chance."

With eyes glistening she touched his hand. "Oh, Charlie, I've waited so long to hear those words."

He smiled broadly and took her hand in his, squeezing tightly. "I need a little more time to work things out, but please know that I plan to court you soon, Lori Barnes."

Lori laughed. When he dropped her off and bade her good night, she gave him a kiss—a kiss with promise.

After their night at the brewery, Lori was called back to Iowa and spent all of December and early January occupied with her father's care, and then his funeral.

While she was gone, Charlie worked on his own issues. With his counselor's help, he discovered how his own unmet needs had led him to Caroline. His strong desire to build a family blinded him to Caroline's reluctance; he was trying to forgive himself for the pregnancy betrayal.

He thought stopping by Mitch Crowley's office to sign papers would just be an errand to check off of his list. But when handed the papers, his knees buckled. Mitch steered him to a chair.

"The finality gets to folks. I'll give you a moment."

Images flitted across Charlie's mind. The giddy days he courted Caroline, the first days of their marriage and exploring the North Shore, even the early images of the family of three once Grace came. Then, the newsreel grew dark with Grace in trouble and Caroline out of camera range. He hung his head and allowed his body to sag for a long moment until he felt ready to go on. *I can't go back.* He signed the document and took his first step forward on a new path.

While he had never had great hopes for his own family search, he was also ready to let that go. Someday, he hoped to share the whole story with Grace. *Hope and Grace . . . always together in my mind.*

Chapter 51

Dauphin Island, Alabama
Summer 2016

It was late afternoon when they arrived at the sanctuary and nearly dusk when the veterinarians, biologists, and a new crop of volunteers started to unload the birds to check for injuries. Roy and Caroline were ushered into the decontamination area before they were allowed to go anywhere else.

After a hot shower and a few minutes to settle into her quarters, Caroline was led into the office of the sanctuary director, Miles Gardener. "Dr. Booker. Welcome to Audubon's Dauphin Island Bird Sanctuary." He shook her hand with warmth and invited her to sit. "That was quite the dramatic arrival for you."

"Yes, it certainly was." Caroline got right to the point. "What have they discovered about the birds. Did we lose any in the accident?"

"I haven't heard yet. We will know by morning. Some of the birds were injured and being transported for rehabilitation already and others were being moved due to the habitat loss during the storm. Your efforts saved many, of that I have no doubt. Your quick action . . . commendable."

"I felt helpless, really. All we could do was to try to save those frightened birds. Roy was the hero. He did the yeoman's work of pulling the trapped birds out of the water. I'd like to go see the birds now." Suddenly, Caroline was hit by a wave of exhaustion, physical and emotional. She felt herself wobble to her feet.

"Dr. Booker, you must be tired. There will be time for that in the morning. Let the team do their work, and we can check on the birds together then. Right now, I think you should eat something, and then head back to your quarters. Tomorrow is a big day. The special guests are scheduled to be here at ten in the morning. We want you to be rested by then. Why don't I come find you then?"

Caroline fell into a deep sleep. Until the dreams came. She was underwater attempting to open the locked hold of a ship where baby Grace was hidden. She didn't have the strength to open it on her own. She looked for tools but didn't know which would help. She looked for a key and couldn't find one. Finally, she was forced to look for others to help her, but they had all left the ship to save themselves. Caroline woke gasping for air and couldn't go back to sleep until dawn. Then she slept deeply until Miles Gardener knocked on her door, twenty minutes before she was due to meet the prospective donors.

She had just time enough to throw on her clothes. Rushing allowed her to push the dream back for recovery later. She sat before her mirror, combing her hair, thinking about the prospective donors she would persuade that morning. With yesterday's events still fresh, she knew she'd easily draw on her passion. No need to prepare for this group. She just wanted them to dig deep in their pockets.

Miles gave his short introduction, and Caroline stepped up to the podium and presented her case. She described how the effects of the hurricanes had led to the loss of habitat and birding on the island. She talked about the climate stressors that threatened the sanctuary and the importance of a forest canopy to a valuable wildlife habitat. "It takes funds to do this work," she said, flashing an extra-sweet smile, "and we so appreciate your interest in keeping the sanctuary alive."

After taking a few questions, Caroline turned the microphone back to Miles. She was done. She knew she had connected. Now she could go see the birds.

As she left the meeting space, she ran into Roy. "You look better today. Where are the birds we brought in?"

"Good morning." He tipped his hat. "I've been down to check on them once, but I'll take you."

She noticed he didn't give her a condition report. They walked in tandem, again, in silence.

The rehab building was cavernous but efficient in its layout. She heard the cacophony before they arrived. Roy led her to Max, the lead biologist who showed her the birds. In cages, some with splints on their wings, some were recovering from surgery, and still others were moving around and seemed to be reorienting well.

Finally, Max replied to her repeated direct question. "Two of the sixteen have died."

Just then, Roy reappeared. "Max, we have incoming."

In contrast with the larger room, the receiving area was silent but for the high-pitched chirp of spoonbill chicks surrounding their wounded mother in an open box lined with straw, carried in by an islander.

"Thanks for bringing this family in. Did you find them yourself?" Max was cool and professional. He interviewed the islander while putting on his gloves and gently stroking the body of the mother bird, clearly in poor shape. Caroline's heart skipped a beat.

"Yes, Mama here can't fly. Not sure why, but it looks to me like her wing is broken," the islander said, his eyes a little shiny. "She's not gonna leave those chicks."

Max kept his hand on the bird and clucked at her constantly.

"Dr. Booker, we're going to take the mother into X-ray, and I'll have to sedate her. Would you feed these baby birds with an eye dropper? They are probably in danger of dehydration. I doubt if all of them will make it."

An assistant handed Caroline rubber gloves and an eye dropper. "Just a drop at a time. Please feed one chick at a time, so you don't lose track of which is which. I'll check back with you a bit later."

As Caroline took the eye dropper and picked up the first chick, she had a visceral memory of a hungry Grace. The eager mouth, the eyes tightly closed, the wail before the bottle was ready.

Her eyes filled. Images flooded her. Grace. Charlie feeding Grace. She had refused to breastfeed her daughter. Her own baby. *Why?*

Suddenly she felt liquid on her forearm beyond the glove line. She looked down and noted that the baby bird's beak was no longer open, yet she held fast to the eye dropper, still dropping liquid in a steady rhythm, trailing down her hand to bare skin. The birds head had flopped to the side, it had died. Unsure whether she had squeezed it too hard or it had just died naturally, she shuddered, then turned her body to the wall. Silent sobs convulsed her body.

She heard voices behind her and saw Miles entering the lab with a group of donors. She bent her head, unable to stop trembling. She heard Miles's voice behind her then and his rapid movement away, as if he were creating a diversion to give her privacy.

An hour later, when Miles doubled back to check on her, she had finished feeding the baby chicks and was petting them gently.

For the next forty-eight hours, Caroline spent all of her

waking moments with the baby birds. Max kicked her out when he came for his final rounds; otherwise she would have stayed with them all night.

On her last night on the island, she wrapped herself in bed in a fetal position hoping to recapture her earlier dream. This time she started off dreaming about birds' nests falling from trees, and the mother spoonbill frantically gathering her chicks from the marshy grasses, despite her own injury. Then the dream shifted. She was on a raft in the ocean, above the sunken ship, baby Grace asleep in a basket next to her, waiting for rescue. A stork swooped down and pulled the sleeping child up by her blanket corners to carry her to her father.

Startled awake, it took her a few minutes to get her bearings. She walked out on her patio to gaze at the water and felt the breeze gently swishing the trees near her. No raft in sight. No baby Grace. She considered going back to the rehab building, but she checked the time and realized three in the morning was not a good time to make an appearance. In a rare moment of self-reflection, she made an effort to decipher her dreams, always coming to the same question. *Why couldn't I save my own baby?* After growing weary of it, she gave up. Finally, fatigue took over, and a long yawn slowly turned into a wide smile. *I wasn't equipped to save my daughter, but I do know how to save birds.* She rewarded herself with a luxurious stretch and headed back to bed, calmer than she had felt in days. This time, she fell into a deep, dreamless sleep and woke refreshed, with new resolve. Her life's work was to move forward, doing what she could to save the birds.

Caroline worked out of the New York City office for a month. When she returned to Lisbon, she didn't expect anything important to be waiting for her, but a large manila envelope with a Duluth postmark caught her eye. Lewis Keith? What could he need now?

She scanned the cover letter: "We need to sort out the final details of your will. I have taken out the name of your ex-husband. If you approve of this change, email me and I will use your e-signature and file it."

Caroline trembled slightly as her body began to lose the equilibrium she had finally won on Dauphine Island. She threw the papers to the floor. At least she'd had the foresight to make a reunion date with one of her lovers.

She took extra pains with her clothes and makeup. Before she left, she looked more carefully at the will. Charlie was off. *Yes, thank you.* But then she saw the beneficiary line: Grace Tate Booker was not.

She stared at the name, focusing on the name Tate. Her family name, her legacy. An image came to her. Grace as a tween, wrapped up tight in outdoor gear, her face barely showing behind her binoculars as she scanned the sky at the Hawk Ridge overlook.

She sat down at her computer and sent a quick email to Lewis Keith. "Approved."

I have no time for regret. She left for her liaison looking like two million dollars.

Chapter 52

>-

Drive to Chicago
January 15, 2017

"Your daughter needs help. Now." The words reverberated in Charlie's head. He wished he had superpowers and could beam himself to Chicago somehow. *Breathe, and keep your eyes on the road.*

He thought back to the short visit with Lori. The mental image of her cornflower-blue eyes helped him steady his breathing. He hated to wake her so early, since she had just come back from her father's funeral. She was drained already. On the sixth ring, her sleepy hello quickly changed to wide-awake alert after he identified himself. "Charlie? What's happened?"

He heard her fumble with her phone. Her voice changed registers as she fought to control it. "Is it Grace? Has she been found? Is she. . .?"

They had supported each other through various parenting crises before, but after fourteen months of no news, this was different. He heard the ragged sigh when he explained Grace was in a Chicago hospital and not found dead, the unspoken fear as time wore on.

He had wanted the next conversation with Lori to be about their future, but that would have to wait. Grace was his priority now, again. He knew Lori wouldn't have it any other way, but would it ever be their time?

A single porch light cast a feeble beam through the driving snow on the block of bungalows near the Two Harbors lighthouse. Lori Barnes met him at the steps. Her tall thin frame wrapped in a worn flannel robe, it was her cornflower-blue eyes that always caught his attention. Now, they looked concerned. His body warmed at the sight of her.

As he approached her, his usual restraint didn't work. He pulled her to him and breathed in her warm, sleepy essence until he felt her body soften and cling to him. "Lori, I don't deserve you, but I don't know what I would do without you."

"I know." She moved back a bit and stroked his face, tears in her eyes. "Go get our girl back. I'll be waiting right here. First things first." She kissed him gently on the cheek. There was no need for more discussion.

His heart filled with love and strength for the task at hand. He carted in Bailey's supplies, the dog loping beside him to get to Lori. "Not sure how long I'll be."

Lori bent down to accept the dog's affection. "Be careful. This has the makings of a blizzard and it's going your way."

"Yeah, I know." He had made first tracks on the road into town, and it hadn't been easy. But, after almost twenty years on the North Shore of Lake Superior, he knew how to drive in snow, and his four-wheel drive pickup would manage. "Good thing I'm leaving now." He glanced at his watch. 4:30 a.m. It had taken him forty minutes to drive in from his place on the Scenic Drive, midway between Two Harbors and Duluth. In the wrong direction.

"Good luck." She leaned in and gave him a tender hug. "Call me as often as you can."

"I will." He forced himself to move away from her. She handed him a thermos of coffee and a bag.

"Let me guess. Your homemade bread and P and J, right?" They shared the slightest of smiles before he followed his path through the six inches of fresh snow back to his truck.

Lori to the rescue again. A theme that was on repeat like a record stuck on an old phonograph. He was certain he needed Lori as his life partner going forward. With the mystery surrounding Grace, he knew he could count on her. Still shaken by the call from an unknown voice to get to Chicago as soon as possible, he hadn't questioned the authenticity of the call but had raced out the door, knowing Lori would take Bailey in the middle of the night.

Driving the divided highway between Two Harbors and Duluth was treacherous, but the few cars on the road were at least moving. Swirling snow, which danced as the gusts of snow blew it across the roadway, tricked the eye trying to follow any track through the deepening drifts. The various colors of white, gray, and crystalline contained in the northland light spectrum were designed to foil a driver amid the elements.

Charlie caught a break as the snowplow worked the north side of Highway 61 and he was heading south. It still took him an hour and a half to get to Duluth from Two Harbors, over twice as long as the usual time. He was relieved to get to Duluth, but the traffic was heavier, and it slowed him considerably. He counted fourteen cars off the road between Duluth and Sandstone, and then the freeway was closed at Hinckley. Not yet noon, the highway patrol was diverting traffic into town and recommending drivers hunker down for the duration.

Local hotels built around the casino were in for a midweek bonanza, but Charlie had other ideas.

His Ford-150 pickup could handle the road if a road were open. After a pit stop, he inquired about air travel. The patrolman obliged, "Nope, MSP is closed until further notice. They were down to just two runways earlier this morning, but now they're closed." Charlie's head pivoted back north. "And if you're thinking of the Duluth airport, it also closed early this morning."

If he'd left immediately after getting the call, would he have been able to get a flight out of Duluth? He could have left Bailey for Lori to deal with later, and maybe made it before the airport had closed. What was he thinking?

He got some coffee and gas at the Holiday station and overheard a conversation between a trucker and the cashier. "Yeah, I'm gonna have to haul ass now. Gotta be in Eau Claire by four. Looks like the storm track will wind down around nightfall in Milwaukee. So, I'm in for a hard day's drive."

"Excuse me, could I ask you how you're going to get to Eau Claire?" Charlie was desperate to find a way to Chicago.

The middle-aged trucker wore a scruffy Carhartt hat and jacket. He pushed his cap back farther on his head and studied Charlie. "Well, I'll take old highway twenty-three into the city, then . . . I don't think ninety-four is closed, so will take six ninety-four to get to that and hope that the road isn't too bad. But I've got a big heavy rig, I'm not sure it's a good idea for you, man."

"No, I'm sure it's not a good idea." Charlie smiled, hoping for a connection and some advice from this guy. "I've got to get to my daughter—just got a call that she's in the hospital in Chicago. So, it's not really optional. I do have a tough vehicle." He pointed toward his pickup.

"Ahh . . . I get it. Rough news. I got a few kids of my own." The trucker extended his hand. "Boyd Mueller." As he shook Charlie's hand he added, "Listen, you can follow me if you'd like. I'll have to be moving at a pretty fast clip, but at least you can have a bead on the road."

Charlie followed Boyd. White-knuckle driving. Slow going, then accidents to avoid, tow trucks and snowplows everywhere. Luckily, the interstate was open on the northern edge of the metro suburbs, and they could connect to Interstate 94 going east. Boyd signaled his turn off at Eau Claire and Charlie knew he needed to stop for a bit. He pulled off at a rest stop, ate the sandwich Lori had sent, and dozed off.

The glare of bright beam headlights startled him awake, breadcrumbs spilling from his shirt as he jerked, bumping his knee hard on the steering wheel. He glanced at his watch, thankful he had only napped a couple of hours. It was six o'clock at night. The lights from the rest stop building were bright against a dark sky, but the snow still swirled. He unspooled his body from the tight coil of a blanket he had wrapped himself in and rummaged around for the scraper. Three new inches piled on the cab of the truck. The rate of snow was at least diminishing.

He cleaned off the snow, cleared his windshield wipers, and bought some tea and a chocolate bar from the rest stop. He checked his navigation app and figured he could get to Madison in about three hours in good weather. He hoped for four tonight.

The roads were better. Plows had been out. There were few cars on the road. As he drove past the Wisconsin Dells, he recalled the trip to the water park that Mack's family and he and Lori and the girls had taken when they were around eleven years old . . . when Grace still loved him and thought of him as her hero. *I wonder what she thinks of me now.*

He pulled into a gas station outside of Madison just after nine thirty. He made a quick call to Lori to let her know where he was and that he was all right.

"We were so worried with the roads and airports closed. How did you do it?" she asked. Even Northlanders knew this had been a storm for the record books.

"Well, it wasn't easy, but I made it. Who's 'we'?"

"Mack knows. He was checking on my roof for snow load and noticed Bailey. He told Walt. Is there anything any of us can do?"

A lump formed in Charlie's throat as he considered his caring friends, still a revelation to the lost boy he often considered himself to be. "No, but it's nice to hear about the support. I'll let you know when I know something. I should get off the phone now. I'm going to call the hospital and try to make arrangements to see her whenever I get there, which should be in a few hours."

He gassed up the pickup, bought a large coffee, and swallowed some cheese crackers, then searched for the hospital number on his phone and called, nearly losing patience with how many taps it took to get to a human voice. Now that he was close and had come this far, he was keyed up to get to his daughter.

"I'm sorry, but I can't release the name of our patients, sir."

"I'm her father. A friend called me to come immediately. I'm almost there. I'll be there in a few hours. What can I do to convince you that I am her family?" Too late, he realized he should have taken the name and phone number of last night's caller.

"When you arrive and can demonstrate your family relationship, then we can release information for you if the patient is willing."

He continued arguing with her until he caught himself before becoming a total jerk, aware that his reunion with his daughter would require all of his emotional equilibrium. "I'll be there in three hours." He negotiated for an opening.

"Sir, there may not be any way to see her that late."

As he drew near, the hospital signs acted like well-lit landing beacons—homing devices. The houses in the neighborhood were close together, with some shoveled walks and yard lights. Then followed several in a row with ramshackle porches listing to one side. He stopped for a light, and a car next to him had such loud music on, he couldn't concentrate. His mind buzzed with anxiety that he needed to block, anyway. *How will I be received by my daughter? Does she know I'm coming?*

Fortunately, he found a well-lit underground parking entrance so he could finally get out of the weather, now just a mist of light rain. Bleary-eyed, he took several minutes to locate an elevator to the entry level of the hospital. He approached the entrance and tried the door. Locked. He looked around and found a buzzer to ring after-hours.

He rang and rang again after five minutes had passed. It was one thirty in the morning. He had been on his odyssey for almost twenty-four hours. Finally, he saw a silver-haired security guard ambling toward him. Thank God. But then his spirits sank when the guard didn't move to open the door but spoke to him through an intercom. "How can I help you?"

"I'm Charles Booker. I've just arrived from Minnesota. My daughter is here, and I've got to see her." He tried to speak plainly, so as not to spook the armed guard. He knew he looked disheveled at best.

"Admin is closed for the night. I have no way of confirming your daughter is here or allowing you in."

"I was told she's in trouble and to get here as soon as I could. With the weather, I was delayed. I believe she may be in bad shape. There must be something you can do."

"It would be best if you came back after eight, when admin can help you."

"She's in trouble. Please."

This time the guard replied, "Wait here, I'll check on something—no promises, though. What's her name?"

"Grace Booker. Thank you so much." Charlie finally exhaled.

"Don't thank me yet." The guard walked away.

Charlie, taking inventory of how he would look in preparation for reuniting with his daughter, felt the stubble on his face and put his hand through his hair, straightened up, and tucked his shirt into his pants under his pullover sweater. He just needed to look like himself, he thought, the father who loved her more than anything.

A few minutes later, the guard reappeared. "Your daughter's not here. We have no patient named Grace Booker."

"What?" Charlie's body deflated. "That can't be. I got a call to come quickly. She must be here."

The guard stood his ground while Charlie regrouped. "Hey, I don't know what else I can tell you. I did what I could do tonight. I don't know anything else. What I do know, is that you can't do anything more at two in the morning."

Charlie came to and finally registered the guard's words. "What can I do?" he whispered.

The guard pointed north. "There's a hotel just two blocks away, modest but safe. Go get some sleep and come back in the morning. Someone can help you sort this out. But nobody can help you tonight." The guard walked away. "Sorry."

Charlie couldn't move. His legs wouldn't work. He was stuck in place. Was this a bad joke? Had someone taken advantage of him and played him?

He tried to think back to the actual words spoken by the voice on the phone not quite twenty-four hours ago. "Your daughter's in the hospital. She wants you here. She needs you." He would never forget them. But had he misheard the hospital name? No, because the voice had given him the address in South Chicago, and that is where he was.

The second-guessing started his body moving. He grabbed his bag from the truck and found his way out of the underground garage and trying to stay true to the guard's outstretched directional wave of hand, headed north. After a block, he knew he was on the right track. Precipitation had stopped, and he stayed the course. When he arrived at the hotel, an intercom welcomed him. This time, entrance was granted.

With his last burst of energy coming from anger at possibly having been played, he wrote down three questions on the skinny hotel notepad and fell into bed. This time, he slept hard and fast.

Chapter 53

Y

Chicago, Illinois
January 16, 2017

Charlie woke up disoriented and thirsty. He felt the scratchy blanket on his face and remembered where he was. No reason to jump out of bed if he was the victim of a hoax. But what if he wasn't?

He pivoted in the bed to reach the pad of paper to read his questions from last night and grab the complimentary water bottle on the bedside table. He glanced at the hotel clock: 7:00 a.m. If Grace is not at Memorial, is there another hospital where she could be? How can I find out who called me? How do I get help at Memorial?

He was sure of one thing. He needed to shake off his weariness and find out what was going on. He took a long hot shower, shaved, put on clean clothes, and forced himself to eat breakfast. Then he retraced his steps back to Memorial, noting a clear blue sky and just a bit of ice on the sidewalks from the previous day's weather. January thaw in Chicago. Probably not in Minnesota quite yet.

He went to the main entrance of the hospital and walked into a well-appointed lobby with conversation nooks clustered in an attempt to make the busy hub less chaotic. It was 8:05 a.m. He was calm as he approached the reception desk. "Good morning. I was here early this morning looking for my daughter, who I have reason to believe is a patient here. I'm hoping you can help me."

"I'll need your name and identification, and of course, your daughter's name. How old is your daughter, sir?"

"Grace Booker. She's nineteen. I'm Charles Booker." He handed her his ID and watched her type in the information on her keyboard. After a few beats, she turned away from him to speak to a colleague, then handed him his ID. "Mr. Booker, it'll be a few minutes. Could I ask you to stand by, perhaps get some coffee, and we'll come and find you?" She pointed to the coffee bar in the corner of the lobby and smiled at him.

Charlie settled close by, so he could stay in the receptionist's sight. He texted Lori to let her know he was at the hospital and would give her an update when he could. Twenty minutes later, he was crossing the lobby back to reception to find out why he was still waiting when the young woman he had spoken to walked to meet him. "I was just coming to get you, Mr. Booker. Please come with me."

As they left the elevator to walk down a long corridor, he noted the absence of locked doors, a feature familiar to him from the psychiatric ward in Minnesota. Rather, there was a bustle of activity. He was ushered into an office where two women waited at a small round table. One, an older woman in a white coat and the other, maybe in her thirties, with a mass of curly red hair. The older woman stretched out her hand and spoke first. "Mr. Booker, I'm Dr. Joanna Pries. And this is—"

The younger woman rose and greeted him. "I'm Daisy Morse. I'm the person who called you."

"Yes, I recognize your voice. I appreciate the call. Where's Gracie?"

"There is no easy way to tell you this. You're in for a surprise. Before you see her, we thought it best to prepare you." Dr. Pries spoke slowly.

Charlie crumpled into a chair and heard his own voice distantly asking, "What? Prepare me for what?"

"Grace is recovering nicely." Dr. Pries looked from Charlie to Daisy as if to signal her, and then added, "I understand you have not seen your daughter for over a year?"

"Yes, she ran away from home fourteen months ago. I've been searching for her ever since." His voice caught.

Daisy poured him a glass of water and handed it to him. "Mr. Booker, Grace has been living in a residence with me for the past six months."

"A residence? For her psychological issues?"

"Yes, although I can tell you that she was stable and taking her medications. She was ready to reconcile with you, looking forward to it, but she wanted to finish something first," Daisy said.

Charlie looked to Dr. Pries. "Are you her psychiatrist? What happened? Did she suffer a psychotic break?" Charlie saw the two women share a long look. "Tell me, for God's sake, tell me how she is."

"It's not what you think. Grace is fine. And she just gave birth to a healthy baby girl." Dr. Pries glanced at Daisy quickly. "Grace was a great patient and had a normal childbirth. I'm your daughter's obstetrician."

Charlie gasped. "What?" He glared at both women. *Who are these strangers?*

Daisy spoke. "I know this must be an incredible shock to you. We can answer all of your questions. Dr. Pries can explain to you how she is clinically, or you can wait to hear about that later."

"Childbirth?" Stunned, Charlie scanned the room and noticed a framed diploma on the wall and what looked to be an ultrasound machine in the corner.

"Grace is in a good place. She made all of the necessary accommodations for her pregnancy. She was very motivated to have a healthy outcome." Daisy spoke slowly again.

The doctor said, "She was a model patient. I have a special relationship with patients who are in care with Daisy, and I can tell you that Grace was very excited to become a mother. And to surprise you."

"Her obstetrician." Charlie studied the writing on the doctor's white coat. Dr. Pries, OB-GYN. "This isn't a psychiatric hospital?" Charlie had spent the last forty-eight hours conjuring up worst-case scenarios of how he would find Grace once he got to Chicago. This scenario was so out of the realm of possibilities, he couldn't escape his disbelief.

"Although there is a psychiatric program here and it is where Grace sought care for her psychological issues, she was admitted to the OB unit to deliver her baby," Dr. Pries said.

"Baby. My baby gave birth to a baby?" Charlie tried out the words he didn't yet comprehend.

Relieved, they both replied in unison, "Yes."

"I need to see her—now." He stood up.

"Of course you do. She's resting, but let me take you to her," Daisy said.

Dr. Pries excused herself, and Daisy led Charlie to an elevator and one floor up where patients' rooms lined both sides of a hallway.

"Here we are," Daisy said when they arrived outside of Grace's room, the door ajar. "I'll be down the hall," she said, and she disappeared.

Charlie stood still and took a breath. He took a step into the room and peeked around the door. The lights were low, just an overhead light strip turned down. He entered near the foot of the bed, stepping lightly, and peered at the head of the bed as he approached.

There she was. His beautiful daughter, asleep, her face peaceful. It reminded him of how she looked when she was very young, his sleeping angel. Her hair had grown out, and it spread in dark waves across the pillow. She looked healthy and was so deeply asleep that she didn't hear his approach. *Thank God. It's my girl.*

He quietly left her room and closed the door, finally exhaling in relief.

Daisy was waiting and walked to meet him. "You're right, she needs her rest," he said, but he was beaming.

"Yes, it was a long labor. She's tired. If it's OK with you, I'd like to take you to the residence and show you her room. I believe it will help you to see how she was living."

Charlie nodded. They walked east from the hospital, and Daisy maintained a constant hum of inconsequential chatter. He liked her voice—not a fluffy voice, but resonant and sure. She spoke with authority and confidence. He was glad her voice was in Gracie's life. They arrived at a three-story brownstone with wide steps at the entry and large stone flowerpots with evergreen boughs circled with unlit twinkly lights.

Inside, a coatrack at the entry led to a large room with lamps placed by comfortable reading chairs. A worn couch and decidedly cast-off coffee table marked with many years of cup stains stood at the periphery of the room. A large rag rug brightened the room with its bold colors, which didn't match anything else in the room.

"This is the living room, and the kitchen is in the back. Residents sign up for an evening meal each week, for which they are responsible. Gracie is a good baker, and her snickerdoodle cookies are a favorite of the house."

Charlie walked as if transfixed to the far corner of the room where an old upright piano stood, missing ivory on several keys and a faded and unraveling cushion on the rickety piano seat. He touched it and the keyboard, then glanced back at Daisy.

"Yes, she played. It was an icebreaker to get to know the girls here, and they had a music night each week. In the past several months, she played quite a bit. Said it relaxed her."

She led him up the stairs to Grace's room. Each room's door had a poster board for messages and notes, decorated by the occupant. He stopped to study his daughter's choice—a photo of Lake Superior's Hawk Ridge taken from a magazine. He read a note to her that was pinned on the board—"Are you willing to switch meal nights this week?"—decorated with a smiley face, and one that stopped his heart—"Can't wait to meet your little one"—posted with a picture of a more mature Grace, large with child, smiling broadly. Her skin glowed, and her eyes were bright.

Her room was modest. A single bed, simple chest of drawers, and a small closet with a minimum of clothes hanging. She had several books in a pile on her nightstand. *How to Have a Healthy Baby*, and *Anxiety and Pregnancy*. Charlie picked up the one titled, *How to Survive a Narcissistic Mother* and paged through it to see several highlighted areas.

Daisy noticed his interest. "She was finally able to talk about her mother in therapy. I believe it was helping her."

With that simple statement, Charlie realized how much Daisy knew about his daughter and her trials. "Please tell me how you came to know my daughter and about her time here," he asked.

They sat, Charlie on Grace's bed, and Daisy on the only chair. "I can tell you what I know. But perhaps not all you wish to know. You'll be able to talk to her yourself, at the right time."

"That's fair." After a fourteen-month search for a runaway adult child, he was eager for any information. "Please."

"Grace was living in a shelter when we met. My program, Angels for Angie, stays in touch with the homeless to try to help those ready to get off the street. There are several programs prepared to help, and we all watch over the youth we find to monitor. It was clear that Grace, who went by the name of Janie Blank, was nearing a crisis. We watched her closely. When she bolted into the street, we intervened and had her assessed, with her permission, of course." Daisy glanced out the window, and Charlie realized he didn't want to know more than she was willing to tell him.

"Janie Blank," he repeated.

"During the assessment, we discovered she was pregnant. We also discovered she had been taking a variety of street drugs but wasn't addicted, so we were able to start treating her mental illness. In time, she was able to comprehend her situation. She was not aware she was pregnant and couldn't tell us anything about the paternity of the child. She was likely embarrassed to admit to a level of promiscuity or even the occasional trade of sex for drugs. She never attempted to contact anyone, and nobody has come looking for her. There doesn't seem to be a father candidate in the picture. The only friend she talked about was an Abby, but then only in passing, as she seemed to have felt let down by this friend, who was supposed to meet up with her here in Chicago."

Charlie blanched at the mention of paternity, but he didn't pursue it. At *the right time, when she's ready to share, she'll tell me.* "Abby was a friend from home who was in juvie when Grace left. They had been friends in rehab earlier." Suddenly, he was able to connect the dots on a plan the girls may have hatched to start over together in a big city.

"Ahh . . ." Daisy replied. "That's maybe why Grace held onto the alias for so long."

They both stopped to consider this for a moment. Then Daisy continued, "I want you to understand that her last months, her months here with us, were good. She was making friends with some of the other girls here and had taken some interest in a program we offer to help young women prepare for the work force. Two weeks ago, she passed her GED, and we had a great celebration. She made herself very helpful here at the residence and was realistic but optimistic about her future. She was not a suicide risk. She wanted to live for her baby."

Charlie's eyes were full as he listened to this last bit. He wanted one more piece of information to make sense of the last two days. "When exactly did she give birth?" He had to know if he could have made it to her in time.

Daisy folded her hands in her lap and took a moment, perhaps to gain her own composure. "The baby came just a few hours after I called. I'm so sorry for all of the mystery—to put you through that. I didn't know it was that close." Tears threatened in Daisy's eyes. "I tried for over a month to have Grace reach out to you, but she was committed to waiting until after the birth to inform you. I work hard to gain the trust of my residents and couldn't break the promise I made to Grace. She changed her mind during the last phase of labor and wanted her father to be there with her. I'm not sure if it was the pain talking, or if she realized late that she wanted you to witness this monumental life event." She searched his face for forgiveness.

Charlie rose and went to her. He guided her off the chair. "It's not your fault. I understand. You did so much for my Grace." They stood and cried together, hand in hand.

Daisy finally broke away and left the room briefly. She came back with a letter. "She wanted me to mail this to you the moment the baby was born. I'll give you some privacy to read it. I'll be downstairs."

Charlie felt his legs give way just as he backed into Gracie's bed, where he sat to read the message from his daughter.

Dear Dad,
I hope you are sitting down. I know it's been over a
year since we have been in touch. I'm sorry for that.

And for putting you through the worst nightmare that a parent could have. I did it to save myself and to save you. I know now it was the wrong way to do it, but at the time, I felt it was my only option.

I'm stronger now and have learned to separate out my feelings for you—love—from those I can't help but feel toward my mother—a terrible mix of distrust and guilt. I always worried that you would leave me to join Mom, and that fear took over. I couldn't share the fear with you because I thought maybe you would be better off without me ruining your life. I've been working through these feelings with my therapist and am finally making some headway. Maybe, eventually, I will be able to make sense of it all. I need to try because I have an important new role in my life.

By now, when you receive this letter, you will be a grandfather. Yes, I am a mother! And so excited about it!

Please don't worry about me. I'm in the best shape I've been in for years emotionally, and my illness is under control. I have an amazing support system here in Chicago and have been well taken care of these past months.

Dad, I know this is a shock. I wanted to write you so you could take some time to think about the news and consider my request. I know I have let you down, frightened you, and have no right to expect anything from you. I would love to raise my child in Two Harbors, so that he or she would be able to experience the same love and support I felt during my childhood. I miss you terribly, Dad.

I have no cell phone, but when you are ready, please contact Daisy Morse. She is my best friend in the world and has been keeping me safe.

Love,

Gracie

Charlie reread the message, and then read his daughter's revelation aloud. "I always worried that you would leave me to join Mom." He thought back to when Gracie found the letter to him from Caroline pressuring him to join her in Portugal. He had tried to reassure her, but now he understood it hadn't worked. *Gracie thought she was holding me back!* He was overwhelmed, thinking of the burden she carried alone all of this time. He got up and paced the small room until he could move on.

It was the ask in her letter that nearly broke his heart. Asking for something that he had been praying for . . . having her home with him. The baby—his own flesh and blood—to help raise? He thought about the irony of this happening just as he decided to close the search for his own family of origin. *My own granddaughter.*

He thanked God she had found this room to take refuge in. He needed it himself. His emotions overwhelmed him with past regrets and future opportunities. *I can't blow it this time.*

Chapter 54

Chicago, Illinois
January 16, 2017

The wooden stairs squeaked with Charlie's steps as he finally left Grace's room and headed downstairs. Daisy heard him and met him at the landing.

"Join me in the kitchen for some soup." She led him into a cheery room painted bright yellow and bordered by stencils of flowers and bees near the ceiling. A checkerboard oilcloth on the built-in table and window seat had been laid out with two bowls on simple place settings.

"Tracy made this soup for you as a gesture of goodwill on behalf of all of the girls here. They are very fond of your daughter and wanted you to know how much they thought of Janie—I mean Grace."

"Where are the girls?" Charlie was touched but curious as to where everyone was.

"They're out and about. Some go to school, some are working, and a couple are in day rehab. Each day is a little different." She beckoned him to sit and served the homemade vegetable soup. She brought some bread and butter to the table.

"How are you holding up?" Daisy asked. He ignored the question and sat down.

"Mr. Booker. This situation is a lot for you to cope with. Reuniting with a runaway daughter, trying to understand what she has been through over these past months, then discovering that she has given birth to a child is a tough, tough thing to cope with. I want you to know that you can take some time to take it all in. It's the best way."

"I appreciate your concern. I saw my daughter through a suicide attempt, a long hospitalization and rehab follow-up, a very rough patch after that, and then the unknown when she went missing. I can tell you with certainty that the unknown was the worst of all of it." Charlie caught himself, then corrected. "I just need to process all of this . . . news." He picked up his spoon but didn't use it.

She started on her soup and gestured for him to do the same. "You need to eat and keep yourself nourished. Try to get rest when you can. You'll have some decisions to make soon."

After they finished eating, she put on her jacket and pulled her hair back into a clip. "Let's take a walk while I tell you about the baby. They'll be ready for our visit in forty-five minutes." She led him out of the kitchen, then quickly doubled back for a small bag that was on the countertop, wrapped with ribbon. "Snickerdoodles. For later."

As they walked a longer route back to the hospital, she started to talk. "The baby, a girl, is healthy and arrived just a week before her due date. The toxicology screen was clear. We expected that. Grace hasn't taken any street drugs since she came to the program and has been on pregnancy safe medications for her depression."

Charlie was quiet, but as if Daisy could read his mind, she went on. "While there is a familial factor to certain conditions, in Grace's case, it is a small likelihood. Nurture or environment often is the deciding factor over nature or genetic factors. It doesn't follow that this baby will suffer due to her mother's health issues. As I told you earlier, we don't know about paternity, so we can't state any medical history on that side."

Charlie's body was shaky in anticipation of meeting his new granddaughter. "Will I be able to hold her?"

"I believe you will." Daisy smiled. "We'll ask."

"Mr. Booker, I have not read the letter that Grace wrote to you, but she disclosed to me her intent about the baby. I advised her to contact you earlier, but as I mentioned, she wanted to wait until she had an accomplishment to announce, as she had let you down so often. The State of Illinois regards Grace as the responsible party as she is over eighteen. It was Grace's wish for you to care for the child in the event of her death. She is fully capable of making a life for herself and her child, but perhaps not right now. I know Grace's hope was to go home to Minnesota and live with you and her baby. Are you willing to take on this responsibility?" She stopped and looked directly at him.

He gaped at her. *Does she actually think I would consider leaving Gracie on her own?* "Yes. Yes, Daisy, of course, absolutely," he practically shouted. "I wouldn't have it any other way. I can't believe you would even question that. How could you think—" but his words were cut off when Daisy wrapped her arms around him and gave him a bear hug.

"Thank God!" Daisy said aloud as she let him loose. "Mr. Booker, let's go meet your granddaughter."

Feeling lighter yet more grounded than at any other time that day, Charlie matched her stride as they finished the short walk to the hospital and this time went to the hospital nursery.

His first impression as they rounded the corner from the elevator was how whisper quiet it seemed. All the doors off the corridor were closed, and Daisy went ahead of him to find the doctor who was expecting them. As he waited, he was aware of how calm he felt. No matter how uncommon the feeling was for him, he decided not to let it make him anxious but just to accept the moment for what it was. A miracle.

"Mr. Booker, I'm Dr. Balmadi. Baby Booker's pediatrician. I would love the privilege of introducing you to your granddaughter." She shook his hand and kept it in hers. "Would you like that?"

"Yes, very much." Charlie instantly liked this warm personality.

Still holding his hand, she continued to smile, and asked softly, "Are you ready?"

Charlie looked at Daisy and then replied with confidence, "I'm ready."

Dr. Balmadi took his arm and led him to the small nursery. "Your baby Booker is a very healthy young lady. She is a pediatrician's dream and has passed all of her baby tests already." She included Daisy in the conversation. "Daisy has visited her several times to make sure she isn't lonely, isn't that right, Daisy?"

The two women escorted him to the middle of the nursery where a small isolette held this precious baby, Grace's daughter. Swaddled in hospital-issue print and a pink beanie, she was sleeping peacefully, unaware of the world beyond. He thought back to Grace as a newborn; beyond the pink skin and tiny nose, he couldn't claim a resemblance. But he could instantly claim his love for her.

He felt the tears stream down his face as he said, "She's beautiful."

The two women joined him and gazed down at his baby. "Yes, she's very beautiful," Daisy said, a little tremor in her voice.

"And healthy, too!" Dr. Balmadi added, placing her hand on his shoulder. "Would you like to hold her? She is due to wake up hungry in about ten minutes. And then we'll be waking Mom, your daughter. You can do the honors if you're up for it?"

"I am. I hope I haven't lost my touch. It's been nineteen years since I held a baby."

"No worries. It comes back in a flash. There's a rocker over here for your use." She directed him to a corner of the nursery to wash up and put on a gown. As if on cue, Baby Booker started to whimper and her bottom lip quivered.

Charlie, washed and gowned, waited for a nod from the doctor before he scooped the child up and held her close. As he nestled her in his arms, he took in her baby smell and felt her heft. He would get used to this again. His eyes clear and his heartbeat even, he felt himself exude a strength that he hoped would transmit directly to this new little person because that's what fathers and grandfathers did.

Both the doctor and Daisy left him to get acquainted with Baby Booker. One thought still fought for his attention. *I need to see my daughter.*

Chapter 55

Chicago, Illinois
January 16, 2017

Grace awakened slowly, as if from a dream, with conflicting sensations. First, her body felt empty, and yet, her breasts were swollen. She put it together fast and got up quickly to look around for her baby. Near panic, she remembered the nurse had taken the baby back to the nursery to allow her some uninterrupted sleep. "You'll thank me when you get some rest," she had said cheerfully.

She sat again, hard, then realized she was sore. She put her hand on her heart to try to physically stop it from racing. *The baby's in the nursery!* She let the smile starting at the corners of her mouth spread wide and hugged her body in joy. From the moment she was told she was pregnant, she had focused on how to keep her baby safe. *The baby, my baby, I did it!*

Grace felt her chest expand. It took her a minute to recognize the feeling—pride. It had been so long. Now, she thought she might float away on it. Her baby was healthy, she was a high school graduate, and she was looking forward to living a full life. Others had supported her getting to where she was now, but it was time for her to acknowledge how hard she herself had worked. She was confident in her ability to find her way, although she knew she'd need some help.

Dad. Daisy had called him, but would he come? She wished now she had not insisted that Daisy call him, and that she had stuck with the plan to send a letter, which he could ignore if he chose. She had treated him so badly that he had reasons not to want anything more to do with her. Was he with her mother, and was she even in Minnesota with him now? Had he left to join her in Portugal? She couldn't face her mother, she knew that. Why would she think her father would still want her in his life, especially now that she had a baby? Why had she ever thought this would work?

Not every father would accept this grandchild. But, not every father was an orphan. She hoped her intuition was right; her father would want to help her and would lovingly accept this grandchild.

She got up and took several deep breaths. She remembered Dr. Spencer warned her that the wild ride of childbirth might play havoc with her meds. She decided to walk down to the nursery, growing anxious to see her newborn.

She was slowly taking steps in the hallway when she saw him heading her way. Time stopped. He had aged, by more than just a year. The straight bearing, flannel shirt, jeans, and hiking boots all spelled Dad. She wished she could watch him awhile, maybe catch something in his expression that would give her a hint about how he felt about her, but he was focused on checking room numbers and hadn't yet noticed her. Suddenly aware that she was dressed in a wrinkled hospital gown covered with a thin robe, she quickly tied the sash and wished she were wearing something more appropriate for this important meeting.

When he was about to close the distance between them, she spoke. "Daddy. You came."

He stopped in his tracks at her voice. Grace trembled as she locked eyes with her father. He moved to her quickly with outstretched arms to embrace the daughter he hadn't seen in fourteen months.

"I'm here." Tears came easily then, and they held onto each other for a long time, swaying in each other's arms. As he allowed them up for air, he said, "I'll always be here, Gracie."

Grace's nurse approached to tell them she would bring the baby to her room in a few minutes, so they could catch up a bit first. Charlie took her hand in his and put his arm around her shoulder as they returned to her room. When he had tucked her into her bed, she whispered through her tears, "I'm so sorry for running away like I did."

"I know you are. I'm sorry you felt you needed to."

"Can you ever forgive me?"

"Of course. You were always forgiven. I'm so happy you were ready to be found, and that Daisy was in your life to help you when you needed it so badly. I am forever grateful to her."

"Yes, she saved me." Grace smiled broadly. "I'm so glad you're here. When did you get here? Have you seen the baby? Why didn't you wake me?"

Charlie laughed lightly. "Got here in the wee hours of the morning, too late to come in. Didn't wake you as you clearly needed to sleep, but I did sneak a peek at you to settle my heart . . . and yes, I did see the baby. She's beautiful. Perfect. Does she have a name yet?"

"No, but I have some ideas." A flash of caution reminded her that tomorrow would come soon enough to get to that.

"Well, princess, I'm sure you'll pick the perfect name for her when it's time. I know you'll be an incredible mother."

Grace appreciated the vote of confidence. There were so many things to be discussed; she was no longer willing to be estranged from her father, her only parent. If her life and the health of her baby were to be secure, she and her father would have to dig deep into their past relationship to find a way to trust one another again. The question in the air, that she dared not yet ask, would he invite her and the baby to come home with him?

For today, it was enough to witness the first family gathering of her father, herself, and her daughter. She'd deal with the rest of it tomorrow.

Chapter 56

Y

Chicago, Illinois
January 16, 2017

Later that afternoon, Charlie had a long and emotional phone conversation with Lori. While he had barely been able to process the information over the course of the entire day, recounting it to someone else made it real. He was ecstatic and a wreck all over again.

"She's beautiful," he said with a tremulous voice. "My granddaughter is a beauty."

"I can barely take it all in. I'm so relieved that our Gracie is well, and whole." Charlie could almost see Lori's eyes light up as she spoke. "And you know this means that we'll have the fun of a grandchild! Does she have a name yet?"

Charlie laughed. "Nope, but Gracie says she has a few ideas. She'll choose well, I'm sure."

Daisy stayed with him. At her urging, they moved his truck from the expensive hospital parking ramp to the free hotel parking garage, and then had snickerdoodles in the truck before heading back to the hospital to check on Grace and the baby. By now, she was finally calling him Charlie.

Over dinner in the hotel restaurant, Daisy raised the question of Caroline. "I gather that Grace's mom hasn't been in the picture for quite some time."

Charlie felt the old defenses rise up at the sound of Caroline's name. "That's right. She's been teaching in Europe for a few years now. Quite the reputation as a world-class ornithologist."

He realized she was trying to tell him someone should notify Caroline of their daughter's whereabouts and about the baby. His body grew cold, as if a stiff wind had just knocked him down. For a moment, he couldn't breathe.

"Charlie, what's wrong?" Daisy asked, concerned.

"I guess I hadn't thought that far about Grace's mother being told." He tried to regulate his breathing. "That will be difficult."

"Difficult how? You don't know how to reach her, or the conversation will be difficult?"

Daisy asked.

He was silent a beat too long. Reading his discomfort, Daisy said, "Well, think about it overnight. We've got some other things to discuss and arrangements to be made, but it can all wait until morning. You look exhausted, with good reason. Let's call it a night."

"Daisy, there's something you should know. Caroline and I are divorced. It's pretty recent. Of course Grace doesn't know. I'd like your advice on how this should be handled, given Grace's feelings toward her mother." He played with the napkin on his plate.

"That does change things somewhat regarding communicating with Caroline." Daisy drummed her fingers on the tabletop, her brow furrowed.

"How so?"

"Well, Grace is nineteen and independent and wishes for you to be her responsible support. She has asked to go home with you to Two Harbors and with your assistance, raise her child." Daisy counted off each point on her fingers. "It's up to her to communicate this information to her mother, if and when she chooses. It's not your responsibility."

"It's her news to share, and I play no role here?"

"That's one way of saying it." Daisy and Charlie shared a long look before Daisy continued.

"Grace is still dealing with the effects of what she considers to be a toxic mother. It's up to her to decide the timing of any such reconciliation. She has two big transitions to get through right now: motherhood and a return to your home. That's enough to deal with."

Charlie puzzled between Caroline and Grace as he had for so many years. He knew Daisy was right. It was Grace's decision, and she was his priority. However, it felt wrong not to tell Caroline.

Until he remembered the stunt she pulled not listing Grace as a dependent on the divorce papers. He felt a seismic shift in his universe that shook him to the core but left him weightless.

He left Daisy and was just back in his room when his phone rang. It was Lori.

"Mack and I are flying out day after tomorrow, in the morning. It's all arranged, but I need the name of your hotel. We'll probably have to stay a night or two to help you get everything sorted out."

As if she expected him to start to fuss, she was ready with her argument. "There's no way you can get Grace and a newborn baby back home without help. Accept it, Charlie. It's happening."

He knew that voice. "Lori, I'm thrilled with this plan and thank you for your kind offer. We're family. Of course I want you here. I'm so excited for you to see Grace and meet the baby."

With that image in his head, he slept better than he had in months. Tomorrow he would have help to sort out the rest of it.

Chapter 57

Chicago, Illinois
January 17, 2017

As sleepy as Grace was, she couldn't nap. She gazed at the bassinet, just three feet from her own hospital bed. The little pink cherub bundle slept still as a statue, but then her little mouth suddenly quivered and made a sucking motion. Grace beamed as she pulled up the blankets to her chest, careful to avoid too much pressure on her breasts.

She thought back to the previous afternoon when her father excused himself so she could nurse her baby, commenting, "Your mom didn't nurse you. I'm glad you made this choice."

She didn't trust her response. "I wouldn't have it any other way. It's the best nutrition choice you can make, and my immunities pass right to her. I'll be nursing her. Do you think she looks like me?" She steered the subject away from the topic of her mother.

"She does. I know the hair is right. And the shape of her head." He shrugged. "It's been a while, princess. Babies don't come into their own for a few months. We'll see a resemblance when she's home for a bit, I'm sure."

She felt her body tense, jostling the baby a bit. When she trusted herself to sound calm, she asked, "When you say home, does that mean Two Harbors?"

"Of course it does." Charlie realized his intentions had not been clear to her. He dashed over to put his hand on her shoulder. "That's still your home. I'm thrilled to have found you and to bring you and the baby home. It's exactly right. I've missed you, Grace. I've worried about you for so long, it's like a dream come true to find you."

"Daisy gave you my letter then?"

"Yes, she did." Charlie met her eyes. "I'm so sorry you worried that I would leave you to join your mother. I didn't know." He kissed her cheek. "I would never have abandoned you."

"I know that now but didn't at the time." She hesitated slightly. "I was pretty messed up about things then. It was a hard time for me."

"I understand." Charlie's voice was steady and sure. "But now, thanks to Daisy, we have our family back."

"Our family. That has a nice ring to it, doesn't it?"

"Yes, you, me, and the baby."

"You know I've been staying on my meds and will do whatever it takes to stay healthy."

"Yes, I know."

"Do you have any questions about anything? Anything that's happened?" Grace dared to ask, her voice a bit shaky.

"Not anything that needs discussion now. It's enough that you are healthy, we have a beautiful baby to raise, and you want to bring her home."

"Thanks." Grace exhaled slowly. *That's the Dad I remember.* However, it didn't stop her from wondering where her mother was.

Chapter 58

Chicago, Illinois
January 17, 2017

Daisy caught up with Charlie having breakfast in the hotel restaurant. "Mind if I join you for a cup of coffee before you head to the hospital?"

He noticed a slight strained look on her face as he flagged down the waitress for another cup. "How are you Daisy? Anything wrong?"

She smiled at him. "Sorry, I'm just a bit distracted." She pulled her puffy coat off and settled in the booth. "Overall, I'd say things are going very well. Grace is so forward-thinking. She's motivated to make a new life for herself and be strong for her baby. I'm amazed, actually."

"But?" Charlie poured coffee into her newly arrived cup.

"Well, these things tend to go smoothly until they don't, and I want to avoid any bumps." Her eyes fell to the book, *How to Survive a Narcissistic Mother,* which she slid over to him on the tabletop.

"The book Grace was reading, right?"

"Yes. It was helpful in getting Grace to open up about her feelings, talking about how she felt growing up, how she related to her mother." She took a sip of coffee. "Last night I was boxing up a few of Grace's belongings, and I found a letter in the book. She had not shared it with me earlier."

Charlie paged through the book and found a piece of light blue stationery, folded and folded again. He opened it to find *CTB* scripted at the top. What was Caroline's stationery doing in this book? He read it.

Dear Charlie,

My patience is rapidly giving way to bitterness. I have asked you repeatedly to join me. Now that Grace is not a factor, there's nothing to keep you in Two Harbors. You can't possibly be satisfied with that hick town and plebeian job teaching high school—you are better than that! That is not the life for us!

I'm truly sorry Grace is sick, but now she can be placed in a facility that can handle people like her. You recall how I didn't want a baby. I think of this as fate. A chance for us to have the life we were meant to have.

I want you. I need you. But I won't wait forever.

Charlie rubbed his chin. "My God, this one passed by me. I've never seen this." Gracie must have picked up the mail before he did one day and taken this letter. He remembered how upset she had been when Caroline's letter had arrived in the fall of her junior year, which probably caused her relapse. She must have been watching for other letters, not knowing he had taken himself out of Caroline's orbit. This one would have shaken her the most. If only she had talked to him about it. However, by then, she didn't trust him to keep her safe.

He crumpled the letter in his fist. "What a terrible thing for Grace to read, and then keep to herself. Did she ever speak to you about it in general?" he asked.

"No. I worked hard on having her open up and share her fears and to talk about her mother with her therapist. This letter is clearly motivation for Grace to panic. Knowing what her mother declared about her hopes, in a letter to her father, certainly gave Grace plenty of reasons to run away from that situation. I've seen lots of situations of conflict with couples over troubled children. It's not unheard of for one partner to want to abandon their child, unable or unwilling to cope. It can be a tough life to help a child navigate through their issues."

"Caroline didn't want children." He carefully opened that door a crack to Daisy wondering if she would open it. He clenched his jaw. "Basically, she wanted me to shelve our daughter and join her on her romps around the world . . ." With that statement, he signaled the end of making excuses for his ex-wife.

"Given what I've learned about Caroline, Grace had every reason to react to her mother's behavior toward her. Clearly, she was fragile, and it's my guess that Caroline's emotional abuse exacerbated her anxiety and depression to crisis proportions at various times."

Daisy caught her breath, her rapid-fire words like bullets in intensity. She slowed down. A sad half-smile appeared on her face before she continued. "Children can be badly damaged by toxic mothers. Grace's escape was a cry for help, for her own survival. Her desire to reconnect with you and have you help her raise her child is proof she realized she had misjudged you—that you were her staunch supporter throughout her life. She believes that."

"I hope so." He exhaled finally. "You really think so?"

"Yes, I believe she trusts you. This letter clearly explains why Grace was motivated to run away."

Charlie stared at the crumpled letter on the table. Neither spoke for a few minutes. "I failed my daughter miserably. She didn't feel protected from her mother. She thought I might have given up on her. What should I do? How can I make this right?"

"Has Grace asked you anything about her mother since you've been here?"

"No. The last thing she knew about her mom was that she was in Lisbon teaching and in no hurry to come back to Minnesota. She may just assume that's the situation."

"Or she's afraid to ask," Daisy replied. "Let's give her a little more time. Are you OK if I sit with the two of you to counsel you a bit about the transition home?"

"Thank God." Charlie let out a deep breath. "As happy as I am to have Grace and the baby with me, I can admit to you that I'm a little nervous about what she'll need and whether I'm equipped." His thoughts of past worries and events came to the forefront of his mind.

"This will be the perfect opening to set the expectation for family counseling for the two of you going forward." Daisy took out her phone to make a note. "I assume you have someone in the area?"

Charlie had felt exposed when Daisy learned the worst of his family problems and was grateful she knew him now as a loving parent trying to do his best. He thought of Dr. Chester and Mrs. Schiff and how perhaps he should have insisted on more than just a session or two when she was first discharged to home. "Yes and yes."

"This will be ongoing. There's no quick fix to any of this."

"What do I say about Caroline?"

"Follow my lead on that part, and we'll see how that goes."

Chapter 59

Chicago, Illinois
January 17, 2017

Daisy pulled the door of the small conference room shut and sat across from Grace and Charlie, her demeanor professional, her smile warm. "I'm happy to give you two a little advice to guide your transition home." Grace watched her dad as he leaned in attentively.

"I know you are both very happy to be reunited and highly motivated to make your family work. The challenge is that you have been apart for the past fourteen months. You will need to build trust with one another based on your changed circumstances. It won't all be easy." Daisy paused. "It's OK to acknowledge that neither of you have a one hundred percent trust level to fall back on right now. Your relationship has been strained."

Grace's face flushed.

"You need to give yourselves time and space to get to know one another again. Be patient and respectful to each other as adults. Communicate honestly. Hear each other out. I recommend starting a habit of check-ins with each other as a regular part of each day."

Grace shifted in her chair so that she was angled to see her dad's face. He turned slightly and smiled at her as he put his arm on the back of her chair.

"We can do that, right, Gracie?" he asked.

Grace nodded.

"It's not a secret that Grace is emotionally vulnerable and needs support to manage her anxiety and depression. Grace and Dr. Spencer, her doctor here, have agreed on a plan for her care in Minnesota. I'm also very happy that both of you have agreed to counseling with a mutually agreeable therapist on a regular basis."

Daisy pulled a stray curl out of her face. "I know you two will make a success of it." She smiled brightly. "Your newborn will keep you both on your toes!" Daisy chuckled then and Charlie and Grace joined in, all of them a bit more relaxed.

"Now, before I leave you two, is there anything we haven't covered?" Daisy asked.

"Yes." Grace turned to face her dad. She forced her voice to sound even. "Where's Mom in all of this? You haven't mentioned her at all. Daisy hasn't said anything about her. What's going on?" Grace clutched the arms of her seat with both hands. "Tell me, please."

Charlie met Grace's eyes, then looked to Daisy for confirmation to go forward.

"Your mother and I are divorced. I haven't seen her since she flew over when you were first hospitalized in Minneapolis. The divorce was handled through attorneys and was final about a month ago."

Grace loosened her fingers from the chair. She tried to swallow, but her throat tightened. She finally got the words out. "Why, Dad? Tell me why. It's because of me, isn't it?" She thought back to the years of feeling that she was the spoiler between her parents, the reason her mother was never happy with her around.

Charlie took her hands from the chair. "No, it's not because of you. It's because of who your mother revealed herself to be, and it just took me a long time to realize that."

"You're just saying that. You have to blame me for it. You'd be with her now, if it weren't for me, my illness. Be honest with me." Grace's voice was barely a whisper.

"I'm being totally honest. I feel very guilty not to have seen the damage she was causing both of us. I'm sorry, Gracie." Charlie's voice cracked, and his eyes filled with tears.

"You don't communicate with her at all?" Grace asked her father.

"No. The last time we talked was when I told her you had run away."

Grace's face grew thoughtful, and then she asked Daisy. "Is there any requirement that we have to tell her about the baby, or that I'm safe?"

"No. You're over eighteen and a fully responsible adult. Your parents are divorced, and your father will be taking you home to Minnesota. It's up to you what you communicate to your mother, if anything," Daisy stated.

A peace descended on Grace that she hadn't known for years. She allowed herself a small smile.

"Grace, you—" Charlie began.

"Dad, I know we just agreed to listen to each other. But please don't make this hard for me. It's my decision, and I won't do it. I will not subject my daughter to my mother. End of discussion." Grace looked to Daisy, then both turned to Charlie.

"Princess, what I was going to say is that you have my full support on whatever you decide."

Grace broke the tension with a loud exhalation followed by a hearty laugh. "Oh, Dad!"

They all joined in Grace's laugh of relief.

Chapter 60

Chicago, Illinois
January 18, 2017

Charlie slept in and then immediately went to the hospital to see Grace and the baby. He stopped by the nursery first but found it empty. All the babies were rooming in with their moms. He headed toward Grace's room and heard the baby squealing loudly when he knocked on her door. Baby Booker was bonding with her mom.

"Good morning. Sounds like someone is hungry?" Charlie's heart filled when he saw Grace picking up the baby from the bassinet.

"Yes, she slept longer than I expected. But she's anxious to be fed now."

He walked over to admire the two of them. "Well, I just stopped by to tell you that Lori and Mack are on their way. They're going to help us get home."

"That's great." Grace smiled broadly. "I've missed Lori so much."

"She's very excited to see you," Charlie replied. Baby Booker let out a loud cry. "I'll leave for now. Daisy offered to pack up your personal items so we can load them in the truck later today."

"Good, that helps." Grace put the baby on her shoulder. "Dad, before you go, I think it's time Baby Booker had a name. Don't you?"

"I do. Shoot."

"Remember our rules. You have to be honest with your reaction." Grace swayed a bit to quiet the baby. "I want to name her Serenity."

Charlie felt his heart skip a beat as he took in the image of his daughter, stronger than he had any right to expect and his surprise granddaughter, the bonus he already knew would enrich his life beyond his imaginings. *Serenity says it all. Our hopes, wrapped up in pink.*

Tears threatened. "I love it," he said, then added softly. "Serenity Grace?"

Grace scrunched up her nose. "Hmmm . . . Serenity Grace, but we'll call her Sara Grace or Sara for every day. Does that work?"

"I like that," Charlie said lightly. "It fits."

"Perfect. Thanks, Dad." She waved goodbye as he left the room.

Charlie received a text from Lori when they arrived at the airport, and he waited for them at the hotel. He hung around the lobby and then impatiently walked up and down the block using this precious time to review the past couple of days. He wanted to pinch himself to make sure he wasn't dreaming. *Can I trust this feeling of hope?*

He saw Lori exit the taxi at the drop-off in front of the hotel. In a burst of emotion, he ran to the car and pulled her into his arms. He kissed her full on the mouth, much to her surprise and Mack's delight.

He paid the cab driver and shuttled them out of the cold and into the hotel. After a quick lunch, they were at the hospital, where he had the pleasure of introducing them to his new grandchild while Grace napped.

"She looks just like Gracie!" a tearful Lori whispered. Heads together over Sara Grace, they silently remembered when Charlie had learned about parenting from Lori. "She's beautiful. What a gift to be a grandparent. We're going to have such fun with this baby!"

"Yes, we are." Charlie squeezed Lori's shoulder. His hope grew, lifting him up, confident now he would have his life's partner with him. "I'm so happy we'll have this experience together."

Lori held the baby close and smiled up at him.

Dr. Basmati joined them. "Mr. Booker, I see you've enlisted help."

Introductions made, the doctor asked, "Do you have a physician in Minnesota to whom you would like me to transfer care?"

Lori glanced at Charlie and quickly answered, "Yes, Dr. Walt Riley has accepted that responsibility. He'll be the baby's doctor."

"Good, so I'll just need his address and we'll send the medical records to him. Sara Grace is ready to be discharged whenever you are ready to take her home."

"Ahhh—" Charlie began.

Lori finished. "We'll be ready in the morning."

Chapter 61

Chicago, Illinois
January 18, 2017

Grace sensed Lori's presence before she saw her peeking around the half-open doorway. "Come in! I'm so happy you're here."

"Oh, my girl." Lori stepped into the room and got the words out before she started to sob, holding her hand over her mouth. "Look at you. You're a mother!" Lori tiptoed over to give Grace a kiss on the cheek and pulled a chair close. Grace looked carefully at Lori, hoping she would find what she expected—the total acceptance by the mother Lori had always been to her.

Lori put a hand on Grace's shoulder, and Grace leaned in for a hug. "Thank you for coming. It's so good to see you."

"And you!" Lori squeezed her close. "We can't wait to get you two home. Your dad is over the moon, as am I, that you are coming back to us. And, with a new little person."

"Thanks. I hope I haven't disappointed you too much." Grace teared up but continued, "I'll need lots of support."

"You know you have that. You always will." Lori held her eyes. "How are you feeling? Up to the flight home in the morning?"

"Absolutely. I've missed you all, and the lake." Grace smiled, buoyed by similar answers of forever love from both her dad and Lori, the woman she considered her mom. She chanced asking the questions that loomed large. "Lori, can I ask you something?"

"Of course."

"How did my dad get through these last months? He looks older to me, and now that I know he and my mother are divorced, it must have been a rocky time." Grace wanted the truth, and she knew Lori would be the one to tell her.

Lori was thoughtful. "Gracie, your dad is human. I'm not going to tell you everything was good. It came close to break-ing him to have you gone; the unknown was the worst part. Thinking too much. We tried to keep him going, but it was hard on him."

"And the divorce?"

"Hmmm. That was perhaps a relief? He didn't know he needed it." Lori paused. "I understand from your dad that you don't want to communicate with your mom now."

"That's right," Grace answered immediately and tried to relax. "Do you think that's wrong?"

"I think you know what you need right now, and that should guide you. What's right for you is what I will support for you."

"Thanks. And thanks for being there for my dad. I know what you mean to him and to me. I also know he got through this because you were there for him."

"That's what family does, Gracie." Lori blushed and added quickly, "Speaking of family, Ashley wanted me to give you a big hug and tell you how excited she is that you're OK and coming home."

Grace's smile diminished. "Oh, Lori, I want a thorough update on her and everyone. Do you really think they will all be happy to have me back? A mental case who ran away, got wild, had a baby, father unknown?" Grace's eyes met Lori's as if to a beacon, and she read the signal clearly.

Don't worry. We've got your back.

Lori tousled Grace's hair. "We love you, kiddo. Let's get you home."

The next morning, Mack left right after breakfast. He drove Charlie's pickup packed with Gracie's belongings, an infant car seat from the hospital, and most of the gifts that seemed to appear for the baby from the people who were close to Grace.

Grace, Lori, and Charlie had a ten o'clock flight out. Daisy had borrowed an infant car seat from the hospital and drove them to the airport herself. Three-day-old Sara Grace slept all the way.

"Lori, go ahead in with the baby. I'll grab all of this stuff and meet you just inside." Charlie held back with Grace.

Suddenly Grace felt shy. She said, "Amazing how well supplied we are for the baby—that pink bunny snowsuit for the trip home is too cute. Daisy, please make sure you tell the girls that I love it. Pink is my favorite color."

They shared a smile, and then Charlie got serious. "Daisy, I can't ever thank you enough for saving my daughter. By doing so, you also saved me. Please know that. I'll never forget it."

"I'll never forget Grace. I'm so happy for you both and for the baby. You all have each other. I wish you the best of everything!" Daisy stepped forward to give each of them a hug. "Stay in touch. I'd like to hear from you with baby milestones."

A security officer approached Daisy's car. "Yes, I'm moving," she said to him.

"Grace, you know where I'll be. Remember. Don't expect smooth sailing forever. It's all normal for this journey. I'm available whenever you need me."

Lori peeked through the lobby glass, holding Sara Grace. Grace took her dad's arm and started toward them, ready for the trip home, Daisy's business card safe in her pocket.

In that moment, Grace became aware she had won the battle and shifted the burdens of the last years to the past.

I'm finally ready to find my future!

Chapter 62

Two Harbors, Minnesota
January 19, 2017

Charlie gazed out the airplane window at blue skies and smooth air. The three of them were in the bulkhead seats with plenty of leg space and took turns holding the baby, who continued to sleep until they landed at MSP. Gracie fed her while waiting for their flight to Duluth, and she slept soundly through the last part of the flight.

"First grandchild for you two?" the attendant asked him and Lori, as Grace napped.

Charlie smiled and turned to Lori, holding a sleeping Serenity on her shoulder, with a question in his eyes.

"Yes, and we're thrilled." Lori answered instantly. Her blue eyes held his, and they shared a conspiratorial giggle.

The moment mirrored his thoughts. *Can I promise her good times, finally? A future with her in it?*

Walt greeted them at the airport. His warm eyes landed on Grace first. "Gracie! You look wonderful." He enfolded her into a gentle squeeze. "So glad you're coming home." Grace hugged him back.

"Welcome home, Charlie." He grasped him into a bear hug, then released him to study the baby. "Well, hello, little one! Don't you look snug in your bunny suit." He turned to Lori and gave her a peck on the cheek and a wink. "Ready to go home?"

Charlie watched his tiny granddaughter in the car seat and thought of all the paraphernalia they would need for her. He owed it to his daughter and granddaughter to move forward in the best way possible. Right now, though, he just wanted to get his girls home.

As they drove the Scenic Highway out of Duluth toward home, big piles of snow and ice encroached on the edges of the road at the intersections, some over twenty feet tall. "Eighteen inches in thirty hours, a record snowfall for January," Walt said. "School was off for two days, and travel was discouraged throughout the state and through Wisconsin. Amazing that you got to Chicago through it all, Charlie. You're a brave guy. Not many could do it."

Charlie knew he'd had no choice. He now started to think about his own driveway and how they would get into his house. Did the furnace stay on during the worst of the wind? He noticed the snow piled high around the neighbors' driveways and worried.

As they approached his home, he saw the driveway plowed out, the mailbox shoveled, and smoke coming from the chimney. Lights on at four o'clock in the afternoon in January was not unusual. However, it was unexpected with nobody home. Then he saw the balloons. A bouquet of pink balloons was tied to the light fixture by the front door.

Walt drove as close to the front door as possible, and as he stopped, the door opened. Bailey ran out of the house and got to Gracie before she could get out of the car, then Walt's wife, Claire, and Mack's wife, Dottie.

"Welcome home! Come in! Let's get that baby out of the cold!"

Charlie was speechless. Walt took the baby out of his arms so he could reunite with Bailey, after he got his fill of Grace. Lori hung back a minute and said, "It will all be OK, Charlie. One day at a time."

Claire and Dottie surrounded Grace and clucked over her. "Gracie, you look wonderful! You have that new-mother glow. Congratulations!"

"It's so good to be home. Please meet my baby, Sara Grace." She pulled Walt over to give them a look before they followed Charlie into the house.

Charlie's senses perked up when he walked into the house. The smell of cinnamon and cloves from the pumpkin bread on the dining room table, the warmth of a fire in the fireplace, the visual treat of flowers in January, the continued touch of Bailey by his side. With his hands in his pockets and his eyes trained on Walt, he made a short speech in a quivering voice. "I don't know what to say. This is amazing. You are amazing. What a generous thing to do, making our homecoming so welcoming. Thank you all."

He sensed a twittering among his guests. Then Claire took Grace by the arm and led her to her bedroom door. She opened it. "Dad, come see." Inside, he saw a crib, a changing table set up on the low set of drawers, and boxes of disposable diapers. The bed was still there but moved to the corner of the room.

"We know you'll need these things, and we hope it's all right that we kept Gracie's room the same, just added to it, for the baby."

Grace said through her tears, "I can't believe you did all of this in the past three days. Where did all this stuff come from?" She examined the room closely. "Lori, this is the rocker from your house, isn't it?" Grace gave Lori a big smile.

Charlie added, "Fresh linens on the bed, and the distinct smell of Lysol and lemon—you've done it all!"

Dottie spoke up. "Our kids are way beyond cribs, so that was easy. The changing table came from my neighbor, and we thought you'd recognize the rocker."

"Yes, I remember using it a time or two at Lori's to calm a fussing Gracie or Ashley," Charlie said and smiled his approval at Lori. "I also have to say, I'm glad about the diapers. It's coming back to me how many we'll need." The laughter got him through the moment.

The women went to help Lori and Grace unpack the few items they had brought from the hospital and put the baby in her crib.

Walt took Charlie aside. "Gracie looks fantastic. All OK with you?"

"I'm great. Overcome with the surprise of it all, but in a good way."

They saw headlights turning into the driveway and Mack driving the truck into the garage. He came in the side door. "I like the ride, Charlie."

"Took you long enough," he teased, fist bumping his friend on the upper arm and softly adding, "Thanks, Mack."

Dottie came out of the bedroom. "I thought I heard you out here." She walked over to Mack and gave him a solid kiss. "Glad you made it safe and sound, honey."

Claire and Lori joined them. Claire said, "Now that everybody is here who belongs here, the rest of us should go home. Charlie, the porchetta is ready when you are, and there are some groceries in the pantry and fridge that should keep you for a few days."

Mack grabbed Walt. "Come help me unload the truck. Charlie, how about I put the stuff in the back porch for now, and you can pull it in as you get to it?"

"Yeah, that sounds good." Charlie ducked into the bedroom to watch his granddaughter breathe, a habit he had developed long ago with Grace.

Lori joined him. "I'm staying. Just so you know."

"Good, I hoped you would."

"Me, too." Grace had slipped into the room and hooked her arms round their shoulders.

Chapter 63

Two Harbors, Minnesota
January 2017

There were three of them in the house to hear Sara Grace cry. Each time, one of them would rise, change the baby, and walk her. The routine of daily living had saved Charlie from melancholy in the past. This time he savored the moments when his granddaughter needed attention, every few hours like clockwork. He didn't have time to dwell on all that had happened; he simply enjoyed each moment as it came.

"Dad, I dreamed about this breakfast!" Grace came into the kitchen just as he was putting a plate of scrambled eggs with salsa on her plate next to a side of rye toast. She patted her stomach and sat next to Lori at the breakfast table.

"Gee, they look great; if you're taking orders, I'm ready now." Lori took the last swallow of her coffee.

"Ready for more coffee, too?" Charlie walked over with the coffeepot. "Yes, these eggs are a specialty of the house. Yours will be coming right up." He winked at Lori and marveled at how lucky he was that his three favorite women were all in his life now.

Grace spent every minute she could looking out at the lake. She checked the color of the horizon, the lake ice, and the snow swirls for changes every hour. She lifted the baby up to look out at the lake each time "I really love this lake. I didn't realize how much until I didn't have it close by. And the piano." She walked over to it and let her hands float along the keys while still holding the baby.

Ashley called from college in Eau Claire, and Lori and Charlie shared a smile when Grace handed the baby off to her dad so she could take the phone into her room to have some privacy to talk to her oldest and dearest friend. When she reappeared from her room, she appeared wistful, "I can't believe she's halfway through her freshman year. It makes me realize how long I've been gone. She's doing so well."

"Yes," Lori commented, while she folded clothes fresh from the dryer. "She seems to be happy there. College agrees with her. Did you catch up?"

"Kind of, I guess," Grace replied. "It's not like I can tell her much, as so much is blank in my memory." She stopped and stared out at the lake. "She didn't seem to judge me, though. I got the feeling she's happy I'm back here."

"Of course she is, Gracie. And I think she'll be very helpful as you find your way."

"Do you think I will?"

"What?" Lori looked at Charlie, then back at Grace. "Do I think you will what?"

"Find my way?"

"Yes, I do, Grace." This time Lori held Grace's eyes. "I know you will."

Hot pork sandwiches and a full refrigerator of food had sustained them through to the day when Lori had to go home. While Charlie was taking family leave generously offered by Patricia, his principal, Lori had used her family leave through the fall to care for her dad and needed to go back to work. She took a run to Duluth to shop first.

Charlie saw her drive in and met her at the porch door to help unload groceries and more baby supplies before she would leave them on their own. "Cold out there, Charlie, and it looks like we may be getting some snow soon. I found a good sale on baby clothes and hope you don't mind that I spent a lot of your money."

She laughed, chattier than usual, possibly to cover her feelings about leaving.

He wished Lori could stay, but she insisted that his priority right now was to spend time with Grace and not complicate things. "Grace needs you to herself right now. There will be time ahead, soon, for us."

They put the groceries away, and Lori sat at the kitchen table to open the packages to show Grace the new clothes as she pulled the tags off and set them aside to put in the washer.

Charlie admired the purchases and pulled out the last of the baby gifts they had brought home from Chicago. It was from Daisy. He handed it to Grace for opening. Packed carefully in layers of bubble wrap and tissue paper, she finally got to the delicate gift itself. A lovely wooden box hand-painted with pink and yellow flowers. As she opened the box, he saw a ballerina rise up and heard the lovely notes of a Mozart sonata that he knew well.

Grace's quick intake of breath was telling. "I can't describe how it felt when I first played the piano at the Refuge. It felt joyful." She laughed. "I think I drove the girls nuts with all of my playing."

"The baby will love it." Grace took the music box to the piano and sat and played the same sonata.

Grace brought Lori into the bedroom to take a last look at the sleeping baby, and then thanked her for being there for her, again.

"Always," Lori said.

Charlie carried her bag from the guest room to the car, and they made a detour to the garage for a passionate kiss before he released her.

With Lori gone, Grace returned to the piano, and Charlie listened to her play. He studied her face. She hadn't been this peaceful since she was fifteen years old. He breathed deeply. *I'm going to do whatever it takes to keep her safe and secure.*

After a few minutes, he busied himself setting up the music box near the baby's crib, and when Sara Grace awoke, he started the music, changed her, talked to her gently, and walked her around the house, describing all of the fun adventures they would have together. He added a few comments about her mother, and which adventures were her favorites. Grace heard them approach and stood up to feed her daughter. When she was finished, Grace placed the baby back in her crib and left the door open so Bailey could watch over her, settling on the rug beside her crib.

"I love how protective Bailey is of the baby. It's so good to be home." Grace stretched and yawned, curling her legs under her on the couch. "How about if we call Mrs. Schiff tomorrow to make an appointment for our first counseling session? Dr. Riley wants to see Sara Grace in his office soon, also. Anything else on the early list?"

"How do you feel about a visit with Pastor Swenson to plan a baptism?" Charlie asked.

"Oh, yes, and Ashley told me when she'll be home for her winter break. Could we plan it around her schedule?"

"Sounds good," he said. "How about if we finish the last of the porchetta and play a little Scrabble before bed?"

"OK. Can we get groceries tomorrow? I'm getting tired of pork."

"Yep, me too."

They laughed together.

Chapter 64

Two Harbors, Minnesota
January 2017

Their relationship remained agreeable through the next day when Grace badly wanted to accompany her dad to the SuperOne to experience the opportunity to choose her own groceries and take in the abundance of choices.

"Well, Sara Grace is not yet ten days old, and I'm not sure we should take her out to such a public place yet. What do you think?"

Grace chided herself for not thinking that through herself and frowned. "You're absolutely right, Dad, it's too soon. Maybe when we see Dr. Riley later this week, he can advise us." She worried then about her maternal instinct and asked, "What about the flight? Should we have done that differently? Do you think Sara is OK?"

"Well, the difference is that we had to travel to get home. It was a necessary trip. The grocery run is something we can do by just sending me." He teased her by saying, "I promise I'll bring you all the special treats you've missed if you put them on the grocery list." He handed her a pad and pencil. "Go crazy, princess."

"This parenting stuff is tough, knowing the right things to do." She needed more reassurance. "I really wanted to go to the store and not stay home with the baby."

"It is, but you haven't made a false move yet. Remember, you will. That's how it works. All parents make mistakes." Charlie's voice dropped as he was reminded of the gravity of his own. "I clearly did."

Grace saw the hurt in her dad's eyes and let it linger there before she smiled at him. "I should have been stronger."

"Nope, you should have had more protection." He moved toward her and kissed her forehead.

While her dad shopped, Grace hunted through her bedroom closet for more clothes that fit. She pulled out jeans of various sizes and remembered how her weight had fluctuated when they were first trying meds for her. Fortunately, she had thinned out, and then grown skinny when she was on the streets. Now, even just after childbirth, her body was normalizing in a good way. Her midsection was tightening back up. Evidently the nursing helped with that, and the meds she was on now didn't seem to affect her weight.

She started a pile of clothes to give to charity and another of warm winter clothes to wear now. She knew her dad would buy her new things, but why bother when he would now have to buy baby clothes for Sara Grace. She didn't want to be a burden. Soon, she would start thinking about how she could contribute to the family. She wanted to find a pathway for herself.

In the chest at the foot of her bed, she found her down jacket. She put it on and was happy to find her warm mittens in one of the pockets. She laughed at how happy such a thing could make her. She hugged herself in the warm cozy coat. As she put the mittens back into her pockets, a slip of yellow notebook paper fell out. Just one word on it—Abby—and the scrawl of a phone number.

"Abby." Grace said the name out loud. Just the sound of the name made her sad all over again. The one person Grace had trusted, whom she thought she could trust. It was time to face it. Abby had let her down. She hadn't told anyone the whole story. Now, she knew their plan had been ridiculous.

She took the jacket off. Bailey's eyes followed her as she left the room and took it to the back closet to hang it up. "It's OK, Bailey, I'm not going to get upset about Abby. I'm a mother now, and I need to move forward. I need to move past that dark time." Almost unconsciously, she stuffed the piece of paper in her pants pocket.

"I could use a little help here," her dad called.

He had both arms full and stood outside, unable to open the door.

"OMG. How much did you buy?"

He handed each bag to her and then went back to the car for three more. "Your list was meager, and I felt like a few treats were in order."

Grace unloaded the grocery bags onto the countertops in the kitchen, and then needed the kitchen table as well. By the time her dad was in with his coat and boots off, there was no counter or tabletop space visible.

"How did I do?"

"Great. I'm guessing you want me to make snickerdoodles. Am I right? How about if I do that this afternoon and then maybe we can make that pasta dish we like together?"

Charlie rubbed his hands together. "Lovely."

Grace pulled out a mixing bowl and measuring cups to start the snickerdoodles. Just then, they both heard the beginning whimper of a waking baby. She looked at her dad. "Hmm. I'd guess we have about ten minutes. Maybe I'll measure and then mix the cookies up after feeding her."

Charlie nodded and watched his daughter take over the kitchen.

"By the way. Do you remember the girl I met in rehab after my stay in the psych ward? The one who lived in Duluth that I saw a few times, and went to juvie with? Her name was Abby?" When he didn't respond, she went on: "Well, I found her phone number in my winter coat pocket. I think you knew her grandfather a little. Do you know how she is?"

Her dad disappeared from the kitchen. "Dad?"

"I'm going to change the baby."

Chapter 65

Two Harbors, Minnesota
January 2017

Charlie needed to get out of the kitchen. He was failing his first test. He didn't know what to do or say. He had to think. *How will she handle Abby's death?*

He swaddled his granddaughter with expertise. His hands did not shake; he was in control. His body was doing what it was supposed to do.

"Dad?" Grace appeared at the door with flour on her hands." Let me wash up, and I'll come in there to nurse."

"Sounds good," he answered. "I'm going to go and do a little shoveling around the garage while you do that. I'll be back in shortly and then we can talk."

The bracing chill outside calmed him. The repetitive motion of shoveling moved his brain out of neutral. He thought of Daisy's rules. Be honest, be respectful, give each other space. You need to rebuild trust. *What if she falls apart? What if she tells me something I can't bear to hear?*

Charlie went around the entire garage and moved the snow away from the foundation as much as he could. It was useless, as there would be more snow this winter, and the foundation would be snow-covered ten to fifteen more times. However, it kept him busy long enough to realize there was only one way to handle this.

When he reentered the house and put another log on the fire, Gracie was back in the kitchen putting the snickerdoodles in the oven. "Good timing. Fresh cookies in twelve minutes."

Charlie stood tall. "Grace, I'm ready to talk about Abby."

She faced him.

"I'm sorry to tell you. Abby died about two months after you left."

Grace crumpled to a chair, her mouth fell open. Finally, with great effort, she asked "How?"

"Suicide. She took too many pills."

Grace placed her arms on the table, cushioning her face and leaned forward. The hollow silence of dry sobs racked her shoulders. He pulled a chair close and covered her body with his, trying with all his might to send the strength of his love through to her. "I'm so sorry, Gracie, so sorry."

The insistent ding of the oven timer broke their embrace minutes later. Charlie was about to hunt for the oven mitt when Grace rose, found it in the right drawer, pulled the piping hot cookies from the oven, and carefully put them on a cooling rack.

The next morning Grace was more subdued than she had been on previous days. She surprised him when she said, "Dad, I'd like to talk to Abby's grandfather. Would you ask him to come over tomorrow?"

He felt like being honest with her had been the right thing to do. He questioned whether Lucas coming to talk about his dead granddaughter was also the right thing to do. Again, he went back to Daisy's guidelines. They needed to rebuild trust between each other. He decided to ask her to trust his judgment.

"Lucas and his wife have been through so much." Charlie leaned forward in his easy chair and gazed out at the lake before meeting Grace's eyes. "I don't think that's the right thing to do right now." He thought hard about how to explain the pain Lucas and Karin had experienced without dragging him and Grace through it vicariously. "It's just over a year since Abby passed, and they are still finding the peace they need to move forward."

Grace's eyes filled with tears. "I never even met her grandmother, and I'm not sure I would even recognize her grandfather. It seems like I should pay my respects."

"I know, princess, and the sentiment is correct." He smiled at her. "How about if we put it off for a bit, and then, make it into a visit to them later to introduce Sara Grace?"

Grace smiled. "Make it a happy visit, instead of . . ." Her smiled faded as her body tensed. "Dad, it could have been me."

"I know. But it wasn't. Here you are, and Sara Grace is with us, needing us to love her and keep her safe. I know Lucas and Kristin can celebrate that at the right time."

Her body posture relaxed as she accepted this plan, and his own heart rhythm returned to normal.

Chapter 66

Two Harbors, Minnesota
February 2017

Grace welcomed the Minnesota February even with its brevity. It could be a cruel month on the North Shore. Deep winter, overcast skies, the snow no longer the novelty it was in December—slushy one day and crusty the next. The roads were often dangerous and ice levels sometimes fickle for the ice fishing that sustained many through the short, dark days. Even with the fatigue of carrying for a newborn, she was grateful to be home.

With the turning of the calendar page, people appeared at their door bearing gifts. "They want to show their support for you. Dropping by with a casserole or a baby gift is their way of doing that," Lori had explained.

Grace and her father shared a chuckle. "We should expect to find another Tupperware container of mystery food left on our doorstep whenever we go out?" For each visit, Grace dutifully thanked them and accepted their baby gifts as they "oohed" and "ahhed" over the baby. She was also in a good mood, excited to show off her baby to Dr. Riley after almost a month at home.

She called Lori to ask her to join them for Sara Grace's first checkup with Dr. Riley.

"Oh, I'd love that! I can almost hear Walt clucking his approval at how this little one has been doing." Lori laughed. "Thanks for including me, Gracie."

"I really want you there. Would you mind staying with Sara Grace for a couple of hours so Dad and I can go to see Mrs. Schiff in Duluth afterward?"

"It would be my pleasure. How about if I cook dinner for us all while you're in Duluth?" Lori offered eagerly.

Grace smiled to herself. She had intercepted enough signals between Lori and her dad to detect a change in their relationship.

This will be fun to watch...

"You're doing everything right. This baby is up a few ounces." Walt reviewed the digital history Dr. Basmati had sent to him, along with a personal note describing the baby's birth. "She looks very healthy. I take it she's eating well?"

"Very well. Fortunately, she's sleeping almost five hours straight overnight, which is good," Grace replied.

"It's been a while since I needed to know about well-baby visits or shots," Charlie said. "Do you have a schedule we should have?"

"Yes, we're quite modernized now. You'll get a printout with this visit summary that lists all the shots and visits required up to age five. Then, of course, school readiness comes into play. We don't need to worry about that now." Walt smiled at his three friends. "Actually, it goes by fast, doesn't it? Gracie, it wasn't that long ago for you!"

"Well, it certainly feels different this time around! "Charlie pointed to his daughter and Lori and laughed. "This time, I'm not in charge, just a coach!" His comment caused Grace to reflect on what it must have been like for him dutifully bringing her in for her well-baby visits before or after school, alone.

They started to pack Sara Grace up and Walt handed them the promised printout. "Next checkup in two months. And Charlie, we should have a Saturday breakfast soon. I've missed that," Walt said.

Lori jumped in. "Yes, you two should do that, and Gracie, if you want some personal time, I can take Sara Grace."

"Great! This Saturday then, Vanilla Bean at nine o'clock." Walt smiled and said to Grace, "Good to have you home, kiddo!"

Chapter 67

Y

Two Harbors, Minnesota
March 2017

Charlie wasn't sure how the baptism would go. Grace had planned it on her own for weeks. He hoped enough people would attend to make her feel good about the effort. Pastor Swenson assured him the congregation would be there in support. "This is the perfect way to allow the congregation and the town to welcome Grace back and to celebrate a new life."

When baptism day came, Charlie was a little nervous until he watched his daughter clothe Sara Grace in the special baptismal gown Ashley had picked out.

"It's so delicate, Ashley. Perfect for her." Grace smiled broadly. Ashley and Lori joined Charlie and Grace for this church event as they had all others during the years, except this time with one new addition.

Mack, serving as usher, guided them all to the front pew. Charlie helped Grace settle the baby on her lap. She whispered to him, wide-eyed and smiling, "Wow, I didn't expect such a crowd."

He looked around and saw a full row of his biology students sitting next to Patricia near the middle of the church, and many of Grace's friends from church and school scattered about.

Grace had selected the organ music with her long-time piano teacher, now the church organist. The service was planned to create a mood of celebration to welcome babies into the church family, but Charlie hoped it would also serve to welcome a young woman home, after being lost in a tangle of family dysfunction and emotional distress.

As Pastor Swenson called them to the baptismal font near the front left of the sanctuary, he greeted them and another family baptizing their baby, too, and extended a personal message to Grace. "Today we welcome Grace back to us. No longer fearful and lost, she was helped by good people who encouraged her. Now, she is looking forward to raising her child, Serenity Grace. Let us all take comfort from her choice and support it. After living in the darkness, she has chosen life."

Grace's smile trembled slightly as she listened; her head held high, holding tight to Sara Grace. Charlie fought back his tears in solidarity with his brave daughter, thankful that she was trusting him to help her raise her baby.

Huddling close to Lori, Ashley, Grace, and the baby, he welcomed a moment of truth. *This is my family. Finally.* They would all work together and be there for one another for this next chapter, he was confident of that. He looked up just as Pastor Swenson gently patted the water on Sara Grace's head and laughed out loud with the entire congregation when her piercing cry shot through to the eaves.

Familiar and melodic hymns filled the church and as a benediction, Pastor Swenson invited all to join the family downstairs for a light lunch. Ashley and Lori surrounded them and led the way through the church and downstairs. They stood together in an informal receiving line as teachers from school, some of his students, Grace's classmates, and church members spoke to them briefly, welcoming Grace home and wishing them well with the new baby. After a while, he took Sara Grace from her mother and mingled with those who were noshing on food from the buffet.

When the baby started to fuss, he settled her on his shoulder and moved around the room, gazing at the familiar surroundings and watching his daughter catch up with friends and well-wishers.

Unguarded, his thoughts floated to Caroline and how much she had missed. He caught himself, correcting his own narrative. Family life was never what she wanted, so she would never consider it a regret or something she missed. She had avoided it—actively worked against it.

A memory came to him: the image clear, the betrayal vivid. Caroline wore gloves in the bedroom since it was so cold. "Bring me my pill." He saw his younger self opening up the medicine cabinet and looking at the contents, picking up the circular packet of birth control pills and putting it down again. Such a simple trick of swapping out pills—an action that could not be undone—that had wreaked havoc for his wife but opened the world to him.

He forced his mind to skip over the pain. It was time to make peace with the facts. In the end, Caroline did get what she wanted. A life built around her wanderlust without family ties. He knew his action to realize his own family would always be tinged with guilt. But it was time to make room for the joy of his family dream coming true.

The crowd was thinning. He watched Lori, Ashley, and Grace walk toward him, chatting happily. He walked to meet his family with Serenity asleep on his shoulder, content.

Epilogue

Grace pulled her dad's truck into the arrivals parking area of Duluth International Airport and checked her image in the truck's mirror. Her face was now smooth and glowing, her hair softly curling in the shoulder-length style she now favored, pulled back from her face. She wanted Daisy to see that she had made big changes in her appearance beyond the internal reset she had undertaken since Daisy rescued her from the street. This new Grace, who was confident, happy, stable, and positive about her future, owed Daisy a debt of gratitude she could never repay. She would make sure Daisy saw the difference she had made in her life.

Parked between two Uber drivers, Grace texted Daisy her location and waited. Daisy was flying in from Minneapolis after spending a few days there at a conference and had eagerly accepted the invitation to join them for Sara's first birthday. Grace jumped out of the car when she saw Daisy's wild red hair blowing in the wind as she came through the arrivals doorway and stopped to look at her phone.

"I'm here, Daisy!" Grace hugged her tight. "Welcome to the Northland. It's wonderful to see you."

Daisy said, "Wow, look at you! You're gorgeous." She handed her roller bag off to Grace, searching for something as she was led toward the truck. "No baby with you?"

"Nope. I'm being selfish. I wanted some time alone with you first. You'll fall in love with her soon enough. Everybody does." She laughed lightly. "Dad and Lori are with her. They expect us after lunch. Hope you're hungry?"

"Always. How nice to have some time together. Thanks for planning it."

They chatted about the conference and Minneapolis as they drove to the restaurant. "I chose a place with a lake view. You'll be seeing a lot of it during your stay. It's our star attraction, so I'm starting with it." Pier B was a newer place that featured a view of the boat traffic that was a signature attraction of Duluth. "There's still some open water. However the harbor is closed for the winter now. Ice abounds, as you can see. It's beautiful, though."

Daisy took in the grandeur of the multiple shades of gray and blue, and the crystalline formations of ice covering almost all surfaces that touched the lake. The wind was brisk, but the brilliant sunshine reflecting on the ice featured a full spectrum of colors and kept the temperature bearable. Grace pointed out the Aerial Bridge and the Wisconsin side of the port as they waited for menus.

"Truly, you look great, Grace. You got your figure back, which always makes a girl feel good. Everything from your manner to the way you carry yourself speaks to a new level of confidence."

"I'm glad it shows. My big news is that I've been accepted at the University of Minnesota at Duluth starting next fall. I'm thinking of nursing."

"Yes!" Daisy clapped her hands. "Great choice! I can absolutely see it. I bet your dad is happy. How are things with him?"

"Excellent. As you predicted, we did need some time to learn to trust one another. We had a breakthrough when he confided in me how tough the months after I ran away had been for him. It was like he finally dared show me his vulnerable side."

Grace recalled the tough conversation when she had provoked his shouting at her.

"You put me through hell! I'm still trying to process that you're back. Of all the scenarios I worried about after you ran away, this one wasn't even on the radar. Suicide was on my mind a lot. Losing you to prostitution and drugs, locked up somewhere after a psychotic break, even murdered for your car . . . all were on my mind through the months you were away."

"Maybe even bigger news is that my dad and Lori are together and engaged!" Grace announced with a broad smile.

Daisy clapped her hands. "I knew that would happen. How wonderful."

"It took a while for my dad to feel like it was the right time." Grace giggled. "It was fun to watch it all play out. I'm so happy for them."

After lunch, Grace drove them home on the Scenic Highway, and Daisy gave her an update on Angie's Refuge and any news of girls that Grace had known while she'd stayed there.

"My big news is that my benefactrix, the original Angie's mom, has agreed to provide some seed money for a program like ours to be developed in Minneapolis or maybe St. Paul, yet to be determined."

"That's so great!" Grace congratulated Daisy. "The program saved me. You saved me, Daisy."

"I was just there when you were ready to take a new road. Glad I was. You did the work. Always remember that, and how strong you are."

Sara Grace was napping when they arrived, and Lori was putting tomorrow's birthday cake in the oven. "How great that you can join us for the special occasion. Can you believe

Sara Grace is one year old tomorrow?" Lori, gracious as ever, greeted their guest warmly.

Her dad, smiling from ear to ear, ushered all of them into the living room. "What a difference a year makes. Daisy, we are so grateful to you. To say that things have changed for the better is such an incredible understatement. You literally saved us, and we are so thankful."

"Well, I may have helped, but it appears that all of you have done your part to move toward a healthy and happy future."

Grace knew Daisy would turn the attention away from herself but could tell from her eyes she was touched. "So, Charlie and Lori, I understand you have some news to share with me?"

As Lori showed off her engagement ring and Charlie glowed, Grace said a silent prayer that her father would spend the remaining years of his life as happy as he appeared today. Tomorrow, as Sara Grace attempted to blow out her birthday candle, she would be celebrated by family who had surrounded them for years: Ashley and Lori, Walt and Claire, Mack and Dottie, and Daisy, an honorary family member who helped them survive. *What a difference a year makes, indeed.*

Grace still felt the pull to know more about her mother and why she could be the way she was. Her own motherhood was a joy she couldn't have imagined. It was difficult to understand how her own mother could have so easily abandoned her. She continued to work on this in therapy.

She had not reached out to her mother and wasn't sure she ever would. But every trip she took to Hawk Ridge, she was compelled to search the sky for a peregrine falcon, the bird she always considered her mother's bird. The wanderer.

She hoped that someday she would be strong enough to reach closure. But now she had a life to build and a daughter to protect.

Acknowledgments

The full moon is tinged red from where I write on the North Shore of Lake Superior today. Fires in the Superior National Forest this summer of 2021 were tragic in their scope and speed, endangering what many have come to depend on as a forever sanctuary for city dwellers in need of a nature fix. It's amazing what a bit of lightning can do during a drought.

My intent for *Finding Grace* was to write a complicated family story. My choice of location was fixed from the beginning—Lake Superior as a backdrop to signify reliability in its very wildness and changeability. In an era of certain climate change, securing our natural wonders for the future requires careful handling. Let's hope we take on the challenge

Thank you to the steady hand of my editor, Annie Tucker, for keeping me on a narrative track with the meanderings of my characters. Always a joy to work with Annie! Thanks also to Brooke Warner and all of the talented professionals at She Writes Press who take the design and production of books seriously and partner with their authors so seamlessly.

Also, sincere thanks to my early readers—Mary Brodehl, Gabrielle Lawrence, Sharon Abrahamsen, and Elizabeth Super—who provided support and feedback for my early drafts and shared valuable insight into my characters as they developed. The collaboration was much appreciated.

About the Author

Maren Cooper grew up in the Midwest and now resides in St. Paul, Minnesota. She currently serves as a volunteer for various nonprofits and retreats frequently to the shore of Lake Superior, where she loves to hike and watch the deer devour her hosta. Her debut novel, *A Better Next*, was published in May of 2019 by She Writes Press. Visit her at www.marencooper.com.

Author photo © Leslie Plesser

SELECTED TITLES FROM SHE WRITES PRESS

She Writes Press is an independent publishing
company founded to serve women writers everywhere.
Visit us at www.shewritespress.com.

A Better Next by Maren Cooper. $16.95, 978-1-63152-493-6. At the top of her career, twenty plus years married, and with one child left to launch, Jess Lawson is blindsided by her husband's decision to move across the country without her—news that shakes her personal and professional life and forces her to make surprising new choices moving forward.

Eden by Jeanne Blasberg. $16.95, 978-1-63152-188-1. As her children and grandchildren assemble for Fourth of July weekend at Eden, the Meister family's grand summer cottage on the Rhode Island shore, Becca decides it's time to introduce the daughter she gave up for adoption fifty years ago.

Our Love Could Light the World by Anne Leigh Parrish. $15.95, 978-1-938314-44-5. Twelve stories depicting a dysfunctional and chaotic—yet lovable—family that has to band together in order to survive.

How to Grow an Addict by J.A. Wright. $16.95, 978-1-63152-991-7. Raised by an abusive father, a detached mother, and a loving aunt and uncle, Randall Grange is built for addiction. By twenty-three, she knows that together, pills and booze have the power to cure just about any problem she could possibly have . . . right?

Stella Rose by Tammy Flanders Hetrick. $16.95, 978-1-63152-921-4. When her dying best friend asks her to take care of her sixteen-year-old daughter, Abby says yes—but as she grapples with raising a grieving teenager, she realizes she didn't know her best friend as well as she thought she did.

Tzippy the Thief by Pat Rohner. $16.95, 978-1-63152-153-9. Tzippy has lived her life as a selfish, materialistic woman and mother. Now that she is turning eighty, there is not an infinite amount of time left—and she wonders if she'll be able to repair the damage she's done to her family before it's too late.